Samantha Young is the *New York Times* and *USA Today* bestselling author of the On Dublin Street series, the Hart's Boardwalk series and the standalone novels *Hero* and *Fight or Flight*. She resides in Scotland.

Visit Samantha Young online:

www.authorsamanthayoung.com
@AuthorSamYoung
Instagram & Facebook @AuthorSamanthaYoung

ALSO BY SAMANTHA YOUNG

Much Ado About You

SAMANTHA YOUNG

PIATKUS

PIATKUS

First published in the US by Berkley, an imprint of Penguin Random House LLC
First published in Great Britain in 2021 by Piatkus

A CIP catalogue record for this book
is available from the British Library.

ISBN 978-0-349-42924-3

Cover design and illustration by Colleen Reinhart
Book design by Elke Sigal

Printed and bound in Great Britain by Clays Ltd, Elcograf S.p.A.

Papers used by Piatkus are from well-managed forests
and other responsible sources.

Piatkus
An imprint of
Little, Brown Book Group
Carmelite House
50 Victoria Embankment
London EC4Y 0DZ

An Hachette UK Company
www.hachette.co.uk

www.littlebrown.co.uk

I do love nothing in the world so well as you.

—William Shakespeare,
Much Ado About Nothing

One

I had not gone on a date in two years.

That would explain the riot of butterflies in my stomach and the overwhelming and panic-inducing sensation building up in my gut. My foot tapped nervously against the floor.

I took another sip of the water the waiter had brought me and tried to look like I didn't care that my date was fifteen minutes late.

It didn't make sense.

Aaron and I had been talking for four weeks, but it felt longer. We met on a dating site, and when we realized how much we had in common (a thirst for travel, an obsession with cooking and renovation shows, a true appreciation for Shakespeare, a love for quiet nights in and the occasional nonquiet night out . . .), we'd graduated to sending each other Snapchats.

Four weeks of daily snaps.

My cheeks burned with the heat of rejection, and I flicked my fingertips across my phone screen to open the app. I'd saved huge chunks of conversation between us because the banter was so great, and I liked to reread them.

I looked at our snaps from last night.

AARON T

So what are you like in the mornings?

> **ME**
>
> Useless without that first coffee.

AARON T

Note to self–priorities: bring Evie coffee in bed first thing in the morning. I need her useful there.

> **ME**
>
> 😄
>
> **ME**
>
> Why do I need to be useful? Surely your priority in the morning is to be useful to me. 😉

AARON T

Okay, here's the plan of action. I'm useful to you first.
Then I get you a coffee. This will be followed by you returning the favor of usefulness.

AARON T

You know "useful" is a euphemism for going downtown, right?

> **ME**
>
> *snort* I did but thank you for clarifying so charmingly.

AARON T

Oh that was me being a gentleman about it.

Frowning, I turned my phone over on the restaurant table and eyeballed the entrance again. At first our flirtation had been sweet, but as Aaron and I got to know each other, things had heated up. For me, it was a weird mix of feeling reckless and safe flirting with him since I'd never met him, but he'd been so upfront with me. I had rules against dating younger men because I'd attempted it a few times and those relationships always failed due to the men's immaturity. Aaron was twenty-eight—five years younger than me. However, within the first week, I lost all concerns about his maturity because he was so open, confiding in me about how awful his ex made him feel about himself. He'd quit law school because he was miserable and instead started over again, studying to be a vet. I loved animals, so I loved that about him. But his ex never supported him. Then when he started missing gym visits because he was studying so much, and not eating great, she'd crushed his confidence with her pointed comments about his body.

He'd sent me snaps of himself, and Aaron was not fat. He just wasn't built like a cover model. Who cared? He seemed like a great guy. Aaron was the two *h*'s: honest and handsome.

Dating was not my favorite thing, especially online dating, and I had walls up for miles. However, because Aaron had been so forthcoming, I told him that for the last five years I'd had one bad date after another. How on my thirty-first birthday I'd declared I was taking some time out from dating. Most of my friends tried to be supportive, but you could see the worry in their eyes.

Poor Evie. She's in her thirties and still single. Shouldn't she be working harder to find a man, not taking a break?

Only my best friend and soul mate, Greer, genuinely sup-

AARON T

My self-awareness. I know when I'm being a dick. I either
try to stop myself or I apologize right away.

ME

Self-awareness is also underrated. I like that you're self-aware.

AARON T

But not that I can be a dick, right?

ME

No one's perfect. We all have dick days.

AARON T

So what don't you like about yourself?

ME

If I'm being honest, I have physical insecurities.
I've gotten more confident over the years,
but I still have days I don't feel great about myself.

AARON T

Why do you have insecurities? You're fucking gorgeous.

ME

Thanks. But I'm tall and I'm not skinny. Far from it.
I've gotten a lot of "you're big for a woman" comments
on first dates, followed by them never calling me again.

It was true. At five foot ten, I *was* tall. In my four-inch heels, that put me at six foot two. But I didn't think that was what bothered some guys. I had plentiful boobs, an ass, hips, and although I had a waist, it wasn't super trim. Neither was my belly. Either guys loved my tall voluptuousness, or they labeled me fat. I hated that word. It made me physically flinch. But there were days, usually around my period, where I felt overweight and wondered how anyone could be attracted to me.

Most days I was content enough with myself, even had days where I felt sexy. However, maybe I'd feel confident *every* day if I were a few inches shorter and a dress size or two smaller. Who knew? Didn't we all sometimes wish we were the opposite of what we were? I gave myself a break when I had those kinds of thoughts because on most days I liked myself, inside and out.

The trick was to guard against allowing other people to dictate how I felt about my physical appearance. However, I noticed a correlation between periods of high self-worth and low self-esteem and when I was online dating. Shallowness in men was a huge turnoff for me, yet that didn't mean those who rejected me based on my appearance hadn't had a subconscious effect on me.

AARON T

So you said you're an editor. Where? What? Tell me more.

ME

I'm an editorial assistant at Reel Film, the film magazine.

AARON T

That's cool. What does that mean exactly?
Do you write reviews and stuff?

ME

No, I'm assistant to an editor. I started out in an administrative position but over the last few years I've helped my editor, editing the journalists' articles.

ME

My editor is retiring, and his position is open.
It's likely I'll get it.

AARON T

That's awesome. Maybe I can take you out to celebrate?

ME

Maybe 👀 What's your idea of celebrating?

AARON T

Whatever you want it to be. I aim to please 😉

I sighed heavily, trying to alleviate the churning in my stomach. I'd been working at *Reel Film* for ten years, had been passed over many times for an editor's job, but finally my long wait was over. I was excited about it, but I was also distracted by my interactions with Aaron. He'd stolen my focus and we hadn't even met. There was something addictive about our conversations—they made me feel young in a way I hadn't in a long time.

And now . . . now was he standing me up?

I looked at the very last snap sent last night.

ME

Can't wait to see you tomorrow.

I could see he'd opened it only a few hours ago.

My fingers hovered over the keyboard. Glancing at the time on the phone, noting he was now twenty minutes late, I quickly sent a snap.

ME
I'm at the restaurant. Are you running late?

A few anxious minutes passed, and then I saw he'd opened it. Relief filled me.

But as a minute turned into five and there was no sign of a reply, a sick feeling rose within me. Five minutes turned into ten.

What an idiot I'd been.

Yet, even as I sat there, I did that thing people do when they turn over all the other possibilities in their head.

Someone had stolen his phone and it wasn't him opening the messages.

Maybe he'd been in an accident.

He was already in love with me and it was all just a little overwhelming.

I gave a bark of laughter at that one and ignored the bemused look the couple at the next table gave me.

It was then I sensed the hovering waiter. I glanced to my left and gave him a forced smile. "You need the table back, don't you?"

He shook his head. "No, you're fine. I just wondered if you wanted to order anything?"

"Do you have an alternate-reality special on the menu? You know, the kind where I don't get stood up?"

The waiter gave me a sympathetic smile. "Sorry, we don't. If it makes you feel better, a lot of people would order it if we did."

I laughed. "Yeah? See a lot of this, do you? I wonder what his excuse will be. If he offers an excuse, that is."

"Maybe his dog died."

"Or his dog ate his goldfish and he had to do the Heimlich maneuver."

The waiter chuckled. "I once got stood up and he texted me to tell me that his visa had expired, and he'd left the country that day. I saw him in Andersonville two weeks later."

"No way."

"Yes way."

Feeling a little better at the reminder I wasn't the only person to have ever been stood up, I told the friendly waiter I was going to head home, and he offered me a bolstering smile as I left the restaurant.

Despite joking around about it, I felt stupid for making myself vulnerable to someone who would stand me up.

As I strode toward the L, I kept checking my phone to see if Aaron had replied, but nothing. I tried to figure out how the guy I'd spent hours talking to for four weeks could do this. If he'd changed his mind, why hadn't he just said so? He'd seemed like the kind of guy who would just be brutally honest with me.

Not a coward.

Not a dick.

I winced.

Well, he had warned me he could be a dick.

But I'd thought it was real of him to admit that. I didn't think beyond our cute banter and the fact that he loved Shakespeare just as much as I did. We'd discussed our favorite Shakespearean tragedies and argued over which of Shakespeare's comedies were best. He said *Two Gentlemen of Verona*; I said *Twelfth Night*. I'd been pretty excited to find someone who enjoyed my favorite playwright so much in this day and age. On top of everything else, he really had seemed too good to be true.

It all was too good to be true, apparently.

Or . . . what if Aaron had shown, saw me, and decided I was too fat or too tall or too—

Evie, shut up! I yelled at myself.

I would not let him do this to me.

Enraged, I pulled out my phone.

ME

You at least could have had the decency to say you
were no longer interested in meeting me.

My heart raced and my palms were clammy as I saw he immediately opened it.

But no reply was forthcoming.

What the hell?

Hurt, sad, angry, confused, all of it mingled as I jumped on
the Blue Line to get to my tiny studio apartment in Wicker Park.
All that emotion I'd kept buried at the restaurant started to flood
up out of me. By the time I got into the apartment, tears were
streaming down my face. I brushed them away with frustration,
cursing myself not only for letting Aaron upset me but for how
much of myself I'd put out there to someone I hadn't met in
person.

What a naive moron! I knew better than that.

No. I shook my head. I couldn't do that to myself. He wasn't
worth my tears. And he didn't get to make me feel like I'd done
something wrong.

Maybe he was just another boring, judgmental jerk that was
looking for the kind of woman who didn't exist outside of movies
and airbrushed magazines.

Did that sound bitter?

"That sounded bitter," I murmured to myself.

Okay. So maybe I was a little bitter.

But this was why I avoided dating, because even in my thirties it could reduce me to feeling like a rejected sixteen-year-old.

My phone buzzed in my purse, making my heart jump into my throat. There was a text on the screen from my best friend, Greer. Disappointment filled me and then I felt instantly horrible about it. I tapped to open the message.

How did the date go? Or is it still going? 😉

I snorted, my lips trembling as I bit back more tears and quickly texted back. **He never showed. I messaged him, he opened them, but he never replied.**

That rat bastard! Do you need me to come over?

She would too. I smiled through my tears but shook my head as I texted, **I'm fine. He's a dick. It's done. I'm just going to bed. I have a big day ahead of me tomorrow.**

My phone buzzed again in my hand, but this time Greer was calling. Not really in the mood to pretend I was fine during the call, I hesitated a second. But then I picked up. This was Greer. I knew she was probably worried about me.

"Hey."

"First off," she said, "he *is* a dick. Forget about him. Any guy who claims to be a Shakespeare fan but hates *Romeo and Juliet* isn't worth shit. Second, yay for tomorrow! You have to call me as soon as they give you that freaking editor's office."

I hated that Aaron's mixed signals had dampened what was an important time in my life. "I will."

"And third . . . so okay, I was going to wait to meet face-to-face to tell you this, but I think you need something to cheer you up right now."

"Okay."

"Evie, babe . . . you're going to be an aunt!"

Trying to make the words make sense, I shook my head. "Uh . . . how . . . what? I don't have . . ." I was an only child. Greer knew that.

"Oh my God, you're slow tonight. I'm pregnant, Evie! Yay!"

I blinked in confusion. "Are you joking? To cheer me up?" Because Greer had told me more than once that she didn't want kids. Or to get married. She'd been dating Andre for two years, but it was a very relaxed relationship.

"No!" Greer giggled. "Andre and I have been talking about it for a while and I'm thirty-four, I'm not getting any younger, and well . . . we decided to try. And I'm pregnant!"

Holy Mother of God.

Greer and I were two of six friends who had met at Northwestern and stayed in Chicago after college. Over the years, my friends had dropped like flies. First marriage, then kids, until the only times we saw one another were at their kids' christenings and birthday parties, and once every couple of months for dinner when they found a babysitter.

The knowledge that Greer never wanted to settle down and have kids had made me think we wanted the same things and I wasn't alone.

Now, my last friend standing was going down with the baby ship.

"That's great!" I forced a happy tone and cursed myself for my utter selfishness. "What a surprise!"

"I was going to tell you at lunch on Saturday, but I thought you needed this news now."

"I'm so happy for you!" Those words weren't a lie. I wanted only happiness for Greer. But I felt conflicted about her news. "Well, I'm gonna hit the hay. I'll let you know about tomorrow. And we'll still do Saturday lunch, right? To celebrate your news. Tell Andre I said congrats."

"I will, babe. And yes, Saturday, definitely. To celebrate both our news."

We hung up.

Striding over to my bed, I flopped down on my back and stared up at my cracked ceiling. I could hear the murmur of my upstairs neighbor's TV.

Greer was pregnant.

If I was honest with myself, I was scared I was about to be left behind.

My phone buzzed again, and my heart beat at triple speed at the sight of the Snapchat symbol.

I opened it up.

AARON T

I'm sorry. I'm not ready for something serious after all and I know that's what you want. Sorry I was a dick about it. You deserve better. Hope you find what you're looking for.

Fresh tears filled my eyes. I didn't know if he was telling the truth, but I would be honest one last time.

ME

I'm sorry too.

Sorry for the last four weeks of wasted emotional energy.

When the status remained as delivered, I tapped on his profile and noted I could no longer see his Snapchat points. He'd deleted me from his friends list.

Well, that was final.

Despairing, I lay in the dark trying to figure out if I was sad over facing another romantic disappointment or if my pride was merely hurt.

Maybe both.

"Tomorrow," I whispered to myself. "Things will pick up tomorrow."

Two

"There you are, Evie." My editor, Patrick, lifted his hand and curled his fingers, gesturing me to follow him.

My boss had jolted me out of concentration mode. Outside of work hours, I offered freelance editing services to self-published authors to supplement my income, and one of my clients was a crime writer. An old friend of mine from Northwestern worked with the FBI, and I'd emailed him three days ago with facts I needed checked. The author had gotten her info online, and I just wanted to make sure it was correct. I'd received my friend's response minutes after coming into the office. Fascinated with the information he'd sent me, I'd forgotten I was at work.

Patrick's sudden appearance caused giddiness to fill me, swamping the melancholy that lingered. I strode through the open-plan office, smiling at my colleagues as I made my way toward Patrick's office. My desk sat in front of the glass cube that housed his space.

Picking up speed, I hurried to follow him inside.

"Close the door."

Despite everyone being able to see what was going on in the office, once that door closed, the cube was soundproof. It was pretty cool. I glanced around. Patrick's desk sat near the bank of windows that looked down over East Washington Street downtown.

Boxes containing my boss's belongings filled the space.

I'd worked for Patrick for ten years. He was a good enough boss. Thanked me for my work. Seemed to appreciate me. However, we'd had our differences over the years, mostly because he'd never championed me the three times an editor job opened up at the magazine.

Now he was retiring, and as I was his loyal, long-standing editorial assistant, everyone at the magazine predicted that I would get his job.

"You've packed up really early," I observed. "The job is still yours for six weeks."

Patrick nodded distractedly. "Evie, take a seat."

Not liking his tone, I slowly lowered onto the seat in front of his desk. "Is everything okay?"

Come to think of it, when was the last time Patrick beat me into work? I usually arrived at least fifteen minutes earlier than him every day.

"Evie . . . you know I think you're a great assistant. And you'll make a damn good editor one day . . . but the higher-ups have decided to hire an experienced editor. Young guy, twenty-five, certified as an editor, been working at a small press for two years. He's coming in next Monday so I can show him the ropes."

It was like the floor fell out from beneath my feet. "Wait . . . what?"

My boss frowned. "Gary Slater. He's going to be your new boss."

Was the room spinning?

Or was that just the anger building inside me so much that my body couldn't handle it? "More experience? Certified?" I stood up on shaking legs. Not only had I been editing here for seven years, Patrick knew I was a freelance editor too. Experienced? "*I'm* certified. You know I am." Although I'd come into the job with an English degree, I'd gotten into the editing program at the Graham School at the University of Chicago and worked my ass off after hours to get certified. "This guy is twenty-five. I've been doing this job for ten years, and they want to make this barely-out-of-college kid my boss?"

"Evie, lower your voice," Patrick scolded.

I struggled to calm down. "Is this a joke?"

He shook his head. "I'm afraid not."

"And you." I curled my lip in utter disappointment. "Did you even fight for me on this?"

Patrick sighed. "Of course I did. I told them you had enough experience, but they want someone who's been editing."

"*I've* been editing. I've been editing work you were supposed to edit for the last seven years. But I guess that doesn't matter because I lack the one appendage that apparently makes a person more qualified—I don't have a dick!"

My boss blanched. "Evie."

I didn't care if I was losing it. There were five editors at *Reel Films*—none of them were women. There was only one female critic. And you only needed one guess to know what kind of movies she was asked to review.

I was done, I realized.

"I quit."

"Evie." Patrick pushed back his chair. "I know you're upset, but don't do anything hasty."

"Hasty?" I guffawed and turned to throw open his door. "I've done this job for ten goddamn years and this is the thanks I get? No."

Feeling my colleagues' burning stares, I ignored them as I swiped all of my belongings into my big slouchy purse.

"Evie, will you stop?" Patrick sidled up to me.

I closed my bulging purse and turned to glare at him. We were eye level. "I hope this stuck-in-the-nineteen-fifties publication goes down the toilet, Patrick. As for you . . . thanks for ten years of nothing." On that note, I stormed out of the office, not looking at anyone, focused entirely on getting the hell out of there.

As the elevator stopped on the ground floor, my legs began to tremble so badly, I thought they might just take me out. Splatter me right across the marble floor. It would be the perfect end to the grotesqueness of the last twenty-four hours.

Yet, somehow, I walked out of there.

I just kept walking.

Walking and walking.

My mind whirled as I attempted to figure out what I would do with my life. How had I ended up here—with no promising prospects for my future?

When I thought my despair couldn't get any worse, my cell rang. I pulled it out and saw it was my stepfather calling. I loved Phil, but his call was bad timing. Considering he rarely called me when he knew (or thought) I'd be at work, however, I felt compelled to answer.

"Evie, sweetheart, I just called your office and they told me you quit."

"Yes."

"Why didn't you tell me?"

"It was . . . kind of a recent decision." I stared around, realizing I was in Millennium Park, next to the Jay Pritzker Pavilion. A woman with a six-pack ran past me in workout gear, while a guy spilled his latte down the front of his shirt and started cursing profusely.

I couldn't even remember walking here.

I was losing it.

". . . so I thought I better call you right away," Phil said.

What?

"Sorry, Phil, what?"

"Your mother," he repeated patiently. "I just got off the phone with her. I'm picking her up from rehab this Saturday and she wants me to take her to see you."

Feeling my stomach lurch, I staggered toward the nearest bench and slumped down onto it.

I loved my mom.

But this was shitty news on top of a shitty day.

I couldn't take any more disappointment from my mother.

"Phil, I can't talk about this right now. I need to go." I hung up, feeling bad about it because Phil was great. However, I couldn't concentrate on the guilt.

Instead, all I could think about was the need to escape.

I thought of the money sitting in several savings accounts. Life insurance money left to me when my dad died. I'd used a bit for tuition, but with interest my savings were substantial. I'd been holding on to the money to buy a house, for that day when I finally met Prince Fucking Charming and settled down.

Since that seemed like a dream that would never come true, I pulled up the search engine on my phone and typed in "vacation escapes in England." It was moronic considering I no longer had a full-time job and should probably be concentrating on finding another in Chicago. Besides, I doubted Patrick would give me a reference, so that was going to be a much harder feat than usual.

However, in that moment, nothing else mattered but getting away from my life.

As a fan of all things classic literature—Jane Austen, Charles Dickens, Geoffrey Chaucer, Charlotte Brontë—England was on the top of my bucket list.

I scrolled somewhat frantically through the vacation listings until my eyes caught on a link.

MUCH ADO ABOUT BOOKS—A BOOKSHOP HOLIDAY!

The nod to Shakespeare made me click on the link.

The advertising copy made my hands shake with excitement.

Much Ado About Books was a small bookshop in the quaint fishing village of Alnster in Northumberland. I googled it and that was northern England, near the border with Scotland. At Much Ado About Books, not only did you rent the apartment above the bookstore, but the owner let you run her bookshop.

It was a booklover's dream vacation getaway.

I could do that.

I could totally run away from my life and manage a bookstore in a little village in England, where none of my troubles or worries could get to me. And come on, someone named the bookstore after a Shakespearean play. It was fate.

It had to be.

No more men who made me doubt myself.

No more job that made me feel like a failure.

In fact, no more entire life circumstances that made me feel like a failure.

And I wasn't just going to England for a two-week break either. No way.

Hands shaking, I dialed the number on the ad after checking the country code for the UK. It rang five times before a woman with a wonderful English accent answered.

"Much Ado About Books, how can I help?"

"Uh, yes, hello, I'd like to speak to someone about booking a stay at the bookshop."

"Oh . . . okay. Well, I'm the owner, Penny Peterson."

Butterflies fluttered to life in my belly. "Hi, Penny, my name is Evie Starling, and I'd like to book the store for a whole month. Starting Monday. Please tell me that's doable?"

Three

If it weren't for the slightly darker shade of gray in the line of the horizon, it would have been almost impossible to see where the sky met the sea on my first day in England.

Yet, I'd never seen anything more beautiful than the harbor village I now found myself in. The harbor itself was small, a semi-circle carved into the coastline with stone arms curving out to almost meet. There was just enough space in the gap for the small fishing boats to escape out into the sea.

A small rocky beach led up to a pathway, and beyond that pathway to the left was a low stone wall that demarcated where row upon row of individual gardens began.

The gray of the day was broken up by a riot of colorful flowers and plants that blossomed in gardens. In each garden was a wrought-iron gate that led onto the harbor at one end and the street on the other. I gathered the gardens belonged to the terraced houses across the street behind me because small notices on the gates stated they were private.

Looking down at an older couple sitting in a garden that was decked and covered in flowerpots, staring out at the water, I thought how lovely it must be to own one. A place to sit and enjoy the harbor without tourists venturing into their sanctuary.

My eyes moved back to the water as I swayed a little against the large suitcase sitting by my side. As soon as the cab drove past the quaint English cottages and turned with the bend in the road, the water appeared on the horizon before me . . . and I knew.

I knew this was where I was meant to be, and the agitation I'd felt since saying goodbye to Greer finally settled.

"I know you better than you think I do," Greer had said last night, clutching my elbows as we stood on the sidewalk outside O'Hare. "You feel like I'm abandoning you, don't you? Now you're acting insane and running away to England."

Concern shone dark in her eyes.

Guilt suffused me. "Greer, no. I love you and I want nothing but your happiness . . ." I winced, feeling ashamed. "Okay, yes, it's a little weird for me you're pregnant. But this baby isn't about me. It's about you and Andre. I can't expect everyone to stay standing still with me just because my life isn't what I expected it to be at thirty-three years old." I mirrored her, taking hold of her elbows. "I will not stand still anymore."

Her fingers bit into my skin. "So, running away is the answer?"

"I know it seems like I'm running away, and for a moment I guess that's what I was doing. But I've thought about it and I'm determined that's not what this is. I'm just putting a little distance between myself and my life as it stands in Chicago. To get a little perspective."

"Other people go to Greece for a few weeks. They don't pay to run someone else's store for them in the middle of nowhere England."

I smirked at her dry tone. "I'm not other people."

"I know." She stepped closer to me, eyes filling with tears. "And that's why I love you and I have . . . I have this horrible feeling I'm about to lose you."

Understanding filled me, and I drew her into a tight hug. Greer and I met freshman year of college. We'd been friends for fifteen years, and on more than one occasion she'd told me I was the first and only person in her life she trusted to be true and steadfast to her. She came from a broken family, from parents who used their child as a pawn in their divorce battle. I had my own issues with family, and we'd bonded over the fact.

Even without our respective backgrounds, Greer and I would have always become great friends. There are people you meet in life whom you just connect with. Greer was one of those people for me. The first day we took a stroll around campus together, we lapsed into a comfortable silence. We felt no pressure to ramble awkwardly or to constantly ask questions or try to entertain each other. We could just *be*. Trust came easily to us. Our instincts seemed to tell us we could trust each other absolutely.

Other friends took time to find that comfortable silence and trust. We had it instantly.

I knew then that the idea of soul mates wasn't just a romantic notion. I knew that people could find a soul mate in a friend.

"You could never lose me, Greer Bishop. You're my family and the love of my fucking life."

She laughed but it sounded shaky with her tears. "You're mine too."

"And soon"—I pulled back to glance down at her stomach—"I will be an aunt and little Baby Bishop will be the love of my life too."

Gratitude filled her expression. "Really?"

That she would think any different made me feel a ton of remorse for my selfishness. "I'm in a weird place right now, but never think for a second that I don't want you to have the things that bring you joy. If that's Andre and Baby Bishop, I'll rest easy knowing you're where you want to be."

"I want the same for you." She gave me a sad smile. "I just really hope you find it here and not four thousand miles away."

I chuckled. "I'll be back in four weeks. I promise."

"Don't." Greer took my hand and squeezed it. "Don't make a promise you can't keep."

Her genuine anxiety that I might choose to stay in England seemed ridiculous to me. Of course I was coming home. Yet I couldn't persuade Greer of this, so all I could do was hug her close and leave her standing on that sidewalk. She'd cheer up when I returned. For now, I would enjoy my four weeks in northern England.

After I slept. I'd caught up on edits for one of my loyal indie author clients, so I hadn't slept on the plane.

Jet lag was a bitch.

Reluctantly turning from the spectacular view, I took hold of my suitcase and crossed the road toward the terraced houses. Built of stone, like the cottages around the bend in the road, these were a story taller. Most had a front door and two sash and case wooden windows, one downstairs and one upstairs. Nearly all had been extended into the attic with a dormer window jutting out of the gray slate-tiled roofline.

One house was painted a pale blue, the one next to it was unpainted, showing off the beautiful original stonework. The one next to that was painted white, and so on.

On the end of the terraced row was a detached building—stone built but newer, bigger. Instead of two small windows, there were two large windows, one up, one down. Above the downstairs window was a sign that read:

Much Ado About Books

I smiled, and my suitcase and I trundled down the narrow sidewalk past the other houses until I stopped at the shop door. Unlike the solid wooden doors of its neighboring houses, this one had a large glass pane on the top half, and hanging inside was a notice that read CLOSED.

I knocked loudly.

A second or two later I saw a woman with dark hair appear behind the pane of glass. She smiled, and I heard the movement of the lock before the door swung open. "Evangeline?"

"Evie." I grinned through my exhaustion.

"I'm Penny. It's nice to meet you." She had a lilting English accent, different from the upper-class one in *Downton Abbey* or even the accent of the actors who played the servants. "Let me help you with that." Penny stepped down into the street, took my suitcase from me, and hauled it into the store before I could think to stop her.

Exhaustion made my reflexes slow.

"It's heavy," I said belatedly as I followed her inside. Penny was a sturdy woman, a good few inches shorter than me. Yet she was also, by my guesstimation, at least twenty years older than me, and I didn't want her to throw her back out because of my luggage.

"You're staying for four weeks; I didn't expect anything less." She threw me a smile as we halted in the middle of the store. She pronounced "you're" and "you" like "yur" and "yuh," dropped her g's, and left the final syllables of her words unstressed and short.

"I like your accent."

"Well, thank you. I'm a Geordie but I've lived here nigh on twenty years, so my accent has softened a wee bit."

"What's a Geordie?"

She smiled. "Someone from Tyneside. I'm originally from New-castle upon Tyne."

I vaguely considered how useful it would be to know more about the geography of northern England, but it was not the priority.

Tired. Bed. Sleep.

"The air is very fresh here." I gazed around the store, dazed with weariness. "Our air isn't as nice in Chicago, but I didn't realize that until coming here." On the far left of the room was a small counter. In front of the counter were little trays filled with tourist trinkets to buy, such as key rings and ornaments and candy. The large front window had a ledge with a display of books set up on it, and behind that ledge was a window seat for people to relax.

On the left, just in from the door, was a small, unlit fireplace and two cute old-fashioned armchairs set up on either side of it. Beside it was a wide bookcase filled with books. A sign on top of the bookcase stated they were new releases.

The right side of the room was taken up with stacks of oak bookshelves, each spaced apart with enough room for people to maneuver through them. Although the store was small, each bookcase had a sign on the side with a category on it: ROMANCE, CRIME, POETRY, etc.

Just as I'd hoped when I saw the photographs online, it reminded me of the small bookstore in my hometown that my parents would take me to once a month as a kid. They'd let me pick out a new book or order one if the store didn't have a particular title I wanted.

Nostalgia caused an aching flare in my chest as I continued to take in the space.

The shelves facing out toward the window boasted a display. This one was on the history of Northumberland with books, nonfiction and fiction, about the area.

"Books, books, books," I muttered as the room seemed to sway.

"Fresh sea air is good," Penny said, drawing my gaze back to her. She wore an amused expression. "But it can also make you sleepy when you're not used to it . . . and on top of jet lag I can only imagine how knackered you are."

"Knackered. That's a good word."

"It means 'tired,' pet. And I think we'll go over all the shop stuff tomorrow and just get you settled in."

I barely remembered advancing up the narrow stairs at the back of the building or Penny showing me around the apartment. I did remember her telling me she'd stocked the kitchen with some food, milk, tea, and coffee for me, which was so sweet, but before I knew it, she was gone.

The last thing I remembered was kicking off my shoes and faceplanting on the first bed I found.

$\mathcal{P}$enny was sweet enough to leave a note for me.

> I'll be round at 11 to show you the ropes. The Anchor does
> a wonderful English breakfast. It opens at 7.30. Hope you
> slept well, Penny.

I could hear her saying it in my head and decided hers was my new favorite accent.

Jet lag was evil and I'd awoken at five a.m. After making some coffee and nibbling on cookies Penny had left, I unpacked my suitcase and then snuggled down in the sitting room. The living space was open plan with a kitchen and sitting area, with a large modern window overlooking the water.

There was a wood-burning stove in the corner of the room, but there was also a heating system that must have been on a timer because I wasn't cold, despite the dreary weather outside. After sending a text to Greer to let her know I'd arrived and spending a dreamy hour staring out at the sea, I hopped in the shower in the bathroom that accompanied the master bedroom. By the time I emerged, the sun had broken through the rain and turned the village resplendent with color from the vibrancy of the flowers in the harbor gardens, to the bright painted stonework of some of the buildings.

Deciding to take up Penny's recommendation, I blow-dried my hair, changed into skinny jeans and a T-shirt, and grabbed my purse, excited for breakfast. My belly had been grumbling at me for hours, completely in shock at the time difference.

A fairly strong breeze blew up from the water, but I enjoyed it as I stared across the harbor to the other side. Perched atop the land above the right side of the harbor was a large stone building with a garden. I could see empty benches and chairs outside. Guessing this was The Anchor, I walked the path along the harbor road and followed it as it took a steep turn upward.

There were already a few people milling about, and from their camera-phone snap happiness, I gathered they were tourists. Standing aside to let two cars pass me, I noted another pub called The

Alnster Inn. It too appeared to be open. I wondered why Penny didn't recommend it.

As I hit the summit of the steep hill, the entrance to The Anchor appeared. Its small parking lot was already full, so I took that as a good sign. Again, there were outdoor benches and seating for dining outside, but why would you eat in the parking lot when you could enjoy the view on the other side of the building?

As I ventured inside, my heart delighted at the rustic interior. It was everything I imagined an old English pub to be, with low ceilings and thick dark wooden beams. A long bar top ran along the left side of the room, but the right side was cut in half by a wall. In the front room were tables and chairs with hardly any space in between and a massive fireplace that took up nearly the entire end wall. A bench ran down the outer wall beneath the small, old-fashioned windows with their bottled panes and iron detailing, and tables were situated in a row in front of the bench. The front room was busy, and some diners looked up from their plates at my arrival.

A small bark drew my attention, and I could see the diners sitting near the fireplace had their dogs with them.

Yes, it was everything I thought a pub would be.

I smiled at the blond woman that stood behind the bar.

"Table for one?" she asked.

I nodded. "Please."

"There's a couple of smaller tables free in the back room."

Giving her my thanks, I strolled down the narrow passage along the bar and stepped into the second room. It opened up into a much bigger, more modern space with a bank of doors along one end that led out onto the alfresco dining area I'd seen from the harbor. Spotting a free table near the doors, I sat down and gave a happy sigh at the view.

An English breakfast turned out to be nothing like the version of it I'd had back home in Chicago. It was strange to my palate, but, ultimately, I decided I liked it. Feeling better now that I'd eaten, I reluctantly finished my coffee and got up to pay at the bar.

"Staying in Alnster?" the woman asked.

It took me a minute to understand what she was saying because she pronounced the name of the village differently from how it was spelled. "Anster? I thought it was called Alnster?"

She chuckled. "If it's spelled *A-L-N* round these parts, it's usually pronounced like 'an' with a silent *L*. And *w*'s in place-names are sometimes silent . . . just to confuse you even more."

"Oh." I grinned gratefully at her. "Well, I'm glad I found out now before I pronounce the village name wrong to customers."

At her eyebrow raise, I continued, "I'm renting Much Ado About Books."

The bartender frowned. "Penny's still renting it out?"

I shrugged, wondering at the question. "She rented it to me for four weeks."

"Four weeks? I guess I'll be seeing you around then. I'm Milly Tait. I own this place with my husband, Dexter." She held out her hand to shake.

I took it. "Hi, Milly, I'm Evie. Have you been here long?"

"The Anchor was opened by my granddad seventy-five years ago. Was just a pub back then but Dex is a chef, and he turned the place into a proper gastropub."

"How cool. Does that mean you grew up here?"

"Born and raised. Where in America are you from?"

"Chicago."

"Ah, big-city lass then?" she teased. "Living here will be quite the change of pace."

"A much-needed change of pace."

"I sense a story there. Perhaps you'll come back in this evening and tell me all about it."

I hadn't known what to expect from the locals. Would they resent tourists coming in and running one of their stores, be indifferent, or embrace temporary residents? I was glad Milly was so friendly.

"I'd like that."

After I paid up and said goodbye to Milly, I walked around the small village. The bookstore was on the very end of the coastline. There wasn't anything beyond it but a few houses before the road ended and the cliff tops began. There was a path along the cliffs, made over the years by people traversing them, so I decided I'd put some time aside at some point to take a walk along it. On the opposite side of the village, however, where The Anchor was, was the main hub of Alnster. There was The Alnster Inn, a post office, a convenience store, a butcher shop, a bakery, a tourist shop, a café, and an art gallery/jeweler. There seemed to be two establishments to a building with lanes between each. I ventured down those cobblestoned lanes to find idyllic, quaint cottages tucked away at the end.

Back on the main road, heading away from that central hub, the village opened up into what was a housing development. The houses weren't as quaint here, but they looked out over the water. A playground sat above the sand dunes on the opposite side of the road.

Following the sand-encrusted sidewalk along the houses, I took a turn in the road and realized the homes reached far along the coastal land. Although I spotted a small primary school, there weren't signs of much else, and I deduced that the children more than likely had to get a bus to a high school in a larger nearby town.

After walking back toward the main street, I'd just passed The Anchor when a dog raced past me, yanking my attention away from the details of the village. The dog made my breath catch, and I hurried after it, my heart racing a little.

"Duke?" The name fell from my lips even though I knew it wasn't him.

I drew to a stumbled halt at the sight of the large, black, elegant Great Dane as it followed its nose along an invisible line on the sidewalk. He was the spitting image of my dog Duke. We adopted Duke when he was one year old, and we'd had him until he died of old age at nine. We'd gotten him only three months after my father died, and Duke passed away just after my fifteenth birthday. His death was heartbreaking, and it also brought back a lot of memories. It had been like losing my dad all over again.

"Shadow!" a male voice bellowed from behind me.

I was just about to turn toward that voice when the Great Dane followed whatever it was he smelled into the middle of the road.

Right near the blind bend toward the hill.

My feet moved, seemingly with a mind of their own.

"Shadow, come here, boy!"

Right then I heard the hum of a car engine and quickened my steps as the Great Dane suddenly lifted his head in my direction. Then the car appeared. Before I knew it, I was running, my eyes on the dog and the car.

The car that wasn't slowing!

Heart in my throat, I dashed out onto the road, grabbed the startled Dane by the collar, and hauled him with me to the other side of the street. At the last minute, my foot caught on something, my weak left ankle turning on itself.

Down I went.

Pain scored across my knees and left hand as I shook my head, discombobulated.

A snuffling sound in my ear brought my head up to the side, and my nose met the cold wet one of the Dane. His head bent toward me as he stared inquisitively into my eyes, and I realized I still had a tight grip on his collar.

"Jesus Christ, Shadow, look what you've done." A deep male voice sounded near. "Are you okay?"

Slumping to my side, I turned toward the voice I deduced was addressing me, my head falling back as I looked up.

Blinking against the bright sky, I wondered for a moment if the car had hit me, killed me, and now I was in heaven.

Because the most beautiful man I'd ever seen was staring down at me.

Four

I blinked rapidly, thinking the image before me would disappear, a mirage from the fall . . . but it didn't.

The man lowered to his haunches in front of me, reaching out to get a hold of the dog without removing his gaze from mine. His warm dark brown eyes wandered over my face, his expression seeming to waver between awe and concern. "Are you okay?" he repeated.

The question drew my attention to his mouth. A somewhat scruffy beard surrounded compelling lips, the bottom full in comparison to the top. My mother would call it a Harrison Ford mouth. I'd call it a Matt Davis mouth.

Oh my God, how long had I been staring at his mouth?

"We need to get you off this road." He nodded encouragingly. "Are you okay to move? Or is my dog in danger of being sued?" That devastating mouth of his curled at the corners to let me know he was teasing.

Realizing I was staring at him like a moron, I glanced back at his dog. "I can move."

"Are you hurt?" The stranger stood, pulling the Great Dane into his side with one hand, while he held out the other to me.

Still a little dazed, I reached for the proffered hand. Strong fingers curled around mine, and as he pulled me gently to my feet, his calloused palm rubbed against my softer one. A shiver skated down my spine, and I felt a little breathless. On my feet, I was startled to realize the man was a good few inches taller than me, the powerful breadth of his shoulders making his height seem even more substantial.

He grinned at me, a flash of white teeth, before he said, "We could stay here but Shadow might have to rescue *us* next. He's acting like a wild thing, so I'm not sure he's a good bet as a hero today. Unlike some people."

I realized he had an accent like Milly. Although they both sounded a lot like Penny, the defining character of their accent—the "yuh" instead of "you," the dropped *g*'s, and the abrupt final syllables—was less pronounced and easier to understand than Penny's.

"Shadow, heel," the man said, his tone sharp with demand. Then he tugged on my hand and led me across the road, with Shadow following closely.

Once on the sidewalk, I opened my mouth to thank the man, when a new voice stopped me. "Roane, is she okay?"

The man's gaze moved beyond me, and I turned to see Milly from The Anchor standing at the top of the hill, her eyebrows knitted in concern. A group of people at her back were watching curiously.

"Everything's fine, Milly," the man called up to her.

She scowled at him. "What the bloody hell has gotten into Shadow?"

I felt a squeeze on my hand and looked down to see he was still holding it as he responded, "He's only two and a half, Milly. Sometimes he regresses to puppy."

She harrumphed at that. "You all right, Evie, lass?"

Grateful for her concern but feeling fine, I waved it away. "I'm good, thanks."

With that, Milly nodded and turned back toward her pub.

"Evie, is it?"

My attention lowered to the hand the man had not yet released, before returning to his eyes. He seemed to study my every feature with open appreciation.

I shivered again.

"Did the fall affect your vocal cords? Or do you just not want me to know your name?"

"Evangeline Starling," I blurted out, still feeling disoriented. "But everyone calls me Evie."

His mouth spread into a wide smile, and his grip on my hand tightened as he gave it a little shake. "I'm Roane Robson. It's nice to meet you, Evie Starling."

Flustered by Roane's intense regard, I pulled my hand out of his and took in the rest of him. Thick dark hair with a slight curl to it ruffled in the breeze coming up off the sea. A worn, forest-green cable-knit sweater covered his broad shoulders, a loose thread dangling from the hem. Dark-wash denim jeans, covered in mud splatters, were tucked into knee-high Wellington boots. His skin was olive toned, and considering it was May in England and still somewhat cool, he was naturally tan, or years of laboring out in the sun had given him a permanent tan.

Shadow was sitting at attention by his side, the dog's head level with Roane's waist. Roane rubbed the top of it absentmindedly. He seemed to understand the question in my eyes. "I'm the local farmer hereabouts."

Now his clothing made sense.

Not that I minded his rugged appearance.

He was altogether the most masculine specimen I had ever come across. Even his voice was deep and rumbling. I felt that voice in places I had no business feeling it.

I did not come here to meet a gorgeous farmer. Even if he was looking at me as though he'd like to gobble me up. Seriously, his expression was so transparent and . . . *awestruck*.

A flush moved through me again. I was not a woman who inspired such open and blatant admiration. At least, I never had been.

"It was nice to meet you." I looked down at the dog. "I'm glad he's okay. He's a beauty."

"He's my best pal and that arsehole tourist was too busy looking at his phone and not the road. He would have hit him if you hadn't dragged him out of the middle of the street." Roane stepped toward me, and my skin tingled with awareness. "Please tell me you're not just visiting for one day. I'd love to buy you a drink in thanks."

Curse my luck!

I swear off men. I book a trip to England to find myself.

Instead I find a sexy English farmer who looked at me like he wanted to kiss my feet in thanks and then strip me naked to thank me some more.

Was it genuine attraction, or was he just grateful I'd saved his dog?

"Um . . ." I cleared my throat as I attempted to shake off the ludicrous spell he seemed to have cast over me. Was this what instant lust felt like? "I'm renting the bookstore. From Penny Peterson."

Roane frowned. "She's still renting it out?"

Milly had asked the same thing. What was that about?

I opened my mouth to query this, when he continued. "For how long?"

"Four weeks. I just arrived last night."

His eyebrows raised. "Four weeks?" Curiosity was evident in those twinkling eyes of his, and suddenly he grinned again. And it was wicked. It was the kind of grin that belonged on a womanizing playboy, not a farmer. "Then you can definitely join me for a drink tonight at The Anchor."

Oh boy.

"I'm not sure I can." Suddenly I wanted to run as far and as fast from this gorgeous man as I could. I leaned over to scratch Shadow behind the ears, gave the dog a smile and Roane a grimace. "I need to get back to the store. It was nice meeting you," I repeated.

However, I'd barely made it three steps when Roane and Shadow fell into stride beside me.

I kept walking but shot him a "can I help you?" look.

"I really have to insist that you let me make reparations toward you on behalf of Shadow. He'd do it himself, but he's shy around beautiful women."

A huff of laughter fell from my lips at his flirtation. "That's a shame. He's very handsome."

"I know, the bonny bastard is always stealing female attention away from me."

Chuckling, I shook my head at his nonsense, watching my footing as we strolled past the harbor, in case I took another tumble. When my attention returned to Roane, his eyes were trailing across my face, seeming to linger on my mouth before our gazes locked. Flabbergasted by the interest he did not hide, I stumbled, my foot hitting a crack in the sidewalk.

Roane grabbed my bicep to steady me and I groaned, feeling my cheeks warm. "You must think I'm a klutz."

"You took a tumble saving my dog," he reminded me as he gently led me across the street, checking at his side to make sure Shadow was following. "How does that make you a klutz?"

It wasn't what was making me a klutz. It was his intensity and open attraction to me.

An attraction I reluctantly returned.

"You can let go of my arm," I said, giving it a gentle pull.

His fingers flexed for a second before he released me. Shadow squeezed between our legs and started to trot in front of us. "Stay close," Roane said, and Shadow's ears twitched at the command.

"I don't normally throw myself out in front of cars to save dogs," I confessed, not wanting some idea that I was a champion of animals to give this guy the wrong impression of me. If he was feeling misguided hero worship, I wanted to nip it in the bud so I could go back to swearing off men. "Shadow is the spitting image of my dog Duke. I had him until he was nine years old and he . . . well, he came into my life as a puppy, just when I needed him. I was fifteen when he died." That tight ache in my chest flared anytime I thought of Duke. I cleared my throat. "I saw Shadow shoot right past me, and for a second I could have sworn . . ."

"It was Duke," Roane concluded, his deep voice gentle.

Avoiding his gaze, which I somehow knew would be just as soft as his tone, I nodded. "I've never had a dog since. Great Danes take up a lot of room, cost a lot to house and feed, and my mom didn't want another one, especially with me going off to college. Then I moved to the city and I didn't feel it was right to keep a dog when I worked all the time." Why was I telling a stranger all of this?

"But you miss the company?" Roane asked.

Pulling the key to the store out of my pocket, I nodded. "I guess."

We came to a stop outside the bookshop.

"Shadow, heel," Roane called to the dog. Thankfully, Shadow heeded him this time and trotted back to sit at his side.

I reached out to pet him. "He's so gorgeous," I said, smiling as Shadow bussed into my touch. Thankfully, like Duke, his ears hadn't been cropped and were floppy and silky and beautiful.

"Lucky bastard," Roane muttered.

Surprised, I glanced up to see he was staring at Shadow with genuine envy.

I dropped my hand and stepped toward the store. "Well, thank you for seeing me to the store . . ."

"Wait." Roane moved toward me, his expression eager. "Evie, I don't make a habit of asking tourists out but I can't help myself. You're brave, you love animals. You're stunning. I'm a mere mortal." His chuckle had a slightly disbelieving tone to it, like he couldn't understand himself in that moment. "So please have a drink with me tonight?"

It would be a lie to say I wasn't extremely flattered by Roane Robson's attention. Or that I didn't very much want to know what it would feel like to have the most tempting mouth I'd ever seen on a guy in real life pressed against mine.

But I wasn't here for a fling.

I was here to find myself.

I turned to him, deciding to be as forthright as Roane was being. "I've sworn off men. Not forever. But absolutely while I'm here. No men."

Roane's eyes rounded with surprise, and he reached up to scratch his cheek, the sound of fingernails against the bristles of his beard overly loud in the quiet morning.

And weirdly arousing.

After a few moments of contemplating me, he threw back his shoulders. "Have you sworn off friendships with men?"

Stupid disappointment rose in me, and invisible hands quickly moved to stuff that feeling back down, somewhere deep and dark inside me where I'd forget about its existence. "Friendship is good."

He dipped his head to me, his lips curled at the corner in what seemed to be a perpetually teasing way of his. "Then have a drink with me tonight at The Anchor. Let me say thank you properly. And maybe you can tell me where you come from—why you came here for four weeks and swore off men."

I shouldn't.

I really, really shouldn't.

But didn't I come here to experience something different? A new place, new people, and maybe a new me?

Becoming friends with an English farmer was definitely a new experience. Who cared if he could grace the front cover of "The World's Hottest Farmers" calendar? "Okay." I smiled. "A drink. But I'm warning you, my story isn't that interesting."

Roane's grin widened. "Somehow I doubt that." He glanced down at his dog and then back to me, his expression somber. "In all seriousness . . . thank you, Evie."

Realizing Shadow probably meant just as much to him as Duke had meant to me, I answered quietly, "You're welcome, Roane."

With that, he nodded and took a step back. "I need to return to the farm. I'll see you tonight at eight o'clock."

"I'll see you then."

As he and Shadow turned and strode back in the direction they'd come, I realized how breathless I'd been in Roane's company and sucked in a lungful of air.

"Jesus, Mary, and Joseph," I muttered, watching them disappear.

"You met Roane then—"

"Argh!" I cried out in fright and turned to find Penny standing on the sidewalk, as if she'd appeared out of thin air.

Her lips twitched. "Sorry, pet, didn't mean to scare you."

I let out a shaky breath. "It's not you. It's . . . been an interesting morning."

"Oh, aye, I heard about that from Milly. Saved Roane's dog, did you?"

I frowned, glancing behind me and back to Penny. How could she have heard from Milly, who was in the opposite direction, and then appear at my back as if from nowhere? Had Milly called Penny immediately to tell her what had happened? Obviously.

Village life. News traveled fast.

She chuckled as if she sensed my bemusement, and gestured toward the store. "Open her up then. Let me show you the ropes."

It was as I unlocked the door that I suddenly felt the stinging in my left palm and on my knees. Looking down, my jeans were covered in dust from the fall, and the left kneecap looked a little threadbare too. I must have hissed because Penny queried, "You all right, pet?"

"I'm fine. Probably have a skinned knee or two from the fall."

"There's a first aid kit in the flat. Would you like me to get it?"

"Oh, I'm sure I'm fine, thanks."

She nodded, accepting this. "Okay, let's get to work then."

But before we could, there was a loud rap on the door, and we turned to see a man peering in at us. "You open, Penny?"

She frowned and hurried to open the door, letting the man in. He had graying dark hair and startling pale blue eyes, and he wore a brown lightweight coat with a white apron underneath it. "Did you leave the store?" Penny asked, sounding surprised.

"Young Matthew's watching it." The man threw me a flustered nod. I put him around the same age as Penny and wondered at their connection. Turning to her, he said, "Lella dropped the bomb on me this morning that she's supposed to read *Twelfth Night* by tomorrow for homework. I'm really hoping you have a copy."

"You're in luck." Penny hurried toward the shelves to the one marked POETRY and scoured it for a few seconds before pulling out a thin paperback.

The man seemed to sag in relief. "You're a star, Pen. How much?"

"Take it." Penny held it out to him. "My next steak and ale pie is free."

He grinned, the smile transforming his glowering expression. With those unusual eyes of his, he was quite handsome. As if sensing my attention, he nodded to me. "New owner?"

Penny sighed and threw me a small smile. "New renter." Seeing his eyebrows draw together, she shrugged. "I'll explain later."

"Right. Well, I best get back. Thank you again."

"You're welcome, Jed. Remember that pie."

"I'll go one better," he said, pulling the door open, "Cerys and I'll have you round for tea, so you don't have to cook it yourself."

"I won't say no to that."

After the door closed, Penny wandered back to me and explained, "Jed's the butcher. Sad tale." Her eyes darkened. "He and Cerys, his wife, lost their daughter in a car crash two years go. Cerys was in the car. She's in a wheelchair now. Their daughter left behind her daughter Arabella. Everyone calls her Lella, a nickname from a young neighbor's son that just kind of stuck." She leaned against the counter. "Poor couple lost their bairn, Cerys her mobility, and gained full guardianship of their granddaughter all at the same time. Lella just turned thirteen. Raising a teenage girl again. It's not easy."

My heart hurt for the butcher and his wife. "That's awful, Penny."

She patted my shoulder. "Don't worry. It's a good community here. When my Arthur died, they rallied around me, like we rallied around Jed, Cerys, and Lella."

Realizing her words meant she was widowed, I offered, "I'm so sorry."

"It was four years ago now. Sometimes . . ." Her gaze drifted off into the distance, to someplace no one else could get to. "Sometimes it feels like yesterday. Other times like . . . like it was another lifetime."

A silence I didn't know how to break without being disrespectful fell between us. Finally, I said, "You and Jed seem close."

"Cerys and I have been friends since Arthur and I moved here. The four of us were good friends for years." Seeing my somber expression, Penny suddenly clapped her hands together. "Let's get on then. You've got a bookstore to run."

Five

For a moment it was like I was six years old again with all of my toys set up in a row in my bedroom as I pretended to own a toy shop, forcing my parents to play my customers.

Except this was real.

The cash register was an app on the laptop hidden behind the counter. I just had to use a barcode scanner connected to the computer when ringing up books and other items. There was a stockroom behind a door at the back of the store, next to the private downstairs restroom. The stockroom was filled not only with books, but with all kinds of ornaments and objects for renters to use for the window display.

I had free rein to create whatever display I wanted.

When Penny left after showing me the ropes, leaving me her number in case I needed help, I'd felt a little apprehensive. How brave Penny was to leave her store to the charge of inexperienced bookish tourists?

As for other tourists, several passed by the store throughout

the day, peering in, trying to catch my eye as if that would somehow force me to open the door.

I ignored them, even though I felt rude. However, after discussing it with Penny, I decided while I was in charge, the store
would be open four days a week. Wednesday through Saturday. I
had two editing jobs lined up with authors I'd worked with before,
and even though I imagined I'd have free time during opening
hours to work on those, I still liked the idea of having free days to
edit. It gave me time in the week to sightsee around Northumberland. I'd need to arrange a rental car, but other than the nerve-
racking prospect of driving on the opposite side of the road, I was
kind of excited about it.

I wondered if I'd get to see Roane's farm and then threw the
thought away.

Roane? Roane who?

First things first. Arranging a display in the storefront window.
I started unloading the boxes marked DISPLAY and noted what was
there. There were little sheep and cattle, and I wondered if they
were for an agriculture display about Northumberland.

Did another woman come here, meet Roane, and decide to pay
homage to him? Was he the tourist trap?

I shook my head.

Roane? Roane who?

When I saw the painted bust of Shakespeare's head among the
items, I knew Penny and I were secretly soul mates. Giddy with excitement, I grabbed my favorite playwright's head, intending to use
it. There was a weird and wonderful collection of ornaments that
seemed to make no sense, but my love for Shakespeare meant my
brain automatically put them all together and came up with *A Midsummer Night's Dream*. Penny had several garden fairies, and there

was even a miniature donkey. Finding a crib and a manger, I suspected the donkey was part of a Christmas nativity set. But all I saw was Nick Bottom. Sure, *he* only had a donkey's head, but I had to work with what was available, and that didn't include a half-human, half-donkey doll.

Because that would be creepy.

I wondered if Roane liked Shakespeare.

Who cares? I admonished myself.

Grabbing piles of green sparkly tinsel, I arranged it on the wide window ledge to look like grass. Penny had several small, twiggy Christmas trees, and I attached paper blossoms I'd found to the branches. The blossoms had clips on them, like they were hair decorations to be worn for a luau or something, and I transformed two of the miniature Christmas trees into blossom trees. The others I plugged in so they lit up.

Finding strings of fairy lights, I draped them around the window. Then I placed the garden fairies and the donkey across the ledge surrounded by tinsel and lights. There were several copies of *A Midsummer's Night Dream* in the store, and I opened those just enough that they stood in place among the display.

The bust of Shakespeare took center stage.

To finish the scene, I found gold stars, glued them to string, and taped them to the wall above the window so they cascaded down above the display at differing lengths. Using the laptop, I printed quotes from the play onto white cards and propped them against the fairies.

A few hours later, I stepped outside in the pleasantly sunny May afternoon and took in the effect of what I'd created. It wouldn't win awards—in fact it looked like six-year-old me had done it—but it was whimsical and made me smile.

I wondered if it would make Roane smile.

"Oh, for goodness' sake," I snapped at myself.

$\mathscr{A}$ s focused as I was on preparing the bookstore for opening (and trying to distract myself from invading thoughts of a certain farmer), I completely forgot to eat lunch. Deciding to dine at The Anchor, I left for the pub before seven o'clock. My belly rumbled furiously at me, and I felt a little light-headed.

Dressing for the evening had been tricky. I didn't want to encourage flirtation from Roane, but I wanted to wear what I wanted to wear without thinking about how it would affect the farmer. I loved tailored shorts because I had long legs. Where most of my female friends complained of cellulite on their thighs, it didn't plague me on that part of the body. My legs were slender but well formed and strong. As I neared my late twenties, the dreaded cellulite did appear, but it attached itself to the wings of my arms and my belly. A lady couldn't win. However, she could choose to embrace the positives.

I mused over the decision to wear my favorite clothing item or stick with jeans.

Would Roane think I was showing off my legs for him?

Would the locals think I was a silly American who didn't know how to dress for cooler weather?

Ludicrous. I lived in Chicago. I knew cold weather.

Finally deciding the whole purpose of this trip was to embrace the things I wanted and liked, I pulled on a pair of black tailored shorts, a plain green crew-neck T-shirt, which I tucked into them, a short black blazer with the sleeves rolled up to the elbow, and a pair of slouchy green leather ankle boots with a low heel. I had a bruise on my left knee from today's fall, but it wasn't too bad once I applied a little concealer.

I released my dark hair from the ponytail I'd worn during the day and wore it in loose beachy waves so the caramel ombré highlights were noticeable.

Studying my image in the full-length mirror, I stuck my hands in my shorts pockets and bit my lip. I did not look like I was venturing out to a pub in Northumberland.

Yet I looked like me.

Snapping a mirror selfie, I sent the photo to Greer with the text message:

Does the bruise look bad? xx

I'd messaged her earlier to tell her about rescuing Shadow and the consequent fall. I left his handsome owner out of the story.

As I was heading downstairs to leave, my phone buzzed.

Babe, I can't see a bruise. xx

My cell beeped again.

I am worried a horny fisherman or two might try to kidnap you. You know those legs are lethal. xx

I grinned at her teasing and stuffed the cell in my purse. The cool evening air took me by surprise as I stepped outside the store and locked up. Yeah, the breeze off the sea had interrupted the temperate day, but it had been pleasant. Plus, it was still light out.

The flutter of butterflies I'd been trying to ignore the past few hours made themselves known. Shaking my head at the stupidity of those butterflies, I glanced at the garden Penny said belonged to the store. I noted its bench and how it was angled toward the sea and decided my next day off would be spent reading there.

It was better to think of these things than to think of a man.

The rejection from Aaron was less than a week old. My pride had healed, and I realized my hope of finding love had been crushed more than my hope of finding love *with Aaron*, but that didn't mean I was ready to put myself out there again.

Especially not with a man I'd never see after my visit to England was up.

A sound similar to that of a motorbike drew my gaze from the water and my attention from my musings. From the brow of the hill before the main street of the village appeared a woman.

On a quad bike.

She blew past me and turned left toward the road that led out of Alnster.

The image of her made me smile.

She wore no helmet, her blond curly hair blowing behind her on the breeze, her open jacket fluttering in the wind as she confidently rode the quad bike like she did it every day.

And I got the feeling she did.

How badass.

Was she a local? If so, I wondered if I'd get to meet her.

The parking lot of The Anchor was worryingly busy, suggesting I might not get a table. Those fears were supported by the wave of warmth and the loud murmur of voices that hit me as I stepped inside.

The pub was packed with people dining.

I stared around, more than a little bemused that such a tiny village could have such a busy pub. Sure, I'd understand if it were the height of summer and tourists were crawling all over the place . . .

"Evie." Milly drew my gaze as she strode toward me behind the bar. Almost every stool at the bar was occupied. "In for tea?"

It took me a moment to realize "tea" meant dinner. Stepping up to the end of the bar, I gave her a weak smile. "It doesn't look like there's a table." And I was hungry. So, so hungry. The smell of delicious food was intoxicating me.

"Not to brag, lass, but my Dexter's food is known all over Northumberland. We keep busy at teatime. If you want to eat here, you let me know and I'll reserve a table for you. For now, if you're happy to, you can eat at the bar."

I nodded eagerly. "Yeah, please."

Perhaps my relief was palpable because Milly chuckled and gestured for me to follow. I rounded the bar, ignoring some men on stools who blatantly ogled my legs.

The second dining room was just as busy as the first.

Sliding onto the stool Milly gestured to, I gave the woman next to me a small smile when she turned to see who her new neighbor was. She returned the smile before giving her attention to the man beside her.

"There, lass." Milly placed a menu in front of me. "Now what can I get you to drink?"

"Oi, I was next, Milly!" a male voice shouted from the other end of the bar.

She raised an eyebrow in that direction. "I say who's next in my pub."

"Fine, but I'm next after Legs," he shouted back.

Presuming "Legs" was me, I scowled.

"Her name is Evie," Milly informed him crisply.

I wanted to hide under the bar.

"I prefer Legs."

"Oh, aye? Do you prefer going somewhere else to drink, man? Because I don't cater to rudeness in my pub."

"Aw, I was only joking, Milly. Get the lass a drink and put it on my tab."

She nodded and turned back to me with a smirk.

"I'll pay for my own drink," I replied.

She grinned. "And what will that be?"

"A cider."

"What kind?"

I shrugged. "Whatever you recommend."

While Milly disappeared to get my cider, I perused the menu. After googling it, I'd discovered The Anchor, just as Milly had said, was a gastropub. Deciding to continue eating "British," I ordered the battered haddock and chips, remembering that chips in the UK were like a plumper version of fries, and crisps were what we in the US called chips.

My fish and chips arrived on a wooden tray, the chips served in a miniature frying basket, with sides of tartar sauce and mushy peas in little ceramic pots. Everything was delicious, and although I'd had a fish and chips dish at a British bar in Chicago, the tartar sauce I'd had there didn't even compare to Dexter's.

"Enjoying that?" Milly asked as she passed me to serve someone a drink.

I swallowed a chip I'd layered with mushy peas and replied, "Your husband's a genius."

She guffawed. "For Christ's sake, keep your voice down. His ego's big enough."

I chuckled at her teasing and continued to clean my plate.

Stuffed full, I wished I were in a chair with a back so I could slump down in sleepy satisfaction. Between the food and jet lag, I was almost ready for bed. Milly took hold of the tray with one hand and popped a smaller menu in front of me with the other. "Dessert."

Oh God, I couldn't eat another—

Sticky toffee pudding.

The British bar back home had sticky toffee pudding on the menu. I'd bet my entire shorts collection that Dexter's was yummier.

"Well?" Milly returned to me a few minutes later.

I made a face of distress. "I want the sticky toffee pudding and ice cream so bad, but I don't think I'll manage it."

"Then why don't we split one?" Roane suddenly appeared at my side, and I jerked with surprise. He smirked, those dark eyes twinkling mischievously.

Before I could speak and reprimand him for the fright, Milly said, "Excellent idea. And a table has opened up by the fireplace so you can sit there with Shadow."

Glancing down, I found Shadow at his side and focused on the dog. Scratching his ears, I welcomed him warmly, laughing when he licked my wrist in response.

It was so much easier to focus on Shadow because the Roane before me differed from the Roane this morning. Sure, he still had the beard and wild thick hair, but now he wore a dark red plaid shirt with the sleeves rolled up, a pair of dark-wash jeans that didn't have mud stains on them, and a pair of hiking boots instead of Wellingtons. I focused in on his strong tan forearms and shivered.

He smelled amazing. At first, I was hit with something musky, woodsy, like his cologne had a strong sandalwood base note. Then this overlying ocean scent drifted over me, layered with something citrusy. It was fresh and heady at the same time, and it made a woman want to nuzzle her face in his strong throat and run her fingers through the bristles of his beard.

Well, it made this woman want to.

"Is Shadow the only one you're going to say hello to?"

Realizing I was being rude, I straightened and gave him what I hoped was a natural smile. "Hey."

Roane grinned that boyish, wicked smile of his. "Hi. Let's grab that table before someone else does." He shot Milly a look. "Can I get a pint too, Milly?"

"I'll bring it over with the pudding. Another cider, Evie?"

I nodded. A little fortification might be just the thing. Throwing off lingering exhaustion, I slid from the stool to follow Roane.

He looked over his shoulder to make sure I was behind him, and did a double take. His gaze dropped to my legs and slowly traveled back upward, and I swore I saw the crests of his cheeks redden before he looked away.

Ignoring my smugness, I studied the back of him and cursed our maker for creating men with such fine asses.

You're objectifying the farmer, I scolded myself.

It was hard not to appreciate those wide shoulders, the tapered waist, and the way he moved through the tables with an easy, loose-limbed gait. Shadow trotted behind him, and they both drew admiring gazes.

Roane stopped at the lit fireplace and pulled out a chair, gesturing me to it.

I did *not* swoon at the gentlemanliness. I was merely lightheaded from all the food and was forced to collapse quickly into the chair. The heat from the fire caused goose bumps on my arms and legs as Shadow sprawled out in front of the fireplace as if he'd done it many times before. Roane took the seat opposite me.

We were both so tall, our knees knocked together under the table.

The corner of his lips tipped upward as if this amused him. Those dark eyes studied my face as they had earlier today. I squirmed in my seat, hoping I didn't have crumbs at the corners of my mouth. Or that he'd look lower to where my belly rolls were visible and particularly prominent after the fish and chips.

Are you listening to yourself?

Weren't these the thoughts I'd tried to banish over the years? Was a stupid four-week social media encounter really going to screw with my self-esteem? And hadn't I just repeatedly told myself that Roane Robson was off-limits? So what the hell did I care what he thought about my body?

I relaxed back in my chair, and Roane's gaze automatically flickered downward.

He never got farther than my boobs. Visibly swallowing, he looked quickly away. There was a definite flush on the tops of his cheeks. "The place will quiet down in a bit." His voice sounded extra rumbly, maybe even a little hoarse.

Hating how charmed I was that such a sexy man was flushing like a schoolboy, I picked up a menu from the table and started to fan my heated skin. "Is it always this busy?"

Roane's gaze moved back to mine. "It gets busy April through October because it's heavily advertised by Visit Northumberland—the tourist board." He gestured to the room. "It usually quiets down around nine o'clock, leaving mostly locals."

"Is your farm in Alnster?"

"Just outside."

Before I could ask any more questions, Milly appeared with our drinks and was accompanied by a man the same height as her. He was a handsome bald man, with dark umber skin, lots of gray stubble on his cheeks and chin, and warm, laughing dark eyes. He wore chef whites. He placed a delicious-looking sticky toffee pudding and ice cream on the middle of the table along with a spoon for me and one for Roane.

"Evie, this is my husband, Dexter. Dexter, Evie."

I held out my hand, beaming at him. "So nice to meet you. Your food is amazing."

"I told you you'd like her," Milly muttered.

Dexter chuckled and brought my hand to his lips for a quick kiss. "It's a pleasure, Evie. I'm chuffed to bits you like the food, considering you're from Chicago." Dexter released my hand and leaned on the table, his head bent toward mine conspiratorially. "Have you ever eaten at Alinea? It's on my bucket list."

Alinea was a fine dining restaurant in the city. It had three Michelin stars and was ranked in the top fifty best restaurants in the world. I chuckled at the feverish look in his eyes. "I'm afraid not. Alinea is a little out of my price range."

The chef opened his mouth to say something else, but Milly caught him by the arm. "Let them eat their pudding." Milly smiled at me. "We'll come over later when the pub is quieter and join you for a pint."

Something in me relaxed. Having Milly and Dexter as a buffer between me and Roane did not sound like a bad thing. "Great!"

When they'd gone, Roane waved a hand at the plate. "Ladies first."

Sharing a dessert was strangely intimate. It did not help that we kept locking gazes. His eyes appeared darker than they really were because of the sable outer rims of his irises. However, on close inspection, I found a lighter shade of brown encircled his pupils, a dark mahogany, and between the sable and mahogany were embers of a fire. Copper in the sunlight. Bright autumn leaves on dark soil.

I could have stared into Roane's eyes all night.

Most discomforting in all this was the fact that I wasn't uncomfortable. Despite my hyperawareness of him, I was weirdly at ease in his company.

"So." Roane pushed the plate aside. "Chicago?"

"I grew up in the suburbs of Indiana. Carmel, north of Indianapolis. But I graduated from Northwestern University, which is north of Chicago, and I just never left. What about you? Born and raised in Northumberland?"

"Aye. The farm is a couple of miles from here. I went to school, traveled a bit, but the Northumberland Coast is home."

I smiled, imagining him wandering the world only to be drawn back to the beauty here. "What a home it is."

Roane smiled appreciatively. "You like it here so far then?"

"So far. Alnster is beautiful, and I haven't even walked along the beach yet."

"There's a lot more to see."

"I know. I've decided the store will only be open four days a week. That way the rest of the time I'll sightsee."

"Good plan. You know, it was a surprise to hear you rented from Penny. Last we heard, she was selling the place."

This news surprised and saddened me. I hadn't even been open one day as the "owner," and yet it had already brought me the peace and relaxation I'd been looking for. To be surrounded by books in such a beautiful place. "I booked last minute, maybe that's why."

Roane asked me why renting a bookstore was my idea of a vacation, and I told him of my love of all things books and Shakespeare.

His lips twitched and he stared at me, gaze warm, like he

thought I was adorable. "I've never really been a fan of Shakespeare, to be honest."

I narrowed my eyes, teasing, "How can you not be a fan of Shakespeare?"

Roane shrugged.

"Now is the winter of our discontent."

His eyes danced with laughter.

"Some are born great, some achieve greatness, and some have greatness thrust upon them."

His smile grew.

"Cowards die many times before their deaths; the valiant never taste of death but once."

The warmth in his eyes darkened. "That's a good one. I like that."

Pleased, I nodded and continued, "If you prick us, do we not bleed? If you tickle us, do we not laugh? If you poison us, do we not die? And if you wrong us, shall we not revenge?" I leaned forward, and Roane's gaze flickered to my mouth. "How can you not be a fan of Shakespeare when his characters say epic shit like that?"

Roane laughed and leaned toward me. "Well, when you put it like that . . . Also, I'm impressed you know all that by heart."

"Do you want the truth?"

"Aye, always, unless it's something negative about Shadow. I won't hear a bad word against him, even if he shit on your marigolds."

I threw my head back in laughter. How could a guy be both adorable and sexy? I hadn't thought it possible until I met Farmer Robson.

Roane's eyes glittered, his lips twitching with amusement. "You were saying?"

"Oh. Yeah. Well, I love Shakespeare. I do. But I memorized a bunch of lines in college to impress my hot lit professor and they stuck."

"Your dedication to get his attention is impressive."

"How do you know my professor wasn't a woman?"

Surprise flickered across his face, and if I wasn't wrong, disappointment. "You're right. I shouldn't have presumed."

"I'm teasing." I drank the last of my cider and smirked at him. "He was a guy."

Giving me a mock scowl, Roane stood up. "I'll get us another round."

When he returned, the pub was quiet enough that Milly and Dexter joined us. They sat at the table beside us, and I turned my chair so my back wasn't to them; however, this situated me closer to Roane. My hyperawareness went into overdrive. The first time his arm brushed mine, I swear my heart leapt into my throat.

Before I knew it, I'd consumed another cider and was on my fourth. I was feeling a little drunk and a lot loose-tongued when the conversation turned more personal.

Milly asked what had brought me to Alnster, and I ended up telling them about the wreck of my life, how much of a failure I was, about Aaron being the end of a long list of bad online dating experiences, my lack of a job, and my friends all moving on with their lives. The only thing I, thankfully, kept to myself was my mom.

"So now I'm here, putting a little distance between me and Chicago, and trying to figure out what I want." I couldn't look at Roane as I added, "And that means no men for a while."

"Why swear off men entirely?" Dexter's gaze flickered to Roane and back to me. "Surely after all the dating you've done, you know what it is you want and what you don't want?"

"Oh, I know what I emphatically *don't* want." I raised my bottle of cider to punctuate this point.

"That being?"

I turned to Roane. He sat forward, his arms crossed in front of him, his head bent toward mine, his dark gaze focused entirely on me. For a moment he discombobulated me. Then I shook myself. "No younger men and no guys with money."

He frowned. "Isn't that a little judgmental?"

I winced and dragged my gaze from his to Milly, thinking a woman might understand my reasoning better as I explained, "I've dated two younger men—"

"How old are you?" Milly interrupted.

"Thirty-three."

Her face was expressionless as she nodded.

"As I was saying, I've dated two younger men—well, I've dated one and then there was Aaron, who was twenty-eight, but he doesn't count as a boyfriend. Although, it weirdly felt like we were dating. I don't know. Anyway, they both proved to be emotionally immature and a waste of my energy. It just makes sense to me I don't go down that road again.

"As for my rule against dating men with money, well, I've had that one since college. Chace. Chace Miller. My high school sweetheart. He grew up on the West Side and I grew up on the East. I didn't have money. He did. We met at the movies when I was fifteen, got into Northwestern together, and we dated until sophomore year of college." I looked down at Shadow, suddenly unable to meet anybody's eyes. "I knew deep down he'd never treated me well. But it wasn't until my best friend Greer started to hound me about his behavior, I realized I had to break it off. He always made these comments, little offhand comments that he tried to sell as jokes, that I was lucky to be dating him. And he'd condescend to me about things, especially about cars and clothes and anything materialistic, mansplaining these things because I hadn't grown up with money like he had.

"And I realized Greer was right. I'd been so *grateful* to him for choosing me, and he made me feel ashamed of where I came from. Inferior. There was no balance between us." Finally, I looked up and saw Milly staring at me in sympathy. "Years of this subtle negativity had a big effect. He fucked with my self-esteem and it took a long time for me to fix what he broke."

"He sounds like a prick," Roane said. "You shouldn't shut yourself off from different people because of one bad example."

I smiled at him. "You're probably right but I'd rather not take the chance, Farmer Robson."

For a moment we just looked at each other, his lips pressed together as if I'd displeased him. The desire to lean over and kiss those gorgeous lips was so strong, I reared back to stop myself.

Roane's eyebrows drew together.

"I'll get us another round," Dexter said. "Give us a hand, Roane."

The men left and my cheeks burned as I realized I'd just spread most of my life story out before these strangers. I glanced sheepishly at Milly. "I don't think I should have another."

"Don't be embarrassed, lass," she offered kindly. "By the time your holiday is over, you'll know all of our entire life stories. That's just the way it is in Alnster."

My eyes seemed to move across the room to Roane with a mind of their own. "Everyone knows each other, huh?"

"Aye. And Roane Robson is a well-known bachelor along the entire coast."

This knowledge irritated and disappointed me. "A player?"

"Oh God, no."

Milly's vehemence surprised me.

She shook her head. "You must have noticed he's a grand-looking man. He's got his share of admirers, locals and tourists, but he's no lothario. In fact, he's the opposite. Never met a man more monogamous than Roane. He gets a right ribbing from the men round here for it. But he is who he is, and he never shows an interest in tourists." She grinned. "Unless they save his best friend's life." She nodded to Shadow before looking back at me. "And have legs that go on forever."

I rolled my eyes. "I've already told him I've sworn off men. This is a friendly drink to say thank you for saving Shadow."

Milly chuckled. "If you say so."

A few minutes later Dexter and Roane returned, and over the course of the next few hours I overimbibed as I was introduced to more locals; people whose names I forgot as soon as they said them . . . because things got very foggy. The last thing I remembered was finishing the sixth bottle of cider.

Which was probably why the *next* thing I remembered was waking up in bed with Roane Robson.

Six

The shock of seeing Roane's handsome sleeping face on the pillow next to mine caused me to jolt upward, and with that sudden movement, a huge wave of nausea rose from my gut. Clasping my mouth, I threw myself off the bed and momentarily panicked as the world spun. Pushing through the dizziness, I lurched into the master bathroom and got the toilet lid up in time.

Ugh, vomiting was miserable.

And my body just didn't seem to want to stop.

As the worst of it began to settle and I rested my head over the bowl, trying to catch my breath and pretty much luxuriate in my misery, I realized there were gentle hands on me. One was holding my hair away from my face, while the other rubbed my back in comfort.

Roane.

An image of what I'd woken up to flashed across my mind.

Roane, fully dressed, sleeping above the duvet on my bed.

Spitting up the last of the bile, I flinched at the sudden appearance of a washcloth in my face and with shaking hands took it from Roane. Wiping my mouth, I slumped back against the side of the bathtub and watched, pained, as Roane flushed the toilet.

Fragile.

The best word to describe how I felt with the hangover from hell was "fragile." Like I might break apart at any second. My head pounded, my throat burned, and I felt sick, light-headed, and shaky.

Basically, I felt like I'd poisoned myself, which I had.

Why was Roane here?

I glanced down at myself. I was still wearing the same clothes from last night, so I hadn't gotten undressed at any point. I didn't think.

Looking none the worse for wear, Roane strolled out of the bathroom and returned a minute later with two glasses of water and Shadow on his heels. The huge dog came right up to me, towering over me as Roane handed me the glass of water and two pills.

"Take those and then I'll make a quick breakfast before I leave for the farm."

Seriously, why was he here? Had something happened last night between us?

Oh God. I hoped not. Not like that.

Not at all! I reminded myself.

"What time is it?" I asked, scratching Shadow behind the ear.

"Just before five in the morning."

I nodded and took the pills, finishing the water in a few gulps.

While I did this, I watched Roane's expression veer between amusement and concern.

There was no way I didn't look like shit. Still in my clothes from last night, I studied my legs for any new bruises and was grateful to find none. Hopefully that meant I hadn't done any falling down.

"Come on." Roane held out his hand. "Let's get some food in you."

My stomach revolted at the idea. "Please no," I begged, even though I took his hand.

He slowly helped me to my feet, and although there was nausea and dizziness, I seemed to have emptied all the contents of my stomach for now. "You have to eat something."

Leading me by the hand, Roane brought me to the living area and sat me down on a stool at the kitchen counter. It was still dark outside, so the kitchen lights felt overly bright to my sore, hungover eyes.

"Why are you here?" I finally asked.

He glanced at me over his shoulder as he opened the refrigerator. "You were wasted last night. So drunk I was worried you might get sick in your sleep. I brought you home and stayed to watch over you." He turned back to the refrigerator. "I must have fallen asleep too."

Warmth spread through me. "That was a nice thing to do."

"Aye, well." Roane grinned as he pulled eggs out of the fridge. "I owe you."

Somehow I thought it was something Roane would do for a friend even if that friend hadn't saved his dog's life. Watching him as he pottered around the kitchen making me a breakfast of scrambled eggs and toast (which I did not want to eat), I realized I wasn't embarrassed.

Shouldn't I be mortified to have this gorgeous man witness me drunk and then throwing up the next morning? There was no way I didn't have mascara streaks on my cheeks and that my pallor wasn't deathly pale.

All of this should have made me self-conscious, uneasy. Especially since he was a stranger.

And yet, just like last night, I felt weirdly comfortable sitting in silence as he made breakfast while Shadow waited patiently at his feet for any scraps.

"Thank you," I said as he placed a plate before me. He took the stool beside me to dig into his own plate of food. "For everything."

He gave me that boyish smile I liked too much. "It's what friends do."

"And you want to be friends, even though I'm leaving in less than four weeks?"

Swallowing the bite of food he'd taken, Roane nodded. "I do."

Forcing myself to take a forkful of eggs into my mouth, I concentrated on keeping them down before replying, "Is it because I saved Shadow?"

"What?"

"That you're going out of your way"—I gestured to the food, but the gesture encapsulated the entire night—"to be my friend?"

Roane shook his head. "It started with that. Now it's because I like you."

I snorted. "I got drunk, blurted out nearly my entire life story to a pub full of strangers, and then you had to babysit me all night and hold my hair back while I threw up. Yes, I can absolutely see why all of that would endear me to you."

Chuckling, he shrugged. "You do have a certain charm, that's true."

Rolling my eyes, I pushed the food around on my plate. "I'm a mess."

I hadn't meant for those words to sound so melancholy, but they brought about my companion's intense regard.

"Let me ask you a question." Roane turned his body toward me. "Why did you really come here?"

My head was pounding, I still felt nauseated and irritable with it, but out of gratitude I indulged a question that had a very complicated answer. At least it felt that way. "If I stayed, I would have spiraled into a depression, and it's harder to pull yourself out of that black hole than to fight getting sucked into it in the first place. So, I came here."

"Why would you have been depressed? What are you avoiding feeling?"

"Feeling like a failure. I came here to find some meaning in my life. To find out what I want from my life."

"Career-wise?"

"That. And . . ." I glanced shyly down at my plate. "And love."

"In what way?"

Looking up at Roane, seeing the genuine curiosity in his expression, the shyness, the vulnerability I felt about my love life—or lack thereof—eased. "Am I really lonely, or do I only think I should feel lonely because society dictates that I should be in a long-term relationship?"

His brow furrowed and he gestured for me to continue.

"Sometimes after a long day at work where I'd been especially productive and useful, I'd come home, I'd order takeout, watch Netflix, and then I'd get in my big comfy bed that takes up most of my studio apartment and I'd switch on my e-reader. For an hour before bed, I'd sit there, warm, safe, and engrossed in a great story. And I'd feel content." I turned toward him so our knees touched. "Because not everyone has that in their life. There is a lot of darkness out there, a darkness that some people don't want to think about. Human trafficking, modern slave labor, extreme poverty, homelessness . . . Not everyone gets to spend their nights in a warm bed, enjoying books. Maybe some people think my life is pathetic, but my life would be a *dream* to some people. What right do I have to whine about wanting more from my life, when what I have is more than some people can ever imagine having? I'm privileged in a way that doesn't have to do with great wealth. I'm privileged by comforts we take for granted, like education, having food in the refrigerator, a roof over my head, heat, clean water, and easy access to books. A life that has been blessedly free of violence.

"So why do I have days where I feel miserable and lonely?" I asked him, wondering if I'd ever work out the answer. "Is it because I'm *genuinely* lonely and looking for love? Or is it because all of my friends have found companionship, even love in most cases, and I feel their quiet pity for me because I haven't? Is it because society tells me that's what I should want out of life? Or do I really want it? Am I so spoiled by my upbringing, I'm conditioned to continually want more than what I have?" I shook my head and then immediately stopped when the room shifted off its axis. I gripped the counter and took a deep breath. "I thought if I came here and put some distance between myself and my life, I might figure out what I wanted so I could finally do something about it."

"Do something about it?"

"If I'm content, truly content, to live alone, then I'll make peace with the fact that society judges it unusual for me to stay single. But if I really want to find someone to share my life with, then I need to start making more of an effort to find that person. Even though it's hard and it hurts, and I may never find him."

At Roane's silence, I suddenly felt stupid for telling this man things I hadn't even told Greer.

"It all must sound silly to you."

"No," he said emphatically, his hand coming down to rest on top of mine. I saw a light of understanding in his eyes. "I realize the pressure is worse for a woman—which is bloody ridiculous in this day and age—but men feel the pressure too." He released my hand, his small smile almost self-deprecating, as his gaze dropped to his plate. "I've never been that guy who could sleep around, have one-night stands. And living in a small community hasn't made finding someone easy. I've had a few long-term relationships but the last was two years ago. And the men round here, they don't mean anything by it, but they give me a good ribbing for not *availing* myself of willing tourists and women from other villages who've made it clear they'd be happy to see me.

"I've never wanted that." I felt a little breathless at the intensity in his eyes. "It doesn't do it for me. I need to feel more than just the presence of a warm body. Sex is better for me when I care about the woman I'm with."

Already warm from my hangover, I flushed uncomfortably hot at his words. "Oh."

His smirk was somewhat bitter. "Men aren't supposed to want that, let alone say it, right? It makes them less of a man not to be out there sowing his wild oats. There's something effeminate about a man who is turned off by sex with a stranger and believes wholeheartedly in monogamy."

"Women don't think that." I certainly didn't. In fact, I found his honesty way too intriguing for my own good.

"No. But like you said, everyone has this idea of what you should want out of life. And you're right. There are places in this world where folk are just trying to survive. We're privileged enough that our lives have moved beyond basic survival, but it means we have time to impress these stupid ideas of 'normality' upon each other." He ran a hand through his bed-mussed hair. "My mum, Milly, and all the like, they badger me almost every week about 'settling down and finding a woman to keep me company.'" Our eyes locked as he continued, "But unlike you, I know that I want that. Definitely. I want someone to love, to share life's difficulties with, to have bairns and watch them grow. To make a little world with someone. Which means there are days, thankfully few but they exist, when it doesn't feel so nice for all those people who are supposed to care about me to hound me about the thing I want most in life."

Emotion clogged my throat.

Not just because I was sad that Roane felt that way.

But because for the first time in a very long time, I felt like someone saw me. Understood me. Truly.

Tears I didn't even feel embarrassed about shimmered in my eyes as I reached for Roane Robson's hand and curled mine tight around it. "You'll find it, Roane." I believed he would.

"You don't know that." He squeezed my hand, giving me a small smile. "You don't know me or the future."

"I don't know the future, agreed. I do know you a little, and I *see* you a lot."

He understood. I saw it in the way he studied my face and by the way his hand tightened in mine. "I see you too, Evie."

It was too big a moment to share with an almost stranger, but it was happening, and it was real.

I made a decision in that moment. To put aside my attraction for Roane and embrace the connection between us. I'd felt something similar the instant I met Greer. Just like with Greer, I was determined to make a friend of Roane.

"When I have a day off and don't feel like upchucking, do you think you can show me your farm?"

"Friends then?" he surmised, his expression relaxed and happy again.

"I just told you some of my deepest worries. We're friends or I have to kill you."

Chuckling at my teasing, Roane nodded. "I'll take friendship over death."

"Wise choice. I'm inexperienced at murder. It could get messy."

He shook his head at my nonsense. "Hurry and eat the rest of your breakfast. Shadow and I need to get to work, but we're not leaving until you've had at least three more bites."

Groaning, I glared at my plate. "I don't think I can."

"Well, it's that or I remind you of the moment last night you started singing a song called 'When You're Good to Mama' to Old Man Thompson."

My eyes widened in horror, and Roane began to shake with laughter. "From *Chicago*?"

He shrugged. "You said it was from some musical."

Yes. The musical *Chicago*.

"'When you're good to Mama, Mama's good to you,'" I squeaked out.

Roane gave a bark of laughter. "It was the best night of Old Man Thompson's life. We thought he'd need his pacemaker checked."

"You did not!" I gasped, aghast.

Seeing him bury his face in his hand with laughter, I smacked him playfully across the back. "Stop!"

Unfortunately, that only made him laugh harder.

Seven

It was opening day, and while I should have been excited, I was thankful for the heavy rain falling outside because it meant I could sit behind the counter and nurse my hangover without interruptions from customers.

Penny had informed me it was time to order titles for the new releases bookcase, and she trusted me to do this. I thought that was huge. She gave me a budget, and the distributor resources that offered some insight into what titles were popular for the season. As a reader of all genres, and part of the online book community, I felt I had a finger on that particular pulse. Still, I was grateful Penny trusted me to order new stock, and it was fun! For a moment, I forgot I was ordering them for the store, and not for myself.

However, the work also opened my eyes to the complexity of stock rotation for an independent bookstore. Hours passed as I attempted to work out Penny's ordering history. I knew she worked with the local schools and ordered titles the kids would be reading in school every term. That had already been done for the current term.

There also appeared to be a seasonal pattern. For example, she ordered any new books about the area around late spring/summer along with the latest bestselling children's books. Yet, as I fell farther down the stock-taking rabbit hole, I discovered there were a lot of nonfiction titles that just weren't selling. I itched to plump Penny's summer stock with beach reads.

As I opened more files for previous years' sales, trying to get a grasp of what worked and what didn't depending on the season, it suddenly occurred to me that it was none of my business. I was getting carried away. I was there to temporarily run the store.

Deprived of the many hours, probably days, it would take to look through sales history and the current stock situation, I turned to my other work: content edits from another client who wrote crime fiction. While I'd felt okay scrolling through stock and sales history, as I worked on the edits, the screen made me feel slightly nauseated, and my hangover began to catch up with me. All I really wanted to do was curl up in bed and listen to the rain.

Instead I sipped at my coffee, worked for a bit, and then gazed distractedly out at the rain bouncing off the sea. Perhaps, after my experience with Aaron, I was a fool to believe in the connection I felt with Roane. But unlike with Aaron, I'd actually *met* Roane. Sat face-to-face with him and gotten a real measure of the man. My instincts told me I could trust him, and I wouldn't let some stranger I'd mistaken for a confidant cause me to be mistrustful of new friends.

That's all Roane was. I'd friend-zoned him to protect myself. Despite his earlier attraction to me, he seemed fine with that. No doubt that had something to do with my drunken escapades the night before and then his watching me vomit.

Not sexy.

I gave a huff of sheepish laughter and then groaned when the sound ricocheted around my head.

Around noon the rain slowed to a drizzle, and I was contemplating closing the shop for a half hour when a small figure appeared at the door and pushed it open.

Folding back the large hood that had obscured her face, a young woman let the door slam shut behind her and gave me a tremulous smile. She unzipped her raincoat and gave it a little flick, rainwater splattering on the door behind her. Holding out a Tupperware box, she slowly approached the counter.

Her bright red hair was pulled back in a severe bun that was so tight it elongated her eyes. She had a pretty face with charming freckles sprinkled across her nose and the crest of her cheeks. It was hard to guess at her age because without a speck of makeup on she looked very young, but she was dressed much older and dowdier than her years. Her raincoat came to her knees, and beneath it was a light-knit navy sweater with a high neck and a pleated beige skirt that hit her ankles. Plain, somewhat clunky Mary Janes completed the look. She wore no jewelry except for the simple gold cross around her neck.

I grinned at her in welcome and slid off my stool, pretending the movement didn't make the room spin. My first customer! "Welcome to Much Ado About Books."

She smiled a shy but very pretty smile. "Hello."

When no other words were forthcoming, I glanced down at the Tupperware box. Looking back at the woman, I asked, "Can I help you?"

"Oh. My name is Caroline." She licked her lips nervously. "I, uh, well, I heard what you did for Shadow yesterday." Her accent was more *Downton Abbey* than Alnster. I wondered if she was a tourist. But if so, how did she know Shadow? Caroline pushed the Tupperware box toward me. "This is to thank you."

Looking down at the cakes, I was a little flabbergasted.

Who was Caroline to Roane and Shadow?

"Uh, okay." I took the box and peeled open the lid. There were cupcakes inside, decorated with pink frosting that looked like roses. "These are beautiful. Thanks." Surprisingly, my stomach rumbled.

"I'm Roane's cousin," Caroline explained.

Oh. Okay. The accent threw me, but looking at her again, I realized she and Roane shared the same beautiful chestnut eyes. "Right." My grin widened. "Well, it was nothing, really, but thank you for the cupcakes."

She shook her head. "It was everything, Ms. Starling. Shadow is Roane's best friend. He's a wonderful dog." Her eyes brightened with tears. "I don't know what we would have done if something happened to him." Caroline's cheeks suddenly flushed, and she looked down at her shoes. "You must think me such a goose getting upset over a dog."

My lips twitched at the way she talked. Seriously, how old was she? "I don't think you're a goose at all. I'm a dog person. I get it. They're family."

Some of her embarrassment faded, and she nodded. "They are."

Intrigued by Roane's cousin, I leaned against the counter. "So, do you live in Alnster?"

"On the outskirts, yes. I live with my aunt. Do you know the road that cuts into the woodlands? We live up there."

I remembered there being woodlands on the road that led into Alnster, but that was about it. Surmising that's where she meant, I nodded. "So is your aunt Roane's aunt?"

"No. We're cousins on our paternal side, and Aunt Helena was my mother's sister."

"So you're a Robson."

Her lips pinched together. "Technically yes. But Aunt Helena had my name changed when I came to live with her."

There was something unhappy in Caroline's eyes. That and her indeterminate age intrigued me. I wanted to ask more questions, but she started backing away toward the door. "Well, I better get home. Thank you again."

"It was no problem, really. Thanks for the cupcakes. Maybe I'll see you at The Anchor sometime?"

Instead of answering, Caroline gave me a weak smile and hurried out of the door and back into the drizzly day.

"Well, that was weird," I mumbled.

Looking at the cupcakes, I decided to take that break after all.

A few minutes later I was in the apartment, preparing a sandwich, and eyeing the delicious cupcakes the whole time. Arranging them on a platter, I snapped a photo and posted it on my Instagram. My friends were enjoying my shots of England. I captioned this one with "A gift from a friendly neighbor."

Then, like an impatient kid, I took a bite out of one instead of waiting until I'd eaten my sandwich.

The sponge cake melted in my mouth, sharp, flavorful strawberry jam oozing onto my tongue from the center. The buttercream frosting was perfect. Not too sweet, light and creamy.

It was the best freaking cupcake I'd ever had in my life!

I wondered if Caroline worked at the bakery in town.

Finishing the cupcake, forcing myself not to eat another, I put them back into the Tupperware box to keep them fresh. "Note to self," I murmured just as I was about to sit down to my sandwich, "ask Roane about his cousin."

It was as if I'd conjured him.

A loud banging had me rushing to the window. Peering down onto the street below, I saw a familiar figure at the front door. Shadow stood at his side.

Heart rate increasing, I hurried out of the apartment and down to the bookstore, regretting the faster pace almost immediately. Light-headed, I gripped the store door for balance and yanked it open.

Roane pushed his way inside as he brushed off the hood of his raincoat. Shadow followed, and as I closed the door and locked it, the dog shook his body and sprayed everything in his vicinity with rainwater.

Me included.

He was forgiven when he trotted over to me and jumped up to say hello. Despite my light-headedness, which was seriously worsened by a huge dog putting his wet paws on my shoulders, I stumbled, laughing and jerking my chin away to avoid his kisses.

"Shadow, down," Roane said, not sounding amused.

"It's fine," I promised, petting the Dane just before he heeded Roane's orders. I had two muddy marks on my shoulders from his paws, and Roane's expression clearly said that it wasn't fine.

"It'll come out," I said, waving off his concern. "What brings you back so soon?"

He held up two paper bags that had rain splatter on them. "Lunch from the bakery. I wanted to make sure you were eating."

"I was actually just about to sit down to a sandwich I'd made,"

I told him as I took one of the bags from him and peered inside. The smell of chicken hit me hard, and my belly rumbled. "But screw my crappy ham and cheese sandwich, this will do much better."

Roane chuckled and made to move past the counter, but my laptop caught his attention. Shooting me a curious look, he dipped his head toward the screen. "What's this? Do you write?"

I made a face. "No, Nosey. I'm a freelance editor."

He frowned at me. "You never mentioned that last night."

"It's about the only thing I didn't mention." I made a face, remembering all the personal stuff I'd blurted at The Anchor.

With a commiserating smile, Roane led me into the back hallway. Shadow trotted at our heels. "So," Roane said as he kicked off his muddy Wellington boots at the bottom of the stairs. "Do you edit fiction books for a publisher?"

"No, I edit books for indie authors. People who self-publish."

"Oh yeah, that's a thing now, isn't it."

I grinned as I followed him up to the apartment. "It's been a thing for a while now, Farmer Robson."

"And you make money from this?" He glanced over his shoulder at me as he walked into the kitchen.

"Yeah. I did it to supplement my income. Chicago is an expensive place to live."

"What made you decide to be an editor then?"

The question made me halt in the doorway. No one had ever asked me that question. That couldn't be right. I thought on it and decided it *was* right. Not even Greer had asked me. I guessed, however, my best friend just assumed she already knew the answer: I loved words. "I didn't know I wanted to be an editor until I started working for the film mag. I just knew I wanted to be in publishing, to be surrounded by the written word. I can't explain my love for words. Not well, anyway. They're like a golden sunset across a tranquil sea, viewed from a run-down shack. They can turn even the most ordinary of feelings or thoughts into poetry."

Roane smiled at me.

I shrugged, smiling back. "When I started working at the magazine, I realized an editor got to have a part in creating something interesting and meaningful. After I started taking on fiction writers as clients, I knew I loved that more than the magazine. Not only do I get to read books before everyone else, I get to read some pretty great books and help tighten the plots, make the characters richer, guide the author a little. It's fun for a book nerd. That's why I edit."

Roane considered me with a soft look on his face that was becoming familiar. "Good. Everyone should love what they do for a living."

"Yeah. Except I no longer do it for a living. And book editing on the side merely supplemented my income."

The farmer was quiet for a second or two as we pulled out plates and put the roast chicken sandwiches onto them.

"Coffee?"

"Aye, please," he said, taking a third bag I hadn't seen out of his jacket pocket. Seeing my questioning gaze, he nodded to Shadow. "I'm quite strict about what he eats, but every now and then he gets a wee treat." After rummaging in the cupboards, Roane produced a dog bowl. Obviously, the apartment was pet friendly. Penny seemed to think of everything. Roane opened the bag and removed slices of deli meat. "Corned beef from the butcher."

I laughed at the way the dog's eyes grew huge as Shadow dug the side of his head into Roane's waist, waiting impatiently.

Roane broke it up into pieces and put it into Shadow's bowl. "Good boy," he said affectionately as he set the bowl on the ground. Then he sat down at the counter like he had this morning.

Warmth suffused me at his proximity, and I was just about to ask him if farming made him happy, when he asked, "Why don't you make a career out of it? Book editing?"

The truth was I had thought about it. Especially these last few days. However, I wasn't sure it was plausible. "It's crossed my mind. But one, I don't have enough clients yet, and two, I'd have to line up three full-time projects a month to make it financially viable, and I don't know if that's doable. Besides, I'd have to funnel money into promoting the business. Turning it into a brand. I have a website and testimonials, but not enough authors know about me just yet. So far I've gotten work through word of mouth."

"Your schedule is open now, though. Maybe if they knew this was full time, your current clients would recommend you more."

"That's true. But self-employment is scary, right? And I don't want to have to work sixteen hours a day just to make ends meet."

"Right you are," he agreed. "It's a lot of stress and responsibility. Especially when you have employees. But on the plus side it's bloody nice to be your own boss."

I smiled, envious. I'd love to make editing a full-time gig, but for now it was just a nice way to keep me afloat without having to dip too far into my savings. Trying to push away my worries, I asked, "Does farming make you happy?"

Roane swallowed the bite of sandwich he'd taken as I slid onto the stool next to him. His gaze wandered to Shadow, who had finished the deli meat and was sniffing all around the bowl as if he might magically find more. "Aye."

I frowned at the slight hesitation I'd heard. "You don't sound so sure."

"No, I am. I've always liked the physicality of it. It's straight-forward, the results of your productivity are tangible, and I like going to bed physically exhausted rather than mentally."

"You're never mentally exhausted?" God, I envied him.

"Sometimes." He looked at me for the first time since I'd asked him about his happiness. "I do a bit of maintenance for the tourist board as well. Looking after homes that are rented out to tourists. Farming and tourism aren't easy industries. There's a lot of stress involved."

I mentally berated myself for thinking he had it easy. "Of course there is. Now that you mention it, I'm sure I read some-where that farming is one of the most stressful jobs out there."

Roane nodded, studying his sandwich intently. "It can be."

"But it does make you happy?" I pushed.

Our eyes met, his warm with something I couldn't name. "Aye, Evie. I'm happy."

I couldn't help my wide smile. "I'm glad."

His eyes flitted past me and landed on the Tupperware box. Sur-prise flickered across his expression. "Where did you get those?"

"Oh. Your cousin."

"Caro came here?"

At his shock, I grinned. "Is that unusual? Because she's unbe-lievably shy?"

Roane nodded but then he looked at Shadow. "Mind you, she loves him almost as much as me. She cried when I told her what happened."

"Yeah, I got that. By the way, her cupcakes are delicious. Does she work at the bakery?"

"No." His expression clouded over.

Aha!

I sensed a story.

Letting Roane take a few more bites of his sandwich, I pounced. "What does a cupcake master do if she's not working for the local bakery and why is she so shy? And why is her accent different from yours?"

He rolled his eyes. "What's with the twenty questions?"

"Caroline is intriguing. She dresses like my great-grandmother, is of indeterminate age, impossibly adorable, and is a shit-hot baker. I want to know more."

Instead of laughing at my nosiness, Roane's gaze darkened when he turned to me. "Caro lives with her aunt on her mum's side, so Helena's nothing to do with the Robsons. She's an uppity bitch from money who got custody of Caro when her parents died in the Boxing Day tsunami in 2004. Caro was only seven years old.

"She was staying with us for Christmas." His expression was sad. "Mum told me that Caro's mum, Amelia, was never really meant for motherhood. She was too selfish. Amelia was a bit of a jet-setter and never wanted to take Caro with her, so she got left behind to stay with us or with Helena whenever her parents traveled. Her dad, my uncle Heath, was different from my father. Weaker, I suppose. Gave in to Caro's mum's demands all the time. Blinded by his love for her, Mum said. And poor Caro was the one that suffered for it." He sighed heavily. "Though no one deserves to die how they died."

I remembered that earthquake and tsunami in Indonesia. I was eighteen at the time, and it was world news for weeks because of its far-reaching effects. It killed almost a quarter of a million people.

"That's awful." For Caro's parents, but also for Caro. To have had such neglectful parents, and then to lose them in such a way.

"Aye. Our nana Robson was still alive at the time, but she wasn't well enough to take care of Caro. Mum and Dad wanted custody, but Amelia and Heath had made it clear in their will that guardianship was to be granted to Caro's aunt Helena. She was Caro's mum's twin sister, you see."

There was something hard in his tone, and putting that together with what I'd witnessed in Caro, I felt a little knot in my gut. "I'm guessing she's not exactly a great guardian."

Roane met my gaze, and I was surprised by the anger I saw there. "I don't hate many people, Evie, if at all . . . but I *hate* that woman."

I flinched. "Wow. That bad, huh?"

"She controls every aspect of Caro's life."

Calculating the dates quickly in my head, I replied, "But Caro's twenty-two now."

"Aye. But she's lived with that woman for most of her life. I've tried my best. My mum has tried her best, but she's got this grip on Caro." The anger dimmed from his eyes, leaving only the melancholy. "I'm the closest thing she's ever had to a best friend . . . She's tried but her aunt always managed to chase off her friends. And she's never had a boyfriend. Helena takes religion to the extreme, and she's filled Caro's head with all this toxic stuff about purity and what it means to be a 'good girl.' It's all bullshit. It's all meant to keep Caro living in that house, looking after the old cow into her dotage."

Indignation for Caroline simmered inside me as I remembered how shy she'd been. I glanced at her beautiful cupcakes.

"That's just the tip of the icing." Roane gestured to them. "The lass is a born baker. Everything that comes out of her kitchen is heaven on a plate."

"She should be working at the bakery then. Or opening her own!"

His eyes twinkled at my passionate exclaim. "Aye, but you try telling *her* that. I've offered to get her a place of her own, to break away from that woman and start living her life. But she won't. She's trapped by guilt."

We fell into a companionable silence as I pondered Caroline's situation. Maybe I could talk to Caroline. Roane was perhaps too close. Besides, he was a guy. It was presumptuous to assume a stranger could have more success than her closest relative, but maybe Caroline needed encouragement from an independent, mature woman who lived alone. I could show her how great it was. Plus, praise from a stranger about her baking was always better than support from family. The bias was removed.

"I can practically hear your thoughts turning," Roane commented, his gaze roaming my face. "I'm not even going to tell you not to do whatever you're thinking about doing."

It was a little unnerving how quickly he was beginning to understand me. "I'll be gentle," I teased.

Something dark, hot, flashed in his eyes, and he quickly looked away.

Tension immediately sprung between us, and I scrambled to think of something to say to defuse it.

Roane beat me to it. "What are you doing for dinner?"

Grateful for the subject change, I replied, "Well, I was going to see what they had at the convenience store. I haven't booked a rental yet to go to the supermarket."

"The convenience store doesn't have much. Why don't we eat

together at The Anchor, and I can find some time tomorrow to take you to get a rental car? Maybe give you a lesson on how to drive here," he added pointedly.

"Is it that hard? I thought we just drove on opposite sides of the road." I knew that it would be a little discombobulating at first, but did I really need a lesson?

"Which is harder than you think. But there's more to it than that. We have different rules of the road here. And roundabouts. Lots of roundabouts."

Hmm, when he put it that way. "Okay, I'd be grateful. Are you sure you have time?" I was under the impression farmers worked around the clock, and was more than a little surprised he'd joined me for lunch.

His dark, autumnal eyes locked on mine. "I'll make time."

A rush of attraction swept over me like a wave, and I tensed on my stool. *Friend zone, friend zone, friend zone*, I began to chant inwardly, wrenching my gaze from his. It was so unfair. If I looked into his eyes too long, I got flutters in my belly. If I stared at his mouth too long, I got tingles a little farther south than my belly.

The only place to look was his nose, and that was just weird.

Deciding that not to look at him at all was the best option, I studied my dwindling sandwich.

It seemed to work, and I relaxed long enough to pepper Roane with more questions about his life. It turned out he'd taken over management of what sounded like a fairly sizable farm from his parents. They had retired to their second home in Greece, which made me assume the farm was financially successful. But I soon learned Roane had to work extremely hard to make it so.

"We're a commercial mixed farm," he explained. "Meaning we farm to sell at market. Our arable farming is on the eastern part of the estate, where we grow crops of winter wheat and barley, oil-seed rape, and spring beans. On this side of our estate"—he gestured to the room, so I gathered he meant "right here on the coast"—"we have our sheep farming. We also sell hay."

That sounded like a pretty big enterprise to me. "And you run it yourself?"

He shrugged. "I manage and work it, but we have employees." Suddenly he slipped off the stool. "Speaking of which, I need to get back. We'll be here at seven for dinner. I've already reserved a table."

"That was presumptuous," I teased.

"Well, I figured you might need a buffer before venturing back into the local." He chuckled before pressing a quick, surprising kiss to my cheek. "See you at seven."

Ignoring the flush of pleasure I felt from the kiss, I focused on his comment. Why would I need a buffer?

"What does that mean?" I asked as he gestured to Shadow to follow him.

Roane just shot me another boyish smile before descending the stairs out of view.

"Roane!" I called after him. "What does that mean?"

The only answer I got was the sound of his deep chuckle.

However, hours later, as I walked into The Anchor accompanied by Roane and Shadow, I finally got my answer.

A roomful of eyes met us as we strolled in, and I felt suddenly self-conscious. This only worsened when four men turned on their stools at the busy bar, saw me, shared a knowing look, and then burst out into song.

"When you're good to Mama, Mama's good to you!" They gestured to me comically.

While most diners stared on in confusion, others let out barks of laughter, including Roane, whose guffaw was the loudest.

Realizing I'd met these men the night before and had no memory of it, I made eye contact with Milly, who was hee-hawing behind the bar.

Mortification flooded me but so did something else.

They were teasing me.

Like I was one of them even though I was a visitor.

Much like how Roane had befriended me even though Milly said he usually steered clear of tourists, I somehow sensed this was unusual behavior for the locals.

Pleasure seeped into the mortification, and I couldn't help but laugh through my groans of embarrassment.

$\mathcal{E}$ vie, you can do whatever you want, pet. That's the point." Penny gave me a reassuring smile.

The next day the rain had cleared, the sunshine bringing more tourists with it. A few came into the store to browse and I tried not to act giddy at my first sale. The woman had called my window display adorable and purchased a copy of *A Midsummer's Night Dream* along with a few little key rings with the Northumbrian flag on it.

Not long after, while I was pondering splitting the display with all the books and information on Northumberland so I could continue the Shakespeare theme, Penny had come to the store to see how I was doing.

I'd told her about the sale and asked her if I could put the books on Northumberland on the bottom half of the case and more Shakespeare titles on the top half.

Grinning at her answer, I was antsy to start riffling through stock for more Shakespeare plays.

"So, you're doing fine then?" Penny asked.

"Oh, I'm doing great."

Her smile widened. "You've made quite an impression here." She nodded to the window. "The locals love your display when it's lit up at night."

People had talked about my homemade, whimsical display? Pleasure suffused me. "Really?"

"Aye. It's very cute. Probably the most memorable display I've had at the shop."

"Well, yay me."

"And everyone up at The Anchor loves you. The folks here have never been so taken with a renter before."

Remembering how welcoming everyone had been after the teasing last night, I beamed. Roane and I had stayed at The Anchor until closing, but this time I didn't consume alcohol. Instead I enjoyed the company of the locals, including Penny, as they told me their life stories without artifice. I'd also learned that Roane's closest friend from university lived in Scotland, just across the border, so his closest friend in Alnster, from what I could tell, was Bobby Hopeton. Bobby worked with Roane in some capacity. I wasn't sure in what way—they kind of brushed over that when we were chatting last night. He was around the same age as Roane and me, and married to a woman named Jill, whom I hadn't met yet because she was at home with their two kids.

Bobby wasn't much of a drinker from what I could see, and sounded like a homebody. He gave me the impression he was only at The Anchor to get a look at me. This made me wonder what Roane had said about me.

"Everyone is so welcoming."

Penny snorted. "Not usually, pet. Folks don't want to be friendly with someone who isn't sticking around. But they can't seem to help themselves with you. Especially with Roane being so taken with you."

"We're friends."

"Oh, aye." She nodded but didn't look convinced.

Hmm. Let her think what she wanted to think. Let them all think it. Roane and I knew what we were and that's what mattered.

"Anyway, I best be letting you get on."

"Wait, Penny." When she turned back to me, eyebrows raised in question, I hesitated. What I wanted to ask wasn't really my business, but I couldn't help my curiosity. "I heard you're selling this place, is that true?"

Her expression tightened.

"Sorry, not my business."

Sighing, she turned fully toward me. "It's all right. Aye, I've been thinking about selling it."

"But why?"

Penny laughed at my nosiness. It wasn't a happy sound. "Oh, pet, it's complicated."

"Do you want to sell it? Is it not financially viable?" As soon as the words were out of my mouth, I cursed myself. "God, I *am* nosy."

This time when she laughed, it sounded genuine. "Aye, you are." She glanced around at the shop. "The bookstore itself makes enough during the summer months to tide me over for the whole year. It's the renting it out that really makes the cash, though."

"Then why sell?"

We locked gazes, hers strangely intense as she replied softly, "Everyone has asked that, and I just tell them that it's time, but the truth is, I'm not sure. Time for what? My sister lives in Australia, and she thinks I'm wasting what's left of my life in a small village where I can't meet anyone. She wants me out there with her. She thinks I can't move on from Arthur if I stay here. I'm not sure she's right. But I'm not sure she's wrong."

Sympathy ached in my chest as we stood quietly for a moment. Then I asked, "Are you happy here, Penny?"

Her sigh was heavy, weighed down. "With the business, aye. And I love the people, my friends . . . but I think . . ." She trailed off, lowering her gaze.

"You think?"

Her small smile was chagrined. "Maybe I *am* lonely." Her eyes widened as soon as the words were out of her mouth, and she suddenly gave a bark of confused laughter. "Now how did I end up telling you that?"

My answering smile was kind. "Because maybe you needed someone to tell." I stepped forward and placed a comforting hand on Penny's shoulder. "Follow your gut. I followed mine here and I already know it's the best decision I've made in years."

$\mathcal{A}$fter lunch I began working on my new display. I moved everything from the top shelves of the front-facing bookcase to the two bottom shelves, and then took out the copies of Shakespeare that Penny had in stock. There were a few more copies of his completed works in the storeroom, so I brought those out too. She had multiple copies of *Much Ado About Nothing*, which made sense since the store name was clearly inspired by it.

For a while I stared at what I had, trying to figure out what I wanted to do with this display.

Flicking through plays to pull out quotes, I realized that I'd only ever read *Much Ado About Nothing* once, and before I knew it, I was standing in front of the bookcase, engrossed in the play. I decided Hero was an awesome name for a little girl, but that Shakespeare did her a disservice by matching her with Claudio in the end. Claudio believed the deception of Don John and Borachio, who convinced everyone that Hero had had sex with another guy before her wedding to Claudio. Claudio humiliated her at the altar, her family convinced everyone she died of shock and grief, and when her innocence was finally proven, they forced a devastated Claudio to marry her "cousin," only for her cousin to be revealed as Hero. And they lived happily ever after.

"Bad call, Will," I muttered, closing the play. Claudio was undeserving of Hero. He was supposed to love her and yet he believed the deceptions of others over her. And then she was just supposed to be happy she got to marry him in the end? Nope. I preferred the other couple in *Much Ado About Nothing*: Benedick and Beatrice. They were hilarious together, trading barbs and witticisms, until their friends decided to play matchmaking tricks to get them to admit they were actually in love. Plus, Beatrice was badass. Not only did she banter as well as Benedick, but she was a feminist of her day, not wanting to marry where she didn't love, or be a pawn in the games of men; furious at Claudio on Hero's behalf, wishing she weren't constrained by the trappings of gender so she could avenge Hero like only a man could back then.

The play was all about deception. Hero's story was actually tragic and yet it had been depicted as a romantic comedy. But I guess that was me thinking as a twenty-first-century woman.

Or maybe I was just too unforgiving?

"Renegades" by X Ambassadors suddenly blasted into the

room, jolting me from my musings and my untouched display. The song was my ringtone.

Hurrying over to the counter where I'd left my cell, I smiled at the name flashing on my screen.

Roane and I had exchanged numbers last night.

That smile turned to a frown as I caught sight of the time on my phone. I'd spent over an hour reading the play instead of working.

Maybe there *was* a downside to a book nerd running a bookstore.

"Hey," I said a little breathlessly as I answered.

"Sorry, did I catch you at a bad time?"

Ignoring the way my heart sped up a little at the sound of his deep voice, I shook my head, even though he couldn't see me. "No. Is everything okay?"

"Not really." He sounded glum. "I'm sorry, Evie, but I need to cancel our plans this afternoon."

We'd planned for me to close the shop a little early so Roane could drive me into Alnwick, the largest nearest town, to pick up a rental car. Disappointed I wouldn't see him, I pasted on a breezy smile and hoped it translated in my reply. "That's okay. What's going on?"

"I've been called away from the farm to one of the houses we maintain. A neighbor reported a loud party to the police last night, and I've turned up and the renters have smashed up the place, including the kitchen window."

"Oh my God."

"Aye, I've had to call the police again, as well as the owners, so I don't know how long it'll take to sort this mess out. I'm sorry."

Irritated for him, I sighed. "You have nothing to be sorry for. That's awful. Is there anything I can do?" It was probably a stupid question, considering I was carless.

"You're doing it." I thought I heard a smile in his voice. "Meet me at The Anchor after dinner? Eight o'clock?"

"Of course."

I wished him luck sorting out the vacation home crisis and we hung up. Staring out at the sea, I thought about how disappointed I was that I wouldn't get to spend the afternoon with Roane and wondered if maybe bonding with this guy so quickly wasn't a very foolish idea after all.

Yet I knew I wasn't going to do a damn thing to stop myself.

Eight

Before I knew it, my first two weeks in Alnster were almost up. It was a frustrating quirk of human nature that time seemed to slow when you were going through something difficult or when you were bored. Yet it sped up, racing away from your control when life was pretty darn good.

My second Sunday arrived with alarming alacrity, and it followed a busy Saturday at the bookstore. Saturday morning had started with a book bang. The books I'd ordered for the new releases bookcase arrived. I was a kid in a candy store! Pulling the beautiful paperback and hardback books out of the boxes; smelling that new book smell and feeling crisp, unread pages beneath my fingers; and wishing they were all mine. Organizing the books on the shelves, I'd posted a selfie on Instagram of me hugging the bookcase with longing in my eyes.

Apparently, Saturday was the store's sweet spot, because almost as soon as I'd finished organizing the new titles, the bell above the door tinkled. A couple ventured in, each holding the hand of the little girl between them. Nostalgia filled me as I watched them peruse the children's titles with her, remembering days when my mom and dad had done the same thing with me.

I loved how the hours melted away as I engaged with my customers. As it turned out, my bookworm tendencies did come in handy when customers asked for recommendations or asked if I'd read a certain book and had an opinion about it. As a voracious reader, I was super helpful.

Unless a customer asked me about Northumberland and the best I could do was direct them to the books written about the area.

I was counting that as helpful too.

My daylight hours during my first two weeks were spent at the store, working on edits when things were quiet, and then taking walks on the beach during my lunch hour if the day was dry. In the evening, I met Roane and Shadow at The Anchor. Sometimes we met early to eat, other times at night just to catch up on our day and chat among the locals.

The mystery of why we never socialized at The Alnster Inn was finally solved my first Friday night when Mr. Thompson cracked a joke about Milly leaving Dexter for someone called West Elliot. To me it was an offhand comment based on the fact that Milly was rushed off her feet behind the bar at weekend nights, with waitstaff jumping on to help her out because Dexter insisted they needn't hire another bartender. Milly had joked, "It's because he wants the cash for his precious produce, never mind his precious wife."

However, after Mr. Thompson's (or Old Man Thompson as Roane called him) crack about some guy called West Elliot, Milly shot him a frosty look and tension descended over the occupants of the pub.

Waiting until we were alone at our table by the fire, I asked Roane about it. It turned out West Elliot owned The Alnster Inn and, like Milly, had inherited it from his parents. Back when they were teenagers, Milly and West were in love, but while West stayed in Alnster to run the family business, Milly took off for Newcastle to attend university. It was there she met Dexter.

"You've met Milly." Roane leaned in to whisper in my ear, goose bumps shivering down my neck at the ghost of his words on my skin. "She's a good woman. She never meant for anyone to get hurt, but when you know, you know, and Dex was it for her."

I winced. "It's a shitty situation."

Roane nodded. "And West has never made it easy. Even though he married a girl from Alnwick and they had kids together who are now grown, he's never let it go. His love for Milly turned into bitterness, even though he knows things haven't been easy for her."

I frowned. "In what way?"

"Well, you know they have a daughter, Viola?"

I nodded. Milly had proudly shown me photos of Viola, a beautiful young woman currently finishing her sophomore year at Newcastle University. She was excited because Viola would be home soon for the summer.

"They tried many times before they had Vi." Roane's dark eyes filled with sympathy. "After a number of miscarriages, Milly couldn't take it anymore. They stopped trying."

My heart ached for her, for them both. "Poor Milly. Poor Dexter."

"Aye." Roane sighed, his gaze darting to The Anchor's owner.

"But once they stopped trying, it miraculously happened. Viola was born."

I was glad it had worked out for them. From what I'd witnessed, Milly and Dexter were an example of a marriage to aspire to. Married thirty years and, yes, they still loved each other, but more impressively they still *liked* each other. After a moment's contemplation, I whispered, "I do feel kind of bad for West. He must have loved Milly a lot."

Roane nodded, his expression thoughtful. "Aye, I wouldn't wish having to live in the same village with the object of your affection, watching her live her life with some other man, on my enemy. But he made a choice to move on, marry Kathy, have kids. That should have been it. Instead he turned it into a war with everyone taking sides. Some locals patronize here, others The Alnster Inn—some are people who didn't even live here thirty years ago but have somehow gotten caught up in their story. And worse, they have two boys. Lucas, the youngest, is Viola's age. The war continued with them. The two of them are forever at each other's throats when they're home. Kathy has to see that. Can you imagine marrying a man and standing by his side while his bitterness over losing the love of another woman pervades an entire village and affects your kids?"

Sometimes I loved the way Roane talked. Realizing I was staring at his mouth, I shook my head and returned my attention to our conversation. "Poor Kathy."

My friend contemplated me a moment, those entrancing lips of his twisting into a smirk. "Aye, poor Kathy. Poor Milly. Poor Dexter. Maybe poor West. You could write a book about this place."

I chuckled. "One day I might."

Over a week after our conversation about Milly and West,

Roane had commandeered my day off. I hadn't had time to rent a car just yet. Penny drove me along the coast on one of my days off, and I'd visited a few of the coastal towns. As for food, I'd had groceries delivered to the apartment. When Roane found out, he'd insisted on taking the following Sunday off work to drive me into Alnwick so I could buy some groceries and check out the car rental place. Upon our return Roane would cook dinner for me.

The man was perfect.

I had to find a flaw. It was imperative that I find a flaw.

He picked me up in his old Land Rover Defender, and I bubbled with excitement at the prospect of finally venturing into Alnwick. Roane laughed as I settled into the SUV. "You're like a five-year-old going to her birthday party."

"I feel like a five-year-old going to my birthday party."

"Aye, well, I'm not far off that feeling myself." He shot me an affectionate look. "It's my first day off in I don't know how long."

This surprised and dismayed me. "Seriously?"

He nodded, pulling the Defender away from the curb. We waved at a few locals as we drove out of the village.

"So, do you not have time for a day off?"

"I've got people to cover me . . . I've just not seen the need to for a while."

That was miserable. Roane deserved better than to be working 24/7. "Well, I'm glad to give you an excuse to relax. Roane, you need to take better care of yourself. Everyone needs a day off."

He grunted as only men can grunt, and I couldn't decide if that was an agreement grunt or an "it is what it is" grunt.

"Where's Shadow?" I changed the subject.

"He's with Caro. I didn't want to leave him in the car when we go to the supermarket. I'll pick him up after tea."

I nodded and we lapsed into comfortable silence as I watched the beautiful countryside pass us by.

"I was thinking I could take you to Barter Books before we go to the supermarket."

My eyes lit up. "Ooh. A bookstore?"

Smiling, possibly at my utter nerdiness, Roane replied, "Not just any bookstore. It's a used bookstore inside the old Alnwick railway station. It's famous round here."

"You sure know how to show a girl a good time, Roane Robson."

"See, from any other woman that could be construed as sarcasm, but I think you actually mean it."

"I do." I chuckled. "Books are life."

He took his eyes off the road for a second to flash me that teasing smile of his, and I pretended not to feel the effects of it in places a friend shouldn't.

I was in love.

Inside the old station with its vaulted aluminum roof with shafts of light pouring in through skylights, I stared at the rows upon rows of bookcases. Through the bustle of people, there was something to catch the eye at every turn. Not just books, but interesting chandeliers that looked like something out of a steampunk novel. Reading areas set up in breaks between stacks, tables with chairs so people could lounge, read, drink their coffee as crowds milled around them. The rows of bookcases down the middle of the large room were connected at the top by strips of wood painted white and printed with a verse I recognized from the Song of Solomon. Each strip was a line from The Beloved's Request: The Shulamite.

My favorite line from the verse they'd used was "For lo, the winter is past, the rain is over *and* gone." I took out my phone and snapped a shot of it.

"So pretty," I murmured, wondering at the choice behind using the verse.

Roane took my hand, drawing my attention to him, and he nodded to our right. There was a café in the bookshop called the Station Buffet.

There was a possibility I would die at the whimsy of it all.

"It's like something out of Harry Potter."

Laughing at my overexcitement, Roane squeezed my hand. "You're very cute."

Something in his eyes made me feel flushed. I looked away and tugged on his hand. "Let's explore."

I expected him to let go of my hand, but he didn't, and I should have questioned it, but I didn't.

"You know they filmed scenes from the Harry Potter films right here in Alnwick," Roane told me as he followed me through the stacks. "At Alnwick Castle and Gardens."

"Really? Will you take me there sometime?"

I was too busy studying the shelves to see his expression, but I heard the affection in his tone when he replied, "I'll take you anywhere you want to go, Evie."

That's when I discovered there was such a thing as a word-provoked heart flutter.

Commencing "ignore heart flutter."

To do that, I found a way to release his hold on my hand without it being too obvious, using the crowds as obstacles. However, Roane stayed with me, seeming content to watch me peruse the shelves, moving from bookcase to bookcase. The book titles quickly became a blur as my awareness zeroed in on one thing, one person.

Him.

I felt the warmth of his presence, hovering at my back, and felt the heat of his gaze on my face. The skin on my cheek tingled, and I wondered if it had turned red under his intense regard.

My breathing grew more shallow as Roane's fingertips brushed against the small of my back, as if he were afraid that without that lack of connection I'd somehow disappear as I moved along the stacks.

What the hell was I supposed to do with this inconvenient attraction?

Most times we hung out at The Anchor with other people as buffers. There were moments we were alone, and we were comfortable, but then I'd catch Roane looking at me in a certain way or he'd notice I'd been staring at his mouth, and the sexual tension would fill the air between us.

Like now.

Busy frantically pondering how to defuse the chemistry we shared, I hadn't realized what book I'd halted in front of until it was too late.

A historical romance novel with a couple in a sexy clinch on the cover.

Perfect.

My cheeks were definitely bright red.

Roane's fingertips pressed deeper against my lower back, and then I felt the whisper of his lips on my ear as he commented, "Interesting choice."

I made the mistake of turning my head toward him and found

his nose inches from mine. Our eyes locked for a second before his gaze dropped to my mouth.

Today he smelled like freshly mown grass sprinkled with musky male spice.

My body swayed slightly toward his, and Roane apparently took the movement as an invitation, his head dipping those last few inches.

"Excuse me."

A voice, loud and close, jolted me away from Roane, whose mouth had been millimeters from touching mine—so close, I'd felt his breath tickle my lips.

"I just . . . want that book." An arm reached between us, and dazed, I looked down to see a petite brunette with glasses that took up most of her face. She seemed unfazed by the fact she'd clearly interrupted an almost clinch. Instead her determined eagle eyes were on the historical romance novel.

Despite my disappointment, I decided I was ultimately grateful for the interruption. I was leaving in two weeks, and there was no point in giving in to this attraction. Neither of us would be happy with a casual physical encounter. Furthermore, I was running out of time to discover what I wanted from life. I did not need a guy muddling up my already confused headspace.

I grabbed the book for the woman, who was straining to reach the shelf, and handed it to her. She gave me a thin-lipped smile and darted away. After a second or two of staring after her, I finally drew up the courage to look at my friend.

Roane's expression was unreadable.

Uncomfortable for the first time in his presence, I flickered my gaze over his shoulder, looking for something to distract us. Across the room, I spotted a shelf dedicated to Harry Potter.

That would do.

"Ooh," I said, hurrying across the bookshop. Spotting the first book in the series, I removed it. Roane had followed, as I'd expected, and I turned to him, smiling through the awkwardness. "I have to get this."

Roane bent his head toward mine to peer at the book. "*Have* to?"

Our eyes met, and just like that we were much too close for my body to handle. I swallowed hard, wondering how obvious it would be if I physically retreated. Pretty obvious, I guessed. "It's, uh, well . . . the first book has a different title in the States. It would be cool to own a copy with the original UK title."

His eyes trained on my mouth as he murmured, "What's it called in the States?"

"*The Sorcerer's Stone*, not *The Philosopher's Stone*. Apparently, the publisher didn't think Americans would associate the word 'philosophy' with magic." I sounded breathless. Most likely because I was.

"Hmm." Roane wasn't even listening to my words at this point. His focus was on my mouth, his eyes were hooded, and he was definitely going to attempt another kiss.

Stop him! a voice screeched in my head.

It was the voice of reason.

I jerked away from him. "Anyway, I'm going to go buy it." Wow, my voice sounded high. Unable to meet his gaze, I strode away toward the front of the store, where I'd seen the cash register.

As I waited to be served, I took a bunch of photos of the store to share on Instagram, and by the time the line moved down, Roane had returned to my side. He didn't say a word, just waited patiently for the guy behind the counter to ring up my book, and when I was ready to leave, he placed his hand on my lower back and guided me out through the crowds.

"You liked it then?" Roane asked, as if he hadn't just tried to kiss me twice, been interrupted and then rebuffed.

"Yes," I replied, deciding to follow his lead and pretend the encounter hadn't happened. "I loved it. Thank you for bringing me here. I'll have to come back before I leave."

He flicked me an unreadable look and yanked open the driver's-side door of his SUV.

Despite our pretense of normality, tensions were high between us as Roane drove me to the rental car place. Unfortunately, it was closed so we'd have to come back another day. When? I didn't know. I was already halfway through my vacation. The thought depressed me.

Our last stop was the supermarket, and as we strolled through the aisles, Roane pushing the cart, it felt weirdly more intimate than the two near kisses at the bookstore.

So domestic.

People stared at us. I didn't know if it was because it was difficult *not* to notice Roane, or if it was the two of us together that was causing the stir. Then I caught sight of us in one of the mirrors in the clothing department, and my uneasiness increased.

We looked good together.

We looked . . . *right*.

"We should invite Caroline to dinner," I blurted out, almost desperately.

A buffer. Caroline would be the perfect buffer, and it would give me an opportunity to get to know her better. I hadn't seen her again these last two weeks.

If Roane suspected my reasons, he didn't let on. Instead he frowned. "Caro won't leave Helena alone for tea on such short notice. Believe me, I've tried inviting her to different things and she declines every time. I stopped asking ages ago."

It was my turn to frown. "Well, maybe that's the problem. You stopped asking."

Roane drew to a halt in the middle of the canned food aisle. "I think I know my cousin well enough to know what the answer will be, but if you insist." Clearly irritated, he yanked his cell out of his back pocket to call her. His irritation was strangely amusing, probably because he was usually so laid-back about everything. Holding out my hand, I said, "Let me."

His brows puckered. *"You* want to call her?"

"Maybe she'll find it harder to turn me down."

Roane's lips twitched as he slapped the cell into my palm. "Aye, anyone would."

I couldn't help my answering smile, even though I shouldn't encourage his flirtation. He'd already pulled up Caroline's number, so I just hit the call button. After a few rings, she answered, "Hi, Roane."

"No, it's Evie using Roane's cell. How are you?"

"Oh. Oh, I'm very well, thank you, Evie. How are you?"

God, I loved the way she talked. "I'm good but I'd be even better if you agreed to join Roane and me for dinner tonight at my place. Roane's cooking. We'll pick you up in"—I glanced at the time and calculated how long it would take us to get the groceries and return to Alnster—"an hour. Okay? Great. We'll see you then." I hung up before she could respond.

Roane stared at his cell as I held it out to him, and then me, then his cell, then back to me. Suddenly he burst out laughing as he took it from me. Throwing his arm around my shoulders, Roane pulled me into his side to kiss my temple. "You're mental, lass," he declared, still chuckling.

"It worked, didn't it?"

"We'll see." He released me to push the cart up the aisle. "If she doesn't call back in the next fifteen minutes, it worked."

Turns out . . . it did work.

$\mathscr{S}$omewhere in the back of my mind, I knew that making connections with anyone in Alnster was akin to running with a knife. At some point I was going to trip over and land on the pointy end. It would be painful, even debilitating.

Yet I couldn't seem to stop myself.

Not with Roane.

And apparently not with Caroline.

I'd stopped thinking about time and what it meant. Quantity didn't matter in life. Quality did. Roane was a quality human being, and there was something about Caroline that drew me to her. Maybe it was because they were cousins and for some reason I could sense they both possessed a soul-deep kindness. Surprisingly, I'd also stopped questioning my own naivete. I was choosing to risk following my instincts, and there would be no more second-guessing.

I would befriend Caroline just as I had Roane, even if it hurt when I had to say goodbye.

How much could it hurt after only a month anyway?

Roane had been amused when we pulled up to a large cottage on the outskirts of Alnster. A tarmac road led all the way up to the house through the woodland. I could see from the SUV that the woods ended here, the view beyond the cottage that of fields.

"It's a pity it's one story. An upper floor would give views of the village," Roane had told me just before he opened the door to get out.

His actions had been halted by the sight of Caroline bursting out of the front door, Shadow bounding at her back. She wore a calf-length navy skirt, the same Mary Janes from before, a navy sweater with a Peter Pan collar, and a pink long-line cardigan over the ensemble. In her hands was another Tupperware box.

Yay!

Shadow had jumped into the back of the Defender, saying a happy hello to Roane before giving my neck a swipe with his tongue. I'd giggled and scratched his ears, giving him the attention he desired as Caro got in beside him. She'd helped Shadow settle into the back seat and beamed brightly at Roane. Her smile had dimmed when she turned to me, but I hoped it was out of shyness and not dislike. "Hello. Let's go."

"Helena all right about this, Caro?" Roane had asked as he turned the SUV around. I'd caught a glimpse of a face peering out from the front window of the cottage as we left.

"Well—"

"Be honest, treasure," Roane had coaxed softly.

Hearing him so tender with his cousin made my heart squishy.

He called her "treasure."

"S-She wasn't entirely on board with the idea," Caroline had admitted quietly.

I'd twisted around in my seat to meet her gaze. "You told her I didn't give you a choice, right?"

Her answering smile had been more confident, even a little mischievous. "I did. Very clever of you."

Grinning back, I'd replied airily, "I do try my best."

The cousins had shared a smile, and when we arrived at the bookstore, I'd tried to ignore the meaningful look of gratitude that bordered on adoration from Roane. He'd squeezed my hand before hopping out to get the groceries.

He really had to stop looking at me like that.

Over an hour later we were seated at the small dining table in the apartment above the store, talking and laughing as the cousins shared stories about village life and growing up there. Shadow was sprawled in front of the wood burner despite the fact there was no fire blazing in it. His light snoring was a gentle backing track to our conversation.

Sometimes the cousins would share these secret, wary looks and seem to hesitate before talking, but I gathered it had something to do with the way Caro had been raised. Roane was probably checking with her before speaking to reassure her that he wouldn't mention how it was for her with Helena.

At least that was my guess.

As for me, I spent time waxing lyrical about living life as an independent woman. "I come and go as I please. I get to travel. Right now, I'm working on making my editing business a full-time gig."

"You're doing it then?" Roane asked, sounding pleased.

"I'm going to try. It probably won't be feasible, but at least it's something to concentrate on while I try to find another editing job in Chicago."

Roane frowned a little but nodded. "Good plan."

Was it the mention of Chicago that made him frown?

It was making me frown too.

Two weeks would be up before I knew it, and I still hadn't figured out what I wanted from my life.

But Caro didn't need to know that. "It was really scary moving out on my own at first, but I love it now. The sense of freedom is amazing."

This time Roane shot me a knowing, teasing look, but I ignored it. I was determined to plant as many seeds in Caro's mind as possible about grabbing hold of the reins of her life from her controlling aunt.

We were eating the light-as-air Victoria sponge cake Caro had baked when Roane excused himself to use the restroom.

As soon as he was out of earshot, I turned to his cousin. "Your baking is off-the-charts delicious, and Roane says you're good enough to bake professionally. Have you ever considered approaching the baker for a job?"

I'd met the baker when I'd gone there to buy lunch. His name was Antony Graham. I'd gotten his life story from him when I went in—early forties, divorced, had his kids every other weekend, and he'd run the bakery in Alnster for twenty years.

Caro shot a look at the door where Roane had disappeared out of, and then turned to me. Her dark eyes were bright with frustration. "I have. Two years ago I went to Tony with my baking. I was so nervous."

"What happened?"

With a heavy sigh, she lowered her eyes to the table. "He said he thought I was a good baker but asked me if Aunt Helena knew I'd come to him about a job. When I said no"—she met my gaze again, anger mingling with the frustration—"he said he wouldn't employ me, knowing it was going directly against the wishes of my aunt. I said, 'But I'm twenty years old,' and he said . . . 'Everyone knows Helena's in charge of your life, and I don't want to deal with her wrath. Go home, little girl.'"

"He said what?"

I closed my eyes, wincing at the fury in Roane's voice. When I opened them, Roane was rounding the table, indignation etched into every feature of his face. He placed his palms on the table and bent toward Caro, who was wide-eyed with concern.

"He really said that?" Roane asked, clearly forcing calm into his voice.

"Roane, it's not worth getting upset over."

"I beg to differ. Why didn't you come to me, treasure? I didn't . . ." He slid into his seat, his expression changing to one of guilt. "If I'd known you were trying to make a career out of baking, I would have helped. I would have gone to that spineless prick of a man and—"

"And what, Roane?" Caro placed her hand over his. "Threatened him? I don't want a job that way. I just . . . I just wanted to see if other people liked my baking . . . if I was good enough to do something with it."

"You are," he promised. "Let me speak to Tony."

Seeing Caro's lips pinch together, I found myself intervening. "Caro is right," I butted in. "She doesn't want a job because you threatened the baker. She wants it on her own merit." My brain kicked into high gear. "I . . . what if you set up a market stall on Main Street just outside The Anchor? You could sell your baking and get some reactions." Although I already knew those reactions would be positive.

For some reason this idea caused panic to flitter across Caro's face.

Deducing she was too shy to put herself at the center of attention, I hurried to add, "We could see if anyone else is interested in putting up a stall. Have a market day. I could ask Penny if I can sell some books."

She relaxed. "That might work."

"You'll need permits," Roane said, his brows drawn together, "and Caro would need to register with the Food Standards Agency, and that takes time. I can see about pushing the permits through, but not the FSA. You need to register with them twenty-eight days before the event."

"You can push the permits through?" I asked, curious about his influence in town.

"I sell livestock to market," he explained, but he wouldn't meet my eye. "I know people."

There was something cagey about his explanation—

"Do you really think we could do it?" Caro seemed brighter now, hopeful.

Realizing I wouldn't be there for it made me sad. But I could still help organize it before I left. "Absolutely."

Roane frowned. "You're really not worried about Helena trying to put a stop to it?"

"I'm a little worried," she replied softly. "But . . ."

"But . . ."

She swallowed hard and stared Roane right in the eye. "I-I've been thinking about it for a while and I need to know if I can do this. Because maybe if I can do this one thing . . ." She stared forlornly at the table now.

"You'll feel strong enough to leave her?" Roane guessed, his tone hesitant, like he was afraid of pushing too hard.

"Perhaps."

Roane looked at me, his expression determined. "Get sign-ups for the market by Wednesday and I'll see about getting what you need to hold it in four weeks' time."

I knew my expression was equally determined. "You got it, Robson."

"I do wish you could be there, Evie," Caro said.

Sadness threatened to take hold, and I couldn't quite meet Roane's gaze. "I'll be there in spirit," I replied far more brightly than I felt inside.

Nine

It was the first week of June and the end of my third week in England.

A gentle breeze kissed my bare arms and legs as I clasped the old photograph in my hand and shook with laughter.

"Give it here," Roane demanded. "Caro, you'll pay for this."

Caro, wearing a light summer dress that still managed to cover everything but her arms and throat, giggled. "I'm sorry. I felt it was in Evie's best interest to see this side of you. I wouldn't want her to think you're perfect."

I snorted and shot him a teasing look. "I'm keeping this."

Just as he had last Sunday, Roane decided to take a day off to join me on a walk along the beach. Considering my attraction to him had only deepened over the last week, I felt it prudent to invite Caro to join us. Shadow danced in and out of the water, entertaining us with his exuberance.

And then Caro had produced an old photograph of Roane she'd found.

She told me he was fourteen years old in the photo.

Once upon a time Roane was a gangly, long-limbed, skinny teen whose face hadn't quite grown into his ears.

Oh, and he was wearing a Spider-Man costume in the photograph.

Scowling, Roane turned to Caro. "Mum and Dad guilted me into wearing that costume for your bloody birthday party because you loved Spider-Man. I took shit from everyone for it and this is the thanks I get."

She giggled harder.

Sensing he'd get no remorse from his cousin, he narrowed his eyes on me. "Give it here. I'm destroying the evidence."

"No!" I held the photo behind my back. "This is priceless."

"Evie, give it here," he warned, striding toward me.

I stumbled back into the tepid sea, my sandals in one hand, the photo in the other, and held the latter out of his reach. "You'll have to fight me for it."

Something flashed in his gaze. "Challenge accepted."

Suddenly he was on me, forcing me farther into the sea, my feet sinking into wet sand as the water encircled my calves. Roane wrapped one arm around my waist, hauling my body against his as he attempted to reach around my back for the photograph with his other hand.

I'd been laughing until that moment.

Any amusement died as soon as my breasts crushed against his hard chest.

We both stilled at the contact, our eyes locking.

The crest of Roane's cheeks turned red, and he swallowed hard. His voice was hoarse as he practically begged, "Give it to me, Evie."

Dirty-minded me gasped at the request.

Roane squeezed his eyes closed, his arm tightening around me as he let out a little groan. When he opened his eyes, his voice was thick as he clarified, "The photo. Give me the photo."

The sensible side of my personality was screaming to wriggle out of his hold, but the part that wanted to reassure him stayed where I was. "I like it. You're adorable."

"Every man's dream, that," he said gruffly. "To be called adorable."

"You were a boy then. You can be adorable when you're a boy. What you did for Caro is adorable. If I give it back, don't destroy it. It means something to your cousin."

"I wouldn't destroy it," he replied, his eyes dropping to my mouth. "It was just an excuse to put my arms around you."

My eyes widened at his confession, and he gave me a self-deprecating smile as he gently let me go and stepped back.

"But that wasn't such a great idea after all."

Disappointment I tried to hide washed over me.

As if he read my mind, Roane whispered, "It's a form of torture, Evie."

Aware that Caro was still on the beach with us, within hearing distance, I could only gape at him like a landed fish.

"Evie!" A voice carried along the beach, interrupting the tension-fraught moment.

My befuddled gaze moved past Roane. First, I saw Caro, who was watching me and her cousin with open fascination. Beyond her was a stretch of sandy beach, shadowed beneath high sand dunes.

Hurrying alongside the bottom of the dunes was Penny.

I strode out of the water, avoiding contact with Roane, and hurried to meet Penny. Shadow beat me to it, almost knocking

Penny over with his exuberance. She laughed and petted him, but her eyes never left mine. I'd sensed Roane and Caro following me and knew they were at my back when Penny's eyes moved over my shoulder.

"Hey, what's up?" I asked as the bookstore owner and I drew to a halt a few feet from her.

Shadow loped away from her, pressed his cold nose to my hand, and then stopped beside Roane, who absentmindedly petted him. He was too busy staring at Penny in concern.

In truth she looked agitated, which *was* concerning.

Penny gave Roane and Caro a tight smile before turning her attention to me. "Evie, can we speak in private?"

My pulse started to race.

What if Penny needed to cancel the last week of my vacation? No!

I wasn't ready to leave yet.

Heart pounding, I tried to hide my distress as I suggested to Roane and Caro that they walk on ahead and I'd catch up with them.

They seemed reluctant to leave, but they did, with Shadow bounding through the shore ahead of them. Worry seized my chest.

Roane and Caro, Millie and Dexter, and Penny had all become important to me so quickly. I didn't know if it was because I needed people to cling to during a difficult time in my life, or if I'd genuinely found special friendships with them all.

No, that wasn't true.

I knew for a fact that I'd found something special with Roane, and I was afraid of it. Yet, thinking of leaving him, now or in a week, was a scary thought.

I reluctantly faced Penny. "What's going on?"

She held her hair in a tight fist to stop it blowing around in the breeze. The wind was picking up as if to mirror my mood, and I shivered in my T-shirt and shorts. Although it was the warmest day of the year so far, that didn't mean it was superhot and that sea breeze was cool.

"Evie, I have a proposition for you, and you'll probably think I'm mad for even asking but I'm going to do it anyway."

I felt a flutter in my stomach. "Okay."

"Remember I told you my sister wants me to sell up and move to Australia?"

"Yeah."

"Well, I've been thinking about it, and what's stopping me is the unknown. I don't want to sell my store and leave my life here only to go over there and three months in discover I bloody hate the place."

"That makes sense." But what did this have to do with me?

Penny's gaze sharpened. "Evie, we haven't known each other long, but I have good instincts about people, and I trust you. I know from our talks that things are a little unsettled for you right now, and I think we can help each other."

"Help each other how?"

"I'm going out to Australia for three months as a trial run. I'm gonna rent out my own flat while I'm gone, but I'll still need someone to look after the store and its apartment. I want that person to be you."

Stunned, I gaped at her. The ramifications of her proposition cluttered my headspace instantly. Greer would be upset. So would my mother. Phil would be concerned too. But it would give me more time to figure out a path.

And I'd get to spend more time with Roane.

"Now I can't pay you much, like, but you can stay in the apartment rent-free."

A tremor of excitement ran through me. My immediate reaction was to scream *YES!* at the top of my voice, but that goddamn sensible side of me took control first. "I'm only here as a tourist. I'd need a work visa for that."

Penny waved her hand in a dismissive gesture. "Already looked into it." She pulled a folded-up piece of paper out of the back pocket of her jean shorts. "I filled out the employer form and I have the address you need to send it to, to update them about the change in situation of your stay."

I gaped.

But what about Greer?

"My friend is pregnant—"

"I thought she had her boyfriend, Anders, or something?"

"Andre."

Penny took a step toward me. "Before you come up with excuses not to do it . . . can I ask if you *want* to do it?"

The only thing back in Chicago for me was Greer. The thought of missing out on the majority of her pregnancy made my heart twinge in my chest . . . but . . .

Three more months running the bookstore, getting paid to do something I was loving more and more by the minute.

Three more months with Caroline, Milly, and Dexter.

Three more months with Roane.

Something stressful that had been knotted tight in my belly for a week, something I didn't want to put a name to because it seemed ridiculous to feel so strongly about a person when we'd known each other only a few weeks . . . well, that something began to dissolve, loosening, relaxing.

I was relieved.

"Yes." I nodded a little frantically. "Yeah, I want to do it."

Penny smiled, and gripped my hand. "Then why not do it?"

Why not indeed?

Three months was plenty of time to figure out my life, and I'd get to do it during the summer on the coast of England. Rent-free.

I'd be crazy to turn this down, even if a certain farmer and his friends weren't a factor.

"If they give me a work visa, I'll do it."

Smiling from ear to ear, Penny pulled me into her arms and squeezed me tight. "Thank you, Evie. You're a godsend, lass."

We were lucky to procure the table and benches in the garden of The Anchor an hour later. On a day like today, on a Sunday, the pub was heaving with tourists. We'd walked in just as a family was leaving, however, and Caro nabbed the table outside before anyone else could.

The three of us sat sipping our drinks, Roane and I drinking cider, Caro a soda, while Shadow lounged at my sand-dusted feet.

The cousins had kept quiet about Penny's visit with me on the beach, but I could see they were growing impatient. They'd obviously expected me to offer up the reason for her tracking me down. I wasn't sure what to say. I didn't want to get their hopes up in case my work visa was denied.

Not that I should presume to think their hopes would be high at the possibility of my staying.

Yet, somehow, I knew they would be.

"So what—"

"Caroline Robson." Roane was cut off by the appearance of a familiar blond woman.

She stood over our table, staring down at Caro, wearing calf-length army pants and a khaki tank top. Her calves and arms were enviously toned, while her face was somewhat weather-beaten. It made it hard to determine what age she was.

But I recognized her.

She was the quad bike blonde.

I'd seen her a few times driving through the village on her quad bike, but I'd forgotten to ask Roane about her.

"Uh, it's Mordue," Caro corrected shyly.

"No, it's not." The blonde scoffed and shot Roane a commiserating look. " 'Bout time you took back your legal name, girl. Hell can stuff it."

Hell? I mouthed at Roane. Did she mean Helena?

At the twitch of Roane's lips, I made a strangled noise to cover my amusement.

"You must be the American." The blonde turned her eyes on me. They shone an indeterminate color in the sun. Green or blue. It was difficult to tell. "I hear you're behind the market, along with this one." She gestured to Caro.

"That's right." I stuck out my hand. "I'm Evie."

The blonde took my hand and shook it vigorously. "Annie Foster."

Foster?

I'd met a Foster already. Maggie Foster was an older woman who owned the art gallery/jewelry store. I'd been in and bought a bracelet for Greer. Maggie was sweet and affable and a good listener. She'd questioned me about my stay, and I'd spent an entire lunch break chatting her ear off. Not that she'd minded. In fact, I got the distinct sense she enjoyed company.

I really ought to stop in to see her more.

"Any relation to Maggie?"

Annie dropped my hand, her expression turning blank, before she looked at Caro. "Is it too late to set up a stall?"

Surprised by her abruptness and more than sensing I'd said something out of turn, I shot a look at Roane. He squeezed my knee under the table, giving me quiet reassurance, but I knew all of his expressions well enough to know I had definitely said something wrong.

"What are you selling?" Roane asked her.

"Lizzie's paintings."

Caro's eyes widened. "Oh, I'm not sure people shopping the market could afford those, Annie."

"The wee ones." Annie shrugged. "She won't be charging near as much as she normally would."

Roane frowned. "But they'll be worth a fortune."

"Aye, so?"

Lost, I blurted out, "Who's Lizzie?"

"My wife." Annie stared stonily at me.

Confused by her attitude, I asked, "Is she a famous painter?"

As if a switch had flipped inside of her, Annie grinned at me. "Aye. A bloody good one."

"She's famous in the art world, Evie," Roane explained before smirking at Annie, "which is why it's baffling she wants to sell her work at a wee village market, when she could make a fortune on those paintings."

"We have enough money. So, we're in?"

Roane sighed. "I'll see what I can do to add you to the permits, and let you know."

"You know where I am. Nice to meet you, Evie. Caroline Robson." Annie stared pointedly at Caro before marching away.

Caro rolled her eyes. "I think I need to legally change my name just to get Annie off my back."

"She's not wrong." Roane shrugged.

"I'm aware." Caro rested her elbow on the table and cupped her cheek in her hand. "I'm just tired of people looking at me like I'm some kind of weak little girl."

I reached across the bench and squeezed her wrist. "I don't think that was Annie's intention. I think she's trying to remind you of who you really are."

She gave me a sad smile. "Yes, you're probably right."

"What's her story?" I settled back on the bench seat, gazing from Roane at my side to Caro across the table. "Annie's, I mean. Why did she avoid my question about Maggie?"

The cousins exchanged an uncomfortable look before Roane explained, "Maggie's Annie's mum. She and Annie's dad disowned Annie when she told them she was gay."

Shock froze me to the spot.

Maggie had seemed like such a sweet soul.

"I don't get it."

"It's hard to understand for anyone who isn't a closed-minded, judgmental prig." Caro sighed unhappily. "Annie's father and my aunt Helena are among the few who shun Annie."

"In this day and age?"

"Small-village mentality. We're not as bad as some, but there's still people round here old-fashioned and narrow-minded." Roane's tone was clipped with disdain. "Some who even patronize The Alnster Inn over The Anchor because Dex is black."

Horrified, I could only gape as hot indignation choked me. "But . . . b-but," I spluttered. "What bullshit! And Maggie . . . she seemed so nice."

Caro's expression was pained. "She is, Evie. But her husband is a controlling man and she . . . well, she let him drive Annie away and refused to speak to Annie publicly."

"Probably for fear of the man. But that's no excuse now. Horace Foster had a stroke a year ago and is now paralyzed, bedridden, and taken care of by a full-time nurse. Maggie could have a relationship with Annie if she wanted to." Roane vibrated with disapproval. "He can't stop her now. It's up to her to make that move. A year passed and she still hasn't? That's not right."

"I think it's a little more complicated than that," Caro suggested softly.

Roane grunted in answer, clearly disagreeing.

Perhaps Caro was right, but I had to agree with Roane. It was up to Maggie to bridge that distance with Annie after the way she'd allowed her to be treated.

A tension fell over the table at the quiet disagreement between the cousins.

So I blurted out my news. "Penny's asked me to stay and run her store for three months."

Roane's head whipped around to look at me so fast, I could only imagine he got whiplash. "What?"

I stared into his warm eyes and felt a flutter of something I didn't want to feel at his hopeful countenance. "It's not a done deal," I hurried to say, "I have to apply for a work visa. Penny's got all that figured out and is going to try to push it through as quickly as possible. She thinks it'll take two weeks, so she's letting me stay a week longer free of charge. So no matter what happens, I'm here for another two weeks instead of just one. I need to postpone my flights home but that shouldn't be a problem."

"That's wonderful." Caro beamed from ear to ear. "I really

hope they grant you the visa, Evie. I can't imagine the summer here without you now."

Pleased to be wanted, I smiled. "Me too."

Then I felt Roane's hand on my knee again and shivered at the feel of his calloused palm on my skin. My gaze flew to his, and he squeezed my knee. "I'll see what I can do to make sure you get that visa."

The flutters in my belly went wild. "What could you do?"

"I know people," he said.

He'd said that before. "Who are these mysterious people you know?"

"People who help me get what I want."

My breath caught at the heat in his eyes, and he gave my knee one last squeeze before releasing me. Roane smirked as if he knew how he affected me and wrenched his gaze from mine to say to Caro, "If I invite people to The Anchor to celebrate Evie's prolonged stay, you're coming. No arguments. Helena can go to hell."

Ten

"I'm staying in England for another three months."

At the deafening silence on the other end of the line, I slumped onto the sofa and stared out at the dark sea. Broken streams of moonlight glinted off the water, moving with every gentle wave like fluttering silver fairy wings dancing across the surface.

Yet not even the beauty of my surroundings could ease the rising tide of concern as the silence continued.

To my shock, I received an email along with my digital work visa that day. Only nine days after I'd spoken to Penny. Last week, I'd called Greer and told her I was staying for an extra week because Penny offered me a deal. I hadn't seen any point alarming her about the prospect of my staying in England for longer until it was for certain.

Now it was certain.

"Greer?"

She cleared her throat, and then her words came out tight, as though she were clenching her teeth. "How is that possible?"

Quietly, as though I were afraid a loud tone would spook her, I explained Penny's situation, her proposition, and the arrival of my work visa.

More silence followed the explanation.

"Greer?"

"I knew it," she replied sadly. "I knew you would go there and not come back. I just felt it in my gut."

Guilt that I was hurting her, worrying her, made me flinch. "Oh, Greer, that's not true. It's just these past four weeks flew, just like a vacation, and I didn't have time to figure anything out. Now I have three months to do that, and I am certain I'll know what my next step is going to be when I get back to Chicago."

"Yeah but you might decide Chicago isn't your next step." She huffed. "And please don't tell me your decision to stay has nothing to do with the hot farmer."

"It doesn't," I snapped.

It didn't.

Not really.

Not like that.

I'd posted an Instagram photo of Roane holding an impressive pair of melons to his chest beside a fruit stall at Alnwick Markets last week, with the caption "Some people are just blessed by nature's bounty ;)"

Almost as soon as I'd posted that photo, I was inundated with comments from friends. Who was the mysterious hottie, and what was he to me? Mostly I ignored the comments, but I couldn't ignore Greer's phone call later that day.

I'd explained who Roane was and that we were just friends.

I thought she'd bought it.

Not that there was anything to buy. We *were* just friends. Even though he constantly flirted with me and was generally making every day harder to resist the temptation he presented.

"Oh, please." I could practically hear the curl in Greer's upper lip. "You went to England to get some distance from your life, met a gorgeous guy, and are allowing your vagina to dictate the next three months."

For a moment I couldn't speak. I was hardly ever on the end of Greer's sharp tongue, but I knew she had one. She used it to eviscerate lazy colleagues at her design firm. Greer was a UX designer, specializing in the design of digital products like websites and apps. We'd shared the experience of working in a male-dominated office, and Greer had decided that to be seen, heard, and respected she'd be the resident ballbuster.

It worked for her.

I just never thought it would be directed at me one day.

The urge to snap back was great, but I reminded myself my best friend was pregnant. Shouting at your pregnant best friend was not cool.

"That's not what I'm doing." I kept my voice gentle, calm. "This is about me. What I want."

"Then tell me this guy hasn't got something to do with you wanting to stay?"

"You know not everything has to be about a guy, but if you want the truth, yes, he factored into the decision but not the way you think. We're friends." My chest ached whenever I thought of Roane. "And not just acquaintance friends or good friends but friends like you and I are friends. We connected immediately in a way I can't explain. So, yes, part of staying for a little longer is so I can have more time with him."

"Are you listening to yourself? Are you deliberately deluding yourself? A heterosexual man and woman cannot have that kind of connection and it not turn sexual. Are you saying there isn't even a tiny bit of you that's attracted to this guy?"

"So what if there is?" I snapped, forgetting my vow not to argue with her. "I'm not going to do anything about it. I didn't come here for that. I came here because I was so goddamn lonely in Chicago, I couldn't bear it, and until I figure out why that was, I'm staying here."

As soon as the words were out of my mouth, I squeezed my eyes closed in regret.

This time I wasn't surprised by Greer's silence.

"I didn't mean that," I whispered.

"Yeah, you did. And it breaks my heart that I didn't know that." She released a heavy sigh. "I'm sorry. I'm . . . just sad that you'll miss out on most of my pregnancy, which is selfish. We're all following your Instagram here and you . . . God, you look so happy over there. I'm just worried. I miss my best friend."

Tears stung my eyes. "You don't think I miss you? You were the only thing holding me back from making this decision, and *I* feel selfish as hell for staying here while you're pregnant."

"Don't. I was a snippy bitch before. Don't feel guilty about this, Evie. This is your life, and what you said before you left is true. Your friends can't stand still for you, but you can't be our sidekick as our lives move forward. I don't want you to be lonely," she sniffled. "It kills me that you were lonely here."

The tears that had been threatening let loose.

"You're not lonely there, are you?"

"No." I wiped at my cheeks, a small, fond smile softening my lips. "I'm not lonely here. It's not like Chicago. This is a small village, Greer. Even when you're single, you're surrounded by friends.

We meet at the pub almost every night and keep each other company. It's nice."

"It sounds nice. It's also why I'm afraid you won't come back."

"My life is back in Chicago," I said, the words automatic.

"Is it?"

For the first time, I paused.

Was my life back there?

Surely I couldn't question that after only a month of staying in Alnster?

I gave a huff of laughter. "I'm sure after three months I will be sick and tired of tiny-village life. I'm a city girl."

"Hmm." Greer sighed again. "Have you told Josie?"

Josie was my mom.

My decision to stay in Alnster for three more months was based on a few factors. My mom was one of them, and I didn't want to face her yet. "I left Phil a voice mail."

"Evie," Greer groaned. "That's not fair."

Feeling defensive, I scowled. "What? I tried to call. It went to his voice mail."

"Did you try calling Josie?"

Indignation bubbled up within me, and I had to work hard not to sound irritated as I replied, "This isn't about her. For once. So, no."

"Okay, I won't push it. You're right, this is about you. You do what you gotta do."

And just like that I melted, grateful to have a friend—no, a sister—like Greer in my life. "It means a lot to me that you would say that."

"Well, I'm trying very hard right now not to be a self-involved dipshit, partly because it's the right thing to do and partly because when I get off this phone and tell Andre you're staying, he'll give me this really disappointed look if he thinks I've been an unsupportive friend."

I chuckled. "That must be some disappointed look."

"Oh, you have no idea."

"I love you, dipshit," I said, trying not to get overly emotional on her.

"I love you too." Her voice had started to break. "Okay, see you later."

She hung up quickly, and I knew it was because she was seconds from bursting into tears. I told myself it was her hormones because Greer usually had a better handle on her emotions than this.

It didn't make it any easier to know that I'd made my best friend cry.

As I got ready for bed, my stomach churned with my decision. Not because I wasn't happy to stay in England for three more months, but because Greer's worries had begun to make a dent in my stubborn belief I'd return to Chicago.

What if she was right?

What if what I discovered about myself meant Chicago wasn't right for me anymore?

This trip to Northumberland was my first international trip. As a kid, we'd vacationed within the States and Canada. Growing up, reading Roald Dahl and Enid Blyton, I'd dreamed of England. Of visiting. Living there. As I got older, plans changed. I lost myself in the minutiae of adulthood. England became merely a wish on a vacation bucket list. It didn't occur to adult me to live somewhere other than Chicago.

It never occurred to me there could be somewhere outside the States that would suit me so well.

My thoughts unsettled me, crashing into me like a massive wave and pulling me out to sea. I floated in that endless sea for hours, until finally, exhaustion dragged me into sleep, relieving me of my worries for just a little while.

$\mathcal{S}$omewhere around five in the morning, I was jolted out of the peace of slumber by Tom Grennan. Confused, heart racing, I blinked into the dark of the bedroom, trying to figure out where the noise was coming from.

Then I remembered I'd changed my ringtone to "Found What I've Been Looking For" by Tom Grennan.

Panicked, I turned to fumble for it on my bedside table, thinking there must be some kind of emergency for someone to be calling me at this hour, when the song stopped. Grabbing my phone, I pushed up to sitting and unlocked it to see the missed call was from my mom.

I stared blearily at the screen for a moment.

Obviously, Phil had passed along my message to Mom that I was staying in England for another three months. What was she thinking? Would she think I was abandoning her? That I was done? Would this cause her to fall off the wagon? This was why I didn't want to talk to her in the first place, because I didn't want my concern for her dictating my choice. Not this time. At some point, I had to put myself first. Horrible flutters flapped around in my belly.

I'd only been staring at my phone a few minutes when it beeped, and an envelope appeared to let me know I had voice mail.

Oh God.

Just delete it, Evie.

But I couldn't.

My curiosity was too great.

"Hey, baby girl." My mom's husky voice sounded in my ear as I listened to her message. An ache flared across my chest. "I just realized it's probably really early where you are . . . so I'm sorry if I woke you."

I relaxed at how clear she sounded.

No slurring.

Not off the wagon, then.

"I just . . . Phil told me you're staying in England for another three months, and I couldn't wait that long to say to you . . ." She sucked in a shaky breath and released it slowly, causing static on the line. "How sorry I am. Again. And . . . uh . . . well, I need you to know that if you can't forgive me, if you can't find it in you to give me another shot, that I understand, baby girl." Her voice broke, her words filled with tears I knew were rolling down her face. "I need you to do what's right for you, even if that means letting me go. I've been selfish with you for too long. So . . ." She paused, and when she spoke again, her voice was stronger. "You make the right choice for you, my beautiful girl, and don't worry about me. You've been the parent in this relationship for way too long. It's my turn to do right by you . . . I'm sorry I let you down so much. I'm sorry I never found a way to let you know that I love you more than I love anything in this world."

The message cut off and I struggled to breathe through the tears that had started falling from the moment I heard her voice.

In all the times she'd apologized, my mom had never once said, *I need you to do what's right for you.*

It sparked a hope.

But that hope had been crushed too many times to count.

Turmoil washed through me, and I knew there was no going

back to sleep after that message. Instead I got up, brushed my teeth, washed the tears off my face, and pulled on a boyfriend cardigan I'd brought with me.

I made coffee, slipped on shoes, and went outside to watch the sunrise from the apartment's private garden across the street. The village was eerily silent, no sound but that of the sea lapping at the small shore of the harbor.

The sky was a dark purple color, slowly brightening to pale blue streaked with orange as the sun began to rise.

Sipping my coffee, I forced tears back as I pondered the message from my mother. For weeks now I'd purposefully forgotten everything about the States except Greer.

It was all waiting for me when I eventually got back, and with the exception of my best friend, I wasn't sure I wanted to face any of it. Which was why Greer's suspicions about my reasons for staying longer in England didn't sound so silly to me anymore.

The heartbreaking truth was that I'd been happier, more content, these past few weeks than I remembered feeling in a long time. Suddenly, I felt brittle with confusion.

The sound of a car engine broke through the peaceful silence, and I turned my head, surprised to see Roane's Land Rover. The beam of his lights blinded me for a second as the SUV turned toward the center of the village.

But then suddenly he stopped, reversed, and swung left toward me.

He'd obviously caught sight of me.

My heart began to beat just that little bit faster.

Roane pulled up against the curb and jumped out. He strode unhurriedly toward the garden and jumped over the small gate rather than open it.

"Evie?" He took the steps two at a time down into the garden.

"Hey."

"What are you doing up so early?" Roane sat down on the bench beside me, resting his arm along the back of it, almost cocooning me.

That's all it took.

The man did something to my defenses.

Obliterated them.

An ugly-sounding sob burst out of me.

"Fuck, Evie." Roane wrapped his arms around me, pulling me into his warm strength. I burrowed into him, my tears soaking the front of his sweater. "Shh, angel." He rubbed my back. "I'm here, I've got you."

He did. Nothing felt safer than his arms around me, and I wondered if anything ever had. More confusion flooded me, so big it got stuck in my throat, the emotion choking me. I burrowed harder into Roane, fighting for breath through my tears, and wished for the feeling to pass.

When my tears eventually subsided, I panted a little, trying to catch my breath, and neither of us moved for a minute.

Turning my face on his chest, I looked up to the sky. It was lighter, almost completely blue, and cloudless.

"Do you want to talk about it?"

At Roane's gentle query, I straightened, lifting my head. His hands smoothed down my back as I moved, one falling away, the other settling on my hip.

I met his concerned gaze, knowing I was probably a snot-nosed mess.

"My mom is an alcoholic," I confessed.

Concern gave way to sympathy. "Evie." He squeezed my hip.

I proceeded to tell him the things only Greer knew. The things I'd kept from previous boyfriends because Chace had used the knowledge as part of his arsenal in his cold war against my self-esteem. He'd used it to support the idea that I was ungrateful trash.

"My dad died of a heart defect when I was eight. One day he was there, the next he was gone. No one knew about the defect until it was too late. I only have a few memories of him that are sharp, clear, as if they happened yesterday. The rest are just impressions of him as a dad, as a husband. I was so young. But he was the kind of dad who sat patiently removing gum from your hair when you had a little-girl freak-out at the idea of the gum being cut out." My smile was watery. "The kind of dad who cheered you on at Little League like you were the next Frank Thomas when in truth you couldn't bat for shit. And he was the kind of husband who kissed his wife every morning before he left for work and every evening when he got home. The kind of husband who dried the dishes she washed and made her laugh when she'd had a bad day."

"He sounds like a good man."

"He was. The best. And when he died, Mom started drinking to cope. She went to rehab when social services got involved, I was in foster care during that time, and then she got me back a few months out of rehab. But she fell on and off that wagon for a few years. Then when I was thirteen, she met Phil. My stepfather. That's when she got help again, and she was sober for a long while. I was lulled into the idea that it was over.

"But then when I was nineteen, at college, Mom had a breast cancer scare. Nothing came of it, but it screwed with her head. She started to drink again." I knew what Roane could see in my eyes. Despair. Pure and simple. "She's been in and out of rehab for fourteen years. Her sobriety can last years and then something happens—losing a job, a friend dying—and she starts drinking again. Anytime life gets a little bit hard.

"Phil adores her. He's a great guy and has been a wonderful stepfather, but he seems to have this unending reserve of patience and support for her."

"And you?"

"I'm tired." I smiled sadly through the tears that slipped quietly down my cheeks. "I'm tired of disappointment. For years it's been a cycle of picking her up off the kitchen floor and putting her to bed, or getting a call from some stranger in a supermarket because my mom is so far gone, she can't even remember how she got there. And then her remorse, her determination to get sober.

"And . . . it's the hope, Roane. No matter how many times she disappoints me, that stupid, fucking useless *hope* won't go away. It won't listen to reason. Because she's not a bad person. She's a really good person, funny and sweet, with a big heart. She just has this huge weakness . . . and I don't know how much more *my* heart can take."

He pulled me back into his embrace, his lips against my temple, and I clung to him. I'd met him just a little over four weeks ago, and yet I felt like I'd known him my whole life. Like he'd been waiting here for me my whole life.

"What do I do?" I whispered, clinging to this human life raft he offered. "I don't know what to do. Do I walk away for good or do I try again?"

"I wish I could give you an answer." His voice sounded husky, as if abraded by a wound. Like he was hurting for me. The thought made my heart ache even more. "But only you can decide that, Evie. The good thing is, you're here. You're not there. And you have time to make that decision. You don't have to make it right now. Just be here, Evie, with me. Your mum, Chicago, all of that . . . for once it can wait. Until *you're* ready. Just be here with me," he repeated in a whisper.

I held on tighter, inhaling Roane's now familiar scent, feeling his hard strength wrapped around me.

The ache in my chest settled, dissipated.

"I can do that," I whispered in return.

His embrace tightened.

Eleven

As if the weather gods knew today was a big day for Caro, the sun was out, the sea breeze was held in check by the buildings surrounding us, and there wasn't a cloud in the sky.

It was Market Day.

For the past few weeks, Roane had been dropping off leaflets at shops and with acquaintances, advertising Market Day. The hope was that they'd spread the news.

Apparently, they had.

The streets were lined with cars before we'd even finished setting up our stalls. The residents had agreed for us to block off Main Street for our market, so they knew if they wanted to drive out of the village today, they'd need to take the back road through the woodlands.

My stall with books and tourist trinkets was situated right next to Caro's stall so I could be on hand if she needed me. Her hands shook as she set everything up. After scouring the internet, Caro had found clear cabinets to display her baked goods all the while keeping them fresh. Mini chalkboards were placed in front of each row detailing what they were and how much they cost. The kitchen at my apartment looked like a hurricane had passed through it because her aunt Helena, furious about the market, wouldn't let her use the kitchen at home to bake. Caro had used mine through the night so that her food would still be fresh for sale.

I was keeping a careful eye on her, worried that she hadn't slept. Even more worried at the sight of those shaking hands.

"Can I help?" I asked, approaching her cautiously.

Her lovely red hair was pulled back in a loose ponytail, mostly because she'd had little time to get dressed this morning, and it softened her. Wisps of hair curled around her face, so different from the severe bun she usually wore.

She'd only brought a sweater with her to wear with her long skirt, and I'd somehow managed to convince her she'd be too hot. I'd given her a plain white crew-neck T-shirt of mine. It was too big, so I'd pulled it tight and knotted it at the base of her spine. The knot-tied shirt worked nicely with the loose, flowing skirt and showed off Caro's teeny-tiny waist. For once she looked effortlessly stylish and her age. When she'd seen her appearance, her mouth opened in obvious protest but quickly clamped shut as she narrowed her gaze on her reflection.

After a quick perusal, she'd tilted her head in thought and smoothed her hands down her skirt. In that moment, I knew she'd made the decision to be brave and wear something her aunt would disapprove of. We'd left the apartment to load up carts, or trolleys as they called them here, with our stuff without another word.

Roane had been in the square with a few other villagers, setting up the stalls we'd rented. He'd left to park the rental van that had transported the stalls at his farm, and we hadn't seen him since.

"I'm quite all right," Caro replied softly, her eyebrows pinched together in a frown as her gaze darted toward the crowd that was waiting for us to announce the market was open. Annie Foster and her wife, Liz, had their stall of Liz's artwork set up nearest to the crowd. Every now and then when someone would take a step toward the market, Annie would cough, look deliberately at her watch, and then glare at them.

I smirked as she did it again.

My smile fell, however, when I saw her wife shoot concerned looks somewhere over my shoulder. I didn't need to turn to know the concern was because Maggie Foster had set up a stall with the artwork and jewelry she sold beside me. No one had told Maggie that her daughter and daughter-in-law would be there, if the pale shock on Maggie's face was any evidence.

Shrugging off my worry about this new development, I decided I could only deal with one problem at a time, and my priority was Caro's nerves. "You'll do great," I promised.

"Of course she will." Roane's voice brought my head around to see him approaching from the parking lot of The Anchor with a girl at his side. "And I brought reinforcements."

My eyes went to his companion, and I beamed. I knew who she was, not because we'd met, but because Milly had proudly shown me photographs.

She was Milly and Dex's daughter, Viola.

And she was even lovelier in real life.

To my surprise, Caro perked up at the sight. "Viola!" She hurried around the back of her stall, and the two young women met for a hug. The affection and ease between them surprised me considering Caro had not struck me as someone who made friends easily.

Roane came to my side, bumping me with his shoulder. "How are you?"

"Confused. I thought you said Caro had no friends?"

"Viola and Caro are as close as is possible with Helena breathing down Caro's neck. All the other girls faded out of her life because she was always declining to do things with them. Viola's different. She's like Milly. Understanding. She's there for Caro whenever she needs her, even if they don't spend much time together."

I liked her already.

Even more so as the stunning young woman walked straight toward me with a beautiful smile on her face. "You must be Evie." She held out her arms for a hug, and I bent down toward her to immediately acquiesce. She gave me a squeeze. "Mam has told me all about you."

"She's told me all about you too."

Viola eyed me in open curiosity. "She said you could be a model, and she wasn't lying." Her large hazel eyes swept down my bare legs. I was wearing shorts. "God, I'd give anything for your legs."

I laughed. "Well, thanks, but you're gorgeous. Nothing about you needs to change."

It was true. Viola had been blessed with smooth, blemish-free skin. It was lighter than her father's, a warm, tawny color, and she had Milly's eye color but Dex's eye shape. With her complexion those light hazel eyes were extraordinarily striking, huge, feline, and long lashed. She had a cute button of a nose and ample lips with an exaggerated cupid's bow. Like mine, Viola's dark hair was highlighted with a caramel ombré effect. There were masses of it fall-ing to the base of her back in fluffy waves.

In shorts, cute sneakers with gold glitter on them, and a cropped belly top, Viola gave the appearance of a confident twenty-year-old. And with her tiny waist, rounded ass, and slender legs, she had every reason to be. I imagined she had many admirers at college. Not just because she was beautiful, but because of the way she smiled. Even if I hadn't heard what a great, kind girl she was, I'd be able to tell by the warmth that radiated from her.

"I love your accent." Viola grinned at me and then turned to Caro. "You ready, chickie?" Caro gave a tremulous smile and her friend laughed, throwing an arm around her shoulder. "Don't worry, it'll be great."

"When did you get back from college?" I asked.

"Last night. It's nice to be home. Mam says you're staying for another three months, which is awesome. We'll get to hang out."

I smiled and gave Roane an amused look he returned. Why a twenty-year-old would want to hang out with me, I had no idea, but I wouldn't shoot her down.

"Looks like everyone's ready." Roane nodded toward the other stalls. We had people from outside the village who had asked to set up their stalls, selling everything from tea towels and jewelry to fresh produce. He looked at me as he brushed his knuckles down my arm. "You ready?"

Since my little breakdown at the beginning of the week, Roane had been even more attentive. The man was killing me.

I shivered at his touch, and his dark eyes glimmered with heat at the reaction. Trying not to blush, I took a step back from him. "Yeah, let's do this."

"I've got to work, but I'll be back later to check in." He strode over to Caro, took her by the shoulders, and pressed a sweet kiss to her forehead. I was not jealous of her forehead. No sirree. "Good luck, treasure. Call if you need me."

All three of us watched him stride across the street, nodding hello to Annie and Liz as he passed.

"I know he's your cousin, Caro, but that man is sex on a stick." Viola sighed, fanning herself dramatically.

Did she have a crush on Roane? My gaze cut to her in concern and found her smirking at me. Almost assessing. Huh?

"He's like a brother to you, Viola, so stop your nonsense." Caro shot me a pointed look before frowning at her friend.

Mischief sparked in Viola's gaze. "True, but I was speaking for Evie."

Realizing Milly had probably filled her daughter's head with speculation about Roane and me, I rolled my eyes and wandered over to my stall, calling over my shoulder, "I'm perfectly able to speak for myself, thank you."

"I'm so happy I'll be home to be there for the day you do," Viola called back with a wink.

I laughed and shook my head, thinking she reminded me a lot of Milly.

The market opened minutes later, and the day began.

My concentration was split between running my stall and watching out for Caro. I soon learned, however, that Viola was the best person for that job. She was bright and shining, her friendly appeal bringing people to Caro's stall, and Caro's baking bringing them back for more. When Caro's smile grew pained under the praise of strangers, Viola would deflect with questions about where they were from and whether they were on vacation.

Safe in the knowledge that my friend was in good hands, I

moved my focus elsewhere, to the bakery. Tony, the baker, kept popping his head out of the door to shoot Caro dark looks. I'd seen very few customers approach the store once word of Caro's amazing cakes and treats filled the market. I reminded myself to keep an eye out and let Roane know Tony clearly wasn't happy about this development.

Another distraction came in the form of the Fosters. I watched with a growing ache in my chest as Maggie Foster stared at her daughter. There was a slight tightness to her mouth that might have pointed at disapproval if it weren't for the melancholy sentiment I caught every now and again in her eyes.

As for Annie, she never once looked her mother's way.

Liz did. She would shoot Maggie worried looks before shifting that anxiety to her wife.

It wasn't right. A mother and daughter separated by the prejudices of the father. Something surely could be done to mend the breach.

I pondered the problem between customers, and it was only after lunch that something new caught my attention.

"What do you want, Luc*as*?" Viola's snappish tone brought my head around in surprise. She'd emphasized the last syllable of the name so it sounded like "ass." A tall young man stood in front of Caro's stall, his arms crossed as he perused what was left of the baked goods, and there wasn't much.

He was a little young for me to usually notice him, but Viola's reaction to him was enough to draw my attention. Whoever he was, he was extremely good-looking, with thick dark blond hair, high cheekbones, a roman nose, and a pouting lower lip. With his angular jaw, long limbs, and broad shoulders, if anyone could be a model, it was him.

His strong biceps were visible in his dark blue T-shirt, and Viola eyed him with distaste.

I raised an eyebrow.

She was obviously unimpressed with his masculine beauty. Good. It meant the darling girl saw beyond these things to what mattered.

At that thought, my protective instincts kicked in.

Who was this kid that upset her with his mere presence?

"I came to sample your wares," he announced loudly, eyes flickering up from the leftovers to Viola. "But unsurprisingly I'm not tempted."

That little shit.

About to step forward, I was stopped by Viola's cool reply. "Impotence *is* a problem for someone who finds no joy in life."

I smirked.

The young man narrowed his eyes. "My problem is only around you. Funny that."

"The fact that you find no joy in the company of a smart and witty woman is not surprising to me, Lucas Elliot. You prefer them dumb and silent, right?"

Ah. Lucas Elliot.

West Elliot's youngest son.

Also home for summer vacation, I presumed.

Roane had said that he and Viola did not get along, but witnessing it in real life was something else. They visibly bristled as they interacted.

Lucas braced his hands on the stall and leaned forward, bringing his head closer to Viola's. She didn't even flinch. "I prefer them sweet like honey." His gaze dropped to her mouth. "Not sour like vinegar."

"Oh, Lucas." Viola fluttered her lashes comically. "With original metaphors like that, you should be a poet."

I tried to contain my snort.

A muscle twitched in her opponent's jaw, and he straightened to his full height. Both of them seemed to have completely forgotten Caro was there and watching their interaction with avid curiosity. That would make two of us.

"Heard your boyfriend dumped you for a cheerleader. Might be something in that, Viola."

If she could have killed him with looks, he'd be dead. "Oh, please, I'm all aflutter to hear romantic advice from a *boy* who rumor has it arrives way too early *every* time."

My eyes bugged out of my head, and I had to cover my mouth to stifle my shocked gasp. I was even more shocked when Lucas just smirked at her response. "Oh, my stats are clear on that count. I always make sure a woman is satisfied multiple times."

"Well, you've certainly made sure there's enough data to draw that conclusion. Better watch that, Elliot. An overabundance of research could lead to an STD in your spreadsheets."

I was shaking now with the urge to belly laugh.

These two were entertaining with a capital *E*.

"You're awfully concerned about my sheets. Maybe if you'd been more concerned about your own, the boyfriend wouldn't have ended up tangled in the cheerleader's. Her thread count must have been higher." He grinned evilly.

A flicker of pain moved across Viola's features before she smoothed it with a look of indifference, and my amusement instantly died.

I glared at Lucas, only to see he was no longer smiling. In fact, he was watching Viola warily. Perhaps he knew he'd crossed the line.

"Well"—she crossed her arms over her chest—"if you're not going to buy anything, take your toxic attitude elsewhere. I've had my fill of immature dickhead for the day."

Lucas's expression hardened and he cut Caro a look. "You might want to think about who mans your stall in the future, or you'll lose business."

"I'm a *wo*man." Viola's hands flew to her hips. "You may not recognize the breed since you're only capable of attracting shallow *girls*. Now run along."

With one last dark look, Lucas Elliot turned on his heel and strode across Main Street. He pushed open the door to The Alnster Inn but shot Viola a scowl over his shoulder before disappearing inside.

It was as we were packing up for the day, Caro's baked goods long sold, that I spotted a woman watching us from the lane between the butcher's and the inn. She dressed in much the same way Caro normally did and wore a severe frown of disapproval on her face.

Caro didn't notice her as she and Viola laughed at something together.

It was her aunt Helena. I knew it in my gut.

I braced myself in case the woman was here to make a scene, but to my relief, after a few minutes of glaring at her niece, Helena turned around and walked back down the lane whence she'd come.

An uneasy feeling stuck with me, and I decided I'd ask Caroline if she wanted to stay with me again tonight. Her face was lit with joy as she talked with Viola. Despite her shyness, I could see she was brimming over with happiness that she was the only person to sell out of goods. This, plus the positive comments she got from customers, would surely go a long way to boosting her self-confidence. And I wouldn't have Helena take that away from her on the very same day.

Just as I approached the girls to ask Caro if she wanted to stay over at my apartment, a slamming door pulled all three of our gazes toward The Alnster Inn. Lucas had stepped out of the pub and he wasn't alone. Whether she'd been there all along or had just arrived, a tall blonde wrapped her arm around his waist as he slung his over her shoulders. Without a look in our direction, the young couple sauntered in the direction of the harbor.

I turned to Viola to crack a joke, but closed my mouth immediately.

She was staring after Lucas and the girl with real, true pain in her eyes.

Suddenly, their passionate encounter took on a different edge.

Did Viola have a crush on Lucas Elliot? Was that the reason for their antagonism? Unrequited love?

Thinking of the way everyone else seemed to disappear for him as Lucas took on a battle of wits with Viola, I wondered if it was unrequited after all. Any guy would find indifference toward Viola Tait almost impossible—not just because she was gorgeous (although knowing young guys, that was certainly enough) but because she was quick-witted and self-confident.

Hmm.

Deciding it was best to avoid the topic of Lucas Elliot and his mysterious girl, I asked Caro about staying the night.

"Oh, I don't know. I should probably go home." She bit her lip.

"Stay. We can have a sleepover." Viola grinned at me. "That was me inviting myself too."

I laughed and slung my arm over her small shoulders. "You're very welcome." We both turned to Caro with hopeful gazes. "What do you say? Girls' night?"

Her smile was slow but genuine. "How can I say no?"

"You can't. I won't let you."

Not too long after, Roane arrived with a few more men to load the rented stalls into the van. I stood by the back of the van as Roane shut the door. Caro was waiting for Viola, who was putting together a small bag for their stay at my apartment. We'd said goodbye to all of our market sellers, who thanked us for a great day, and I'd watched Annie and Liz leave without a backward glance at Maggie.

Who stood in the doorway of her store and stared down Main Street until Annie was out of sight.

"She sold everything." Roane crossed his arms over his chest and smiled softly at me. He was dirty and disheveled from working the farm, and sweat glistened on his temples. He smelled musky and warm with exertion, and I had to ignore the impulse to bury my face in his throat.

I didn't know what had gotten into me.

But the urge came over me more frequently these days.

Swallowing hard, I looked toward The Anchor. "Oh yeah. She sold out just after lunchtime."

"Maybe it'll give her the boost she needs."

I nodded. "I saw a woman watching from the lane. Dressed like Caro. Nasty scowl on her face."

Roane frowned. "Helena?"

"I'm pretty sure. Caro didn't see her. Thankfully. But I've invited her to stay with me again tonight. I don't want her to go home to that woman and spoil what has been a great day for our girl."

Suddenly I found myself hauled against Roane, my face pressed to his throat after all, as he squeezed me tight in his arms. I gripped the back of his T-shirt, the fabric damp from all of his physical activity. "What's this for?" My question came out muffled.

He eased his hold, and I stepped back before I did something stupid. However, seeing his expression, I wondered if his arms weren't a safer place. He really needed to stop looking at me like the sun rose and set with me.

"Thank you for looking out for Caro. I tried my best." Roane scrubbed a hand over his face, his beard bristling noisily as he did so. "It wasn't enough. She needed someone like you."

"You've done a great job looking out for your cousin." *But who looks out for you, Roane?* Who made him feel cared for? "I have Caro and Viola at my place tonight for girls' night, but I was thinking tomorrow I could cook you dinner."

His gaze sharpened, and I realized belatedly how that sounded. It sounded like I was asking him on a date.

"Or you know what would be even better, I'll buy you dinner at The Anchor. To thank you for setting this"—I gestured to the van with the stalls—"up."

His long study of me was discomfiting to say the least, and I shifted from one foot to the other. Finally, he looked toward The Anchor with an expression bordering on disappointment. "Aye. Sounds good."

Worryingly, his tone suggested otherwise. I opened my mouth to say something, anything, to take away the sudden weariness I saw in him, but he beat me to it with a tight smile.

"I'll see you tomorrow."

He moved past me without another word, and the amount of uneasiness I felt at his abrupt departure was kind of melodramatic.

"Roane . . ." I followed him as he made his way to the driver's-side door.

He glanced over his shoulder and then stopped. His expression was shuttered, which was completely unlike him. At my silence he frowned. "Evie?"

"We're good. Right?" I was confused by his sudden change in demeanor.

My friend studied my face, and as he did, his hard countenance slowly softened. He walked back to me, and I found my whole body loosening with relief as he clasped my face in his hands and pressed a gentle kiss to my forehead. I could feel every inch of his calloused fingertips on my skin and closed my eyes, much too in love with the feel of his hands on me. "We're good," he whispered. "I'm sorry if I was a bit abrupt with you. I'm tired today."

"Can I do anything?"

Resting his forehead against mine, he chuckled, but it wasn't a happy sound. I brought my hands to his strong arms, curling my fingers around his biceps. For a moment we just held each other. I imagined we looked sweet, affectionate, peaceful. But on the inside my heart was racing like crazy as I fought the battle to ignore our attraction to each other. I even shook a little, feeling as though I might shatter with the force of my restraint.

Deep down I knew why Roane had been disappointed only a mere few seconds ago. I knew why his laugh was weary and unhappy.

He wanted more than I was giving him.

And he deserved to have everything he wanted.

Truthfully, I was flattered and excited that *I* was what he wanted.

However, if I gave in to the desire, I knew I'd lose myself instead of trying to find myself without him.

Perhaps this friendship was unfair to him.

On that thought I pulled out of his hold and couldn't quite meet his gaze. "You know, I know you have a lot going on, so we can do dinner some other time."

Roane's strong fingers gripped my chin, forcing my head up, my gaze to his. He looked somewhere between knowing and annoyed. He bent his head toward mine and I tensed, panic flaring at the thought of him kissing me.

Not just panic.

Stupid, stupid thrill rushed through me too.

I held my breath as his gorgeous lips neared mine.

But he halted, just a hairsbreadth from my mouth. His breath fanned across my lips, making my eyelashes flutter. "I'll see you tomorrow, Evie Starling."

Just as abruptly as he'd captured my chin, Roane let me go and strode away. As I watched him jump into the van, my heart hammered hard in my chest.

Now why did his last words to me sound like more than a promise to meet me for dinner?

Shaken by everything left unsaid between us, I was thankful Viola had invited herself to a "sleepover." I discovered she could be bright, bubbly, and vivacious, but there was a serious, sensitive side to her.

We'd been laughing together in my living room over a British soap they'd introduced me to. The television show was ludicrously depressing. Then, out of nowhere, as the credits rolled, Caro said, "Aunt Helena is going to be so mad at me when I return home."

Viola immediately reached across to grip Caro's hand in hers. "You don't have to go back there, Caro. Mam and Dad will let you stay with us, and I'll go get your things so you don't have to see Helena."

Caro's lips trembled at the idea. "I—I couldn't. The imposition..."

"It's no imposition. Caro, you're a *good* person who deserves to be happy. You know that, right?"

Viola's words seemed to trigger something in Caro, and I knew as she suddenly burst out into heartbreaking sobs that Viola had seen something the rest of us hadn't.

It wasn't just that her aunt had dominated Caroline, taking control of every aspect of her life. She'd done it by making Caro believe she wasn't worthy. That she wasn't *good*. Silent tears rolled down my cheeks as Viola made soft hushing sounds, pulling Caro into her arms. She pressed her cheek to Caro's head and rocked her like a baby.

Wiping at my tears, I got up and crossed the living room to sit down beside them. I took Caro's hand in mine and held back my wince when she squeezed it with all her worth.

"Let it out, Caro. Let it out," Viola whispered.

Just like that our girls' night took a turn I hadn't expected.

And as Caro's story fell from her lips in broken words, I was done taking it slow.

My plan had been to gradually get Caro to a point where she felt comfortable enough to leave Helena. But now I realized why Roane hated the woman so much. This girl was wounded in places no young woman should be. Only abuse could do that. I had known on some level that Helena's control over Caro's life was wrong. Yet the word "abuse" had never entered my mind. Until she shared her story.

Slaps across the face for any attitude considered disobedient.

Locked in her bedroom for a week when she was fifteen for daring to make a date with a boy. She had only a Bible and water to keep her company, her aunt bringing a tray of food once a day.

And every day, being told she was a bad seed, worthless, that she had the devil in her, and only Helena's influence in her life kept him at bay.

Sick to my stomach, I sat in that room, listening to what sounded like something out of a gothic novel, and I realized Caro was so much stronger than she knew. Many people would have given in to such emotional and mental abuse, but deep down Caro knew her aunt was wrong.

We lapsed into silence, Caro's head resting on Viola's shoulder as the young girl hugged her close.

"I don't want to push you, like Helena has bullied you," I announced, "but I think you know you need to make a move and do it now. Move in here, with me, and then we'll find you something more permanent later."

Caro sat up slowly, her big dark eyes round with sorrow and fear. "I know she's wrong . . . but there's a part of me that's scared she's right."

That was the impact of years of mental warfare, and it wouldn't go away with a snap of anyone's fingers.

"She's *wrong*. But no one can make this decision for you. Only you can. I can promise we'll all be here to help you through this."

"Maybe you should speak to someone," Viola offered with a hint of trepidation.

She'd plucked the thought right out of my head.

Caro frowned. "Someone?" Her brow cleared, and her lips

pressed together for a second in displeasure. "You mean a therapist?"

Viola and I shared a look, worried we'd scare Caro away. Coming to a silent decision, we both nodded.

Looking down at the floor, Caro whispered, "I'm scared."

I swear I thought my chest might splinter with the aching pain I felt for her. Roane's cousin was such a gentle soul. How could anyone do what that wicked woman had done to her?

"Anyone would be. But we'll be here." I reached across Viola to take Caro's hand again. "You don't have to go back there. We can get your stuff for you."

Caro shook her head, and I felt my stomach drop with the fear she'd return to that woman. "No." She tilted her chin up with a hint of stubbornness and looked between Viola and me. "I should go back. To get my things." Her lips trembled. "There's not much I want to take with me, but I have a few things I'd like to keep."

Relief swamped me. "Do you want one of us to come with you?"

"I think I'll need you." Anger flashed across her eyes. "She has all the passwords to my bank account details. All the money that my mother and father left me. I haven't been able to touch it."

Fury ripped through me. "Excuse me?"

She swallowed hard and nodded. "I have three savings accounts and a checking account. She took away my bank cards, made me open online accounting, and then changed all the passwords so I couldn't access them. Moreover, we set up investments with my money with a financial adviser, but she has all those details too."

Something dawned on me. "Does she have money of her own?"

Caro took a shuddering breath. "Everyone thinks so because her parents had money, but the majority of it went to my mother because she was the eldest. That money went to me. Helena thinks of it as hers. The only thing she owns is the cottage."

Now it all made sense. She didn't want Caro to exert her independence because it would leave her with very little money.

"Does Roane know this?"

"He suspected, but I lied." Caro's face crumpled. "I told him she didn't have access to my money."

Yeah, I was so done. "Will you move in here?"

She blinked at my abrupt question but nodded slowly. "Yes."

We would talk about therapy later. First things first. "Tomorrow, Roane and I will accompany you to the cottage. While I help you pack, Roane will get everything he needs from Helena regarding your finances."

"What if she won't hand it over?"

"Oh, she will," Viola said. She looked at me, angry determination in her eyes. "Roane has a good friend on the police force at Alnwick. I'm sure he'd be willing to accompany you."

I smirked. "That could work."

"I don't want anyone else to know." Caro shook her head.

"It'll only be Patrick, Caro. You know he won't tell anyone."

After a little back-and-forth, we got Caro to agree, and I disappeared into my bedroom to call Roane. When I was done telling him everything, I had to hold the phone away from my ear while he cursed and railed.

I wished in that moment I could be there in person to comfort him.

"Roane," I soothed. "This is a good development. She'll finally be out from under that woman's thumb."

"That won't fix what she's broken, Evie."

"No it won't. But it's a start."

"And she has Caro's money—" He started cursing again. Then

just as abruptly stopped. "I'll be round tomorrow morning to pick you up. I want this over and done."

"And this police officer Viola mentioned?"

"I don't know if that's a good idea."

"Well, I think it might be a good idea to have an officer of the law there to remind you that murder is a crime."

He gave a snort of laughter. "Aye, you're probably right."

"Okay. Ten o'clock?"

"Aye. And, Evie."

"Yeah?"

"Thank you."

At his heartfelt gratitude I melted. "Roane, it wasn't me. It was Viola."

"No . . . you gave her the confidence to sell her baked goods at the market. Viola might have said the right words to get Caro to open up tonight, but you opened the floodgates long before that."

"You think too well of me," I whispered, worried for us both.

"You're not perfect, Evie, rationally I know that." He let out a long sigh. "But you're perfect to me."

My breath caught, and as I scrambled to find the words to reply to such a comment, Roane said gruffly, "See you in the morning." He hung up.

I must have sat there for a while staring at the bedroom wall, wondering what on earth to do about Mr. Roane Robson, when Viola peeked her head in the room to ask for an update.

Once I'd explained to Caro and Viola that Roane was on board, we settled into the living room again, and Viola and I tried to distract Caro from the thought of tomorrow. We talked about the market, about the villagers, and I took the opportunity to mention Annie and Maggie.

Caro seemed grateful for the distraction. Between the three of us we decided there had to be a way to bring mom and daughter back together, and I'd been elected to plant the first seed of reconciliation. I listened to their suggestions on how to do that, glad we'd found a way to focus Caro's mind on something other than the upcoming biggest confrontation of her life.

Twelve

Jt occurred to me, not for the first time, as I leaned against Roane's Defender, how appearances could be so deceiving. That had never been truer as I looked at the woman standing in the doorway of the chocolate-box cottage in the forest.

Summer was in full bloom in Alnster, the leaves of the surrounding trees thick and lush. Rosebushes and hydrangeas grew lavishly around the double front windows of the house, filling the air with their heady scents.

This place looked like a little paradise tucked away on the outskirts of the village.

Yet for Caro, reality had been the opposite. It had been a place of oppression and abuse.

Well, no more.

Caro stood before the cottage with her hand on Shadow's head, Roane on her other side.

Helena stared warily at us from the doorway, her gaze flickering to the police officer who stepped in front of her.

Patrick O'Malley, I discovered, was around Roane's age. Friendly, all smiles, when we were introduced. However, as soon as he'd gotten out of his car at the cottage, his countenance had turned impressively stern. It had taken Roane over an hour to convince Caro to file a report against Helena for stealing her bank details, knowing that without that report Patrick couldn't act in the capacity of a police officer.

"And what's the meaning of this?" Helena asked calmly, her gaze moving back to Caro. "What have you done now?"

"Ms. Mordue, I'm Officer Patrick O'Malley with the Northumbria police force. Your niece, Caroline Robson Mordue, has filed a report accusing of you illegally accessing her bank accounts."

I tried to keep the smug look off my face as Helena paled. Considerably. Her surprise lasted merely seconds, however, before she straightened her shoulders to peer down her nose at Patrick. "She's lying."

Caro took a step toward her aunt. "L-Let us in, give me my bank cards, my online banking details, and . . . and . . ." She took a deep breath. "I-I'll consider this matter dropped, Aunt Helena."

Her aunt shook her head as if abjectly disappointed. "You ungrateful girl," she whispered, as though Caro had broken her heart. Then she turned to Patrick. "This is my home. You'll need to come back with a warrant." Helena moved to step back into the house, and suddenly Roane was striding forward.

Patrick called out his name and reached for him, but Roane shrugged him off and slammed his hand on the door above Helena's head, pushing his way in.

"You're trespassing!" Helena cried out, cowering beneath his intimidating build.

Roane bent his head toward her, his whole body bristling with restraint, and I found myself moving toward him. "You're lucky I don't sweep in here with a team of police and lawyers and have you put away for years for what you've done to Caro. Physical and mental abuse is a crime, Helena."

Her eyes flashed. "What nonsense."

"Not nonsense. Now you may be an abusive old cow, but you're not a stupid one," he seethed. "You and I both know that if I put my lawyers on it, it is more than likely you'll go to prison for defrauding Caroline of her inheritance. And believe me, Helena, there is nothing I would like more than to drag your wicked, greedy, grasping bony arse through court. I'd do it in a heartbeat and enjoy every minute of it no matter how long it took to put you in prison where you belong. But Caro wants to move on from all of this, and for her I'll play nice. Playing nice involves watching you hand over every piece of financial information pertaining to Caro. All of it. Or I will be back with a court order."

Halfway through his magnificent speech, I'd reached Caro and stopped to take hold of her hand. I squeezed it now, unable to tear my gaze from Roane, who had never been more appealing to me than he was in that moment standing up for his cousin.

Helena stared at him as though she loathed him, and after a moment of contemplation, she leaned back into the door so it swung open. "Very well." She cut Caro a look. "Get your things and then get out. The devil will take care of you."

"Did you just make a threat to Miss Caroline's person in front of a police officer, Ms. Mordue?" Patrick asked.

She shrugged. "A warning."

He stepped toward her, his expression cool, unyielding. "Funny, it sounded like a threat to me. That'll be going in my report."

He brushed past Roane to step into the house, and Roane gestured to us to follow. Caro let go of my hand, and I was so proud of her as she walked past her aunt, ignoring the way the woman stared at her as if she were the serpent in the Garden of Eden. As for me, my skin crawled as I moved past her. I'd forever associate the smell of rosewater with this woman. It was unnerving how normal she seemed for someone who had no soul. Of course, normal went out the window when she started threatening people with the devil. There was nothing I detested more than people who twisted religion to suit their agenda.

The front door led into a large hallway big enough to fit a reading area. There was a doorway on either side of us, and a doorway behind the reading nook.

"Take Caro to get her things." Roane gestured to the door behind the reading nook.

I nodded to Caro to show me the way, concerned by her paleness. Despite her obvious distress, she kept her chin held high as she led me to the dark wooden door. "Watch your step," she murmured as she opened it.

Three small stairs led down into a dark corridor. From the outside the cottage was cute, but inside . . . I shuddered. It was gloomy, dreary, and did not have a good vibe. That pang echoed in my chest again at the thought of Caro spending most of her life here. She turned right and led me to a door at the end of the hall.

Her room was surprisingly bright. A large wooden-framed window allowed a lot of light in despite the surrounding trees outside. The walls were covered in old-fashioned ivory wallpaper with little blue birds all over it. There was a white Shaker-style bedside cabinet to match the dresser, armoire, and single bed.

The floorboards were old and a little warped.

It was a pretty room in the summer, but I could only guess at how cold it was during the winter.

Caro opened a cupboard door on the wall opposite the window and pulled out an old leather suitcase.

"What can I do?" I asked.

She blinked rapidly as if she'd forgotten I was there. "I can manage. I'm not taking much."

True to her word, she only packed underwear, socks, and an extra pair of shoes, and removed a mere two outfits from the armoire. "I . . ." She glanced up at me shyly. "Things are moving so quickly, and I know I shouldn't try to do too much at once, but I think I'd like some new clothes."

I gave her a small smile. "We could make a day or two of it. Maybe go to Newcastle to shop."

Caro nodded and then picked up the picture frame sitting on her bedside cabinet. "My mother and father," she whispered, placing it gently in her case.

According to Roane they hadn't been much in the way of parents, but I'm sure they were a far sight better than her aunt Helena.

When Caro dropped to her knees by the floor at the window, I raised an eyebrow in curiosity. Her small, elegant hands pried at the floorboards, and to my surprise two boards gave way. She reached into the hole in the floor and pulled out a large shoebox. I stepped forward and peered in as Caro removed the lid. Inside was what looked like a journal, a pile of comic books, and to my surprise, three historical romance paperbacks. They looked like they'd been read many, many times.

Caro smiled tremulously. "My contraband."

I crouched beside her, incredibly sad that a twenty-two-year-old woman had to hide these things. My fingers brushed the cover of one of the books. "You're a romance fan."

Her cheeks flushed a lovely rosy color. "They're wonderful escapism."

"They are," I agreed.

"One of the first things I'm going to do once I have access to my accounts is buy an e-reader and just stock it full of romance novels."

She sounded so young in that moment, it broke my heart a little. Her aunt had kept her in a perpetual state of confusion—repression versus teenage rebellion. Caro hadn't been given the chance yet to become an adult. I shrugged off my sadness because she was still so young, and it was happening now. Her life was about to change for the better. I'd called Penny in the early hours of the morning, knowing it was early evening for her in Melbourne, and asked permission to allow Caroline to stay in the second bedroom until we could find her a more permanent situation. Penny, unsurprisingly, had been all for it.

"Buying an e-reader would be the first thing I'd do," I chuckled as I straightened. "Come on. Let's pack this stuff too."

Caro emptied the contents of the shoebox into her suitcase and closed it.

"Ready?"

"Just one last thing." She reached up behind her neck and unclasped the gold cross.

It fell on the wooden bedside cabinet with a delicate clatter and a hiss of the chain. At my questioning look, Caro's expression tightened. "It's the only gift Helena ever gave me. I've had to wear it every day for ten years, shackled to her, not to Christianity, just as she always intended."

I released a slow, heavy breath. "I hope this doesn't sound condescending or patronizing because believe me it's not meant to be taken that way . . . but I am so, so proud of you."

The right corner of her mouth quirked up. "You made me brave enough to do this. All of you—you, Roane, Viola, even Patrick. I—I couldn't have done it without you."

"You could have," I disagreed. "And I think you've been thinking about this for a really long time. This didn't just happen overnight, or because we offered you support to do it. You've mentally prepared yourself for this moment and finally got yourself to a place where you could do this. The credit is all yours."

She released a shaky sigh and gave me a small nod. "Let's go see how Roane and Patrick are faring."

Roane and Patrick were waiting for us in the hall, Roane holding a manila folder in his hand. Shadow loped forward at the sight of us, and Caro reached for him gratefully. As if he knew she needed him, Shadow was loyally sticking by her side. That's what I loved about dogs. Some were very attuned to our emotions and offered their loyalty and love in return for the same.

Affection wasn't a game with dogs like it could be with humans, who often withheld it out of pettiness or in one-upmanship and doled it out when it suited their purposes. I guess that's why I liked dogs more than I did some people. You always knew where you stood with a dog. Either they liked you or they didn't.

"Got everything?" Roane's voice was gentle, but his expression was not.

Caro nodded and he put his arm around her. "Then let's go."

I followed them out, thankfully without having to lay eyes on Helena again.

"You call if you need anything else," Patrick said once we drew to a halt at the vehicles.

"Thanks, Trick." Roane held out his hand to shake his friend's. "I owe you."

"You owe me nothing. It was my pleasure"—he shot the house a dirty look—"believe me."

"Thank you," Caro offered shyly.

"You're going to be fine, Caro." Patrick gave her a soft smile, nodded at us, and then got into his car.

"Let's go." Roane held open the passenger-side door for Caro while I got in the back with Shadow and Caro's small, lonely suitcase. Before Roane put on his seat belt, he handed the manila folder to his cousin.

The tension radiating from Roane was incredible, and I squeezed Caro's shoulder as she shifted uneasily.

We followed Patrick's car down the driveway. He turned left toward Alnwick, and we turned right toward the village. It was only then that Roane spoke, nodding his head toward the folder on Caro's lap. "It holds your bank details. The investment portfolio, everything. Patrick warned her if she changed those passwords, he'd be back to arrest her for theft and fraud, but the first thing *you* do is log on to those accounts and change the passwords. Then contact the financial adviser and see what the bloody hell has been happening to your money. If she's diverting any of it, we need to know immediately."

I understood Roane was concerned that Helena was swindling Caro out of her inheritance, but his hard, demanding tone wasn't exactly what his cousin needed right now. I knew what was eating at him, and I hated it, but we had to talk. Caro didn't need this attitude right now.

Viola was waiting for us in the living area of the apartment and stood up to greet us, only to be stopped by the abrupt thump of Caro's suitcase hitting the floor.

Roane had dumped it. "Do what I said. I'll be back in a bit. Shadow, come."

With that, he strode past us without another word, his dog following at his heels.

"Uh . . . what did I miss?" Viola wrinkled her nose in confusion.

Caro appeared to be seconds from bursting into tears.

"Viola, can you help Caro get settled? I'm going to speak to Roane."

Then I was out the door before either girl could protest, hurrying down the stairs and through the front of the shop. His SUV was still parked out front, and Roane was nowhere in sight toward the harbor or the road up to the main village. Although he had long legs, he couldn't have disappeared that quickly, which meant he'd turned left toward the cliffs.

I hurried around the corner of the building and saw his figure marching up the path that cut along the grassy cliff top behind the bookstore.

"Roane!" I shouted, my voice thrown backward by the sea breeze.

Shadow, however, heard me and hurried to me, causing Roane to halt and look back. His shoulders tensed at my approach. "You should be with Caro," he said.

I reached out for his hand as soon as I drew to a stop. "You should be with Caro."

He tugged on his hand but I refused to let go. He scowled. "Evie, just let me be."

"So you can brood and beat yourself up with guilt and self-condemnation?"

Roane's dark eyes flashed with surprise.

My smile was an unhappy one. "Yeah, I know what's going on

in your head right now, and I won't let you mentally berate yourself. No one shits on my friends. Not even themselves."

His lips twitched, but the sound of my name that followed was pained.

Without thinking, I threw my arms around him, drawing him tight, holding him as close to me as I could get him. "You are not to blame for what happened to her."

Roane fisted my shirt in his hands, his embrace a vise, close to bruising. "I knew it was bad. I knew it was bad, but I didn't know it was *that* bad and I should have known, Evie. I should have known. I failed her."

I pressed my lips to his ear. "You didn't fail her," I whispered, squeezing him to emphasize my point. "You were wonderful today. You make her feel safe. And right now she's probably in that apartment thinking you're pissed that you had to do what you had to do. She doesn't know this reaction is guilt because it hasn't even occurred to her that you could possibly have anything to feel guilty about." I pulled back to clasp his face in my hands, his beard tickling my palms. "Because you have nothing to feel guilty about. And I will tell you that until I'm blue in the face or for however long it takes to sink in."

He gripped my waist, his brows drawn together, his expression fierce. It felt like forever that he just stared at me.

Finally, I smoothed my hands down his neck to his hard chest and gave him an affectionate pat. "Come back. Hug your cousin. And then later we'll all eat out to celebrate today. Because it *is* a day of celebration."

After searching my gaze, Roane finally came to a decision. He nodded, releasing me, and I gestured for us to walk back to the store. The path was single track, so I started walking ahead.

"Evie."

I glanced over my shoulder at Roane, stopping at his pensive expression. When he drew up to me, his gaze searched my face again, and then he almost sounded like he was pleading when he said, "I wish you'd do something to make me like you a little less."

For a moment he looked and sounded so young, it made my breath catch.

With that heart-flipping comment, he brushed past me, he and Shadow striding on ahead.

As I followed him, butterflies fluttered in my belly as it occurred to me Roane Robson was mine for the taking if I wanted him.

Rattled but determined to stay true to myself, I pondered the idea of putting distance between Roane and me.

That would certainly make him like me less.

Except I couldn't do it today. Not with everything going on with Caro. However, if I was to stay in Alnster for another three months, it might be better for both Roane's and my hearts if we saw each other a little less.

The mere thought made me feel panicked and restless.

Thirteen

With tourists descending upon the Northumberland Coast in higher numbers now that it was summer, I'd asked Viola to call her mom to reserve a table at the pub. It was a good thing too. Viola had left just before dinnertime to help her parents out, and when we walked in later that night, the place was packed. Viola and Milly waved at us from behind the bar at the exact same time, in the exact same way, making me smile.

"Usual table," Milly called to us, and I let Roane steer us through the heaving dining room to a table near the unlit fireplace. There was a couple seated at the one closest to it, but Shadow didn't care. Even without a fire in the grate, Shadow promptly took his place sprawled in front of it, making the couple laugh.

I smiled at Roane, who just rolled his eyes as he, Caro, and I took our seats at the larger table against the back wall.

It had been a weird day.

After Roane had returned to the apartment with me and he and Caro had disappeared into her bedroom for a chat, things were easier between the cousins. However, Roane had work to do and took off for a few hours. He'd left Shadow with us since the dog was offering so much comfort to Caro, and Viola and I sought to find a way to distract our friend from the magnitude of the day.

Since Roane insisted I should have a lesson on driving here before I attempted it, I'd taken his advice not to rent a car just yet. Both Viola and Caro could drive, so Viola had us climb into her Fiat 500 to take Shadow for a long walk down the beach. Considering the dog took up most of the back seat, it was kind of hilarious and just what Caro needed.

We didn't travel far, just fifteen miles north to Low Newton-by-the-Sea, a small village with a beautiful stretch of coastline. We struggled to find a place to park because it was so busy. Once on the soft sand, we whiled away the hours walking and playing with Shadow, and generally not talking about the emotional morning Caro had had.

"At least people aren't looking," Caro muttered, glancing shyly around The Anchor.

"No one knows you left Helena," Roane assured her. "Those of us who do aren't going to say anything."

"There's going to be gossip eventually."

He rubbed her shoulder in comfort. "And you'll get through it."

"Roane!"

At the high-pitched noise, almost squeal, we all whipped our heads up to see an attractive brunette maneuvering through the busy tables. At the delight on her face and laser focus on Roane, I stiffened as she drew to a halt at our table. She beamed at Roane, apparently not seeing either Caro or me. "I was hoping I'd see you here."

She had delicate lines around her pretty blue eyes that made me think she was a little older than us, and while she was tall like me, unlike me she was all slender curves in her slim-cut T-shirt and yoga pants.

I turned to Roane, who seemed surprised to see her. "Poppy . . . what are you doing here?"

Poppy's expression made it look like she wanted to eat him up. Irritation made my blood hot. "You mentioned this place so much, a friend and I decided to reserve a table."

He mentioned this place to her?

Was Roane seeing someone this whole time he was making eyes at me?

No. No, Roane wouldn't do that.

Not him.

He wasn't like other men.

He couldn't be.

It would . . . it would break my heart.

My overreaction to this woman was somewhat terrifying, and I sat stiff, unmoving, afraid it would all flood out of me if I did.

"Ah, I see." Roane's smile was polite, a mere pressing of his lips together with a slight curl.

It eased some of my concern.

When Roane liked you, he released the full force of that sexy smile on you.

She didn't seem to notice his lackluster response, but she did finally become aware of Caro and me. A little frown puckered between her brows. "And who is this?" she asked, like she had a right to know.

Did she? that insidious voice whispered.

Roane gestured to Caro first. "My cousin, Caroline." Then he turned his head to me and stared at me a few seconds too long, as if trying to figure out what to call me. Finally he decided: "And this is my friend Evie." He looked back at Poppy. "Ladies, this is Poppy. She just moved to Morpeth a few months ago and frequents Craig's pub."

I knew from talking with Roane that Morpeth was one of the largest towns in Northumberland, and business took him there almost every week. I could only assume "Craig" was a friend.

And Poppy?

Well, it seemed Poppy was on hand to keep Roane company every time he visited.

Our eyes met, hers narrowing on me ever so slightly, before she turned to Roane. "Perhaps you have room for two more at your table."

That forward little . . .

Caro shot me a pained look.

"Actually, we're celebrating something"—Roane gestured between us—"so now's probably not the best time."

"Oh?" She placed a hand on her hip and cocked it, that flirtatious smile still hanging around. Like her. "What are you celebrating?"

How about it's none of your business, I felt like snapping.

Caro ducked her head, her body language screaming, *No one mention me, no one mention me!*

"Life as we know it," I replied vaguely before Roane could come up with something that didn't involve his cousin. I gave Poppy a thin smile.

"Oh, you're American. Just here on holiday then?"

Poppy seemed pleased with the idea. What would it take to make her go away?

"Poppy!"

She whipped around before I could respond with something sarcastic, and I followed her gaze. A blond woman was gesturing from the gap between this dining room and the next. "The food's here."

"Coming." Poppy nodded and turned to us. She eyed Roane with determination and then, to my horror, walked around the back of my chair and settled to a stop at Roane's. The woman leaned down and pressed a lingering kiss to his cheek. "I'll come say hi later."

A flush crested the tops of his cheeks as he nodded stiffly.

Poppy smiled like she thought he was adorable and thankfully turned to leave. Only she did a double take toward the fireplace. "Oh, I wondered where you were, you sweet darling." She moved toward Shadow, who sat up at her arrival and bussed into her petting hand.

For some reason her touching Shadow was almost as infuriating as her kissing Roane!

She *kissed* Roane.

Okay, it was on the cheek, but it was more than just a peck.

There was invitation in that kiss.

And he blushed!

I couldn't look at him, I was so mad.

Which was unfair. I knew that. I never said I was rational *every day.*

This woman knew Shadow. Roane had obviously spent some time with her, and he had never mentioned her even once to me. His *supposed friend.*

As soon as Poppy disappeared into the other dining room, Caro cleared her throat and shot Roane a questioning look. "She's a little full on."

"Aye." He side-eyed me. "But she's just a harmless flirt."

I scoffed inwardly and avoided his gaze by looking over to make sure Shadow was all right. He was back to sleeping. The traitor. He'd licked Poppy like he was happy to see her. "She seemed pretty familiar with Shadow."

"She bought his affection." Roane's voice held amusement, which brought my gaze back to his. "Gives him a biscuit every time she sees him."

"It must be often enough for her to carry biscuits in her pocket on the off chance of seeing him."

Something lit up in Roane's dark eyes as he stared at me. "She has a dog too. Hence the steady supply of biscuits."

Realizing I was not hiding my suspicious jealousy one bit, I felt my cheeks grow heated. "Oh."

He grinned at me. That sexy grin. "Aye. Oh."

The bastard was pleased I was jealous!

I narrowed my eyes, which only made his grin widen.

Looking to Caro for help, I found none. She too looked inordinately pleased by my obvious covetousness of Roane and Shadow.

Feeling uncomfortably hot, I huffed in exasperation and yelled across the dining room toward the bar, "Milly, can we get served, please!"

She startled at my voice but then smirked at my tone. "Aye, keep your knickers on!"

The patrons chuckled at what they assumed was banter, and I tried to let the feeling of being an insider here soften the embarrassment I felt about being so obviously territorial of Roane.

It didn't.

I could feel his searching gaze burning into me, and I longed for the night to be over.

*H*ours later, with dinner service finished, many of the tourists had dispersed and those who stayed were there to drink or socialize. Our table had expanded to Viola, Dex, and a number of the locals. Milly would join us in between serving drinks.

Conversation flew up and down the tables, but thankfully no one mentioned Caro's big move. They did mention how blown away they were by her baking talents and succeeded in pleasing but embarrassing the poor woman into muteness.

It was getting late, and Caro looked a little pale and tired. I was just about to suggest she and I leave, when Roane's gaze moved toward the bar. The sudden tightness in his jaw made me look up, half expecting to see Helena there.

Annoyance flooded me at the sight of Poppy and her blond companion walking toward us.

Hadn't they left already?

Earlier, Roane had thankfully not interrogated me about my reaction, and I'd managed to let the whole incident go by the time dessert arrived.

Now she was back.

Some of the men's eyes followed her swaying hips, and I didn't blame them. Little black dress or body-contouring yoga pants, the woman would look hot. Poppy oozed sex appeal.

And she'd set her sights on Roane.

Yippee.

"Roane, you remember Kylie." She gestured to her blond companion as she drew to a stop beside him.

Roane gave Kylie that same thin-lipped smile he'd given Poppy. "Hi."

"Hi again."

"So"—Poppy dropped her hand to Roane's shoulder—"room for two more?"

He flicked me an apologetic look before he shrugged. "Of course."

My gut churned.

I really hoped it was his inability to be rude that had led to that invitation.

Then, to my shock, Poppy and the blonde grabbed two chairs and placed them between me and Roane. Poppy's was shoved right up against him, and the blonde hit her chair leg off mine and stared down at me when I didn't budge. "Do you mind?"

Disbelieving, I shifted my chair to the left to make room for her, and when she sat down, she turned her back to me, her elbow on the table, effectively blocking me out of any conversation with Roane.

He was too busy with Poppy to notice, considering her face was inches from his as she murmured to him in a low voice about . . . whatever!

Caro was frowning at the entire situation. Sensing my attention, she looked at me and made a face.

It was so unlike her, I couldn't help but smile.

This was my cue to exit with Caro, and I should have. But the sick, masochistic part of me didn't want to leave because I didn't want to miss what would happen between Roane and Poppy. I needed to know if he was going to take her up on what she was clearly offering, because I knew if he did, as unfair as it was of me, whatever spell he had over me would be broken.

The confused, scared part of me that was determined to live the next few months without romantic entanglement almost hoped he would take Poppy up on her offer.

Yet a bigger part of me hated the idea so much, I wanted to cry.

God, I was such a mess.

Our table suddenly jerked upward as Roane let out a muffled curse. My eyes flew to him to see him pulling back from Poppy, and I realized *he'd* caused the table to move. My eyes narrowed at his flushed cheeks and the hard glint in his eyes.

"I think it's time for you to go." His voice carried down the tables, the hum of conversation drawing to a close as all eyes turned toward Roane and Poppy.

She was staring at Roane in disbelief.

Kylie tugged on her friend's wrist. "Poppy, let's go."

With a huff of distaste, the brunette shot to her feet, her chair clattering toward the wall behind her. "No need to be so melodramatic."

Roane glowered at her. "If the shoe was on the other foot, I doubt you'd say that."

What had she done?

Had she touched him inappropriately, because I swear to God—

As if he sensed my growing indignation, Roane looked at me, his gaze softening, becoming reassuring at my obvious agitation.

Poppy huffed. "Come, Kylie, let's go."

Kylie's cheeks were bright red as everyone watched the two of them march out of the pub.

"I hope they paid." Dex broke the awkward silence.

Everyone tittered but kept side-eyeing Roane. He didn't pay them any attention. Instead he got up and moved the now empty chairs back to other tables. When he sat back down, he moved his chair closer to mine.

I waited for conversation to pick up again before I leaned in to him to ask, "What happened?"

He cut Caro a look, and certain she was engaged in conversation with Viola, he bent to whisper in my ear, "She grabbed my cock."

For a second all I felt was the brush of his lips across my ear, and all I heard was the word "cock" in Roane's deep rumble. The low, visceral tug in my womb distracted me for a second, but when his words eventually sunk in, the sexual heat I'd been feeling was overcome by fury.

I jerked my head back from his, eyes blazing, and I instantly felt his hand on my knee under the table. He gave it a reassuring squeeze.

"That's not okay," I hissed. "That's as bad as a guy grabbing a woman's ass or pawing at her breasts without her permission."

"Shh." He shook his head at me, and I bristled, trying to calm. He obviously didn't want anyone else to know.

"It's not okay," I repeated.

It was so not okay, I wanted to march out of the pub and hunt the handsy cow down and teach her some manners!

"I know." A muscle in his jaw twitched. "That's why I asked her to leave."

"Has she tried that before?"

Roane shook his head. "She's been persistently flirtatious these last few weeks, but I haven't done anything to encourage her. She's just . . . determined."

"I'm going to kick her ass," I snapped.

His gaze sharpened. "Why?" He bent his head toward me until our noses were almost touching. "Because she dared to touch me without permission . . . or because she dared to touch me?"

The word "dared" seemed to reverberate between us because the look in his eyes . . . He was *daring* me to speak the truth.

To admit I was jealous. Territorial. Possessive of him.

Suddenly all the air in the room seemed to go out.

"Knocking back another offer, Roane?" Milly's voice suddenly cut through to us.

I leaned away from him, trying to catch my breath, and he shot Milly a barely concealed look of annoyance.

The pub owner took the empty seat on my left, and I glanced around. Dex had disappeared from our table, and the one next to it was entirely female. Milly and Viola; Bobby Hopeton's wife, Hazel; Lottie Mulhern, who was a good friend of Milly's; and Caro and me. They were all staring at Roane. Dex was up at the bar with the men, having taken over serving for Milly.

"What?" Roane asked, clearing the scowl from his brows.

Milly chuckled. "That gorgeous brunette was practically in your lap." Her gaze flicked to me and then back to Roane. "Can't believe you passed that up."

"Milly, don't start."

"We're just looking out for you," Hazel threw in. "We want to see you settled. And you'll never get settled being as choosy as you're being."

A new indignation began to heat my blood.

"Didn't you say you knew someone you thought would be perfect for him, Hazel?" Lottie asked.

Thus began the pestering of Roane on the finding of a romantic partner.

With not just the Poppy incident in mind, but also our conversation a few weeks ago about how shitty he felt when his friends did this, my annoyance built.

Finally, when Hazel, Millie, and Lottie became insistent on setting Roane up with a primary school teacher who lived in nearby Howick, I blurted, "Why are you pushing this right now?"

The three women straightened as if I'd slapped them. "What?"

"You're supposed to be his friend. Friends don't harass friends about their love lives."

"Evie," Roane murmured.

But I was too incensed. "Would you do that to me? Would you sit in a pub and publicly harass me about being single?"

Milly looked uncharacteristically flustered. "We never meant any harm by it, lass."

"Look at him, for Christ's sake." I gestured. "The man is walking lady porn. If he wanted someone, he could have them."

Viola giggled first.

Then Milly and Hazel and Lottie.

I winced, turning to Roane, who was groaning into his hands.

"Lady porn." Milly threw back her head in cackling laughter.

Oh shit.

"Right, we're going." Roane pushed his chair back and took hold of my wrist. "Caro, let's go."

Caro, who was struggling very hard not to laugh, wished everyone good night as Roane practically hauled me out of the pub.

"I'm so sorry," I apologized as soon as we stepped outside into the cool summer night. "I didn't mean to embarrass you."

I could hear Caro behind us, making a gargling sound in her throat, struggling with her laughter.

Roane released my wrist to run a hand through his hair. He heaved a sigh, his long strides not slowing any. "You were just being a friend. It's fine."

"I think my point was getting through . . . until . . ."

"Lady porn," Caro gasped on a laugh.

Roane shot her a semi-annoyed, semi-amused look over his shoulder.

I winced. "I made things worse, didn't I?"

He side-eyed me. "Only time will tell, Evie. Only time will tell."

We fell into silence as we walked by the harbor, me lost in my self-flagellation.

"So"—Roane broke the silence just as we neared the bookstore—"I could get anyone, could I?"

I rolled my eyes at the pleased amusement in his voice.

Caro strolled at her cousin's side, smiling mischievously.

Flushing, I huffed, "Oh, you know you're gorgeous, Robson. You don't need me to stroke your ego."

"I beg to differ." He was suddenly no longer smiling as we drew to a stop in front of the store. "It's getting to the point only you can."

The breath whooshed out of my lungs as our gazes locked and his double entendre had the equivalent effect of him sliding his hand between my legs. My mouth grew dry, and I could only stare. He did not just say that in front of his little cousin.

Roane was the one to break the moment. He turned to Caro and kissed her forehead. "You were amazing today. I hope you sleep well. Call me if you need me, but I'll be in tomorrow to check on you."

"I'm fine," she assured him.

"Even so." He squeezed her shoulder and then looked at me. "Night, Evie."

I swallowed hard, trying to find my voice through the choking emotions building inside me. "Good night, Roane."

Caro and I were silent as we made our way upstairs. Exhausted, we said good night, and I was just about to disappear into my room when the sound of my name on Caro's lips stopped me.

"Yeah?"

She seemed to straighten her shoulders, as if readying for battle. "I . . . I want you to know that I'm very grateful for everything you've done for me but . . ." She exhaled heavily and tilted her chin up stubbornly. "I-If you hurt Roane, I'll come for you."

It might have been funny, this young, shy woman half my size threatening me, but it wasn't. There was sincerity in her voice.

These two cousins, they were more than that. They were like brother and sister. "I believe you," I whispered.

"He—" Caro took a tentative step toward me. "*He* would never hurt *you*, Evie. You must believe that."

The thing was that I *did* believe that. I trusted Roane Robson. And it scared the shit out of me.

Fourteen

$\mathcal{V}$iola seemed to be on a mission to keep Caro occupied. She'd shown up at the store, insisting on driving Caro to Berwick-upon-Tweed for a shopping day. Berwick-upon-Tweed was about an hour north of Alnster, and only a few miles south of the Scottish border.

As I had a shop to run and it was now open Tuesday to Saturday, I couldn't tag along, and Caro, remembering our discussion about Newcastle, didn't want to shop without me. Which was sweet. However, *I* remembered how little she'd brought in the way of clothes and encouraged her to go.

Life in the store was restful. After discussing some changes I wanted to make with Penny, I had the go-ahead to implement them. For others, scrolling through sales and stock history might not sound fun, but for me it was invigorating. I discovered stock that hadn't moved in years, and with Penny's permission I decided to donate them—children's books to children's hospitals, fiction to literary programs, and our local nonfiction to a charity store on the main street in Alnwick.

I really wanted to order beach reads for the summer display, something Penny was wary of doing. It was one thing to lose money on old stock, but new stock was a different story. Especially when she might be selling the store in a few short months. Still, I convinced her to let me order enough copies for a window display.

And it was paying off. Not only were summer tourists purchasing copies, but so were the locals. Caro alone bought five different romantic comedies from the new stock.

Donating gave me an idea that Penny loved. With an advertisement on the shop door, and by word of mouth, I launched a new promotion at Much Ado About Books. If customers brought in their used books for me to donate to different charitable organizations, they'd get a discount on any new books they bought at the store. Judging by the many locals who had taken advantage of the promo, I'd say it was a success.

Running the bookstore didn't feel like a job, especially on days I found myself lounging on one of the armchairs, reading in between customers. I liked to think customers found the sight of the manager actually reading the books she was selling a pretty charming quality.

I'd just finished *Anna Karenina*. Admittedly, some of it was kind of a slog, but it was quite the tale. Now I was rereading *Jane Eyre*. It was one of my absolute favorites. Darcy was surely the OG of book boyfriends, but Rochester came along a few decades later, and although he divided critics, I loved him. Some of the things he said to Jane . . . be still, my beating heart.

I wished men still talked like that. So poetic yet raw and heartfelt.

The sound of the bell over the door brought my head around, and I stood up to greet the customer, only to stiffen when I saw it was Tony the baker. "Can I help?" I asked, wary.

Tony glanced toward the back hallway. "I'm looking for Caroline."

Oh, I bet he was.

But wait . . . how did he know she'd be here?

Seeing the question in my eyes, he said, "People are talking. Said she'd left Helena and is staying here now."

My goodness, village life indeed. I wondered how they'd found out, and marveled at how quickly the rumor mill moved.

"She is staying here, but she's out with a friend. I don't know when she'll be back."

Tony raised an eyebrow. "Seems she's quite the popular wee thing these days."

I thought I should make my dislike for his condescending tone clear, so I crossed my arms over my chest. "Would you like me to pass along a message?"

He mirrored my body language. "You think I want to cause the lass trouble?"

"I don't know you, so I don't know what you want with Caro. But you should know she has a lot of people who care about her, including a six-foot-four cousin who is built like a brick shithouse and sees her as a little sister."

The baker surprised me with a small smile. "Aye, I'm aware Roane Robson would have my head if I caused that lass any more hurt than she's already found. I just wanted to speak with her about a work opportunity."

It was almost on the tip of my tongue to dress him down for coming to Caro now that she'd proven herself popular on Market

Day, when he'd rejected her before. I bit back the snark and gave him a sharp nod. "I'll let her know you're looking to speak with her."

"My thanks." He moved toward the door and then glanced back at me. "You seem like a nice lass, and Penny is a friend of mine . . ."

"Yes?"

"I don't know who started the rumor, but it's milled its way out of The Alnster Inn and found its way among the villagers."

My heart began to race. "What rumor?"

"A lot of the village try to shop local when they can, and always buy and order books through Penny. Rumor out of The Alnster Inn is that in Penny's absence, you've upped the price of books that are already more expensive than what people can get online."

My lips parted in affront. "That's a blatant lie. The prices are the same. Plus, I'm offering my charity discount. Everyone knows that."

"Aye, well, I know Penny counts on parents ordering books here for their kids when they go back to school after the holidays, so you might want to see about killing that rumor before it takes on a life of its own."

"Why would anyone lie about that?"

Tony grimaced. "You decided to settle down awhile, that makes you a villager, and you made your choice clear."

"My choice?"

"Milly."

Just like that it dawned on me what Tony was getting at. "The village feud?" I huffed. "Seriously? Isn't this all a little over-the-top, immature nonsense?"

He chuckled. "Oh, aye . . . but this is also one of the smallest villages on the Northumberland Coast. If drama can be found to spice up life, you'll be sure people will mine that stuff for decades."

"I came here for peace and quiet." I threw my hands up in disbelief.

Tony grinned. "Aye, you'll find that here too. On the beach. At sunset. When no other bugger is around." With a nod he strode out of the store, and I was left there fuming with my hands on my hips.

Had West Elliot started a petty rumor just because I failed to frequent his premises?

Well, that was about to change! That evening, when it was busy, when I knew more locals would be in the pub, I was going to march in there and set them all straight.

Truthfully, I'd felt a lot braver this afternoon when I was planning my onslaught.

As I stepped inside, some of that bravery fled. Although not as busy as The Anchor, most tables were filled and many of the stools at the bar were occupied.

The Alnster Inn was darker, more atmospheric than The Anchor. In all honesty, its low, dark-beamed ceilings and Tudor walls were very charming. The floors were dark wood, as were the simple tables and chairs. Two large circular iron chandeliers hung from the low ceiling with at least ten candle flame bulbs on each.

The lights were cool but lethal for someone of my height. I ducked my head to avoid one as I made my way across the pub floor. I felt only a few pairs of eyes on me, some of their faces familiar enough for me to recognize them as locals.

MUCH ADO ABOUT YOU · *191*

Behind the bar was Lucas Elliot. He was pouring a pint as I approached, but his gaze was trained to me like a hawk. Drawing to a stop at the bar top, I held his open stare.

There was sharp intelligence in that mossy-green gaze.

"Can I help you?" he asked.

"I'm looking for your dad."

Lucas shook his head. "He's not on shift tonight." His eyes narrowed. "What do you want with my dad?"

Two men sitting at the bar turned to look at me. With suspicion.

Ignoring them, I focused on Lucas. "I heard someone at this inn is spreading tall tales about my book prices. I'd like it to stop."

Lucas smirked. "Why the hell would anyone here care about the price of your books?"

The men snickered.

I bristled. "Look, it was just something I heard, okay? Just because I'm friends with Milly doesn't mean my store is open to sabotage."

"Are all Americans this dramatic?"

I narrowed my eyes on the smart-ass. "We both know I'm not the drama queen holding on to a thirty-year-old wound."

A muscle in Lucas's jaw twitched. "You've said what you had to say. You can leave now."

"Aye." The older man next to me looked up from the pint he was clutching. His face was haggard with lines, and if I had to guess, I would say he was well into his eighties. "On you go. We don't want your kind round here. A sympathizer."

What? Really? My thoughts spilled out of my mouth because, man, the melodrama!

"Aye, really." He ran his cloudy eyes down my body and back up again. "I've seen you, friendly with Viola Tait. Better watch, lass, or you'll catch something from her kind."

I swear I felt as if the world had fallen away from my feet.

Did he just say . . . did he just say what I think he said?

Sickening rage flooded up from the pit of my gut. "What did you say?" I asked, my voice hoarse with the strength of my reaction.

"I said—argh!" he cried out in fright as he found himself hauled up by the fist that had tightened in the fabric near the throat of his shirt.

Lucas's face was dark with fury as he held the old man up from his stool and bent into his face to growl, "Get. The. Fuck. Out of my pub." He shoved the old man back with such force, he stumbled off his stool, cursing so loudly, the whole place fell quiet.

He glared at Lucas. "It's not your pub, you little shit!"

"It is while my dad isn't here." Lucas rounded the bar, coming out from behind it.

"Luke." A man at the end of the bar grabbed hold of Lucas's arm. "He's just an ignorant old man. Leave it be."

Lucas strained against him, his chest heaving, but he stopped moving toward the old bigot. He pointed a finger at him. "Racists aren't welcome at The Alnster Inn. You set foot in here again, and I'll physically throw you out, I don't care what fucking age you are."

"Your da will hear about this," the old man blustered, looking around as if for support.

Tourists were affronted by the altercation while locals looked away. I chose to believe it was because they disagreed with him and not because they just didn't want Lucas to assault them. Finding no help, the old man spun on his heel and stumbled out of the dark pub.

I'd never seen him before, but he was obviously a local.

And now he'd do best to stay out of my way.

For a moment I stood stunned, speechless, and it was only as discomfort registered in my hands that I realized I'd clenched them into fists so tight, my fingernails were biting into my skin.

I looked from the doorway, where the racist asshole had departed, to Lucas, who was staring at me. He hadn't moved either.

He'd defended Viola.

Vehemently.

"I thought you weren't friends."

Understanding me perfectly, Lucas narrowed his eyes. "Friend or not, no one talks about her like that around me."

Hmm. Yes, the man was hateful, and anyone who didn't know Viola would have been disgusted.

But people who cared about her would be *enraged*.

Lucas Elliot was still trembling with the strength of his emotion.

Quickly making a decision that dealing with the book price rumor was the last thing on anyone's mind now, I gave the young man a nod of respect, which he returned, and I departed.

As soon as the door of the inn closed behind me, I stared across the road at The Anchor.

I could still picture Lucas straining as he held that old guy by the throat, his anger so fierce, I knew he wanted to throttle the man.

An image of Viola's pained expression as she watched Lucas stride through the village with that mystery blonde came to mind.

Could it be . . . ?

Were Lucas and Viola Alnster's very own Beatrice and Benedick?

As I returned to the bookstore, I considered the possibilities. Watching them interact last Saturday had been so entertaining because the air between them fairly crackled with electricity.

Chemistry.

Did they care for each other beneath the barbs and insults? Only they couldn't do anything about it because of the feud West kept burning between him and Milly.

Like the Montagues and Capulets.

"Except these are real people and it is not a play," I muttered, chastising myself.

These were people's feelings and emotions and—

"I totally want to meddle." I clenched my teeth together, expression sheepish, as I let myself back into the store.

I wanted to *Much Ado About Nothing* the crap out of Viola and Lucas's situation.

But I shouldn't interfere. I shook my head, slumping into the armchair by the unlit fire. West Elliot was clearly a giant man-child who couldn't give a rat's ass that he'd divided a village with something that happened decades before. A man like that wouldn't sit back calmly while his youngest son fell in love with his ex's only daughter.

Viola's sad eyes flashed across my mind again.

She was such a great girl. She deserved happiness, in whatever form that came.

Moreover, Lucas Elliot had just gone up quite a bit in my estimation.

"I shouldn't meddle," I murmured. "I definitely shouldn't meddle."

Meddling was bad.

Oh crap.

"I'm totally going to meddle."

Fifteen

A shade of angry purple had bled through the sky above Alnster, causing it to weep torrentially. Rain pounded off the road outside, and the sea rumbled its displeasure, foaming and discontent.

The damp brought such a chill, I'd lit the fire in the bookstore.

I'd woken up to the rain, and it hadn't let up in its ferocity. Viola had braved it to join Caro and me at the store, but no one else had ventured near Much Ado About Books.

Somehow it was one of the most perfect days I'd spent in England. Caro was curled up on the armchair by the fire with a copy of *The Handmaid's Tale*, while Viola lay sprawled on a faux fur blanket I'd brought down from upstairs. She lay on her side, elbow bent, head in her palm, flicking through the pages of *Wuthering Heights*.

I was on the other armchair, my feet tucked up under me. Still determined to make my way through every Shakespearean play during my stay in England, I was rereading *Hamlet*.

"I'm just going to say it." Viola slammed *Wuthering Heights* closed. "Everyone in this book is unlikable. How am I supposed to care about this romance when I don't like the main bloody characters?"

I grinned. "Maybe because you're reading it as if it's a romance when it's not."

She frowned. "I've seen the movie. It's definitely a romance."

Laughing, I lifted my legs off the counter and turned toward Viola. "Movies and TV adaptations always angle it like an epic romance, thus the misconception that the novel is a romance. If you try to read it like it's a romance, you'll hate it. *Wuthering Heights* is a book about not-very-nice people doing some not-very-nice things. It's not about two people who are in love. It's about two people who are *obsessed* with each other to the point of utter destruction. It's gothic and surreal and addictive once you let go of the idea it's a romance. It's a love story. There's a difference."

Viola thought about this and then nodded. "Okay, maybe I'll give it another shot. Another time, though. I'm in the mood for something a little more romantic."

Indeed.

In fiction or in real life?

"Missing that from your life, are you?"

At my question Caro lowered her book to hear Viola's answer. Viola sighed and sat up, curling her arms around her knees as she drew them toward her chest. "I dumped my boyfriend two weeks before the end of semester." Her upper lip curled into a sneer. "Noah. He plays for the basketball team. He was cheating on me with one of the bloody cheerleaders."

"I'm sorry, Vi," Caro offered gently.

"Yeah, me too. He's a complete moron." I frowned at her self-conscious wince. "You're one of a kind, Viola. Smart, funny, loyal, kind, witty, and although it's not important, you've got the type of stunning beauty that stops people in their tracks."

Caro nodded. "What she said."

Viola smirked. "Well, when you put it like that, I sound fantastic." She glanced between us, her expression somewhat sheepish. "If you want the truth, I think I needed the comedown Noah's cheating gave me." At my glower, Vi explained, "Caro will tell you that it hasn't always been easy growing up in a small village the daughter of a white woman and a black man. Don't get me wrong, most people are fine. They don't see my dad's skin color or mine. But there are some—and I hate to say it—of an older generation, who made it clear they didn't approve of us." Her eyes flashed angrily. "It wasn't just the feud that divided folks here thirty years ago. It was a white girl bringing a black man home."

I shook my head in despair of such blatant ignorance. "I'm sorry, Viola."

She shrugged but I knew she was hiding her real feelings behind indifference. "It wasn't awful growing up here. It's just I think I was made to feel different when I might not have if I grew up in the city. I was glad to leave and go to Newcastle at eighteen. And when I got there . . ." She laughed, sounding embarrassed. "Well, when I got there, aye, I found myself quite popular. Boys asked me out, girls wanted to be friends. Mam and Dad had always raised me to believe in myself, to like what I saw when I looked in the mirror, so it's not like I didn't already have confidence or that I didn't like myself . . . but with all the attention I received, I got arrogant. Knew I was smart. Knew I was pretty.

"Noah cheating on me brought me down to earth a little, and I think I needed it."

I gaped at her.

Viola's brows puckered. "What?"

Taking a minute, I was determined to find the words without lecturing her. My indignation, however, won out. "Did you tear other people down or make them feel inferior to you?"

She looked rankled. "Of course not."

"Then why on earth do you think you needed to be brought low by Noah's cheating? Viola, you're allowed to be confident and to think that you're smart and pretty and deserving of the best. Unfortunately, we live in a society where we tell our kids to be confident and successful and then as soon as they are, we tell them to shut up about it and be humble. Especially women. Guys can get away with cockiness until the end of time, but if a woman is cocky, she's arrogant and superior.

"Even worse, women are just as likely as men to condemn a confident woman for not being modest enough. The only way we can change that attitude is to change it among ourselves. If you're successful at something, celebrate that success. If you know you're smart, then demand that other people treat you as someone of intelligence. If you look in the mirror and you like what you see, then halle-fucking-lujah!" I exclaimed. "Believe me, I spent way too much of my youth, and still do, picking apart my appearance instead of being grateful for what I have. Grateful that all my limbs are intact and that my body is healthy." I leaned toward Viola, who was wide-eyed as she listened to me. "Do not ever apologize for liking who you are. It's a beautiful mindset. And that asshole who cheated on you doesn't deserve to come in touching distance of your life."

Silence settled over the three of us as Viola stared at me in shock.

It was Caro who broke it with a sudden burst of clapping.

We looked at her in confusion.

"I'm sorry but that speech deserved a round of applause," she explained.

She was so adorable, I grinned at her.

"Evie."

I turned to Viola. "Yeah?"

Her smile was slow but genuine. "Thanks. I'm really glad you're here."

"Me too." I settled back in my seat, my thoughts immediately turning to Lucas yesterday. "And I have to tell you something."

She nodded for me to go ahead.

I'd already told Caro about Tony's visit yesterday, but I hadn't mentioned the rumors about my inflated book prices. After I related what Tony had told me, I explained I'd gone to The Alnster Inn to see if there was any truth in it. "I'll never understand how a relationship ending thirty years ago can still resonate with an entire village, but it does. To the point that some old-timer at the bar brought it up."

Caro grimaced. "Because you've been seen at The Anchor."

"Right." I shook my head at the insanity. "Anyway, something not nice was said by this old guy . . ." I paused. After everything Viola had just confessed, why would I want to remind her that there were people out there who saw her as less? Crap, I had not thought this through.

Unfortunately, Viola understood as soon as I trailed off. "About me."

I nodded, mentally berating myself.

Insensitive asshole that I was.

"What happened?" Caro asked.

I'd started this stupid story for a reason so . . . "Lucas reacted."

Viola tensed. "Lucas?"

"He grabbed the guy, and basically threw him out of the pub."

Caro leaned toward me. "For insulting Vi?"

"Yeah."

Viola shook her head, clearly confused. "Why would Lucas defend me?"

"Not just defend you, Viola . . . he was physically shaking with anger." I gave her a small, knowing smile. "Not the actions of someone indifferent or who dislikes you."

Viola scoffed. "Lucas hates me. We've been at war for a long time."

"Why?"

"Because of his dad." She shrugged, a melancholy she couldn't hide darkening her light hazel eyes. "We didn't talk much as kids. We were in the same class, but we had different friends. Lucas stayed away from me because of his dad. When we were thirteen, we got paired up at school for a science project and I tried to befriend him. Lucas was funny and cute." She twisted her lips in derision. "I wanted him to like me, despite the crap between my mam and his dad. He knocked back my offer of friendship. It was brutal. We've been at each other's throats ever since. Then the cocky shit had to follow me to university, so sometimes I can't even escape him there."

"He wanted to kill that old guy for what he said, Viola. I didn't misunderstand his reaction and I'm not making it bigger than it was. He wanted to punch that guy's lights out." Okay, so I was meddling but I wasn't lying.

She shook her head in complete confusion. "Why?"

I grinned at her. "You really can't guess."

Viola guffawed. "You think Lucas *likes* me? *Likes* likes me?"

"Yes," Caro answered for me. "My goodness, Vi, watching you two at Market Day . . . well, it certainly looked like foreplay to me."

Both Viola and I stared in astonishment at Caro, with a surge of laughter bubbling out of me as Viola's tawny cheeks took on a rosy hue. "Caro!" she cried, uncharacteristically embarrassed.

Caro's own cheeks flushed red, but she grinned as she shrugged. "I only speak the truth."

Then I lost it, laughing so hard I was practically cackling.

"Oh, oh, you're one to laugh, Evie Starling," Viola said loudly, cutting through my laughter. "Every encounter you have with Roane is like foreplay."

"Vi, that's my cousin," Caro groaned.

My laughter died as I mock glared at Viola. "Roane and I are just friends."

"Oh really?" Viola looked unconvinced.

I narrowed my eyes at her. "We're as much friends as you and Lucas are not."

Her spine stiffened. Getting my point, she immediately turned to Caro with an abrupt subject change. "What are you going to do about Tony then?"

Caro blinked rapidly, clearly discombobulated by the swift new direction of our conversation. "Well . . . I'm not sure."

"Do you want to work with him?"

"We don't know that's what he wants to talk about."

I made a face. "It's what he wants to talk about."

Caro lowered her gaze, picking at invisible lint on the new pair of jeans she'd bought yesterday. Although her silk blouse with its floppy bow at the neck was still somewhat conservative, it was sleeveless and she'd paired the top with jeans and red pumps. She wore her lovely hair down. Just that simple outfit and hairstyle change had transformed Caro, and she now appeared younger than her twenty-two years.

"I have a meeting with my new financial adviser this week. I'll know more then."

"Know more then . . . ?" I mused. "You have something in mind that you want to do?"

"There's this building in Alnwick that's been up for sale for ages . . . it's in the perfect location for a small bakery."

Excitement for her rushed through me. "Caro, that would be amazing."

"Starting my own business will be difficult. I read that sixty percent of all new businesses in the UK fail in their first year. But . . . I'd like to try."

"Caro Robson, Lady Boss." Viola grinned at her. "I can absolutely see it."

"Robson?" I queried.

She nodded, her little chin set with determination. "First order of business is to have my name legally changed back to Robson."

I wanted to high-five her so badly.

"Caro Robson, Lady Boss indeed," I agreed.

She initially flushed but then I saw her blossom under the enthusiastic faith in her, and it was in that moment I realized I wouldn't be there to see Caro open her business. To see her shine and grow and become a fabulous, independent woman.

That thought hurt more than I could have imagined.

The sun did not return to Alnster the next day, the rain continuing to fall but less heavily. The change from torrents to showers was enough to bring the tourists back. Caro had been out most of the day, busy with meetings with her adviser and such. She'd returned just as I was closing up shop, and the sweetheart made dinner for us both.

Roane had texted me during the day to ask me to join him at the pub that evening, and I promised to do so. It was that promise that prevented me from diving into bed early. I was strangely exhausted for what hadn't been a very busy day, and could only suppose it was the dreary weather.

But I wanted to see Roane. We hadn't spoken much since the weekend, and I missed him.

It was ludicrous to miss someone I'd seen only days before, but it was also true.

After shooting Greer a reply to her latest email, I changed my sweater but not my skinny jeans. Caro wasn't in the mood to socialize and had opted to stay home and read, so I found myself heading up to The Anchor around eight o'clock by myself. Thankfully, it had finally stopped raining. The wet cobbles gleamed under the old-fashioned streetlights as I approached the pub, and I couldn't help but take a photo of the square that made up the main hub of Main Street.

Despite being too early for sunset, the sky was purple from a day of rainfall, and the lights, shadows, stone buildings, and those wrought-iron lamps made a great atmospheric shot for my Instagram.

The pub wasn't packed but it was still busy with diners as I stepped inside. My eyes immediately sought out the table by the fireplace, and sure enough, there was Roane, sitting and talking with Bobby. I knew Shadow would be at their feet.

Roane was laughing at something Bobby said, his white teeth

flashing against his dark beard and tan skin. One large hand rested on the table while his other clutched a pint of lager. I knew every scar and callus on those hands, because like his mouth, those hands drew far too much of my attention.

When I thought of the future, as I had yesterday sitting with Caro and Viola, it left me breathless.

My stepfather, Phil, had a friend who owned stables. Not long after he and Mom started dating, Phil took us there, and I got on a horse for the first and last time.

Because I fell off it.

I'd landed with such force, all the air went out of my lungs. I remember not knowing what was worse—the pain from the fall or the panic of not being able to breathe.

The mere thought of leaving Roane Robson was akin to falling off that horse.

Yet worse.

Much, much worse.

"You all right, Evie, lass?"

I blinked to find Milly in front of me. I stared down at her as her face came into focus. "What?"

She patted my arm and smiled reassuringly. "It happens to the best of us."

"What?" I shook my head, wondering if she'd said something prior to asking after my well-being.

"Go." She nodded her head to Roane and Bobby. "I'll bring you over a cider."

"Okay." I frowned, a little confused by our encounter. As I made my way through the tables toward Roane, he looked up and our eyes met.

That disorientating feeling of thrill mixed with contentment hit me with more force than usual as I drew toward him. Sometimes it felt like we were two magnets, my south seeking his north.

"Hey." I smiled as I reached the table.

Roane reached up to rub his hand along my lower back as he smiled warmly at me. "Evie."

It was something a boyfriend would do. Not a mere friend.

But I didn't care.

I liked his strong hands on me.

Much more than any *mere friend* should.

"Evie." Bobby grinned as he stood up. "I was just leaving."

"Was it something I said?"

"No, no," he hurried to reassure me. "I really do need to get home. See you tomorrow." He nodded at Roane and then winked at me. "Night, lass."

At his abrupt departure, I slipped into the seat he'd vacated. Brows puckering as I reached down to pet a sleepy Shadow, I asked, "He really didn't leave because of me?"

Roane shook his head, his mouth curling up at the corners. "He's just being a good husband. And a good friend."

"A good friend?"

His smile was far too wicked and flirtatious. "Bobby knows I like having you to myself."

Oh, he really had to stop saying such things. Heat pooled low in my belly, and I shifted uncomfortably. "Right," I practically squeaked.

My *friend* laughed, a deep, rumbly, masculine *knowing* laugh that caused me to flush with sexual awareness.

Thankfully, Milly appeared at that moment with my cider and asked me about the store. When she walked back to the bar, I turned the conversation away from the flirtatious tone it had developed. "Caro is thinking of opening a bakery?"

Roane nodded. "Aye. There's a lot to opening a business, but with the money her mum and dad left, even if the bakery failed, she'd be all right. Still, I think she should consider starting smaller—taking on orders for events like birthdays and such and seeing how that goes. If she builds up a strong enough reputation, then I don't see why she shouldn't consider opening up a bakery."

That made sense to me, and I told him so. Over an hour passed as we talked about Caro, the farm, the supposed rumor West had started about book prices. We talked about everything but our no-go areas—my mom, my future departure from Alnster, and the attraction between us that was growing hard to ignore.

I was laughing at a story Roane was telling me about when he and Bobby were in Newcastle for Bobby's bachelor party and Bobby had mistaken a real policewoman for a stripper.

"That doesn't happen in real life." I shook my head, giggling.

"I assure you it bloody does. He spent the night in the clink."

"Are you telling Bobby's stag do story again, Roane Robson?" Hazel appeared beside us, shaking her head in mock disapproval. "You know he hates you telling that story."

"Only when you're around."

"Wait, wait." Milly hurried through the tables to join Hazel beside us. We looked up at the two women in bemusement. "Okay, now you're good." She nudged Hazel.

Bobby's wife removed her hand from her back. In it was a rolled-up piece of white fabric. She held it out to Roane. "A peace offering. For the other night when we were pestering you about your love life."

"Evie here was right." Milly gave him an apologetic smile. "We're going to leave you be from now on."

Roane and I shared a confused smile as he reached for the fabric. "Uh, thank you."

Unfortunately, I made the mistake of taking a gulp of cider just as Roane unrolled the cotton fabric to reveal a T-shirt.

Printed across the front of the chest in bold large print were the words LADY PORN.

Laughter exploded out of me and with it the cider in my mouth.

It sprayed all down the front of the T-shirt as I began to choke in hysterics.

Milly and Hazel burst into peals of laughter as Roane shook his head, shoulders shaking with his own laughter as he used the T-shirt to wipe the cider that had landed on his cheeks.

I couldn't even apologize, I was laughing too hard.

Stumbling out of my chair, I wrapped both my arms around Milly and Hazel. My heroes.

"You have to put it on." I turned to Roane as I fumbled for the cell in my back pocket. "I need to take a photo for posterity."

Although his lips twitched with amusement, he narrowed his eyes. "You're joking, right?"

I took hold of the shirt and pressed it against his shoulders. "This is Instagrammable material right here," I teased.

He eyed me for a few seconds. "You don't think I'll do it."

Of course I didn't. What man would?

Roane pushed back his chair, pulled the T-shirt over the top of the plain one he wore, and he leaned back, his arms by his sides. He raised one eyebrow as if to say, *Well?*

Christ, I adored him.

"Seriously?" I grinned, clutching my phone to my chest.

"Why not?" He gestured to Milly and Hazel. "They went to the trouble and I'm never wearing it again, so you might as well take a picture now."

Practically humming with giddiness, I opened the camera and held it to Milly. "I want to be in it too."

She was still wiping the tears of laughter from her eyes as she took the phone. I lowered to my haunches beside Roane, one hand on his shoulder for balance as I grinned at the camera.

It was only later, after Roane had taken off the silly shirt and said good night to me at the door to the store, that I looked up the photo on my phone to put it on Instagram. I was sitting in bed, still amused over the night's events, when I opened the photo of us.

The smile dropped from my face.

Not because I was unhappy.

But because I was stunned.

While I beamed a bright smile toward the camera, Roane wasn't even looking at Milly.

His head was turned toward me, and the raw, open adoration in his expression was breathtaking.

My eyes burned as I stared at the photo, unable to look away from him. No one had ever looked at me that way.

No one.

My chest suddenly felt tight, packed to the brim as it was with emotion.

I couldn't put that photo on Instagram.

It was too personal.

For my eyes only.

"Fuck," I whispered.

Somehow, I knew that photo had changed everything.

Sixteen

As I handed money to Milly for my breakfast, I reminded her to thank Dex for the delicious omelet I'd just enjoyed.

"Will do, lass." She eyed me speculatively as she handed over my receipt. "Heard you're spending the day at Roane's farm?"

I was no longer surprised by other people knowing my business. It really did come with the territory of living in a tiny village. "Yeah, he's picking me up."

For almost two weeks I'd avoided spending time alone with Roane while I tried to get a handle on my emotions. However, he'd finally invited me out to his farm. It was two Sundays after the infamous LADY PORN photo, and despite my attempts to cajole Caro into joining us, I was going to be alone with Roane.

All day.

Caro had seen the farm. She wasn't interested. Truthfully, I think she just didn't want to be a third wheel.

Great.

"Enjoy that." Milly winked at me.

Over the past few weeks, the winks, hints, and innuendos about my friendship with Roane had increased to the point it was like water off a duck's back for both of us. It felt like the entire patronage of The Anchor was willing me to jump Roane Robson's bones. Belly fluttering at the mere thought, I waved goodbye and headed outside to the parking lot, where Roane said he'd collect me.

The sun shone strong in a cloudless sky, and since we were headed somewhat inland where there wasn't even a sea breeze for relief, I had worn shorts, a loose-flowing tank top, and a pair of Wellington boots I'd bought online. They were dark pink and cute as hell.

I'd pulled my hair up high in a ponytail to keep it off my neck, and I could feel the sun burning hot on my nape as I waited.

Through the brown filter of my sunglasses, I noticed movement across the street and started when I saw Lucas Elliot walking toward The Alnster Inn from the direction of the harbor.

"Hey, Lucas!" I called out before I could stop myself. Shifting my sunglasses into my hair, I skipped across the cobbled road as he stopped midstride. His brow puckered with obvious confusion at my approach. "How are you?"

Lucas crossed his arms over his chest and narrowed his eyes. "I'm all right. What can I do for you?"

Honestly, I'd approached him without really thinking about what I was doing, but the words were out of my mouth before I could stop them. "Viola heard about the altercation at the inn. She was grateful you stuck up for her." She hadn't said as much, but I knew her well enough to know that she was.

Hopefully.

Lucas scowled. "Who told her? She doesn't need to know people say stupid shit like that."

Oh, he so liked her.

It was a struggle to keep a straight face. "Small town." I shrugged. There was no way I was telling him it was my fault.

"Why do you think I care what Viola thinks of me?" His gaze was far too searching, far too perceptive. "Why do *you* care?"

"I care because I care about Viola. And I'd like to think that you're a good guy underneath all your bluster. She doesn't deserve shit from *anyone*."

"Right, well, you don't know us. You've been here all of a few months; that doesn't make you an expert on this village. Stay out of things between Viola and me," he warned. "She's a big girl and she can handle it."

"Can she?"

Lucas's head snapped back like I'd slapped him.

I smirked. "Ah, see, you think you're so smart, that you know everything. Well, I do know Viola. And I know women. As a tough-talking variety of the species myself, I can say with some authority that sometimes we women bust a guy's balls so he won't see just how much his words hurt us."

He shook his head, green eyes flashing with disbelief. "Why would anything I have to say matter enough to hurt Viola?"

"Yeah, Lucas." I made a "duh" face. "Why would your words matter enough to hurt her?"

It took a second but slowly that disbelief and confusion softened to understanding. And then shock. Before veering between disbelief again and something I couldn't quite work out.

He opened his mouth to respond, when a beep of a horn stopped him.

Glancing over my shoulder, I saw the Land Rover. Roane gestured from the driver's seat. Shadow's head was hanging out the window, his tongue lolling from his mouth.

I gave them a quick wave and turned back to Lucas, who was scowling at his feet in thought. "Well, see you around."

He glanced up at me warily. "What are you playing at here?"

This guy was so suspicious. For someone this sharp, he really was blindly clueless about Viola. "I'm just looking out for Viola, that's all."

Lucas curled his upper lip. "Aye, well, I doubt very much Viola would want you telling her enemy that he has the ability to hurt her feelings."

"Her enemy?" I scoffed. "Why on earth would a smart guy like you go out of his way to make an enemy of Viola Tait?" I shook my head at him as if he were a moron. "I've lived in one of the biggest cities in the US, kid. I've met a lot of people in my thirty-odd years on the planet. And she's a singular kind of woman. Intelligent, confident, kind, loyal, fierce, protective, witty as hell, funny, drop-dead gorgeous and no ego to go with it. Whatever guy ends up with Viola will be the luckiest guy in the world."

He smirked. "What are you? Her publicist?"

I narrowed my eyes. "Why did you stick up for her with that old guy if you're so indifferent to her?"

"Again, why do you care?"

"Answer my question first."

With a heavy sigh, he crossed his arms over his chest. "I already told you why. I would stick up for anyone who was the target of that kind of bigotry."

Remembering how he shook with fury over what that old villager had said, I mirrored Lucas's sigh. "You're young and cocky and right now you think you've got years to make mistakes and fix them. But you don't, Lucas. That's why I'm *here*. Because I graduated from college and the next eleven years of my life passed by in the blink of an eye and I found myself with nothing but regrets over the choices that I'd made. I don't want you, or anyone, to wake up in ten, twenty years' time, and wonder what could have been. Such benign little words—'what if.' But at some point in life, those two words become the scariest two words in the English language."

I half expected another sarcastic response. Something immature and lacking in foresight. Yet, to my surprise, Lucas just looked at The Alnster Inn and then back to me, his expression solemn.

"You think I don't already know that, growing up with my dad, then you really don't know anything about this place. Now"— his gaze flickered over my shoulder to Roane before returning to mine—"take this as a gentle warning and not a threat, because I don't want your boyfriend kicking my arse, but putting your nose into people's business round here tends to get the thing lopped off."

I could tell by his expression and tone that it wasn't a threat. That he actually meant well by the warning. So I heeded it, wondering if perhaps I really had crossed a line. "I didn't mean anything by it. I was just . . . trying to be helpful."

"Aye, well, I'm not in need of your matchmaking services, Ms. Starling." With a wry grin and a tip of his invisible hat, he strode past me toward the inn.

I shook my head in disbelief. No wonder young Viola was intrigued by this guy. He was too smart for his own freaking good, and talking to him wasn't like talking to any twenty-year-old guy I'd met before. There was an attractive authority and maturity about Lucas Elliot that made him dangerous to young women everywhere. And he totally had me figured out.

Dammit.

"You getting in anytime soon?" Roane called from his SUV.

With a grin of apology, I hurried over and climbed in. "Sorry."

"What was that about?" He jerked his chin in the direction of The Alnster Inn.

Did I really want to tell Roane about my failed matchmaking attempts?

"Evie?"

Finding myself unable to invent a lie or bad excuse, I told him everything. What I'd witnessed between Lucas and Viola on Market Day, Viola's expression when she saw Lucas with that unknown girl, and then Lucas's reaction to the old racist villager.

"I think they like each other underneath all that animosity."

Roane shot me an amused look as he drove us out of Alnster. "Evie, anyone with eyes can see Lucas Elliot wants Viola Tait."

I gaped. "You know?"

"Oh, aye." He turned left onto the main road, heading south from Alnster. "A few years ago—it must have been early summer, just before the two of them were heading to Newcastle Uni—Viola was in a car accident and ended up in hospital with a broken collarbone and cracked ribs. Word spread round the village fast, but all anyone knew was that Vi was in hospital, that the car she was in was totaled and it was bad. Her friend, the driver, escaped miraculously with very few injuries, but Viola was unconscious when she was pulled from the car by paramedics."

"Jesus," I whispered, thinking of Milly and Dex and how worried they must have been.

"Aye. Well, I was at the hospital to support Milly and Dex. I didn't want to leave them until I was sure Viola was going to be all right. When I came out of her room, I found Lucas skulking around, pale faced—a jittery bloody mess." Roane shook his head, smirking. "When I approached him, he practically jumped me for information about Viola, and I knew then my suspicions were correct. Lucas doesn't just fancy Viola, Evie, he *cares* about her. He might even love her."

My chest ached at the thought. "But—"

"He knew I knew then, and he made me promise I wouldn't tell anyone he'd been there to see how she was. And I haven't told anyone until now."

"Why?"

"Because his name is Lucas *Elliot*. Do you think West, or even Kathy, would ever speak to that boy again if he told them he was getting together with Viola Tait?"

I threw my hands up in despair. "This is ridiculous, Roane! Why should two young people who obviously care about each other have to be at each other's throats to keep the other at bay, because some dude can't get over a lost love?"

My friend was quiet for a moment. And then, voice gentle, he asked, "Have you ever been in love, Evie?"

Surprised by the turn of conversation, I blinked a few times before admitting, "No."

"Then how can you say West Elliot should just get over it? I'm not saying I agree with the shit he's pulled, or that he shouldn't have tried to move on . . . I absolutely don't. I'm just saying that West must have loved Milly with everything he had for it to have twisted him up inside so badly. And that's sad, Evie. That's fucking tragic."

It was. Terribly so. But . . . "Any good father wouldn't wish the same on his son."

"I know you mean well." He gave me a gentle smile to soften the blow of what he said next. "But you need to stop playing matchmaker with those two."

Feeling somewhat foolish and admonished, I turned away, watching the countryside pass us by. "I just . . . I don't want them to end up like me. In their thirties and desperately searching their memory for where it was they took the wrong goddamn turn. It would be worse for them, knowing what was possible between them and they never took the chance on each other."

"Who's to say it would work out with them anyway?"

True.

I nodded, melancholy.

"Hey." I felt a strong sensation squeeze my knee, and I looked down to see Roane's big hand on me. There was a scar across his middle knuckle, and his fingernails were short and blunt. The skin of his hands and arms was just a shade darker than my tan legs. His palm was rough, leathery. A working hand. Masculine against my feminine, slender, soft-skinned knee. There was something visceral about the sight.

I shivered.

"They'll be all right." At his words I wrenched my eyes up. He shot me a quick, meaningful look before he said, "*You'll* be all right too, angel."

Something sweet and heady moved through me at the term of endearment. "Angel." I liked that. I covered his hand with mine and gave him a grateful smile.

As we drove, I was aware of everything. That he hadn't removed his hand, and every now and then he would flex it on my leg, his thumb brushing the bend in my knee. Between the heat and his touch, sweat gathered behind my knees. The only sound between us was the roll of the road beneath us and Shadow's panting from the back seat.

A few minutes later, Roane lifted his hand off my knee as he hit the right turn signal, and we turned off the main road, crossing opposing traffic as soon as there was a break in it to venture down a dirt road that cut through open fields on either side. There were a lot of sheep in the field to my left.

"Is this your farm?" I asked.

"This is some of my farm. The sheep farm."

I remembered Roane telling me he had land to the east for arable farming, and nodded. "About time," I joked. "You kept avoiding taking me out here so much, I was starting to believe it wasn't real."

"It's real. There's just nothing much of excitement to see."

As it turned out, he wasn't wrong, but what I didn't tell him was that just being with him made even the most mundane experiences exciting. Not that the farm was mundane. It was just . . . well, a farm. But it was Roane's farm, and therein lay the difference.

The dirt road led to a small farmhouse with agriculture buildings situated on three sides of it.

"We're surrounded by over a hundred acres of land here for nearly three hundred sheep," Roane said as he jumped out and let Shadow out the back of the vehicle.

I hopped out and rounded the SUV, my eyes on the stone farmhouse. The sound of bleating sheep hit my ears, and although there was a faint hint of sea salt in the air, I mostly smelled grass, hay, and the slight sting of fertilizer. The odors weren't strong, but I imagined on a windy day that breeze swept them from the fields to the farmhouse. "Three hundred sheep? That's a lot, right?"

"Aye, more than some, less than others." He took hold of my hand and led me toward the huge modern barn that sat adjacent to the farmhouse. Shadow trotted at our backs as we walked across a hard dirt road. "We rebuilt the barn five years ago." We stopped at one of three green wooden barn doors that slid open on a wrought-iron rail. I peeked inside, the smell of hay, soil, musk, and something faintly chemical catching my nose. "We use this for lambing season, which you've thankfully missed."

"Thankfully?" I pulled my head out of the large space. "Lambs are adorable."

"This place"—he indicated the barn—"isn't adorable during lambing season. Trust me." With that, he led me around the back of the farmhouse, where an older but pretty substantial rectangular shed stood vertical to the house. There was a pen around the large shed, and the chickens walking around outside gave away its use. "Chicken shed," Roane said anyway as we rounded the house to the other side.

The two largest buildings on this part of the land loomed over us, and I saw Bobby moving around inside one of them among a *lot* of sheep. Hence the bleating I'd heard as soon as we approached. The two buildings had no doors, just steel pens, and the corrugated iron walls curved up and over in a semicircle. The first building was messy with hay, and Bobby appeared to be mucking it out through a small door at the back. The second building, although filled with hay, was empty of sheep.

"They're called hoop houses," Roane explained. "We bring the sheep here during very hot weather, keep them from being out in the sun too long. They were built when we had less sheep, and they just fit, but we'll need to build another to give them more room."

The thought of those poor animals suffering in this heat made me frown. "What about the barn? Can't they go in there?"

He shook his head. "We need that kind of climate for lambing, but we try to keep them out of enclosed spaces. It can cause respiratory problems."

"Evie, Roane." Bobby made his way through the sheep, pitch-fork in hand. His T-shirt was soaked with sweat, and he wiped a hand across his forehead. "This weather is grand, eh."

His tone was bland, but since he was sweating by the buckets and was red in the face, I decided that had been sarcasm.

"How are they?" Roane nodded to the flock in the hoop house.

"Aye, they're fine." Bobby grinned at me. "Enjoying the tour?"

"It's interesting."

"This is the end of it." Roane's lips twitched with amusement. "Nothing else to see, angel, but fields upon fields."

"What about the arable farm?"

He flicked a look at Bobby before glancing over his shoulder to check on Shadow. "It's all just the same except no animals. The hoop houses over there are for keeping hay and the barns for hold-ing grain and barley."

Shadow stood in the shelter of the farmhouse door. "Come." Roane gestured to the house. "I'll show you inside. My great-grandfather built this place."

With a wave to Bobby, I followed Roane to the house. The farmhouse was rectangular with the door jutting out, built into a porch that looked like a mini house with its sharp triangular roof. There were two windows downstairs to either side of the door, and upstairs there were four windows. The windows were made of white wooden frames with six small glass panels in each.

As soon as Roane let us into the porch, I smiled. The porch had two windows on either side, allowing light into the small space. There was a bench under each window, covered in tartan blankets and cushions. An old-fashioned coat and umbrella stand stood in the corner beside a row of men's shoes. It was fairly cool in the porch, a nice reprieve from the heat outside, and Shadow seemed to agree, sprawling across the cool slate tile floor.

Roane sat down on one of the benches and began to remove his Wellingtons. I followed suit, ridiculously relieved to get out of the hot boots. I pulled my sunglasses off my head, useless as they were up there, and set them beside me.

Our eyes met as we sat across the bench from each other, and something in Roane's expression made my breath catch. "What?" I whispered.

He shook his head with a mysterious smile and stood up to hold out his hand. "Want to see the rest?"

Of course I did. I took his hand and let him lead me through the inner porch door and into the farmhouse. A wall of heat hit me, and not for the first time since summer came to Northumberland, I cursed the British and their lack of air-conditioning.

As if he'd read my thoughts, Roane chuckled. "Old houses weren't built with insulation like nowadays where it keeps the house warm during the winter and cool during the summer."

"How do you cope?" I murmured, flapping a hand at my face as I took in the dark space. A spindled staircase sat in the center of the hallway, while there were doors to either side of us. The dark wood of the staircase and sideboard didn't help this windowless room from looking cheerless, and the floral wallpaper was extremely dated.

It surprised me that his parents hadn't updated the place.

Shadow led us to our right, and we stepped into a large, lovely farm kitchen. The ceilings were low for two tall people but just high enough to stop Roane from smacking his head. It appeared as if the kitchen had been updated sometime in the last twenty years. The cabinetry was of the farmhouse style and painted a pale green with bronze handles. An island with a sink sat in the center of the room, while a countertop ran along the back wall, where one large wood-framed window let light in. On the opposite side of the island was a six-seater table situated between the two small wood-framed windows on the front of the house.

But the most eye-catching aspect of the room was the end wall. A huge brick chimney opening took up the entire length of it to accommodate a stunning ceramic farmhouse stove.

It was a cook's kitchen and I loved it. Even though I wasn't much of a chef. The scent of freshly brewed coffee still clung to the air, and I sighed happily. "This kitchen is amazing."

"Aye, it's a good family kitchen. Great place to cook. Caro comes out to bake here sometimes."

On the left side of the house was a large family sitting room. Again, I was bemused by the old-fashioned wallpaper and dark wood. The only sign of Roane's influence in the room was the seventy-inch flat-screen television and the dark leather sofa and armchairs.

Overall, I'd say the house needed a little lightening, a little touch of femininity perhaps.

The smell, however, I would not change. There was no denying this was Roane's home. His woodsy, citrusy, ocean-layered scent was in every room we walked through. I wanted to rub myself against that scent so that I would take it with me.

Aware of Roane's eyes on me as I took in his surroundings, I turned to him, crossing my arms over my chest. Embarrassment flooded me at the idea of his knowing my thoughts, and I asked a little snappishly, "What? Why are you looking at me like that?"

He just smiled. Softly. Tenderly. "I like you here."

At his sweet confession, I felt my cheeks heat.

I liked me here too.

Too much for my own good.

The temptation to give in to my attraction to Roane was great, and my willpower was weakening by the second.

"It's, uh . . . it is a tad warm in here. Isn't there something I could help you do today . . . outside?"

He studied me a moment, expression unreadable, then he nodded. "Aye. We need to bring the rest of the sheep in out of this heat and into the hoop house. It needs to be done in shifts. You can help Shadow and me herd them."

In all the time I'd known Roane and Shadow, it had never occurred to me that Shadow was a working dog. "Wait, Shadow herds sheep? I thought border collies were the best for sheep farming."

"They are." Roane rubbed Shadow's head affectionately as we wandered out of the sitting room to the porch to put our boots back on. "And Danes aren't the go-to for it. But I trained Shadow. He's a big gentle giant and knows when to stop being playful and get down to business."

And that was how I spent my afternoon. I wasn't particularly helpful as we drove out to the fields in a high-bed, high-sided truck with Bobby. The truth was, all I really did was stand there and enjoy watching Roane as he and Bobby unlatched the ramp on the truck so the sheep could climb up into it. Shadow and Roane herded a flock up the ramp onto the truck, while I kept an eye out for any strays.

We then drove back to the second hoop house and unloaded the sheep, only to drive back to the fields to load up more.

It was slow work, and I could feel rivulets of sweat trickling down between my breasts. Roane's T-shirt was soon soaked through like Bobby's, with damp patches across his back and under his arms.

Perhaps it was the heat, or perhaps it was weeks of denying myself, but my body was tingling and throbbing with need as I watched Roane at work. I found myself mesmerized by the beads of sweat that trickled down the back of his neck, and the way the muscles in his biceps flexed as he helped Bobby fix the ramp to the truck.

The veins in his forearms held particular appeal.

I was in a state.

Slick with sweat and need, throbbing deep in my core.

When we got back to the hoop house and unloaded the last of the sheep, my thighs were damp, and my limbs were trembling. After counting the sheep, they realized there were three not accounted for, so Bobby took off to find the strays that had wandered away from the larger flocks.

Roane, completely unaware of how he was affecting me, cursed under his breath once the sheep were behind the pens, and whipped off the T-shirt that was sticking to every inch of his torso.

My jaw hit the floor as he strode past me, oblivious, and bent toward an old-fashioned water pump that I hadn't even noticed situated by the side of the house. He ducked his head under it, yanking on the pump handle, the movement making his muscles *known*.

When he stood, he flicked his head, water flying off the ends of his unruly thick hair.

I think I might have moaned.

It was like watching Darcy coming out of that pond or Poldark cutting the fields with his scythe.

Was I drooling? I felt like I might be drooling.

Roane bent down under the metal channel beneath the pump,

pulled out a water bowl, and began to fill it. Shadow was already at his side, waiting for the offering, and eagerly bent to the bowl when Roane put it down for him.

When Roane straightened, he looked toward the hoop house, his brow furrowed as if he was contemplating something.

And I ogled.

He wasn't roped and ripped the way a man who had time for visits to the gym might have been. No, he was something better. Although broad shouldered, Roane was lean and muscular from daily physical activity on the farm. Plus, he wasn't waxed to an inch of his life. There was a fine sprinkling of hair over his chest, and he had a happy trail.

I hummed under my breath.

He was sexy and strong without making me feel bad about my own lack of gym visits.

Roane was what Greer called "naturally manlicious."

A deep tug low in my belly made me bite my lip to stop a moan, and despite the heat, I felt a familiar tightening in my breasts.

Then he looked at me.

Roane's eyes widened and his nostrils flared at whatever he saw in my expression. His face darkened with heat, and I hungrily watched a droplet of water take a path down the center of his chest, stomach, and then disappear beneath the waistband of his jeans.

"Oh, screw it." I ran.

Actually *ran*.

I threw myself into his arms with the intention of locking our lips together.

Unfortunately, Roane wasn't expecting my assault, and the water from the pump had turned the dirt under his feet soft and slippery.

As his arms closed around me, the impact of my body forced his back and his feet out from under him.

Roane landed on the ground with a pained groan, the impact made all the worse because the weight of my body flattened him.

"Oh my God." I scrambled on top of him, my hands moving off his chest to brace on either side of his head. His handsome face was strained as he blinked up at me, apparently disoriented. "Are you okay?"

After a second of humiliating silence, Roane's hands suddenly tightened on my waist and he rolled, pushing me to the ground. The water from the pump seeped into my tank top, but I couldn't care less. Roane Robson was braced over me, half-naked, his gaze hot and searching. "Are we about to have sex?" he asked bluntly.

The question set my heart to racing.

"Yes," I whispered.

His grin was immediate and oh so wicked. "Then, aye, angel. I'm fan-fucking-tastic."

Seventeen

Roane jumped to his feet with more grace than a big guy like him should have been capable of and then bent down to haul me to my feet. Without a word, he grabbed me by the wrist and began marching us into the house. Shadow barked and followed us inside, and Roane paused momentarily to push the kitchen door open. "In, boy," he directed, closing the door on Shadow, who gave another bark of disgruntlement.

Roane glanced at me. "It's cool in there for him."

I could only nod.

My heart was thundering in my chest, and my already sweat-slicked body was burning now from the inside.

Something voracious and sexual flashed in Roane's eyes, and suddenly he was running up the stairs and I was hurrying to catch up with him. It was only then I realized we were both still wearing our dirty Wellington boots.

Not that we cared. It was the last thing on our minds.

He led me down a dark, narrow corridor and into what I surmised was the master bedroom at the front of the house. It was surprisingly light compared to the rest of the house. There was no heavy floral wallpaper in here. It was all pale gray walls, his large bed covered with dark gray linen.

The two small windows let light pour into the room.

It was stuffy and hot, and made me want to rip my clothes off even more than I already did.

Roane stopped by the side of the bed, turning to me, pulling me close until the length of our bodies pressed together. His hands coasted leisurely up and down my back, while his beautiful eyes searched my face.

"You sure this is what you want?" he asked, but before I could answer, his caresses stopped and his voice became gruff when he confessed, "Because this isn't just sex for me, Evie. I want us to take a chance on each other, for real. And if you can't do that, you need to walk away now." His hands suddenly pushed deeper into my back, holding me tighter, closer, the gesture at odds with his words.

I trembled in his arms, despite the heat, a shiver tickling down my spine. I knew Roane. I knew that it would never just be sex for him. He wasn't that guy. And he didn't look at me like a guy who just wanted one thing.

He looked at me like a guy who wanted *everything*.

It was seductive, compelling, and despite all my concerns about how a relationship might derail me from working out my future plans, I couldn't deny myself him anymore. Hadn't I told myself all those months ago that if I realized love was something I wanted in my life, then I had to actively start pursuing it? Well, Roane Robson was one of a kind, and I'd be an absolute fool to walk away from the chance to see if what was between us could be something real.

Something epic.

In answer, I lifted my arms into the air, inviting him to remove my tank top.

Relief sparked in his eyes, hunger following quickly on its heels. My chest heaved with my labored, excited breaths as Roane's fingers curled into the fabric. He fisted it and then slowly tugged the tank top up and over my head.

He dropped it to the floor, and a feeling of self-consciousness came over me as he dragged his gaze down, drinking in the sight of me in my bra. I might have legs for days and an impressively large chest, but I also had a rounded stomach that turned into belly rolls when I sat.

Maybe I tensed or Roane read my expression because he suddenly cupped my face in his large hands. His palms were hot and rough against my skin. "You're perfect, Evie."

"I'm not perfect." I shook my head with a wry smile as I lifted a hand to tickle my fingertips across one of his pecs. *Not like you.* His eyes fluttered at my touch, a shudder moving through him that made me feel extremely powerful. Okay, maybe I wasn't perfect, but Roane seemed to like all that I was anyway.

"You are to me," he said, supporting my suspicions. He swept his thumbs over my cheeks, the touch tender, but as he moved his hands down my neck, there was a sexy possessiveness to his exploration.

Roane's eyes followed his fingertips as he trailed them with frustrating slowness across my collarbone and down toward the rise of my breasts. His gaze filled with intense want as he stared at them.

"I can almost taste them, feel your nipples on my tongue," he whispered.

My body jerked at his surprising words. I hadn't imagined Roane to be much of a talker during sex. It was arousing, and goose bumps prickled in the wake of his touch as his fingertips lightly caressed the upper curves. My nipples peaked against my bra in anticipation for his mouth. I made a guttural sound in the back of my throat, bringing Roane's gaze back to mine. Whatever he saw there made him cup my face in his hands, and he lowered his head toward mine.

I sucked in a breath as I clasped his biceps, his skin damp from the heat, his muscles hard beneath my fingertips.

Roane was going to kiss me.

I felt the heat of his breath first, the warning before his lips touched mine. And when they did, it was a barely there brush, a hot, glancing touch.

My fingers dug into his arms, silently urging him to *really* kiss me.

I was desperate for it.

But Roane was determined to take his time. Another whisper of a kiss, then a slightly deeper press, a nibble on my lower lip.

A whimper escaped me.

It shattered whatever restraint Roane had lassoed around himself. His hands clasped the back of my neck, hauling me against his body as his mouth pressed hard to mine. I opened my mouth to let him in, and his groan of satisfaction rumbled through me.

The tickle of his beard was surprisingly erotic on my skin. I'd dated guys who had stubble, which was abrasive, but Roane's thicker beard was slightly wiry and softer than the prickle of stubble. It felt rugged, masculine, my opposite, and it was a big turn-on. Roane was aroused too. I could feel evidence of how much he wanted me digging into my stomach as he savored me with tender reverence that was sexier than any kiss that had ever come before his. Sliding my hands down his back, feeling the hot, smooth strength of him under my touch, I melted into him. His hands drifted down from my neck, and with teasing strokes, Roane studied my body—my ribs, my waist. When he touched my stomach, I fumbled the kiss and he broke it to gaze down at me through lust-fogged eyes.

Watching me, he deliberately ran the backs of his knuckles across my belly. "Every inch, angel." His voice was hoarse.

I relaxed, feeling a little embarrassed by my self-consciousness, but that abashment didn't last long as he bent to recapture my mouth. Roane's hands glided around to my ass, where he cupped both cheeks and drew me against his arousal. As he ground into me, his tongue caressed mine in deep, wet strokes, growing wild and almost bruising. I wondered what that beard would feel like between my thighs.

I groaned at the thought.

Roane suddenly broke the kiss, our breaths mingling as we panted against each other.

"Why did you stop?" I whispered.

"Because." He squeezed his eyes closed as he rested his forehead against mine. "There's plenty of time for us to fuck. I don't want that for our first time. I want to make love to you."

Oh my God, this man. "Are you even real?"

He chuckled and squeezed my ass, bringing me closer against his throbbing body. "What do you think?"

I moaned and reached for his mouth, nipping at his lower lip and then frowning when he let go of my ass to ease away from me. Amusement danced in his eyes at my consternation. "It's good to know you want me too, angel."

"Have you ever doubted it?"

He considered this. "When I tried to kiss you and you pulled away . . . aye, I doubted it."

Guilt suffused me. "Roane, I didn't pull away because I didn't want you. I just . . . I didn't come here expecting to find you."

"But now that you have?"

I moved back into his body, sliding my hands to his front to caress his chest, my thumbs catching his nipples. His lashes fluttered, his chest rising and falling with his rapid breathing. "I want you to make love to me. Then after, I'll want that fucking you mentioned."

He grabbed me near the ribs, his squeeze almost bruising as he huffed, "You trying to speed things up, angel?"

I ran my fingertips down his happy trail. "No," I confessed softly as I followed the line of his waistband, feeling his stomach ripple with my touch. "I like the way you savor me."

Gaze hot and tender, Roane gave me an almost imperceptible nod before he reached around to the back of my bra. With excruciating slowness, he unhooked my bra and began to tease the straps down my arms. The cups caught on my nipples, and my breathing faltered as he seemed to become mesmerized by the sight. He gave the straps a slight pull and the bra fell away, dropping to the carpet with barely a sound.

Roane curled his hands around my upper arms, easing them from my side. My breasts weren't delicate or perky. I suffered from the problem of side boob a lot, but if a guy was a breast man, then he usually liked what he saw.

Roane was clearly a breast man.

His hands tightened around my biceps while he devoured me with his eyes. My nipples peaked under his perusal, tight, needy buds that begged for his mouth. For his tongue.

He made a guttural sound in the back of his throat as he reached up and cupped me with both hands. My legs trembled so badly, I felt my knees give a little, and I arched into his touch with a moan. His calloused thumbs caught on my nipples, strumming and pinching them as he played with my breasts, sculpting and kneading. Arousal rippled deep and low inside me. Seriously, I couldn't remember ever being this turned on in my life.

What was he doing to me?

"Roane," I begged, "please—" I was cut off by his mouth crashing down on mine. This kiss was different. It was rough, desperate, greedy as he pinched both my nipples between his forefingers and thumbs. I bowed against his touch, breaking the kiss to gasp for breath. "Roane . . ."

Could I come like this?

I felt like I might.

However, suddenly Roane was no longer touching my breasts but bending to lift my left foot. I grabbed his shoulder for balance as he tugged off my Wellies one by one. And then he was fumbling for the zipper on my shorts. I shuddered with desire as he curled his fingers into the waistband of my underwear and pulled it down my legs along with my shorts. As I stepped out of them, he pressed a kiss between my legs, his beard tickling me, but it was so quick, I barely even had time to register it. Trembling with need, I stood, naked, as Roane stared at me like Christmas had come early. He kicked off his own boots, unbuttoned his jeans, and lowered his zipper before removing them along with his boxer briefs. After he kicked away his jeans and underwear, he gazed at me, a small smile on his lips, completely unabashed by his nakedness.

And rightly so.

Talk about epic.

His muscular calves, strong thighs, and the impressive erection saluting me from between them caused another hard flip in my lower belly. I bit my lip to stop another moan and then lifted my finger and made a circular motion.

Roane let out a huff of laughter, that adorable flush of red cresting the tops of his cheeks, but he did as I requested and slowly turned.

His ass.

My God, his ass needed to be immortalized in sculpture.

He turned to face me and smirked. "Happy now?"

I shook my head. "I won't be happy until I've kissed every inch of you."

His nostrils flared. "I know the feeling, angel." He stepped back and sat on the bed. "Come here."

I'd barely taken two steps toward him when he reached out to grasp me around the waist. Then he guided me to straddle him, his arousal hot against my stomach. My fingers curled into his strong shoulders as he smoothed his hands up my back.

He was such a tall guy that he made me feel feminine, almost delicate, when most men made me feel the opposite. My gaze wandered from his lips to his eyes, and my breath caught. There was so much emotion in his eyes. Desire, need, yes, but something more. Something beyond even tenderness and affection, and it made my chest feel full. Too full. Almost painfully so.

"Roane?"

He slid his hand along the back of my neck, and I felt him pull on the band holding my hair in a ponytail. It had barely begun to fall down my back when he slid his hand into the masses, tangling in it to grab a handful. Then he gently tugged my head back, arched my chest, and covered my left nipple with his mouth.

I gasped as the touch scored down my stomach to between my legs, and as he sucked and licked at me, my hips began to undulate, searching for satisfaction. Tension coiled between my legs, tightening and tightening as he moved between my breasts. My fingernails dug into his shoulders. I was going to come. He'd built me up with his slow seduction, and now I was ready for release just from his mouth on my breasts.

Oh my God.

Abruptly he stopped, and I found myself falling onto my back as he flipped me. I stared up at him, lying atop his duvet, and my lower belly shuddered as he moved off the bed to his knees. I pushed up on my elbows to watch him, my panting growing louder as my anticipation built.

His big hands coasted up the insides of my thighs as he pushed my legs apart and hauled my body down the bed toward him. He made a guttural noise in the back of his throat seconds before his tongue touched me. His tongue, how his beard gently scratched against my skin, his fingers biting into my thighs . . . it was all too much.

I cried out as I moved against his mouth, my climax right there on the horizon of a few more licks. He suckled me, pulling hard, and that was all it took. The tension inside me shattered in a spine-tingling release that coursed deliciously through me. I shuddered against Roane's mouth as he devoured every drop of my orgasm.

I'd never seen a man look so satisfied or triumphant as Roane stood, towering over me as I lay flushed across his bed. Without a word he pulled open the drawer in his bedside cabinet, fumbled inside it for a second, and removed a condom.

My inner thighs quivered as I watched him tear open the foil, heard it crinkle before it hit the floor. I'd barely recovered from my epic orgasm, and I could already feel the slick tension building inside me again as Roane rolled on protection.

Then, as if I weighed nothing, he gripped me under the arms and slid my body up and across the bed before climbing over me.

I panted for air as he hovered above me, eyes locked with mine. Then he lowered his head and kissed me. Slow, deep, seductive. Mesmerizing. Spellbinding kisses that took me somewhere else. We were wrapped in a cocoon of heat, the air in the stuffy bedroom thick with it, with our musk and the scent of sex.

There was nothing for it but to give in to the heat, to build it until it was a fire that set us ablaze.

As I wrapped my legs around Roane's hips and he pushed inside me, that's what we did. We stoked the fire with every stroke, every gasp, until I was mindless with how this felt. The entire time he held me in his gaze, keeping us connected. A man had never looked so deep into my eyes during sex, and it was intense.

It was lovemaking.

For the first time in my life, that burning desire exploded inside me at the same time as his. I'd never come at the same time as a partner before, and as Roane buried his head in my throat, groaning and shuddering through his release, and as I shook against him with mine, I realized nothing had ever compared.

He'd ruined me.

Eighteen

There was no breeze coming in through the wood-framed windows Roane had pushed up to allow fresh air in. Yet it gave the illusion of cooling us as we lay sprawled atop his bed, naked, sunlight gleaming off our sweat-slicked skin.

The crisp hairs on his calves tickled me as he curled his left leg around my right. Our heads were turned toward each other on the pillows—we gazed into each other's eyes while we held hands. Our fingers locked and unlocked as our hands flexed against each other until I smoothed out his palm with mine and began to trace the calluses that had created hard curves at the base of his fingers.

This was thrill and contentment entwined as one, and it made me so hopeful I could almost cry from the sweet ache of it.

"I don't even care it's like an oven in here," I whispered, "I could stay here forever." It was true. I'd never felt so comfortable being completely naked with a man, but Roane made me feel that way. He made me feel like he truly adored every inch of me.

"Me too." He sighed. "Although I suppose I should really nip downstairs to check on Shadow and grab us each a glass of water."

My grip on him tightened even though I knew he should check on Shadow. Roane smiled at my reflexive move, and as he sat up, he brought my hand to his lips and kissed my knuckles. "I'll be quick."

After we'd made love, Roane was ready to go again impressively quickly. The man had the stamina of a twenty-year-old. Not that I was complaining. Especially when he kept his promise and took me less than tenderly the second time. It had been rough, hard, and he talked dirty.

I shivered at the memory as Roane got off the bed and strode out of the room.

God, I had to write an ode to that man's muscular ass.

Wiping sweat off the back of my nape, I grimaced and slumped into the pillow beneath me. We really needed to shower, but there was something thrilling about lying completely naked in the middle of the day with Roane.

He wasn't long in returning with two glasses of water in hand. I took one from him and greedily gulped it down, having underestimated how parched I was. Wiping my lips, I asked, "Is Shadow okay?"

"He's found a cool spot in the shadow of the kitchen. He didn't want to be disturbed. This weather makes him sleepy." Roane grinned, returning to the bed.

"It usually makes me sleepy." My lips trembled with amusement. "Not today."

"I noticed. Thank fuck for summer days." He looked more than a little pleased with himself.

I rolled my eyes. "I couldn't help myself. You were all sweaty and hot, the latter both literally and figuratively. It was too much for one woman to take."

We were quiet a moment as Roane emptied his glass of water and then lay back down beside me. I shimmied toward him, and he lifted his arm, inviting me to curl against him. Resting my head on his strong chest, feeling his heart thud beneath me, I took a deep breath. He smelled of musk and citrus, sweat and sex . . . and me.

My perfume clung to his skin.

A shiver of possession rolled through me.

"We're doing this then, Evie? We're giving this thing between us a real go?"

I nodded, my hair rustling against his skin with the movement. Beginning a relationship with Roane was just asking for confusion and complication. I knew that. Yet I refused to panic. We had time. We still had two months to figure out if what we had was worth upending my whole life. No decisions had to be made right away. "We are. But . . . let's not overthink it or make definitive plans. Let's just enjoy each other and see where this leads us."

He took an expansive breath and let it out slowly. "Okay."

He didn't sound so sure. "Roane?" I lifted my head to meet his gaze.

His gaze was searching. "What does that mean exactly? That no matter what happens you're planning to leave in two months?"

"No." I shook my head. "No, it means I don't want to screw this up"—I gestured between us—"by panicking about what it means. There's no point worrying about getting deep into this with each other because there's an expiration date. Let's not think of there *being* an expiration date. I leave in two months or . . . I don't. But if I said right now, 'Roane, I'm not leaving because of you,' that would put all of this pressure on us. I don't want that. I just want us to see where this goes without some clock ticking or *not* ticking above our heads."

Nodding, he slid his hand to the nape of my neck and gave it a comforting squeeze. "That makes sense, angel."

Settling my head on his chest again, I traced little patterns on his abdomen, and we lay there in perfect silence. Then I had a thought. "Do you think Bobby came back?"

"He must have. He would have called if he hadn't found the sheep."

"Do . . . do you think he heard anything?" Neither of us had exactly been quiet.

Roane shook with laughter. "I could give a shit, angel."

"Maybe I care." But I really didn't.

"You don't. You enjoyed yourself too much to care."

"Cocky."

"I have every right to be. No woman has come as hard around me as you just did."

At the mention of other women, I thought of the last couple of months I'd spent getting to know this man. Although it felt like he knew almost everything about me, I didn't know as much about him. I knew who he was as a person, but his past was made up of vague information he'd dispensed every now and then. Roane Robson was more of a listener than a talker. But I wanted to know more.

"You said before you've only had a few relationships. Tell me about them."

He tensed beneath me. "You . . . you want to hear about other women while you're naked in bed with me?"

I chuckled at his incredulous tone. "Roane, you never talk about yourself. I just want to know more. If you don't want to tell me about the other women, then tell me about your parents. What was it like growing up here? Because in my mind it must have been idyllic."

Little goose bumps prickled along my arm as he began to trace lazy circles on my skin. "I have a wonderful mum and dad. Like Milly and Dex, they struggled to conceive, but I eventually came along five years into their marriage. They tried again but it just never happened. Despite the farm, Dad's family had a long tradition of sending their sons off to boarding school. Dad went, and my grandfather, who died when I was two, made it clear that's what he wanted for me too. But Mum put her foot down and instead I went to school in Alnster and then to the high school in Alnwick, spent my summers learning about the farm.

"Dad wanted me to run things when he retired, but Mum wanted me to have choices. I took her advice and graduated from Durham University with a bachelor's degree in business and finance. Mum and Dad's graduation gift was money to travel. I did that for six months, backpacking through Europe and Asia. And I was glad for it. I met some amazing people, tried new and wonderful food, and had my eyes opened to the world beyond my own borders. But ultimately, I missed Alnster. I missed the farm.

"Three months after I came home, my mum and dad told me they were retiring, moving to Greece, and the farm was mine if I wanted it."

"Wow." I pressed my palm flat to his stomach. "That was a lot of responsibility all of a sudden."

"It was." He gave me a squeeze. "But it meant something to me that they believed I could handle it."

"How many years ago was that?"

Roane seemed to stop breathing at the question, and then his voice was gruff as he replied, "Oh, it was a long time ago. You hungry?"

I blinked at the abrupt subject change. "Um, the heat kind of kills my appetite. Are you hungry?"

"I can wait if you just want to lie for a while."

"I do." I launched back into questioning him. "Do you see your parents often?"

"Every year. They usually come home around July or August for a few months, but they're traveling this year. They'll be home at Christmas instead."

Depending on how things progressed between us, I might not even get to meet Roane's parents. The thought sobered me. No, it more than sobered me. It upset me.

"Have you . . . have you talked to your mum since you got that voice mail?" His voice was gentle, like he didn't want to spook me with a question I might not want to answer.

I pressed a quick, reassuring kiss to his pec before I replied, "No. I've talked to Phil, but I haven't spoken to Mom directly. Phil says she's doing okay. I . . . just don't want things between her and me to affect my time here. I'm being selfish for once."

"It's not selfish, Evie."

"I don't want to talk about my mom," I whispered, turning to look up at him. He stared down at me with that tender expression I'd come to know and love. "Tell me about your ex-girlfriends before I expire of curiosity."

He flashed me a quick, boyish smile. "What do you want to know?"

"Who they were, what they were like, why it ended?"

Roane shook with laughter. "Not much then?"

"Stop teasing and talk."

With a melodramatic sigh, he brought the hand not tracing patterns on my skin to rest above his head, as if settling in to tell a tale. "Excluding primary school sweethearts, at high school there was one serious girlfriend. Justine Miller. She lived in Alnwick and was an absolute swot."

"What's a swot?"

"Someone that prefers school and learning to socializing. That was Justine. But she was cute and funny, and when she made time for me, I liked being around her."

"Did you lose your virginity to her?"

"Aye. She actually was the one that pushed for it. She had a thirst for knowledge about everything, including sex. We were fifteen."

"Wow." My eyes almost bugged out of my head. "That is young."

"I suppose. It didn't seem so to us. We grew up knowing about the mating rituals of animals," he chuckled. "Sex was always around us."

"I guess."

"What age were you?"

"Eighteen. Chace had been pushing for it since we were sixteen, but I wanted to wait. Still pisses me off that he's the guy who took my virginity."

"No regrets, Evie. Justine wasn't the love of my life, but she was my first time. No changing it. And I wouldn't want to. She's a piece of my story. Just like Chace is a piece of yours and without him you'd be a slightly altered version of yourself. Who wants that?"

Huh. That was true. "You're very wise." I snuggled deeper into him. "Okay, tell me more about your women."

Roane chuckled. "You speak as if there was a harem of them.

There wasn't. Justine and I broke up just before graduation. Then first year of uni, I met Saskia. She was from Kent and so gorgeous and popular, I judged her as shallow before I really knew her."

Ugh. She sounded stunning. Her name evoked an image of a tall, tan blonde with feline green eyes. Someone who could play tennis and ski and hobnob with royals.

Jealousy was an ugly creature stirring to life in my chest.

"But . . . well, she fancied me."

I bet she did.

"And she made it her mission to make me her boyfriend." There was a tenderness in his voice I didn't like. "We were different in so many ways, opposites really. But underneath the shallow socialite, there was a loyal girl with a kind heart. Which I broke." He sighed heavily. "We were together all through university. I'd stayed at her parents' place during the summer, she'd stayed at mine. But the closer we got to graduation, the more she was talking about us getting engaged and moving to London to work, and I knew that it wasn't what I wanted. I wanted to travel, aye, but I think I already knew deep in my heart that I wanted to work the farm. And Saskia wasn't made to be a farmer's wife. So, I broke up with her."

Emotion clogged my throat. When I'd asked Roane to tell me about his past relationships, I honestly hadn't thought I'd feel so possessive . . . and so ludicrously upset by what he'd had with this Saskia person.

It was silly.

She was an ex for a reason.

"She must have been devastated," I managed, my voice a little hoarse.

"She might have been but not anymore. She's engaged to a television producer in London."

"Was she it or was there anyone else?"

"The last was Chloe. We split two years ago after dating awhile. She wanted to travel, and I wanted to stay put."

It sounded like neither of the last two relationships had ended because they'd stopped loving each other.

And I had to know. I had to know how he felt about them before I let myself get in any deeper here. I lifted my head to look at him. "Did you love them? Do you still?"

Roane studied the ceiling as he replied, "When I was with them, I thought I did."

What did that mean? "But you don't think so now?"

His gaze returned to mine, and my breath caught at the raw emotion in them. His voice was gruff as he replied, "Now I know I didn't, Evie."

Nineteen

Without saying those three little words, Roane had just implied them. I was sure of that. Even more so when he rolled into me to make love to me once again.

When his phone rang just as we were snuggling in the aftermath, I insisted he answer, knowing it could be some important issue about the farm. Whoever it was on the end of the line, whatever it was they wanted from him, Roane asked them to "deal with it."

"I might as well take the rest of the day off," he said, grinning as he got out of bed. "Now." He turned to reach for my wrist. "We shower."

Showering with Roane was the perfect experience to follow an afternoon of sex. As we soaped each other up with his citrusy-smelling shower gel, we touched and petted and explored. When he spread kisses across my breasts, I confessed, "I love your beard."

I did. I loved the way it felt against my skin. There was something so appealingly masculine and rugged about it.

Roane lifted his head, his grin pleased. "Then the beard stays for however long you want it to stay."

Forever.

But I was too afraid to say that out loud.

Once we were done with the shower, we dressed and hurried downstairs to Shadow, who got up from his cool corner of the kitchen to greet us with lethargy.

"These hot days are no good for dogs, are they, baby," I crooned, scratching behind his ear with one hand while I gave him a rubdown with the other. He swiped me with his warm tongue in thanks. "You need to drink more, gorgeous."

I straightened from petting the dog to find Roane smiling at me. "What?"

"I love that you love my dog."

"He's very easy to love."

"True." He stroked a hand across Shadow's head. "Dinnertime, boy?"

His sudden wagging of the behind suggested he was up for that.

Not long after, all three of us jumped into Roane's Defender and we drove back to Alnster. After parking outside the bookstore, Roane rounded the SUV and took my hand as I let us inside. Shadow ran ahead, his claws clattering on the wooden staircase, and we could hear Caro upstairs greeting him in delight.

I squeezed Roane's hand. "Are we telling people?"

His eyes narrowed. "Considering I can't keep my hands off you, I think it'll be more than obvious. Or do you not want to tell people?"

At the slight irritation I heard in his voice, I tried not to smile and failed. "I think keeping it a secret hardly goes hand in hand with giving us a real shot."

"Agreed."

To my surprise, I didn't feel nervous about telling people. I already knew that mostly everyone wanted us to get together.

My building was almost as stuffy as the farmhouse, but as early evening hit, it grew somewhat cooler. There was a slight break in the air because Caro had opened all the windows and had the electric fan from the shop rotating in the corner of the living room.

I expected Caro to take one look at us and know.

However, she was sitting on a stool at the kitchen counter with her head buried in her laptop. "I've seen some flats and houses I'd like you to look at," she announced without lifting her head. "Some of them are pretty decent but I don't know how much I should pay in rent. I need advice."

"That's your cue," I said to Roane. "I'm going to change out of these clothes."

His eyes flashed at my words, and I sauntered down the hall to my bedroom with a smug swing in my hips. There was nothing like getting thoroughly laid to put you in a good mood.

When I returned in a fresh pair of shorts and a T-shirt, Roane was sitting on the side of the counter adjacent to Caro, looking at the laptop.

"What do you think?" Caro asked, chewing on her bottom lip.

I rounded the counter to Roane's side to see what he was looking at and, without thinking about it, slid my arm around his shoulder and rested my chin on his other. "What are we looking at?" I murmured.

He curled his fingers around my hand, absentmindedly caressing my skin with his thumb. "Two-bed flat in Alnwick." He clicked through the photos with his free hand, and I frowned at the images.

"It's a little dingy."

"That's what I think. It's overpriced."

"And Alnwick?" I frowned over at Caro. "You're not staying in Alnster?"

Her gaze moved between Roane and me, her smile widening as she said, "There's not a lot of options in Alnster, I'm afraid, and when did this happen?" She gestured to us. "Because it's happening, right? You haven't progressed to torturing my cousin?"

Laughing, I slid into the stool next to Roane. "Do you think I'm that evil?"

"Yes," they answered in unison.

I made a face at Roane and he winked at me.

God, he was sexy.

And yes, I'd always thought so, but over the last couple of months this man's appeal had grown exponentially. It was true what they said. When you started to care for someone, they became infinitely more attractive to you.

"So you're together?"

"Yes, we're together," I replied.

Caro's whole face lit up. "Oh, I'm so pleased for you. This is wonderful news. We should go out to celebrate. And to let everyone know so you can get that part over with."

"Over with?"

"You know they'll tease you mercilessly for a while."

True. "Yeah, sure, why not."

"Don't sound so thrilled about it," Roane said drily.

"Are you thrilled about the teasing coming our way?"

"I can't answer that how I really want to answer it, because my wee cousin is sitting right there, but they can tease all they want. It's worth it."

"I'd hate to think how you'd put it if I wasn't here," Caro grumbled, her cheeks flushing as she hopped off the stool. "Why don't I make us some dinner while you look at those other listings for me?"

Thanking her, I pulled my stool closer to Roane so I could look at the apartments and rested my hand on his knee. I couldn't seem to be near him without wanting to touch him. He turned to look at me, and when our eyes met, I could tell by his expression he understood. His hand covered mine, and we returned to looking at the apartments.

"I like this one," I murmured ten minutes later.

All I'd seen so far just wasn't good enough for Caro, and I realized how spoiled we were by the apartment above the bookstore. Not just by its size and views but by its open-plan living space.

Finally, however, we'd come across a house in Beadnell. Roane and I had taken Shadow to Beadnell Bay a few times. It was this long stretch of beautiful sand twenty minutes north of Alnster. A lot of surfers and kitesurfers hung out at the bay.

The house was set back from the beach surrounded by a small development of matching homes. This one sat at the western tip, so it had views of the sea. It had been designed so that the living spaces were transposed. The two bedrooms were on the first floor, along with the bathroom. Upstairs on the second floor was the open-plan kitchen and living space with its vaulted triangular roof. French doors made up the entirety of the sea-facing wall and led out onto a covered balcony so the owner could enjoy the views.

The place was furnished in a beachy look with a comfortable sofa and armchairs, a light oak six-seater dining table, and a modern white glossy kitchen.

"They're holiday homes," Roane said. "We do the maintenance on a few of these. It's unusual to see one of them come up as a year-round rental."

"The living space is beautiful, and that view . . ."

He squeezed my hand. "Aye, that's true. But I'm not sure about the security. Caro's bedroom would be right next to the only way in and out of the building."

"Which is great in the awful event of a fire."

"Not so great if someone breaks in." He scowled at the laptop.

"Is he pooh-poohing the Beadnell property?" Caro asked from her place by the stove.

I shot her a commiserating look. "Yup."

"Damn," she muttered.

Seeing her crestfallen expression, I nudged Roane with my shoulder. "Surely we can make certain it's safe for her."

He exhaled slowly. "It's not just safety. I don't know what kind of heating system is in these homes. They're rented out less frequently in the winter months, and part of that is not just down to demand. It's about high running costs."

I frowned at the screen. "It says they were built less than five years ago. Surely they're built with better insulation than the building we're in right now."

"Maybe," he murmured.

Realizing what the problem was, I cuddled into him. "She has to move out on her own at some point."

Roane nodded slowly. "Aye, I know. Doesn't mean I'm happy about her living alone."

"I've lived alone for years. She'll be fine."

He heaved a sigh and looked over at Caro, who was pretending not to listen. "If you like the Beadnell house, you should make an appointment to view it. But I'd like to be there."

"I'd like you to be there too." Her eyes flicked to me. "Both of you."

Warmed from her inclusion, I smiled. "I'd be happy to."

As we sat down to eat at the dining table that night, Shadow lying beneath an open window, we dug in to the delicious satay sweet potato curry Caro had thrown together, and I felt a contentment I couldn't remember ever feeling.

It scared the crap out of me.

Not because I was afraid of it.

But because it meant there was a very, very difficult decision looming ahead of me.

$\mathcal{N}$o one at The Anchor noticed that Roane and I walked in holding hands. Milly and Viola were run off their feet behind the bar, and the locals hadn't spotted anything unusual as we stood with Shadow at our side. The tables by the fire in the dog-friendly area of the pub were occupied. Thankfully we waited only a few minutes before the two occupants of the smaller table departed. We grabbed it and borrowed an unused seat from another table for Caro.

It was cool. Roane and I were happy to be smooshed up together.

Still, for Caro's sake, I tried not to be too touchy-feely with her cousin. No one enjoyed feeling like a third wheel. It was just after Roane bought us a first round of drinks that the bar started to quiet down a little. We grabbed the larger table when it emptied, and Viola was soon able to join us.

While she and Caro began chatting about the house Caro was interested in renting, Roane leaned in to whisper in my ear, "When can we leave?"

I shivered at the feel of his lips brushing my skin and turned to smile. "Why?"

Except I knew why as soon as I saw his expression.

This time I shivered with a deeper longing. "Oh." My eyes rounded. "Again?"

His teeth flashed. "I'm sore from wanting you all the time, angel."

I moved closer to him, my lips almost touching his as I murmured, "An angel you'll corrupt by turning me into a sex addict."

Roane's reply was low and gruff. "That doesn't sound like a bad thing to me." He brushed his mouth against mine and I leaned in to deepen it.

"What. The. Fuck?"

The high-pitched question halted us, and we drew apart, amusement dancing in our eyes before we turned to Viola. She was half grinning, half gaping.

"No way!" She gestured excitedly to us. "You're together?"

I giggled at her exuberant response. "Yeah, we're together."

Viola turned toward the bar. "Mam!" she yelled, drawing every eye in the place, including her mother's.

"Jesus Christ, what is it, lass?" Milly lifted the bar to exit it, her eyes wide with concern.

"Roane and Evie are together! Together together!"

A rumble of response slowly built among the locals until we started to hear, "Well, who wins the pot then?"

"Is it Dex?"

"It's not Dex." Milly shook her head. "It might be Jed."

"Who's got the list?"

"It's on Vi's phone. Where's your phone, lass?"

"What the hell are you talking about?" I cut in.

Viola grinned mischievously. "I started a pot for everyone to guess how long it would take for you and Roane to get together. There's nearly a thousand quid up for grabs."

Full of disbelief, I turned to Roane, but he was struggling to contain his laughter.

"You're okay about them betting on us?"

His answering grin turned into a chuckle. "Evie . . . they were betting on the eventuality of you in my bed. I can't be mad about that kind of support."

I smacked his arm as those in our vicinity laughed. "You're lucky I liked what you did there, Roane Robson."

That caused a round of wolf whistles and that adorable flush across the crests of Roane's cheeks. It wasn't embarrassment that caused it, I knew. I knew it in the dark look of want he sent my way. The flush was arousal.

It felt heady, I discovered, to be so openly lusted after by a man you wanted desperately in return.

Unfortunately, there was no way I was having sex with Roane while Caro slept in the bedroom down the hall. I whispered this in his ear, and he immediately buried his head in my throat with a groan.

I laughed, trying to ignore the feel of his lips and beard against my skin, and failing. When he lifted his head, I kissed him. Roane clasped my face in his hand and deepened the kiss as another round of wolf whistles met our ears.

I broke the kiss with a chuckle and shook my head. "Please tell me that will stop once they get used to us?"

Roane grinned. "It's hard to say with these people. This could happen every time they see us until the day we die."

Although I laughed, as I turned to Viola to answer her question of "when did this happen?" inside I was thinking, *Until the day we die?*

Had Roane just implied *forever*?

First those three little words were implied and now "forever"?

I tried not to get too excited about it and failed.

"I'm so happy for you, Evie, but I have to admit I'm jealous too." Viola gave me a sheepish smile. "I'd love a little romance in my life."

"Well, look no further than the Romeo across the street," I replied quietly so no one else but our table would hear.

Roane groaned. "Ah, angel, you just can't help yourself."

I really couldn't. I shot him an unrepentant smile and turned back to Viola.

Viola's eyes narrowed. "What are you talking about?"

"Across the street," I repeated. "A certain someone who uses antagonism to cover how he really feels."

"Oh, fuck," Roane muttered.

Viola's frown cleared and turned to something between confusion and, dare I say, hope. In fact, it was a very similar look to the one on Lucas's face this morning. "You *cannot* be serious. Did he say something to you?"

"He didn't need to."

She scowled. "What does that mean?"

"It was written all over his face. And he's way too interested in you. When a guy is indifferent, you know he's not interested. When a guy goes out of his way to bother you, he's interested." I raised an eyebrow at Roane. "Am I wrong?"

He glowered at me, his answer gruff. "No."

I tried not to be too smug. "See."

Rolling her eyes, Viola pushed her chair back and stood. "That's hardly evidence, Evie. Come on, Caro. I've got my laptop upstairs. You can show me the house you're going to look at."

As soon as the girls had left, Roane leaned into me. "You're right. She likes him."

"Told you."

"Don't push this." He curled his hand around my arm, his expression serious. "Just because she likes him doesn't mean something should happen between them. There's too much history there. I don't want Viola hurt."

His protectiveness was something I adored about him. I kissed the tip of his nose and promised, "I won't push it. I'm not going to do anything more. I was just . . . planting a seed."

"Well, let's hope that seed doesn't take root under two houses and cause the earth to shift beneath them."

I grinned. "Very Shakespearean. I think you're a poet who doesn't know it."

Gentle amusement lit his dark eyes, but he said, "I'm serious, Evie."

"Yes. And I hear you. But you're also very sexy, so why don't we stop talking about this and hurry back to the bookstore for a quickie before Caro comes home?"

Roane's chair screeched across the floor before I'd even finished the sentence, and as he hurried out of the pub, my hand in his, shouts of good-natured but mortifying encouragement followed us.

Normally I'd be disconcerted that an entire pub full of people knew I was about to commence having hot sex with my boyfriend.

My boyfriend.

However, due to the aforementioned boyfriend, I was too happy to care about anything but him.

Twenty

Although I had encouraged Caro's venturing out to rent her own place, I missed her when she left. It didn't help that her departure happened so abruptly. We all took time out of work the next day to see the house in Beadnell, and Caro and I fell in love with the place as soon as we walked in.

The kitchen was big enough for her to bake from home, and the views were spectacular.

After Roane asked a bunch of questions about utility bills, council tax, heating costs, maintenance charges, and all the boring but necessary stuff, he gave Caro his blessing.

As long as he got to install a security system.

She agreed.

Two days later she'd moved into her new home. Furthermore, Caro had talked with Tony, and although she didn't want to work for him, they came to an agreement that he could sell a selection of her baked goods two days a week at his bakery, but it would cost him. This snowballed into Caro having business cards designed and asking Roane to hand them out to local businesspeople, some of whom had already tasted Caro's baking over the years. She got bookings within a day.

She'd started to see a therapist, and I could see the positive affects her sessions were having on her. Every day she seemed to grow more confident in her choices. This was helped by the news from Roane that Helena hadn't exactly been destitute—just greedy and spiteful. Caro seemed to relax knowing that she hadn't left Helena in desperate straits. Roane made it clear that Helena wouldn't be coming after Caro for money or to cause her upset. She was too afraid Roane would make good on his promise.

By the end of the first week Roane and I had spent as a couple, Caro was transformed. I'd barely seen her because she was rushed off her feet. I was proud of her, but I was also worried she was trying to do too much too soon to get her business off the ground. Still, I wasn't her mom. She had to be free to do things her way.

Also, I was a little preoccupied myself.

Being in a relationship with a sexy farmer was somewhat challenging time-wise. Roane was a busy guy. He tried to pop into the store at lunchtime every day to see me, and then he and Shadow would appear at my apartment for a late dinner. Sometimes we'd go to the pub, but mostly we stayed in bed. The guy was used to running on less than five hours of sleep but, considering he reached for me in the early hours of the morning every night, pulling me out of sleep to either ravage me or make love to me, it was a miracle he wasn't a zombie at work. He awoke before sunrise, which was around four forty-five a.m. in these parts during the summer. Sometimes I woke up and felt his kiss goodbye and sometimes I didn't, sleeping right through until my alarm went off a few hours later.

There were days I found myself drifting off in the armchair of the bookstore, marveling over Roane's boundless energy. And stamina.

Oh yes, that man had stamina.

Moreover, he was so considerate. Sometimes he'd get phone calls in the evening about work, and he always went downstairs to the bookstore to take them "so he wouldn't disturb me" if I was watching TV or reading a book. I insisted he didn't have to do that, but Roane was always thinking about my needs and wants.

Inside and outside the bedroom.

I was falling for him.

Which was why I'd felt it prudent to call Greer to update her.

Just in case . . . well, just in case I made a decision that would affect how much we saw each other in the future.

It was around eight o'clock in the morning in Chicago when I decided to call. I'd turned the sign on the store door to CLOSED and ventured into the storeroom to multitask. Stock had come in that morning. Cracking open the boxes, I dialed Greer as I sorted through the new books.

She'd listened quietly as I explained what was happening between my farmer and me.

Then said nothing when I drew to a close.

"Greer?"

"What do you want me to say?"

A flicker of annoyance flashed over me, but I kept it out of my voice. "That you're pissed at the implications but, ultimately, happy for me."

"Pissed at the implications? So, you're seriously considering moving to England for a guy you've only known for a few months? A guy you've only been dating a week."

That flicker was suddenly a flame. "Don't make it sound like that. You know it's more complicated than that. And you know me. I don't throw myself into relationships willy-nilly." I scowled ferociously. "What happened to being supportive of this?"

"I don't want to lose my best friend to England, I've said that from the start. But I could get over that if living there made you truly happy. However, I'm worried about you. I'm worried about your heart. You've fallen for some guy you don't even know!"

I could feel my cheeks burning hot with indignation. "I do know him!" I yelled back, momentarily forgetting she was pregnant. "I know him! And he knows me. Better than anyone knows me."

"Ouch."

I winced, softening my tone. "I'm sorry . . . but it's the truth. There are just some things even best friends can't know about you. But Roane gets me and I get him. I didn't come here expecting to find that, Greer, but you should be happy for me. I'm not saying I'm staying in England. But I'm not saying that I'm not either. That's why I called. To prepare you . . . in case . . ."

"You're in love with him," she whispered.

I hesitated a second; the way I felt about Roane seemed too big sometimes. When I thought about it too much, those emotions seemed to fill up my chest, making it hard to breathe. "Yeah I am."

"Evie." She breathed my name. "I wish I could be there. I wish I could meet him so it would make me feel better about all this . . . but I know it's not about me. I just . . . what if you don't come home and you miss . . . I know I'm being selfish."

"If I decide to stay, and there is a huge possibility I might," I answered honestly, "I will fly to Chicago to see you, and then when the baby comes, I'll find a way to fly over again."

"To Chicago. You said 'fly to Chicago' not 'fly home.' That means you're already thinking of England as your home."

"Well, the truth is, if I decide to stay, it wouldn't just be because of Roane, although he's a massive part of the decision-making process. I'm happy here, Greer. I'm not trying to hurt you, and nobody will ever take your place in my heart . . . I'm just being honest. I haven't felt this content in a long time. And I felt that way before Roane and I got together. It's just now . . . I'm no longer just content. I'm blissfully fucking happy with him. I've never felt this way about anyone."

I heard my friend sniffle. "I want that for you. I do. I'll get over myself. I promise."

"You don't have to. You think it'll be easy for me to stay here and not see you every week?"

"It better not be."

I laughed at her petulance, but the laugh broke on a sob that took me by surprise. "I'm not making any decisions just yet. Okay."

Greer sighed. "Evie, I know this isn't easy for you. I can hear that. I'm sorry for making it harder. Don't . . . don't think about anything but what you need. You've put so many people before yourself in the past. This is about what you want. Remember that. And forget my earlier selfishness. Blame my grumpiness on the hormones. Speaking of the baby . . . it's pressing on my bladder and I really need to pee."

"Okay." I felt despondent as we said goodbye.

The reality of the choice looming ahead of me was starting to set in. My eyes stung with tears as I wandered out of the storeroom and into the shop. I came to an abrupt halt to find Roane standing in the middle of the room.

He wore an intense expression on his face. "The door was open."

Oh my God, how much of that conversation had he heard?

"Oh?"

"I didn't mean to eavesdrop."

Shit. "How much did you hear?"

"Not all but enough." With that, he crossed the distance between us, clasped my face in his hands, and pressed his mouth over mine. I clung to him, moaning as his tongue licked against mine, the kiss greedy and deep. When we finally stopped for air, he pressed his forehead to mine and whispered hoarsely, "I'm blissfully fucking happy too, and I've never felt this way about anyone either. Just so you know."

The emotion I felt before I'd seen him welled up inside me, my eyes burning as I determinedly fought back tears. Roane saw the glitter of them and lifted his head to meet my gaze. "That doesn't come with pressure, Evie. I don't want to make this any harder for you."

"I know." I melted against him, pressing my cheek to his chest, and reveling in the feel of his strong arms wrapped around me.

Holding me tight.

No pressure, I thought. He didn't need to put pressure on me to get what he wanted.

Our wants were in sync, as most everything between us was.

And deep down, I was already thinking about applications and visas, and how the next time I flew back to Chicago, my stay would not be a permanent one.

*T*he sun set a little later in this part of the world in July than it did in Chicago. Roane told me that the farther north you traveled into Scotland, the longer the days were. I'd crossed the border into Berwick, so I was happy to say I'd visited Scotland, but I wanted to go to the Highlands so bad and was already planning a romantic getaway in my head.

Not that I needed the Highlands as I walked along Beadnell Bay, enjoying one of the most stunning sunsets I'd ever seen. The water appeared dark purple from shore, slowly turning lighter until it was a shimmering pink and then growing darker again toward the horizon. The sky above the horizon was gold edged in orange. But the clouds in the sky were dark pink, shadowed in purple.

Waves lapped gently at the shore, a lulling rhythm that suffused me with peace as I walked barefoot on the sand, my shoes in one hand, Roane's hand in my other.

Shadow trotted ahead, his nose to the sand, enjoying all the scents he could find there.

We'd spent the evening with Caro after she'd invited us for dinner, and decided to take a walk on the beach before heading back to Alnster. The farther we walked, the fewer people we saw, although there were several dog owners still out on the sand.

Roane and I had been walking in contented silence when he suddenly commented, "You said you've never been in love."

A fluttering occurred in my chest. I had said that.

It wasn't true anymore, and the words had been on the tip of my tongue for days. But Roane hadn't said them yet and I didn't want to push too hard too fast.

"I did say that."

"I find it hard to believe."

"Well, don't." I shot him an unhappy look. "Before I came here, I was exhausted by dating in Chicago, and that was after a two-year break."

"A two-year break?"

"From the age of fifteen to the age of thirty-one, I dated. Sixteen years of dating. Three serious relationships among them. There was Chace, and you know all about him. Then there was Brent, who was five years younger. A funny guy but we only lasted five months because everything was a joke to him. He lost his job while we were together and started living off money from his parents, who didn't have a lot to spare. He didn't know how to care for himself, expected me to do everything, and threw a tantrum when he didn't get his way. A year after that there was Devon. We dated for fourteen months until . . ." I winced, still mortified by the consequences of dating Devon.

"Until?"

"Ugh, let me preface by telling you I have regular health checks and I'm good."

Roane frowned in confusion for a second before it cleared and turned into a scowl. "The fucker gave you something?"

"Chlamydia. And the cherry on top of that cake . . . I went to confront him after my doctor's appointment. He was a free-lance web designer. Expecting me to be at work, he had what I'd soon discover was one of many women on the side over at the apartment. I walked in on him with his head between her legs."

"Fuck, angel." Roane let go of my hand to wrap his arm around my shoulders and pull me into his side. He kissed my temple as I curled my arm around his waist. "You deserve so much better than that shit."

"Well, in between those three relationships there was a lot of first and second dates, a few third dates, and not much else beyond that. When I hit thirty, most of my friends were in love, married, and some were even popping out kids. I was exhausted and I took a break for a couple of years until Greer convinced me to get back on the horse. That led to Aaron, the online guy, and my renewed sense of 'this might not happen for me.'" I squeezed his waist. "Then I came here."

His hold on me tightened as we strolled, and as I thought about my dating life over the years, I realized that I'd never actually believed I'd meet the love of my life. Deep down, I thought it was a fairy tale that other people got to live.

It made me breathless to realize I'd been wrong.

I found him.

I found my one.

As I sighed happily, my gaze wandered across the water and the beach ahead, and I thought how lucky I was that I found my person in beautiful England.

As my eyes caressed the water and followed the gentle ripples back to shore, I saw two figures ahead of us.

Something about them caught my attention.

Perhaps it was the way the tall male figure was looming over the small feminine one . . . or perhaps it was because there was something familiar about them. As we drew closer, the woman gestured dramatically with her hands, and the guy bent his head to her, his lips almost brushing hers as he responded.

"Evie, I need to tell—"

"Is that Viola?" I cut Roane off, squinting at the couple. Realization dawned. "And Lucas?"

"What?" Roane snapped his head forward and narrowed his gaze. He tensed against me. "Aye, it is."

"Maybe we should stop." The words had barely left my mouth when Viola began striding away from Lucas toward us. Lucas watched her go, but I couldn't see his expression clearly from this far away.

Viola, however, didn't react to the sight of us. Her features were tight with pain, and suddenly I felt like an ass for pushing those two together. She drew to a halt in front of us. Without preamble she said, "I didn't bring my car. Can I get a lift from you?"

"Of course," Roane replied. "You okay?"

"Can we not talk about it? Ever."

We nodded solemnly and turned around to walk back the way we came. The walk was silent and tense, the atmosphere staying that way until we parked at the bookstore and watched Viola walk up toward the pub.

I turned to Roane, contrite. "Maybe I fucked up."

He shook his head. "Like you said, you planted a seed, nothing more. It wouldn't have grown if you hadn't been right about how they feel about each other. And obviously there is something between them. We just need to let them sort it out amongst themselves."

Lying in bed that night, I worried about Viola. I worried Lucas had rejected her and I'd opened the door for that to happen to her.

There was a big part of me that wanted to meddle, to fix the problem, since I felt responsible. But, ultimately, I knew I had to take Roane's advice and stay out of it.

However, that didn't mean I had to stay out of every long-standing issue that plagued the village.

Twenty-One

*B*y the last week in July, the countdown was on.

Five more weeks. That's how long I had left before I was supposed to return to the States. Since that phone call with Greer, Roane and I hadn't talked about the future. It was easier just to immerse ourselves in one another and be *blissfully fucking happy*. Despite my suspicions that Roane was in love with me, I still felt a niggle of insecurity and wasn't ready to make a huge life decision about staying in England until I was one hundred percent certain that he loved me.

By one hundred percent sure, I meant until he *told* me he loved me.

Besides, I still wasn't sure I could leave Greer behind . . . or my mom. I didn't know what to do about my mother, and I didn't like thinking about it because it hurt so damn much.

It was a gray day in Alnster, but I was already used to the temperamental weather and kind of glad for it. Summer in Chicago was hot and humid all the time, but moody British weather meant I got a break from the warm climate when I least expected it.

I was sitting behind the counter of the bookstore, working on a manuscript for one of my clients. As much as I'd wanted my freelance editing work to take off, running the bookstore full-time put a kink in those plans. I was pretty much on the same schedule with my editing as I had been in Chicago.

A few tourists had come into the store over the course of the morning, but it was a quiet afternoon, allowing me time to work. Yet I knew when Maggie Foster stepped into the store that my attention was about to be pulled elsewhere. For weeks I'd wanted to talk to Maggie about her daughter, but I just didn't know how to stick my nose into business that was so personal.

Probably because my nose didn't belong there.

At all.

"Maggie." I clicked save on the manuscript and closed my laptop. "How can I help?"

She smiled as she approached the counter. Maggie was a small woman, so I assumed Annie got her height from her father's side. She had the same lovely "are they green, blue, or gray?" eyes as Annie, although hers were slightly dulled with a perpetual hint of sadness.

"Good afternoon, Evie. I'm here to order a book, if possible. My favorite author only releases one book a year and I always ordered it from Penny."

"Of course." I turned to the store's laptop and pulled up the distribution database. "What's the name and title?"

She told me and I found the book and processed the order.

"Shall I just pay when it comes in?"

"Yeah." I looked up from the screen. "I haven't heard of her. What kind of books does she write?"

Maggie smiled. "Mystery. She's like a modern Agatha Christie."

"Cool. Are you a big reader?"

"The gallery can get quiet, so it's nice to have a book under the counter." She gestured around the room. "You have your pick of them."

"I do. I'm kind of living my dream right now."

"You love books like I love art." She leaned against the counter. "Where does it come from, Evie? That passion?"

No one had asked me that. Not even Roane. The answer was a deep pang in my chest. "I . . . uh . . . my dad died when I was eight . . ."

Maggie's face fell. "Oh, I'm so sorry."

"Thank you. It was difficult and, um, my mom fell apart, and books were my solace. My escape." Suddenly realizing the correlation between my relationship with my mother and Annie's, I wondered how much I should reveal. Not a lot of people knew about my relationship with my mother, but Maggie and my mom had something in common. They'd both let down their daughters in a big way. But they also weren't bad people. Not at all.

"My mom's a recovering alcoholic. In and out of rehab for most of my life. She's not a bad person," I hurried to explain. "The very opposite, in fact. But she's disappointed and hurt me a lot over the years."

Tears shimmered in Maggie's eyes as she pressed away from the counter, and I knew those tears weren't for me. They were for her and Annie.

"Despite all that she's done to me, how many times she's broken my heart, I can't stop loving her." It was the truth. I loved my mom. I always would. "But this time it's been harder for me to forgive her. I didn't think I even would but she . . . she left me a voice mail that surprised me. And I think . . . I mean, I know, that I do forgive her. I think I'll always forgive her." My eyes stung as I watched a tear roll down Maggie's cheek. "She's my mom, you know." I walked around the counter and took hold of Maggie's hand. "You're her mom, Maggie."

Her eyes widened and her mouth trembled. "But . . . but it's different. I turned my back on her. How could she ever forgive me for that?"

"Did you turn your back on her because you stopped loving her?"

"No!" She wrenched her hand from mine and crossed her arms over her waist, huddling into herself. "No," she whispered. "I . . . I let him make the choice for me."

"Your husband."

Maggie nodded. "I know no one should speak badly of the unwell, but my husband . . . it wasn't a happy marriage. He's very ill now. I have a full-time care worker who looks after him and he's unable to communicate because of the stroke . . . and the sad thing is, it's the most free I've ever felt since I was girl." Her eyes rounded with horror. "I shouldn't have—"

"Shush." I gripped her elbows. "No judgment here. Nothing you say to me will ever leave this room."

She swallowed hard. "I've wanted to make amends with Annie for years, but I was afraid of him, and then when he got ill, I realized I was more afraid that Annie wouldn't forgive me."

I contemplated Maggie's situation for a moment, trying to organize my thoughts. Finally, I said, "I assume Annie is well aware of the state of your marriage?"

"Aye. Before she came out to us, when she was still a part of our lives, she defended me a lot to him. I need her forgiveness for that too. She was my protector when I was never hers."

"But understanding what you were dealing with, perhaps Annie will be more willing to forgive you than you expect. It's your silence that hurts. I can't tell you if Annie will forgive you, but I can tell you that if you don't try and ask her for that forgiveness, she *can't* give it to you. Be brave and at least you'll know, one way or the other. Don't let yourself regret not doing anything." I squeezed her arms.

Maggie sighed wearily and gave me a sad but affectionate smile. "You're a sweet, sweet girl. But I just don't know if I have that in me." She pulled away and left the shop before I could reply.

I stared after her, slightly shocked she'd confided in me. Neither of us had expected such an intense moment in our short encounter. I felt melancholy for Maggie and Annie, and I really hoped Maggie found the strength to do what was right.

Yet I also felt a weight lifting off my shoulders.

When I returned to the States, the first thing I would do was meet with my mom and tell her that although she'd hurt me over the years, I knew she was a good person, that I would always love her, and I would always forgive her.

She was my mom.

Although I kept to my promise and didn't tell anyone about the words Maggie and I exchanged, I did tell Roane that she'd confided in me. He, unlike me, was unsurprised.

"How does it not surprise you? The woman opened up to me: a passing acquaintance. I mean, I told her a little about Mom, but I hadn't expected the reaction I got," I'd said as I relayed the encounter to him hours later.

"People sense your kindness and they trust you for it, Evie. They tell you things." He'd cuddled me close on the sofa. "And I'm glad you feel better about your mum."

"Thanks." I snuggled deeper into him. "There's a lot to forgive, though."

"She can't help her addiction," he reminded me gently.

"True. But it's how it made her act. Selfish and deceitful. I can't abide liars because of her. She used to hide her drinking from me and lie about it. She even stole money out of my wallet to buy gin and lied about that too. And then there was how she missed important moments in my life because she was passed out on a bathroom floor somewhere." I'd sighed, frustrated with myself for getting upset all over again. "I have to let it go. I'm starting fresh with her. It's a risk I'm willing to take again."

Roane had been extremely quiet after that, and I realized as we went to bed that I'd spoken of returning to Chicago to have the conversation with my mother. However, I hadn't specified whether the trip would be one-way or not.

I wondered if it concerned him.

While it was on my mind to discuss it with him, somehow life just got in the way over the next few days. We were both busy with work; moreover, I'd offered to help Caro with the cupcakes she was baking for a birthday event she'd booked. I'd closed the bookstore to help her in the kitchen as much as I could.

To celebrate her getting the job done and me aiding her, the three of us ventured to The Anchor a few nights after my conversation with Roane about my mom. However, as soon as we walked inside the pub, we drew to a startled halt. It was the busiest I'd ever seen the place. Milly was red-faced behind the bar.

Alone.

Where was Viola?

I turned to Roane. "I'm going to help Milly."

He gave me an affectionate smile followed by a quick kiss to the lips. My mouth tingling with his sweet touch, I strode to the bar and lifted the top to get behind it.

Milly shot me a startled look.

"I used to bartend after college," I explained. "Who's next?"

She almost sagged with relief. "Thanks, pet." She gestured to the opposite end of the bar. "Start down that end."

Time passed quickly as I poured pints and mixed drinks for the seemingly never-ending line of customers. I didn't know how long we'd been working when Milly called from the other end of the bar, "Evie, can you go down to the cellar and get another bottle of Macallan? I'm pouring the last of it now."

I nodded. Weeks ago, Dex had given us a tour of the pub's cellar, where they kept their stock, to show us their personal wine collection. He'd let us select a bottle, and we'd drunk to my staying another three months in Alnster. Hurrying out from behind the bar, I pushed through the door marked STAFF ONLY that led into a large hall. That hall branched off to the stairs that led up to their family apartments, stairs that led down to the cellar, and a door that led to the kitchen.

I'd taken the first flight of stairs down to the cellar, when I heard the murmur of voices. The sounds from the bar area made it hard to hear, but I was pretty sure there was someone down there. Thinking it was probably Dex, I kept walking until I could hear the two voices clearly.

I abruptly stopped, tense as a rabbit in the headlights of a car.

"Do you think I'd be this fucking persistent for just anyone, Vi?" I heard Lucas snap, his voice carrying up to me on the echo of the bare concrete walls.

Holy crap.

"Oh, so I should feel special because the great Lucas Elliot deigns to pursue me?" Viola replied, hurt apparent in her cutting response.

Lucas must have heard it too, because his tone softened. "You know that's not what I meant. I just . . . I can't let this go. I don't think you can either."

Holy double crap.

I pressed a hand to my chest, my heart beating hard for Viola.

"I told you that night on the beach that we can't." Viola sounded so sad. "You were right to push me away all those years ago because of your dad. I don't want to cause problems between you and your family. I don't want to be the person that causes such a rift."

"Aye, you say that, but then every time I touch you, kiss you"— his voice deepened to a masculine huskiness that made my eyes widen—"you light up like a fucking fire. Are we just supposed to ignore that?"

"Maybe it's just lust."

"You think this is just lust? Goddamn it, Viola, if I wanted *just* sex, I could get it anytime."

She snorted in derision. "Aye, I'm aware of that, Lucas. I am *very* aware of that. You're practically legendary at uni. And I'm to believe I'm not just another shag for you."

"You don't believe that. You're just saying that to piss me off."

"Well, you do fuck other girls to piss me off."

"I haven't touched another girl since I realized you feel about me how I feel about you."

"But we can't be together!"

"Do you want me to go? Do you want to see me with someone else . . . because I can't bear the thought of seeing you with another guy. I'd kill him."

"You don't mean that. You can't mean that. *We* can't. We can't." Her voice broke. "I'm sorry."

"The choice about my family should be mine, Vi, not yours. It's bullshit. It's a lie. You're lying . . . you're tearing my fucking heart out, and I think that's what you meant to do all along. You finally got one up on Lucas Elliot."

Just before I heard the slam of the basement door, I heard Viola cry, "Lucas, no!"

Then the door slammed again as Viola chased after him.

I sagged against the wall, wrung out by the angst I'd overheard.

What the hell? How had these two become worse off than they were before my little seed of encouragement?

Twenty-Two

Sundays had become precious to Roane and me. For most people in the village it was a day off work, the day they visited church to worship, and an afternoon they gathered at one another's homes for roast dinner, but agnostic Roane and I loved it for a different reason. It was the only day in the entire week when we could spend every minute together. The man's body clock forced him to wake early every morning, even though we'd both agreed that we wouldn't work that day. My own body clock seemed to have synced to his, and when I felt him stir, I rolled into him and kissed him awake so he wouldn't get out of bed.

Although he rarely slept, he'd stay with me for a few hours, holding me, touching me, sometimes wringing me dry with multiple orgasms before the day had even begun. Then he'd leave me sated in bed while he showered, and I'd force myself into the shower while he made us breakfast.

One Sunday, following a traditional English breakfast, which made it hard to move for at least half an hour afterward, Roane finally drove me to Alnwick Castle & Gardens. It wasn't something we could do without planning ahead because dogs weren't allowed. Caro agreed to watch Shadow all day so Roane could play my personal tour guide.

The gardens were extraordinary. And by extraordinary I meant epic. We took our time, meandering through the twelve-acre estate. There was a beautiful cherry orchard and amazing tiered fountains called the Grand Cascade. We saw kids playing in little diggers and passed large wrought-iron gates with skulls and crossbones on them. Signs on the gates read THESE PLANTS CAN KILL.

"The Poison Garden," Roane explained. "There's around a hundred toxic plants in there. You need to book the guided tour to get inside."

"Next time," I said, morbidly intrigued. "And maybe we can eat at the Treehouse Restaurant then too." The restaurant was exactly what it said on the sign. It was the world's largest tree house restaurant. I absolutely needed to dine inside a tree house at least once in my life.

We ended up walking around the gardens for a couple of hours, my nose filled with the heady scent of roses, which seemed to permeate the entire grounds. Then finally we approached the castle, and Roane led me into the part of the grounds where they filmed Harry Potter.

"Oh my God, this is where they filmed the first flying lesson scene." I gaped, turning around to take in the massive walled courtyard.

Roane grinned. "Well, I couldn't say whether it was or not."

I pointed to him but was still staring at the castle grounds in awe. "One day you'll be Potter mad like me, my friend."

"I doubt that."

Ignoring his muttered comment, I hurried over to an older couple and asked them if they'd take a photo of Roane and me. They obliged and with giddy excitement I pulled Roane over to where I wanted him

"You're so adorable." He pulled me into him and stole a lingering kiss.

When I got my phone back from the woman who'd taken it for us, I discovered she'd snapped a few and one included the kiss. It was a great photo. "Look." I nudged Roane to show him, and his lips curled at the corners as he looked at it. "I love it. I'm posting it to the 'gram."

Roane was not on social media. He was far too busy and indifferent to public opinion for social media. However, he was so laidback he didn't protest about the fact that he'd become the hero of my Instagram profile. My friends back in the States pestered me with questions about him every time I posted a photo, but I never answered because I didn't know how to explain our relationship. The only answer I could give was that he was the most wonderful man in the world and he was mine, but I'd prefer to say that to him first before announcing it on social media.

Posting the photo of us kissing along with a tagline explaining where we were, I had to admit to feeling a petty thrill. Some of those curious Instagram friends were the ones who'd looked on me with pity when I announced I was taking a break from dating at my thirty-first birthday. Some of them even shared smug "thank God it isn't me" looks, thinking I didn't see them. And nearly all of them asked me about my dating life before they asked me about anything else.

I wasn't above a little smugness myself.

Poor Evie, living in beautiful England, having epic sex with a hot Englishman.

"What's that look?" Roane asked as we strolled into the castle.

"This is my 'my boyfriend is better than yours' look, and I'm not ashamed of bragging." I wrinkled my nose. "Okay, I'm a little ashamed, but what can I say, I'm not perfect."

He gave me a confused smile and squeezed my hand. "What are you talking about?"

As we walked into a massive dining hall that made my lips part in awe, I absentmindedly explained.

Not surprisingly Roane was pleased. So pleased, he gave me hot eyes. He couldn't give me hot eyes in a castle filled with tourists! I shot him a quelling look. "Tell me about the castle," I said, hoping to distract him.

He smirked but began to talk as we walked through the opulent rooms. "It's owned by the Duke and Duchess of Northumberland. They're one of the oldest families in England, and this has been their castle since the end of the eleventh century."

"Holy crap," I murmured. "Imagine living with all that history. Knowing exactly who you are and where you come from dating back to nearly a thousand years."

Roane nodded. "Aye, and it being what it is. Northumberland is considered one of the grandest and richest dukedoms, and although the castle is their official seat, they have three other estates across Britain. Moreover, Alnwick Castle is the second-largest inhabited castle next to Windsor."

"Windsor Castle, as in the queen's Windsor Castle?"

"Aye. Now"—Roane glanced at his watch—"we just have time before it closes, so let's hurry."

"What? The castle?"

"No. One of the State Rooms. They're only open to the public for a certain length of time because the family uses them."

"That's so cool," I murmured, hurrying to keep up with him as he maneuvered us through the castle, clearly knowing it like the back of his hand. Then he walked through a doorway, and my breath caught as I followed him in.

A library.

A magnificent, beautifully furnished library with a walking gallery above us.

"I thought you'd like this."

My gaze moved from the rows and rows of leather-bound books to Roane. Love filled me to bursting, until it was a pain in my chest. "I like *you*," I whispered.

I love you.

The words were on the tip of my tongue, but Roane took my hand and pulled me into the room to show me more, and just like that, the fleeting bravery I'd felt disappeared.

Well, that was great," I said, cuddling into Roane's side as we strolled through the grounds back toward the parking lot. "Thank you for bringing me."

Roane raised our clasped hands and pressed a kiss to my knuckles. "Anytime, angel."

We were staring into each other's eyes, probably looking like two people who were sickeningly in love, when someone called out Roane's name.

He stiffened, his step faltering before he continued on.

"Someone's shouting for you," I said when Roane's name bounced down the gardens toward us.

Roane drew to a stop and turned toward the voice. I followed his gaze and saw a tall middle-aged man in the estate's garden uniform hurrying toward us. He was grinning at Roane as he brushed soil from his hands.

"I thought that was you," the man said, drawing to a halt.

The man seemed friendly and happy to see Roane, but Roane maintained a distant, polite expression on his face.

"Fred." Roane gave him a tight smile. "How are you?"

"Good, good." Fred grinned at me. "I'd shake your hand but—" He wiggled his dirty fingers.

"Oh, that's okay. I'm Evie."

"You must be the girlfriend we've been hearing about. It's nice to meet you."

"You too."

"We're in a hurry, Fred," Roane said, tugging on my hand. "I'm supposed to pick Shadow up in ten minutes."

The man's ruddy face fell. "Ah, of course. Sure, sure. Bring Evie to the Lion's Head one evening so we can get to know her."

"Will do." Roane nodded, and before I could say goodbye, I was pulled along with Roane, whose long strides were hard to keep up with.

Tension radiated from him as he frog-marched us to the SUV.

"What is going on?" I finally asked, feeling a little out of breath as we rounded the Defender.

"Nothing. I just . . ." He winced. "Fred would have had us chatting for hours, and we only get today to ourselves."

Not sure I was buying that excuse, I got into the passenger seat and opened my mouth to tell him so, but my cell cut me off. Digging through my purse, I pulled it out and saw it was an international number. Penny. I showed it to Roane before I answered.

"Evie." Penny's familiar voice made me smile.

"Hey. How are you? How's Australia? I'm with Roane, FYI."

"Oh, then put me on speaker."

I did as she asked and waited as she and Roane exchanged pleasantries. As Roane pulled out of the parking lot, Penny dropped her news.

"I'm staying in Melbourne. I'm happy here."

Overjoyed for her, I told her so.

"We'll miss you," Roane added.

"I'll miss you all too. But I think I needed to be here. To move on, finally. It means, however, that I'm selling the store. You're still good to run it for the next four weeks, Evie, but there will be an estate agent coming in to value the store and the flat, so I'll need you to give them access."

I swallowed hard, bitter disappointment filling me as I realized the store would no longer be mine. Neither would the great apartment above it. "Right."

"I'm going to send you an email with the details, who my estate agent is, etc. Okay?"

"Okay." I cleared my throat. "Thanks, Penny."

"No, thank you, pet. I couldn't have done this without you."

When I hung up, a thick tension fell between Roane and me. We still had not discussed the future—and the inevitability of me having to make a choice hung above us like a cloud that blocked out everything else.

Would it turn black and drench us in rain?

Or would it separate to reveal blue skies?

Although I was ninety-eight percent sure I wanted to stay, I didn't know how it was possible. No matter what my decision, I would probably have to go back to the States while I applied for jobs here so I could get an extended work permit.

I was still waiting for the go-ahead from Roane. But he hadn't spoken up. He hadn't asked me to stay.

Once we pulled up to the store, it was only as we got out of the SUV that I realized Roane hadn't gone to collect Shadow from Caro. I would have asked him why, but for the first time since we'd met, Roane had a wall up. His expression was guarded as I let us into the store, and the dark mood rolling off him was so uncharacteristic I didn't know what to say.

I climbed the stairs to the apartment, feeling a burn of panic clog my throat. In an attempt to work off my jitters, I strode into the room and abruptly stopped by the dining table.

In four weeks, this apartment wouldn't be mine anymore.

Would Roane?

I heard his footsteps behind me seconds before he wrapped an arm around my waist and tugged me into his body, my back to his front. My breath hitched as his hand coasted up my stomach to cup my breast and he squeezed it, a deep groan rumbling up from his chest. I could feel his arousal digging into my back as he tugged on my hair with his free hand, arching my neck. As he kneaded my breast, he pressed hot, burning kisses down my throat.

"Roane," I whimpered, reaching for him.

His strong hands pressed down on my upper back until I bowed over the dining table, and he nudged my legs open with his feet.

Arousal flushed through me, and I shivered, pressing my hands to the table for support.

No words passed between us. The only sound was that of our heavy breathing and the unzipping of my shorts and his jeans.

I shuddered when he peeled my underwear down my legs and caressed my cheeks.

Then I was lost as Roane touched me, readying me for him, my moans growing louder as he built me toward climax. Just as everything inside me tightened to near breaking point, he stopped, I heard the sound of foil crinkling, and then seconds later he gripped my hips and pushed inside me.

Sensation overwhelmed me as he powered in and out of me and I rocked back and forth, chasing his hard thrusts. The coil of tension snapped inside me, and as I came around him, his fingers bit into my skin as he pumped faster and harder, racing after his own release.

It was quick and hot.

But it was also different . . .

It had a desperate edge that hadn't been between us before.

His lips were hot on my neck as he bowed over me, his hands coasting soothingly up my sides. His chest rose and fell against my back as his labored breathing eased. I felt his lips on my nape, a tender, sweet touch before he straightened and pulled out of me.

Roane's continued silence worried me, and I didn't look at him as I pushed up off the table to fix myself. However, as I bent to reach for the underwear around my ankles, Roane took hold of my arm to stop me. Finally, I met his gaze, and a renewed flush of desire floored me at the heat in his.

"Don't bother putting it back on," he said, voice thick with want.

A new shiver trembled through me as I followed him into my bedroom, where he undressed me to make love to me.

Slow, languorous, thorough lovemaking that seared me to the very soul, and as we lay panting, staring at the ceiling, skin damp with sweat and our legs entwined, I knew that was what Roane intended. He wanted to dig himself so deep inside me, there was no way I could let him go. I knew it, because he'd succeeded.

Now I just needed him to say those three. Little. Words.

Twenty-Three

The next morning when I woke up, Roane was gone. At some point the previous evening he'd texted Caro to ask if she could look after Shadow all night. We'd barely left the bedroom, and I'd fallen asleep, completely exhausted.

Seriously, the man had way too much stamina.

Okay, that sounded like a complaint.

I wasn't complaining.

I'd be insane to complain about that.

What freaked me out was our lack of discussion about his sudden mood change and the fact that I'd woken up alone. For once I had no clue what was going on in Roane's head, and I didn't like it. The man was usually an open book, which I'd found was a rare quality in a guy.

The slight freak-out progressed into full-blown panic as the day wore on with no word from Roane. Around dinnertime I finally texted him to ask him how he was and if we were meeting at The Anchor.

He didn't reply.

Pissed, heart heavy, I decided I wasn't going to sit around in the apartment all evening waiting for him to decide to call. Instead I threw on my best jeans and a shirt that did amazing things for my cleavage and strolled up to the pub. As it was the first week of August and the beginning of a holiday week, I'd expected the pub to be busy with diners finishing their meals.

However, it was a fairly quiet night, and I recognized all of the faces sitting at the bar. To my delight, I found Caro at a table by the fire, and moved toward her after I greeted Milly.

Caro had her head bent toward her open laptop.

"Hey, you."

Her head snapped up and she broke into a wide smile. "Evie, just the person I wanted to see. I'm trying to design my website and I want your opinion."

"Design your own website," I said, impressed. "Is there anything you can't do?"

She blushed. "I'm afraid I'm unable to flirt in any language including English."

Chuckling, I squeezed her shoulder. "That's something we can fix."

"Ugh, perhaps one day. For now will you look at this and tell me what you think?"

"Sure, just let me grab a drink. Do you want anything?"

"A Coke, please."

I wandered over to the bar, glad to have something to distract me from the horrible butterflies that had taken up residence in my belly. Still, once Milly served me and I sat down at the table beside Caro, the first thing out of my mouth was "Have you heard from your cousin today?"

Caro blinked distractedly at her laptop. "Oh, he collected Shadow at the arse crack of dawn this morning, but I haven't seen him since. Why?"

"No reason." I shrugged, realizing I didn't want anyone to know Roane was making me feel insecure. It felt stupid to be feeling that way. Not even a whole day of lack of communication had passed. He wasn't under any obligation to stay in touch with me every second of every day.

It was just unusual for him not to want to.

Attempting not to scowl ferociously in a public display of my feelings, I leaned into Caro. "Show me the website."

Thankfully, I got so engrossed watching her play around with the design for her site, I would have forgotten about Roane entirely if it weren't for those butterflies reminding me of him. Even so, she must have successfully distracted me enough because it took Shadow sticking his face right into mine for me to realize he and Roane had entered the pub.

"Shadow." I smiled, my heart lightening to see him. I scratched behind his ears as I looked across the table to find Roane standing before us. "Hey."

His expression was almost as intense as it was last night. If we hadn't been in public, I would have demanded to know what was going on with him.

As if he saw the frustration on my face, Roane's eyes flashed, and he rounded the table to me. "Caro, take Shadow," he said without tearing his eyes from mine.

Okay, he was acting so strangely.

Caro did as he asked without a word, taking hold of Shadow by the collar and guiding him around me to her side.

"Roane . . ."

Then quite abruptly Roane Robson lowered to his knee in front of me and it felt like my heart jumped out of my chest and into my throat. I could feel the pulse there throbbing so hard.

That fluttering turned to pounding as he held up the black velvet ring box between us.

A gasp sounded behind me, followed by another, until the loud mingled chatter of the customers lowered to a murmur and then to silence.

He waited, staring into my astonished face, with a flush on his cheeks and a curl at the corners of his lips.

Then . . .

"Evangeline Starling"—Roane's deep voice seemed to fill the whole place—"people will always say this is too soon. That we would be mad to do this. But from the moment you saved my dog, I have been yours. Days that were filled with only work and friendship have become days filled only with hours that I count until I can see you again."

Oh my God. Tears filled my eyes.

"I know, the way the trees know they're rooted to the ground, that I'm rooted to you. That no matter your answer here this evening, I am yours until I'm nothing but dust in the wind. Maybe even then." His eyes burned with all the love I couldn't believe was for me, and he snapped open the box to reveal a stunning teardrop diamond engagement ring. The white gold band glittered with tiny inset diamonds, and the teardrop itself was *significant.*

It was beautiful.

And he wanted me to have it.

My vision blurred as I looked up from the ring to stare into Roane's face. A face I loved more than any other.

Marrying him would mean leaving my life in Chicago behind

for good, but hadn't I already decided I was going to do that as soon as Roane admitted he loved me? But marriage? Marriage was permanent.

"I'm yours, Evie," he said softly. "Forget time, forget everyone else and what they think. What do *you* want? Because I want you to be mine, as I am yours. Will you marry me?"

It wasn't that I didn't want forever with Roane. I did. I'd known that from that first day we made love, maybe even before then. Yet I had to know for certain whether I could leave Greer, Phil, and Mom behind.

They are important to me, but they have their own lives. It's time for me to start mine.

With that last thought ringing in my head, I laughed in disbelief and joy and he blinked as if he didn't quite know what to make of my reaction. Afraid he'd take it the wrong way, I launched myself into his arms, peppering his face with kisses. "I've been yours from day one," I promised him, leaning back to meet his gaze, his beard tickling my palms as I held him. "Roane, I'm yours. I always will be."

He heaved out a shaky exhalation, his smile slow and relieved. "That's a yes then?"

I gave him a huge grin, so huge my cheeks hurt. Everything inside me felt too much, like I might just burst apart from all the feelings that were too big for one person to contain. "That's the biggest yes of my life."

Roane kissed me, hard, no finesse, kissing my cheeks and chin and nose and making me laugh as hollers and shouts of celebration sounded all around us.

I giggled as he finally let me up for air to put the ring on my finger.

"It's beautiful," I whispered against his lips. "It's perfect."

"You're perfect," he murmured, kissing me again.

"That's enough. Let her up." Milly's voice cut through. "Let us congratulate you."

Roane's expression fell for some reason, and I swore I saw anxiety flicker in his eyes as he whispered hurriedly, "Evie, there's something we need to talk about."

A muffled, animalistic roar made me jolt in surprise, and as one the entire pub looked up at the ceiling.

"Dad!" We heard Viola's muted shriek.

My gaze shot to Milly, who paled and started walking away from us toward the bar.

Feet pounding down the stairs halted her, and Roane and I slowly stood as Viola's shouts were overwhelmed by Dex's angry yelling.

Soon enough we knew why, as Lucas appeared out of the STAFF ONLY door still pulling on his shirt. His back was turned toward us, and his hands were held up in defense as Dex followed him out.

Holding a shotgun.

"Where did he get that?" I squeaked.

"It'll be Milly's father's." Roane's voice was tight as he gently pressed me back. "Stay here." *He* didn't, however, stay. He cautiously started walking toward Milly, who was frozen in place with shock.

As was every single patron there.

"Dad!" Viola crashed into the room, her clothes askew, her face flushed, and her hair rumpled.

Oh dear.

Things were becoming clear.

"Vi, get out of here," Lucas demanded.

"Don't you talk to her." Dex waved the gun. "Don't you even look at her. I see you here again and I will fucking kill you."

Dex was a pretty laid-back guy. I'd never seen him pissed, let alone *enraged*.

"Dad, no!" Viola forced herself between them, struggling against Lucas, who was determinedly trying to get her out of the way.

"Will you lower the fucking gun off her!" Lucas yelled at Dex as Viola stubbornly fought to remain between them.

"You leave and I won't have to bother with the gun."

"Dex," Milly called out quietly. "Dex, put away the gun."

"Not until he promises to never see Viola again," Dex demanded, eyes narrowed on Lucas.

Viola's eyes flashed with fury. "I expected this of *his* dad, not mine!"

Dex faltered. "Vi—"

"I love him! If he goes, I go!" She turned to him, all tortured young love, and if I weren't already swooning over Roane's proposal, I would have swooned over this scene. "I love you, Lucas."

He stared down at her with such adoration, I melted. "I love you too, Vi."

I wanted to clap, but taking a gander at the other occupants of the room, I'd say celebrating was a little premature. I seemed to be the only one happy with this revelation. Everyone else looked stunned. Some even a little disapproving.

Milly was one of the astounded observers.

As was Dex, who lowered the shotgun reluctantly.

Roane did clap his hands but only to get everyone's attention. "The Anchor is closing early. Everyone pay up and get out."

Although slow to comply, everyone followed his orders, slapping coins and notes on the bar before ambling out of the pub with dazed expressions.

First a proposal.

Then Alnster's own Beatrice and Benedick.

"Let's go." Roane held his hand out to me and nodded to Caro and Shadow. She grabbed her laptop as I took Roane's hand, his thumbs sweeping over the engagement ring sitting on my fourth finger.

"Thanks," Milly murmured as we passed. "Sorry we ruined your proposal."

"Nothing got ruined, Milly," Roane assured her. "Call if you need me."

I gave her a small smile, my eyes shooting over to Lucas, Vi, and Dex, who were standing in pained silence together.

All three of us let out an exhalation as we stepped outside and Shadow trotted ahead of us.

"You must be feeling pretty pleased with yourself." Roane shot me a wicked smile.

"Because I just bagged myself a hot farmer or because I was right all along about Vi and Lucas?"

Caro giggled at my side as Roane pulled me closer. "Both I suppose," he said.

"Well, of course I'm ecstatic about the former." I studied my engagement ring and felt another wild flutter of excitement in my belly. Dropping my hand, I sighed. "As for Vi and Lucas, I wish it hadn't gone down like that. Not just because they kind of stole our moment," I teased, "but because I think they should have been up-front about what was going on. They were obviously sneaking around. Lying about their relationship only makes it look like they have something to be ashamed of, and it'll make it harder for Milly and Dex to trust them when they say it's love. I know that's how I'd feel."

Hopefully, however, Milly and Dex would come around. I loved Viola. I loved them all and just wanted them to be as happy as I was.

After Caro had gotten in her car and driven home to Beadnell, Roane and I disappeared into my apartment, where I murmured my plans for the future between each of his kisses. "I'll need to call Greer and then book flights to Chicago to clear out my apartment. And I'll need to drive to Indianapolis to talk to my mom and Phil." I kissed Roane harder, crushing my breasts against his chest to let him know I was ready to shut up and have celebration sex. However, as we stumbled toward the bedroom, discarding clothes as we went, I remembered something. "Hey," I reluctantly avoided his searching mouth to say, "you wanted to tell me something."

Roane hesitated for a second and then whispered, "I love you. I wanted to tell you that I love you so much . . ." He let out a shaky breath, something desperate in his gaze. "So much, Evie, I'm terrified you'll disappear. I didn't know this much happiness went hand in hand with fear."

Clasping his face in my hands, I looked him straight in the eye and announced, "I'm not going anywhere. I'm here to stay, mister. For you, for me, for us." My grin was shaky with excitement and hope. "*And* I'm going to see if I can buy the bookstore."

Twenty-Four

It was fair to say that Lucas and Viola's love story eclipsed Roane's proposal and our consequent engagement. Of course people congratulated us when they saw us, and we'd gotten a few free drinks during the past week, but the whole village was abuzz with the young couple who defied a thirty-year-old feud.

West Elliot found out after the scene at the pub. Viola told me tearfully a few nights ago that West had forced Lucas to choose between family and her. He'd chosen Viola, and to no one's surprise, the Taits had taken him in.

"His room is on the other side of the flat to Vi," Milly had told me. "Otherwise Dex would kill him. Funny thing is, I can tell Dex likes the boy. Would probably learn to love him if he wasn't trying to defile his only child."

Unfortunately, I imagined it was difficult for Dex to wipe the imagery of walking in on his daughter having sex.

Viola was mortified and claimed she would never get over it, but then, as I told her, they probably shouldn't have tried to get away with having sex in her bedroom!

"I thought everyone was downstairs working," she'd whined.

Still, I thought it was pretty big of Dex to let Lucas stay with them because he had nowhere else to go, and it confirmed to me that West Elliot was an immature asshole, even though I'd yet to meet the man. I had seen him from afar. He was very much like his son, and it surprised me that age hadn't dulled his handsomeness, considering how bitter he obviously was.

I'd gone out to run errands and found myself standing in the small cookie aisle in the convenience store, trying to decide if I should succumb to the temptation of the rich tea biscuits I liked to dunk into my cup of tea while I watched the store.

My belly could really do without those biscuits, and I had fitting into a wedding dress to think about sometime in the near future.

I was getting married.

It was so surreal.

"Well, the young Elliot and Viola Tait situation has taken attention away from Roane Robson, and it baffles me," I heard a voice say in the aisle behind me and felt my heart pound at overhearing gossip pertaining to Roane.

"Oh, I know," a second woman said, "you would think one of his closest friends would talk to the lad. Obviously, he's let that American overcome his good sense with her talents in the bedroom. I've heard Americans are very loose in that respect."

My jaw dropped.

Say what?

Glaring through the shelves of products, I crossed my arms over my chest and waited to hear if they said more. Their voices began to travel as they moved.

"Clearly she's muddled his good sense. Never mind the ridiculous notion of marrying someone you've only known for three months—"

"Oh yes, we're not the only ones who think he's being reckless."

"He should be settling down with a girl from good English stock. Even a Scot would be better than an American."

"There's nothing wrong with Scottish blood," the other woman sniffed. "I'm Scottish on my mother's side."

"Oh, I meant no offense, Harriet." A gray-haired lady came into view at the top of my aisle. In a light sweater and a long skirt, her back hunched slightly, the woman was named Lilith something or other. I knew who her companion was before the blue-haired lady in the pantsuit appeared at her side. Lilith and Harriet were two of the oldest villagers, but the bracing coastal life had made them hardy. If it weren't for their severely wrinkled faces, it would be hard to tell they were in their eighties by the sturdiness of their bodies and youthful gait.

I'd admired them from afar.

Not so much now.

They turned toward my aisle and both froze in shock to see me there.

Pressing their lips together tightly, they blanched as I walked slowly toward them, eyeballing them in disapproval.

The truth was I'd known there would be talk about how quickly Roane and I had fallen in love and decided to marry. We'd discussed it lying in bed and decided we wouldn't care what other people thought. We knew that this, us together, was what we'd been waiting for our whole lives.

Peering down my nose at Harriet and Lilith, I murmured, "Ladies," as I passed them without confrontation. I saw their expressions slacken with surprise, but I wasn't going to waste energy on two old gossips who had nothing better to do. People would always talk, but as long as the people I cared about were happy for Roane and me, I couldn't care less what anyone else thought.

When I returned to the bookstore, my skin still prickling a little with the encounter despite my inner pep talk, I moved toward the back staircase and stopped when I heard the giggle from upstairs.

Damn.

I'd given Lucas and Viola permission to use my apartment for privacy. Of course, I knew what "privacy" meant and trusted Viola to use the guest bedroom and not mine, but I'd expected them to be done by now. Why I'd naively assumed that, when they were both twenty-year-olds with unending stamina, I didn't know.

Rolling my eyes, I moved back into the store, dumped my stuff behind the counter, and flipped the sign to OPEN.

I had so much to organize over the next two weeks. Penny was ecstatic that I wanted to buy the bookstore. I was less ecstatic about what it would cost to buy the building. It would eat up the entirety of the life insurance money my dad had left me. That money would have bought me a huge house with land in Indiana. On the other hand, I'd need double that to buy a really nice two-bedroom apartment in the heart of the West Loop in Chicago.

Since it would take longer than two weeks for all the legal stuff to be finalized and Roane and I didn't want to rush a wedding, I'd applied for an extension on my work visa. Penny had provided another letter to say I would be continuing on as an employee at the bookstore for three more months.

We were waiting on approval for that, but worst-case scenario, Roane and I would marry at a registrar's office so I could stay in the country, and then we'd plan a proper wedding later. For now, I was planning as if the visa extension would come through. Which meant I had my lawyer on the sale, and myself on organizing a trip to the States to tie up loose ends there. And to say goodbye.

The thought of saying goodbye to Greer, Mom, and Phil choked me up every time. But I knew I was doing the right thing because there was no niggle in my gut that suggested there were hidden doubts somewhere in my conscience. I knew marrying Roane and moving to Alnster was one hundred percent the right thing to do. How many people could really boast such certainty when making a huge decision about their life?

I was lucky. I knew that.

That didn't mean it hadn't been hard to tell Greer about Roane's proposal. Staring at the glittering diamond on my finger, I felt an overwhelming amount of happiness, but it was tinged with sadness when I remembered my friend crying.

I knew she was happy for me, but like me, she was grief-stricken at the idea of having that big ocean between us for the rest of our lives.

"Maybe I can convince Andre to move to England," she'd sniffled.

My smile had been watery as I'd replied with a sad "Maybe."

The call with Phil had been a little better. There were no tears. And he was relieved to hear I was coming back to see them. "I didn't want to call Mom about this. I want to sit down and have a conversation with her face-to-face."

"I get it. I'll let her know. Just keep us updated on when you're getting into Chicago. We'll book a hotel in the city."

"You don't have to do that. I'll come out to you guys."

"Whatever you want. Just keep us posted."

I sighed as I scrolled through a list of comparison flights on my laptop. With almost every penny I had going to Penny, I needed to book something cheap. Roane had offered to pay, but I wasn't sure he had an abundance of cash just lying around. Besides, I didn't want to imagine what kind of money he'd just dropped on my engagement ring.

Mostly, I felt weird about taking money from him. When I said that, he'd scowled ferociously and told me that as his future wife I'd better get used to the fact that our lives were now there for us to share, and that included money. I knew he was right. But I wasn't his wife yet.

Roane's wife.

The thought put a goofy smile on my face, and I was still wearing it when a villager walked into the bookstore. I didn't know the blond woman's name, only that I'd seen her around enough to know she was a resident here. I saw her driving regularly through the village in her SUV with kids in the back.

"Morning." She smiled at me as she approached the counter. "I don't think we've been properly introduced. I'm Erin."

I shook her hand with a smile. "Nice to meet you. What can I do for you?"

"I always order my kids' schoolbooks through Penny. Is that still possible?"

Erin wasn't the first to come in and do so over the last few weeks, and I thought it was pretty cool that the locals spent their money at their independent store rather than get cheaper books at an online retailer.

"Of course."

She handed over the list. Most of the titles on it were already on order, as the local schools had sent me their book lists for the fall term.

"I'll just take your full name and phone number. It's payment up front."

As Erin pulled her bank card out of her purse, she said, "Did you hear?"

I raised an eyebrow at the speculation in her tone. "Hear what?"

Erin leaned across the counter conspiratorially. "I just saw Maggie Foster hugging Annie Foster outside the art gallery. It seems the feud is over."

"Really?"

"Yup." Erin seemed genuinely excited by the gossip, suggesting she was telling the truth.

Delight began to slowly trickle through me.

Annie and Maggie were reconciling? I grinned happily at the thought, and Erin returned the smile.

"It's nice to see families coming together. Speaking of, I heard congratulations are in order." She pointed to my ring finger.

"Oh, thanks."

"What a catch." She flushed. "I mean, of course, you are too, but he *is* easy on the eyes, and you'll never want for anything." With a cheeky wink, Erin strode out of the store after I promised to call her once the books came in.

Her last words made me laugh, thinking she meant it as an innuendo. Considering Roane wasn't exactly a lothario, I wondered how she'd drawn that conclusion. Ach, who was I kidding? You only had to look at Roane to know he was good in bed. It was just something about the way he moved.

And his hands.

God, his hands.

I flushed just thinking about them.

Where was your fiancé when you needed him?

Fiancé.

I had a fiancé.

What a weird and wonderful turn my life had taken in such a short space of time.

"*I* should write a book," I murmured to myself as I heard footsteps coming down the back staircase.

Viola and Lucas appeared, his arms wrapped around her as they shuffled into the store, cheeks flushed but clothes and hair fixed. I almost rolled my eyes at how mushy they were, but I knew Roane and I were just as bad.

"Thanks, Evie," Vi said, grinning so hard, it was a wonder her cheeks didn't crack.

"No problem." I tried not to laugh. I glanced between them. "Are you doing okay with . . . everything?"

Viola's smile fell as she looked up at Lucas.

He gave her a reassuring squeeze. "It's not ideal with my parents, but we go back to uni in two weeks and then we graduate so we're out on our own anyway."

"Are you going to get a place together?"

"Our flats are sorted for this year but when we graduate, yeah."

"And at least Vi's parents are okay with us," Lucas added.

"Yeah, no one saw that coming after the shotgun incident," I joked.

Lucas smirked but his tone was solemn. "I did. The Taits have always been good people. If it was up to Milly, this feud with my dad wouldn't have gotten past the three-month mark, never mind thirty bloody years."

Viola caressed his arm in a soothing manner and gave me another smile. "Thanks for letting us take some time in the apartment this morning. There's not much privacy at mine."

"It's no problem. I was young once," I cracked.

"Oh, aye." Lucas chuckled as he and Viola strolled toward the door. "Was that not yesterday when everyone saw Roane feeling you up at the harbor?"

Viola swatted him on my behalf while I rolled my eyes. "There really is a downside to living in a village."

"You're just learning that now?"

I waved them out, watching Lucas throw his arm around Viola's small shoulders as Roane appeared before them. They exchanged a few words with Shadow bouncing around them for attention, and my heart did that leaping-in-my-chest thing it always did when I saw my fiancé.

My fiancé.

Would that wondrous feeling ever leave? Would I one day settle comfortably into my feelings for Roane?

As he strode inside the store, holding the door open for Shadow to trot through, we shared a loving smile, and then I got down to the business of greeting the dog. Once my hands were sufficiently covered in doggy kisses, I shared a long, lingering kiss with Shadow's owner.

"I need to wash my hands," I murmured against his mouth, noting the brown bag of lunch he clutched.

"Let's go upstairs."

Even though I'd already closed the shop when I shouldn't, I found myself turning over the sign and locking the door. Upstairs, after I'd washed away Shadow's sweet kisses from my hands, I joined Roane in the kitchen.

"From the bakery in Alnwick," he said, pushing a plate with a massive sandwich on it toward me.

"Thank you. Had a good morning?"

"Well, I heard good news. Maggie and Annie Foster have reconciled."

I grinned. "I heard from a customer, but it's nice to have it confirmed by a reliable source."

Roane's gazed washed over my face, bright with tenderness. "Milly says Maggie told her you had something to do with it."

My cheeks felt a little hot under his obvious admiration. He was looking at me the same way he had when I'd pulled Shadow out of the way of that car. "We just talked. The rest was Maggie."

He gave a slight shake of his head. "You have no idea of your effect." He leaned in and brushed a soft kiss to my lips. "I love you, Evie Starling soon-to-be Robson."

A little blissed out on his praise, I reached for another kiss. Deeper, longer. When we broke apart, Roane's eyes were dark with want. "Do you think we have time for a quickie after lunch?"

I chuckled. "I think we can make that happen."

Roane tore a huge chunk of sandwich with his teeth, a hungry look in his eyes. I laughed, almost choking on a bite of my own sandwich.

"So where are you at with everything?" Roane asked. There was an infectious energy about him since I said yes to his proposal. He seemed to buzz with a constant happiness and excitement.

It had led to a lot of sex in the past week.

"I'm waiting on a call from my lawyer about the purchase contract. Apparently, it can take a while, so I'm a little antsy. Um, booking my flights home today. Talked to Phil. Talked to Greer—"

"How did that go?"

I sighed. "She cried. I cried. She's happy for us, but I know she's worried about me missing the birth, so I'll have to find the money to fly back out for that."

Roane stared at me, his eyes searching. "Evie, we can make that happen. I . . . uh . . ." He cleared his throat. "We need to talk—"

My cell suddenly blasted on the kitchen counter, vibrating toward me. "It's my lawyer." I recognized the number, excitement causing little flutters in my belly. I shot Roane an apologetic look. "I need to take this."

He frowned but nodded. "Of course."

I answered, hopping off the stool because I needed to move with the restless energy that bounced between Roane and me.

The call took longer than I'd thought as my lawyer, Sally, went over everything in the contract that she'd like to negotiate so it sat better in my favor. Some things had come up on the survey, like the age of the roof, and Sally was determined to get money off the purchase price because of it. I didn't want to create problems between Penny and me, but Sally was adamant the agent had over-priced the building.

The call took so long, Roane whispered he needed to get back to work, and I waved goodbye with a forlorn look, disappointed we hadn't had time for that quickie.

His eyes promised me "later," and I smiled at the sweet kiss he pressed to my cheek before he and Shadow let themselves out.

Not long after, I got off my cell, only for it to ring again.

This time it was Caro. A very frantic Caro. Her oven had broken, and she had a three-tiered cake to bake, along with individual cupcakes and vol-au-vents for an anniversary party.

I offered her my kitchen.

*C*losing my shop again, however temporarily, was not ideal, but at the sight of Caro's panicked look when she rushed downstairs to tell me she didn't have enough eggs, I couldn't not offer to go get them.

That's why I found myself weighed down by plastic bags filled with eggs as I marched out of the convenience store and abruptly slammed into a hard body.

The eggs!

I winced, not even caring I'd bruised my cheek on someone's shoulder as I looked down into the bags. Oh man, those babies had better be okay.

Glancing up at the person I'd crashed into to belatedly apologize, I gaped in shock.

It was West Elliot, up close and personal.

In the nearly four months I'd lived in Alnster, this was as close as I'd gotten to the man.

Lucas must have inherited his eye color from his mother, because West's were dark. He was a tall, strapping guy, still rugged and handsome. However, there was a hardness to his eyes and his mouth that I didn't like.

He flicked his cold gaze down my body and back up again. "You're the American."

I tried not to roll my eyes.

That was me. The American. I had a feeling I could live twenty years in this village and I'd still always be the American!

"Yup. You're West Elliot."

He gave me a lift of his chin before his gaze fell to my left hand. He scowled. "Rushing into that, are you not?"

I scowled back. "Not sure that's your business."

West's lips pursed as he studied my face.

"Well, if that's all, I have eggs to deliver—"

"I've heard nothing but good things about you."

Surprised, I faltered. "Uh . . . that's nice."

"Which is why I think you should know the truth."

Something about his tone caused a shiver, not the good kind, to skitter down my spine.

Disapproval darkened West's already frosty expression. "I know what it's like to be made a fool by someone you trusted. And if you're a good lass, like everyone says you are, you don't de-serve that."

The uneasiness settling around me made me irritable. "And what's the truth?"

"Roane Robson is lying to you."

I felt my defenses rising. Bad-mouthing Roane was the wrong move with—

"He has all his friends, nearly the whole damn village, cover-ing up his lies for him. I've heard them joking about it. How the American girl had rules about dating, and he lied about who he was so you would give him a chance. Has he told you the truth now that he's got a ring on you?"

Thinking this was just some sick, bitter attempt to cause mis-ery, I huffed, "You're unbelievable."

"He hasn't," West surmised, crossing his big arms over his chest. "Ask him, lass. Ask him his age. Ask him how much younger he is. But more importantly ask him if he was ever planning to tell you that you're not only marrying into a fortune, you're marrying into a baronetcy."

I leaned away from him, shaking my head.

No.

He was lying.

West sighed. "His father is Sir William George Robson, the twelfth Baronet of Alnster, and when he dies, Roane will be Sir

Roane Robson, and if you marry him, you'll be addressed as Lady Robson."

If this was a lie . . . it was a very colorful one.

"Ask him, lass," he repeated before striding by me.

Sick to my stomach, I hurried toward the bookstore. My heart was racing and pounding so fast and hard in my chest, I thought I might throw up. I couldn't remember even getting to the store.

Yet suddenly I was there. In the apartment, staring at Caro.

She stopped in the middle of pouring batter into cake pans as she looked at me. "Evie, what's wrong?"

My throat felt dry, rasping as I forced the words out. "Is it true? Is Roane wealthy? Is he the heir to a title?"

Her face paled as she stepped back from the counter. "Evie . . . he's been trying to tell you."

The bags in my hands dropped, and the room spun.

Oh my God.

What was I doing? How had I not seen he was keeping secrets?

It looked like I didn't know Roane Robson at all.

Twenty-Five

*E*verything felt unreal, the wall and the wood burner merging into one as I stared into space with the cold mug of tea between my hands.

I'd vaguely been aware of Caro calling Roane, sticking a cup of tea in front of me, and packing up her stuff. She left a few moments before with the promise that Roane would be there to explain everything.

Explain everything.

How could he explain this?

When I heard feet pounding up the stairs followed by the familiar clack of dog nails on hardwood, the wall and fireplace unmerged as my vision came back into focus.

I looked toward the doorway as Roane entered the apartment, Shadow skipping across the floor toward me. Numb with shock I could only stare at the dog as he put his face close to mine.

"Hey, boy," I whispered hoarsely.

"Shadow." Roane gestured to the dog to move as he replaced

him, lowering to his haunches in front of me. His eyes glittered with fear. "Evie."

"Tell me it isn't true," I begged, desperately needing him to have a reasonable explanation now that he was in front of me, reminding me just how much I goddamn loved him.

Guilt etched its way into every one of his features, and suddenly I understood why they called it a broken heart.

It felt like mine had shattered inside my chest, the pain so great it was hard to breathe past the piercing, broken shards.

No.

Tears stung my eyes, flowing over and slipping down my cheeks as Roane cursed under his breath and tried to reach for me. I jerked away. "No," I bit out, swiping at my tears. "Explain."

He straightened but only to take the seat beside me.

To my horror, I had to quash the urge to throw myself into his arms. Roane's arms, after all, were the first and only place I wanted to be when . . . well . . . ever. Biting my lip to hold back more tears, I placed the mug on the floor and curled my arms around my waist to keep the sobs inside.

"When . . . all those months ago . . . you told the entire pub that you wouldn't date a younger man or a man who had money."

I flinched, remembering that drunken night. Or at least some of it.

"I never meant to lie to you, Evie . . ." His tone was pleading. "I just . . . I wanted you to give me a chance without my age or money clouding your judgment. I never lied . . . I just omitted things."

Oh my God.

It was true.

It was really true.

Nausea rolled through my stomach.

"And the entire village was in on this? Lying to me . . . making me the village fool?"

"No." He gripped my arm.

"Don't touch me!" I yanked it out of his hold and jerked up off the couch. "Don't touch me."

"Fuck, Evie." Roane's voice shook. "Please . . . it wasn't like that. I tried to tell you so many times over the last month but—"

"The last month!" I spun around to face him, my rage and hurt and disappointment building into something I didn't know if I could control. It was breaking me. "You should have told me from the start!"

"I know." He stood, holding his hands up defensively. "I know. It's just . . . I loved you from the start, and I was afraid you wouldn't give me a chance."

I didn't want to hear his excuses. "How old are you?"

Roane exhaled slowly. "I'm just about to turn twenty-seven."

"You're twenty-six?" Oh my God, he was almost seven years younger than me.

"Aye."

Seven years. How could I not have realized that? When I was forty, he would just be turning the age I was now.

"Oh my God."

"But age doesn't matter. It shouldn't matter."

"But lying does." I cut him a dark look. "*Sir* Roane Robson."

He closed his eyes for a moment, pained. When he opened them, remorse filled them. "Not yet. My father is the baronet . . ." He took a step toward me and stopped when I glared. "The twelfth baronet. It's not like it sounds. I don't know how much you know about British aristocracy, but that's not what a baronetcy is. We're not peerage. It comes somewhere between a baron and a knight-hood. It's—"

"Is it a title? Is it a historical rank? Does everyone in Northumberland know who you are? Do you come from money?"

"Evie . . ."

"Well?"

He nodded slowly. "Aye. But my mum doesn't come from money, Evie. She grew up here in Alnster, the daughter of a fisherman. I didn't want to go to Harrow, so my mum convinced Dad not to send me, and when I started talking like Mum instead of Dad, he never corrected it. My parents wanted me to be who I am, not shape me into something else because of some legacy I would inherit. And I love the farm. I work hard, not because I have to, but because I want to, and they don't expect or want anything from me. What you've seen of me is the truth. This is my life. Nothing about me or what you know about me has changed."

Confused, I thought of the small farmhouse. "Your home . . ."

He flinched. "Evie . . . the farmhouse once belonged to the estate manager. That's Bobby now and he didn't want it. So I took it over. My parents' home is significantly larger. It's on the land where we do our arable farming. And our farm is larger than I let on. We're quite a substantial commercial farm with many employees."

Realization dawned. That's why he didn't take me to that part of the estate.

"Is there anything else I should know?" I asked, my bitterness clear.

"The maintenance on the holiday homes . . . it's a much larger company than I let on. We cover all of Northumberland. Thousands of holiday home owners pay us to maintain their properties, and the revenue for that accounts for a good portion of our income. Moreover, we own properties we let out, as well."

All the business conversations he'd had on the phone, the ones he disappeared downstairs to take, came back to me. I'd thought he was being considerate. He wasn't. He just didn't want me to guess there was more to his business than I'd thought.

Then there was the guy whom Roane had pulled us away from at the Alnwick Garden. Not because he was chatty, no. It was probably because he wasn't a villager in on the deception, and Roane was afraid he'd mention something about the truth.

Not to mention those times when permits and visas got pushed through quicker than I'd expected. Possibly because Roane had political connections?

And then Erin today.

What a catch. I mean, of course, you are too, but he is easy on the eyes and you'll never want for anything.

I stared down at the blinding diamond engagement ring.

"You've got *money*," I surmised.

Roane crossed the room toward me, and I tensed. "Evie." He reached out to me but halted at my warning glare. "Evie, I'm still the same man."

A sob burst forth before I could stop it, unexpected and forceful, and I stumbled away from his attempts to comfort me. Once I could speak, I stared at him through blurry vision. "Don't you get it? It's not what you lied about, Roane . . . it's that you lied at all. You lied, not omitted, *lied*. And you didn't trust me! You think I would have cared about your age or that you had money based on some reckless drunken comment I made about my past relationships? Do you think because I had a couple of bad experiences dating younger men and because of Chace, I would have held that against you once I got to know you? Do *you* know *me* at all?

"Because all this time I thought *I* knew *you* better than I know anyone . . . and a whole village was laughing at me because I got engaged to a man I didn't even know!"

Anger darkened his expression as he gripped my biceps, bending his head to mine. "You do know me," he promised. "You know what counts."

I shook my head. "You're not the same man." My heart broke all over again, the pain too much as I sobbed. I didn't even care that I accepted his comfort as he wrapped his arms around me and begged me to forgive him.

But it was so clear to me now that I'd been living in a fucking fantasy. I'd done with Roane what I'd done with Aaron. I was so desperate to find love that I'd rushed in, given myself over to a man I didn't know at all. Because if he'd lied about this . . . what else had he lied about?

My tears soaked Roane's shirt as I bawled like a baby.

I bawled for a future I'd been so excited about.

I cried for a life that would never be mine now.

Pushing away from him, my jaw, my cheeks, everything aching with grief, I stared at the man who had caused it. Hating him for it. "I can never look at you the same way. I . . . can never trust you again."

Fear exploded across his face as he took in my meaning. "Evie, no, we can get through this."

Shaking my head, I looked down at the glittering diamond on my finger and felt my face crumple again. Sucking in a breath to stop another hysterical meltdown in front of him, I pulled the ring off my finger and held it out to him.

He glared balefully at it, refusing to take it.

I placed it on the counter instead, my hands shaking.

"You don't mean this," Roane whispered hoarsely. "We love

each other too much. We'll figure this out once everything has calmed down. I'm sorry I kept this from you, angel. I'm so sorry, but they're not malicious lies. It was just stupid omissions that got out of hand. Let's just talk about it and you'll see: I'm still me."

But I knew as I looked at him that everything had changed irreparably. No matter what he said, he was no longer Roane. My kind, loving thirtysomething farmer fiancé. He was this stranger, the son of a baronet, who had made me a fool and hurt me deeper than anyone ever had because of it.

Roane paled at my expression because, apparently, he did know me.

"Evie . . ." His voice broke.

There was still a part of me that wanted to comfort him, and the fresh tears that spilled down my cheeks weren't just for me. They were for him.

The sound of him whispering my name over and over again made me choke back a sob as I left him behind in the apartment.

Twenty-Six

My suitcases sat by the store door, waiting to be loaded into the cab that was coming for me. Unlike heartbreaking scenes in a movie, torrential rain didn't accompany the moment. Instead it was a beautiful, too-hot day in Northumberland. Clear skies, bright sun, water glistening with sunlight that cascaded through its gentle waves.

No one knew I was leaving today except Penny.

Poor Penny.

She was thrown by how quickly things had fallen apart. Sally was pretty pissed too that I'd pulled out of the sale.

As I gazed around the bookstore, my chin wobbled and fresh tears stung my eyes. In the last forty-eight hours I'd cried more tears than I knew I had in me. Yet it seemed there was more to come. I had to hold them back until I got back on US soil. Staring around the store made it hard to be strong, because I was going to grieve not only my relationship with Roane, and the village and my friends, but this store.

This beautiful dream that I'd touched with the tips of my fingers.

When I'd returned that awful day to the apartment, Roane and Shadow were gone, and after I'd sobbed a bucketful of tears, I'd pulled out my laptop and googled Roane.

There were images of him at local events when he was younger along with his parents. I'd discovered Roane's family had been granted a baronetcy by the Crown in the seventeenth century, and they had marriage ties to the dukedom way back then. The Alnster baronetcy was one of the oldest left in England, and although, as Roane had explained, they weren't members of the peerage, it was still a respected title.

Roane's grandfather Edward was the first baronet to avoid becoming a member of Parliament, instead concentrating on rebuilding a dwindling estate. Roane's father had inherited it and expanded that wealth by starting the maintenance company, and Roane had continued to expand upon their little empire.

I found an article on the Duke and Duchess of Northumberland's anniversary gala a few years ago, and Roane and his parents were on the list of guests who'd attended.

No wonder he'd known Alnwick Castle like the back of his hand.

He'd been there, mingling with a duke.

Memories flooded me, all the moments I'd forgotten, where he'd hesitated over taking me to the farm or hedged about details regarding his family. Times where I'd heard him say, "Evie, we need to talk," or, "I need to tell you something."

He had attempted to tell me the truth.

I saw that now.

But he hadn't tried hard enough.

And I hadn't thought to look. I'd stared at photos of him on-line, trying to figure out how I'd missed so much, including his age. I blamed that damn beard. But it wasn't the beard, really. It was Roane. He had this innate maturity and authority that made him seem older.

What I wouldn't do, however, was blame myself.

I pulled in a shuddering breath, pain constricting my throat as I fought back the emotion. It was the lies he'd told. The lies were almost inconsequential in the grand scheme of things. Silly even. Truths that would never have stopped me from giving him a chance or loving him.

It was his ability to lie to me.

And the villagers' deception.

All this time I'd thought I was one of them, but they'd kept this from me, like it was a game. Like I wasn't permanent but just that summer's entertainment.

I saw Milly approach the store door, and my stomach plummeted.

Yesterday I'd had to deal with Viola and Caro. I'd told them I was leaving, just not when, and during separate visits they'd both begged me to stay. It was hard with Viola. I was angry at her, at everyone, for lying to me, but I still cared about her. I'd still miss her.

It was heart wrenching with Caro. She'd pleaded with me not to leave before thinking things through, offering to keep me company by staying in my guest room or for me to stay with her, to give me time to fully process the situation with her support. When I refused, Caro cried in my arms, and despite being pissed at her for helping Roane lie, I'd hated hurting her.

So not only did I have Roane to blame for breaking my heart, I could blame him for the guilt I felt in breaking Caro's heart.

Milly pushed open the door I'd left unlocked for my cab's arrival. Even the thought of having to call a cab infuriated me. I'd never rented that car like I'd promised myself I would because I'd become solely dependent on Roane and my friends to take me anywhere I needed to go.

I'd handed over my independence to them in so many ways.

Greer was right. I'd come to Alnster to find myself, and instead I'd just lost myself in a man, and in a fantasy.

The cab wasn't due for another half hour, but I'd thought it would be easier to wait in the store than up in the apartment that held so many memories of intimate moments with Roane.

I'd been wrong. It wasn't easier to be down here.

Losing the bookstore was agony too.

Milly was focused on me but then something caught her attention in her peripheral vision. The luggage. Her head snapped toward it, then back to me, and her eyes widened. "You're leaving now?"

I swallowed my guilt. "My cab is on its way."

"Oh, Evie." She strode toward me, determination etched in her face. "Don't go, lass. Don't be so rash about this. You know you belong here."

Bitterness cut through me. "I don't belong here. You turned me into the village entertainment."

Milly's face hardened. "If you knew anything about us, you'd know that wasn't true."

I clenched my teeth to stop myself from lashing out at her.

"Evie." Her expression softened at whatever she saw in my eyes. "It seemed harmless at first. We all could see how much Roane liked you right off the bat, and we all heard you spouting about those silly rules. We didn't want you to discount him for stupid nonsense like that. We wanted happiness for him. We're protective of him. Of each other. And we let you in, Evie." She reached out to touch my arm. "We let you in from the get-go, and that never happens, lass. We let you in because you shine so bright and you are special indeed. We knew that this place was your home before you even did. And we don't want to lose you."

The tears I'd been fighting slipped free. Not ravaging, desperate tears like those I'd cried in front of Roane, but that didn't mean they hurt any less. "This place isn't my home," I denied. "It never was."

Milly squeezed my arm, giving me a pitying look. "You know that's a lie. Because for someone who supposedly doesn't think that, you sure made yourself at home here, meddling in people's lives. We can't even be sorry for it," she rushed to assure me as my face fell. "Look at all you've done since you came here. You gave Penny the opportunity to see if Melbourne was the right place for her. You helped Caro find the confidence to leave that wicked woman behind and start her life. You brought Annie and Maggie Foster together after years of separation. And I know that it was you that meddled between Viola and Lucas." She gave me a semi-chastising look. "Viola told me you were the one who realized Lucas cared for her, and although I wish some things didn't happen the way they did, I can't say I'm not happy for how things have turned out. That boy looks at my bairn like he'd take a bullet for her . . . and although I was worried about them, how can a mother not be happy that her bairn is blissfully in love with a boy who loves her back just as much. With everything he has. Lucas loves Vi just as much as Roane loves you."

"Milly—"

"And because of you, Kathy Elliot came to me."

Shocked, I shut my mouth.

"Aye. We talked for the first time ever. All because she doesn't want to lose Lucas. She and I made peace, Evie. Not with West. That'll never happen. But Kathy and I made peace for the sake of the kids. And that's because of you." Her eyes shimmered now as she reached up to caress my cheek, her expression almost motherly. "You're a piece of magic, lass, and this place needs you."

The strength I'd been holding on to failed me and I ducked my head as I shuddered and choked on my tears. After a minute of trying to keep it together, I raised my head. "I'm sorry, Milly," I whispered with regret. "I can't stay."

With that, she pulled me into a hug, one that was almost comical with our height difference, but the moment was too sad for humor. She squeezed me tight and without another word pulled away and marched out of the store.

When my cab appeared a little while later, I was still trembling as the driver helped me out with the luggage. As he put my suitcases into the trunk of his car, I locked the bookstore, popped my key into an envelope, and slipped it into the store's mailbox.

With a juddering sigh, I turned on my heel and promptly stumbled at the sight of Roane and Shadow standing beside the cab.

Roane's chest was heaving like he'd been running, sweat glistening on his temples. I glanced beyond him to see the Defender parked near the harbor in the only parking space available.

Shadow tore away from Roane's side and bounded toward me, and renewed grief flooded me as I wrapped my arms around his supple body and made my silent goodbyes.

"Milly called me," Roane said as I straightened from hugging Shadow.

I'd assumed as much.

"We ready?" the driver asked me, glancing between Roane and me.

"Give us a few minutes." Roane handed him some money, and the driver took it before getting into the car to give us a little privacy.

I didn't want privacy.

I didn't want this goodbye.

I wasn't sure my heart could take it.

Staring at his face, I thought I saw his youth now. There weren't any deep laughter lines around his eyes yet, and the beard hid any telltale age lines around his mouth, if there were any. Then there was his energy. Not that a thirtysomething didn't have energy, but Roane had the stamina of twenty-six-year-old, of that there was no doubt.

I shivered in half grief, half longing.

He would never touch me again.

We'd never lie tangled in each other's arms again.

Fuck, it hurt.

It hurt so badly, I wanted to scream at him until he told me it was all a joke, that he'd never lied, that he was just Roane.

Just my Roane.

I wished I could get over it.

I wished I could forgive.

But he was the one person in my life I couldn't handle disappointing me.

And it was time for me to return to reality and stop living in a fucking fantasyland.

"You're making a mistake," he said, taking a step toward me.

Shadow trotted to his side, like he knew Roane needed him more than I did.

"You made the mistake," I whispered.

He flinched. "Evie, I'm not telling you to just get over this. But don't run off back to Chicago right away without giving this time. We're worth figuring this out."

I tried to close my ears, not wanting to hear the pleading tone in his voice. It was killing me.

"I gave the ring to Caro." When I'd returned home after our confrontation, I'd discovered the ring still sitting on the kitchen counter. So, I'd handed it off to Caro when we said goodbye.

The muscle in Roane's jaw twitched. "I know. She gave it to me."

"I have to go." I stepped toward the cab, unable to face him any longer.

"Evie, please," he begged. "Please just forgive me. I'll do anything."

"I have to go," I repeated, my voice breaking.

Tears burned in Roane's eyes. "You get in the taxi, you take everything I am with you. You leave behind a fucking shell of a man. Over two stupid little lies that don't mean anything, that don't have any bearing on who I am or what you mean to me. Evie, please . . ."

Just like that, the pieces left of my heart splintered inside me. On a choked sob, I hauled open the back passenger door of the cab and threw myself in.

"Newcastle airport?" the driver confirmed.

"Yes," I wheezed out.

As he pulled away from the sidewalk, I couldn't help myself.

I turned and looked out the back window of the car and watched as Roane Robson scrubbed the tears from his face, his desolation so acute, there was a flicker . . . a flicker of doubt.

A flicker.

Now who was lying?

The truth was, as I cried in the back seat of the cab, the driver stiff and uncomfortable with my emotional display, I felt more than a flicker of doubt.

Yet I couldn't seem to make myself ask the driver to turn the car around.

The impact of the shattered illusion of the life I thought we were beginning together in Alnster was bigger than my doubts.

I wanted Greer. I wanted Chicago.

My life there had never been a lie, a fantasy.

My life there was real.

I'd been lonely in Chicago, but it had never broken my heart.

Twenty-Seven

My friend was not glowing like people said pregnant women glowed. Her cheeks were flushed, yes, but the skin under her eyes was dark from lack of sleep.

Seven months pregnant, Greer sat on the sofa with her feet up on a stool, hands braced on her rounded stomach as she gazed at me. Pitifully.

We sat in her small apartment, while Andre was out picking up some takeout for dinner. I'd been back in Chicago for a week, and the aches and pains through my whole body would not dissipate.

The last time I remembered feeling like that was when my dad died.

Guilt mingled with my heartache because surely I shouldn't equate breaking up with Roane to losing my father.

"It's not just about him," Greer suddenly said. "The way you talked about them during our catch-ups . . . it's all of them. It's the village and your friends, not just him. You're homesick."

"I'm not homesick," I denied. "I'm going home tomorrow."

It was true. I was renting a car and driving to Carmel to stay with my mom and Phil for a while.

"That's not your home, Evie."

"Greer . . ." I sighed. "Can we not? Can we just talk about the baby?"

"No." She shook her head adamantly. "Once the baby is here, that's all we'll talk about, trust me. So before the baby takes over everything, we're talking about this, even if you hate me for it. Because . . ." She leaned toward me, her expression openly concerned. "I've never seen you like this. Not even about your mom."

"Like what?" I asked dully.

"Like that." Greer gestured to me impatiently. "Voice flat, eyes hard and empty. Every now and then I'll see pain in them, which is a far sight better than nothing at all. You've lost weight."

"I can't lose weight in a week." But it was true. My jeans felt a little looser around the waist.

"Evie . . . you're grieving."

"So what if I am?"

"So what if you are?" she snapped. "Evie, Roane didn't die! The village didn't disappear. You made a choice to leave him and it behind. Are you sure it was the right choice?"

I stared at her in disbelief. "He lied. *They* lied."

"A white lie. Okay, two white lies. But he's not your mom. This doesn't mean he'll lie to you again. Or that everything he showed you about who he is isn't the truth. Don't you think if you can forgive your mom for years of disappointing you, you can forgive him for one slipup?"

I glared at her. "I held him to a higher standard than that."

"Well, that's on you. Not him. He's just a human being."

Astonished, I flew to my feet. "How can you take his side?"

"Because," she replied calmly. "You tore out of there before giving yourself a chance to process what happened. The result being a miserable not even half version of my best friend standing in my sitting room."

"I don't need to take this." I grabbed my purse and turned to leave.

"Evie, stop."

Glancing over my shoulder, I saw Greer pull herself to standing. She gave me an appeasing look.

"Let me just ask one more thing and you can storm out of here after."

I nodded, gesturing for her to continue.

"What terrified you so much that you cut him out without even considering forgiving him?"

Fresh tears welled in my eyes. I shrugged.

"That's not an answer," Greer pushed.

"It was proof, okay. Proof that none of it was real. It was all a lie, a fantasy, and I acted impulsively and naively."

"It was all a fantasy . . . why . . . because you were happy? Do you think it can't be real if it makes you that happy?"

"Apparently not."

"Evie—"

"I just . . . I thought he was better. I thought he would never hurt me." The tears spilled free.

Greer hurried across the room to wrap her arms around me. She was shorter than me and her bump was in the way, but she did her best to hug me. When she finally released me, she said, "No one is perfect, Evie. And no matter how good a person is, it would be rare for them to go through life never hurting anyone, unintentionally or not. Have you?"

I knew I'd hurt people unintentionally in the past. And I knew I'd hurt Roane by leaving.

"No," I whispered.

"Then why," Greer asked gently, "should Roane be held to a higher standard than you hold yourself? Why should all of them be? Sounds to me like they liked you so much, they were willing to band together just to help their boy keep you permanently in his life."

I sucked in a breath, feeling like she'd punched me in the gut.

Confusion swamped me as those doubts I felt from the moment I'd gotten in that cab swam up to the surface.

"Fuck," I breathed.

*C*armel was a very pretty city in Indiana. Driving through its streets brought back wave after wave of nostalgia and memories. Although I'd grown up in the lower-income side of town, when I was in college, Phil got a promotion to management in the industrial equipment manufacturing plant where he worked. This meant he and Mom could move to a nicer house, although I think it was a struggle to keep it since they had Mom's rehab bills to pay.

I'd offered up my inheritance a long time ago to cover those bills, but Phil had stubbornly refused.

They lived on a picture-perfect suburban street, where every house was the same except in color. They all had triangular slate roofs and a Palladian porch, but some were red brick and others were painted pale blue, lemon yellow, or light gray.

Mom and Phil's house was pale gray, but while most others on the street looked like they'd recently had a fresh coat of paint, theirs was looking a little in need of love.

After I parked the rental car in the drive behind Phil's truck,

I'd barely taken a step out of the vehicle when the front door flew open and Phil appeared.

He hurried down the porch steps, and as I got out of the car, he met me with a bear hug.

That's all it took in my fragile state for me to burst into tears.

I'd emailed him with a heads-up about the broken engagement.

His arms tightened around me, and I inhaled the familiar scent of the laundry detergent he and Mom used as I soaked his shirt with the apparently never-ending supply of water my eyes produced.

"There, there," he said gruffly.

I felt his hold ease, and as I looked up, surprised he was pushing me away, I saw the reason why. Mom stood, tears in the hazel eyes I'd inherited from her, holding her arms up to take me into them.

And I went.

Collapsing into her and crying now for so much more than what I'd lost in England.

Sitting in my parents' air-conditioned living room on a hot day in Indiana, holding a glass of iced tea, I told myself at least there was AC in the States.

Phil had grabbed my luggage and brought it into the house as Mom and I took our reunion inside. My stepfather had left soon after with some excuse about buying groceries, but I knew he was getting out of the way so Mom and I could talk.

We'd filled the time so far with wiping our eyes and making small talk while Mom brought a jug of iced tea into the living room with a plate of homemade cookies.

"I've really gotten into baking since I've come home," she said, offering me a cookie.

Not hungry, I promised I'd try one later.

Homemade baking just made me think of Caro.

To distract me, I blurted, "I'm angry at you."

Mom flinched, tensed, but gave me a tight nod. "I know."

"I've tried not to be. But I'm angry that your addiction was stronger than your love for me."

"Oh, Evie, that's not true." Her eyes filled with fresh tears.

"I know that rationally. I know that's not how addiction works. But it felt like that. I can't change what it felt like. Especially when you lied all the time about it and stole from me. And how do I know that this time it'll stick?"

"You don't. I don't." She shook her head. "Honestly, I can't worry about that because it's counterproductive to fighting addiction. I know that now. I can only try and I am trying." She shifted forward on her seat, expression filled with remorse. "If you can't forgive me, I understand."

I shook my head, my gut roiling at the idea of losing my mom for good now that she was in front of me. "I love you. You're not your addiction, Mom. *I love you*. And despite everything I will always forgive you."

When she broke into hard, shuddering sobs, I wondered how much more I could take. Holding her as she clung to me, I couldn't remember a time more emotionally wrought than this past week.

I felt like I'd cried a lifetime's worth of tears.

A while later, we moved to the porch swing. It was a typically humid day, but we had the iced tea in our hands as a coolant.

"Has it rained much?" I asked. It usually rained a fair bit in Carmel during the summers. Hence the humidity.

"Actually, we're having a pretty hot, dry summer. Climate change, I guess." She shot me a semi-amused look. "Are we really going to talk about the weather? Am I allowed to broach the subject of your engagement? Is it my place?"

"Honestly, I'm all talked out. I could sleep for days. But you're my mom. It's always your place," I assured her.

She smiled gratefully and I noticed how well she really did look. Alcoholism had taken a toll on Mom's skin. She had more wrinkles than some women her age, but the yellow tinge to her skin tone was gone. She looked healthy and glowing. My pretty, shiny-eyed mom from when she first met Phil was back. Hope, despite all my best attempts to stifle it, flickered to life inside me.

I guess I always would hope for the best when it came to the people I loved.

Roane's face flashed before my eyes, and those doubts Greer had breathed life into caused a stomach cramp.

"I hope you don't mind, but I read all the emails you sent Phil, and he'd tell me about your phone conversations too when you were over there."

"I don't mind." I'd assumed as much.

"Your young man . . . Roane . . . he sounds like a good man."

"He lied to me," I replied automatically. "And anyway, I didn't go there to fall in love with some guy." God, did I sound bitter. "I went over there, telling myself from the start not to get involved with him, because I was there to find myself, to find out what I wanted from life. Not to find a man. I didn't listen! I didn't listen to myself and look where it got me. I lost the bookstore and a life that should have been my home. Because of him. Because I gave up my independence for him."

"Oh, sweetheart, you've got it all wrong."

I narrowed my eyes. "Excuse me?"

"Love isn't about giving up your independence, and I doubt very much that you of all people gave it up for a man."

I made a face but she was right. With the exception of not learning to drive there, I'd refused Roane's help buying the store, wanting to do that for myself. I ran the store by myself with no help from anyone else. "Okay, maybe I didn't. Entirely. But I still didn't listen to my good sense."

Mom studied me thoughtfully. "Do you think that it's somehow weak to think of a person as 'home'?"

"No one should rely on someone for that. A home should be something outside of a person. They're too unreliable. You lose them, you lose your home."

"Well, I hate to tell you this, sweetheart, but that's life."

"Mom—"

"No. That is what it is to be human. We find people we love and they become our home. Jobs, houses, they can all change, but it's only when we lose someone that we lose that feeling of being anchored to a place. Not a place that's tangible but a place in here." She touched her chest where her heart was. "Your father gave me a home when I had none, and losing him, losing that anchor, devastated me. And yes, it made me weak, because ever since, I've bobbed around in this nameless sea, dragged under by the waves whenever life gets hard. All because I lost my home when I lost him.

"But what I let myself forget"—she clutched at my hand—"is that *you* were my home as much as he was. It took me multiple rehab stays and far too much time to realize that." Her grip tightened to bruising. "Don't make my mistake, Evie. I see the grief in your eyes. I know that grief. But guess what, my sweet girl, your home is still out there. *He's* still out there."

"How . . ." I choked out. "How do I know he's my home?"

"You wouldn't be so shipwrecked right now if he wasn't."

"Mom . . . he's in England," I reminded her.

Her smile was sad. "I know. This decision isn't about me or Phil or Greer . . . it's about you. It's finally about you, Evie. And all I care about is your happiness. What's an ocean between family?"

"I think . . ." My stomach churned as I answered. "I think I acted impulsively. Stupidly impulsively and I . . . I was just so hurt and blindsided. But they were right. I didn't give myself enough time to think it through. I just wanted to run away. And I hurt him. I've hurt him too."

"Do you forgive him?"

The lies still stung and his actions had shaken my trust in him; there was no magic wand for that, other than time. But the thought of never seeing Roane again was unbearable. "I love him," I admitted. "Being this far away from him scares the shit out of me. When I found out what he'd kept from me, all I kept thinking about was that little whisper in the back of my head that had been telling me since I met him that he was too good to be true. I let that whisper become something big and dark. But being away from him . . . I feel like an idiot for leaving over those lies. Those stupid little lies. I remember he told me once that he was so happy with me, he was afraid. Now I get it. It was hard for him to tell me the truth because he thought I'd walk away. It's difficult to stay mad at someone because they love you so much, it made them act like a moron. So, yes, I forgive him."

"Then he'll forgive you too."

"What if he doesn't?"

"Then he's a fool. And I'll be here."

I hugged my mom tight as we swayed gently on the porch swing, but as the minutes passed, the pieces of my heart that belonged to her began to heal, giving way to those that belonged to Roane. They pulled my mind into the fray of their restoration, until I was already back in England before my body was.

Twenty-Eight

I discovered in the whirlwind of organizing my move to England that Penny had not put the store and apartment up for sale yet.

"I knew, deep down, I'd get this call," she'd said when I called to tell her I wanted to continue with the purchase. I apologized for messing her around and promised this time I meant to see the sale through.

She'd promised me she wouldn't tell anyone I was on my way home, and I believed she'd keep that promise.

Roane might not forgive me for running away from us, but that didn't mean I wasn't moving to England either way. With a little distance I saw the villagers' deception with renewed eyes. It wasn't malice. It was the opposite. Greer was right. They wanted me, an outsider, for one of their own, and in a weird, roundabout way, it was actually a huge compliment.

And I'd spat in their faces about it.

Not that I didn't still think what they did was wrong, but hadn't I also meddled with only good intentions in mind?

Ironic, that.

Whether Roane gave me a second chance or not, I was moving to Alnster. I was taking the risk that if we didn't end up together, the village wouldn't hold it against me.

As impatient as I was to return to England, I stayed a few days with Mom and Phil because it would be a while before I'd see them again. Then I'd gone back to Chicago to arrange shipment of all my things to England.

Besides, I had to say goodbye to Greer.

And yes, I had enough tears left for that goodbye.

The eventual trip from Chicago to London, London to Newcastle was torturous. I'd never been so impatient in my life to get anywhere. The drive north from Newcastle was even more so. Jet-lagged, smelling of plane, and pale cheeked, I directed the cab to Roane's estate.

His true estate.

Alnster House.

I needed to see it. It was part of a deceit that had become twisted into something that shouldn't have been as destructive as it was. What I wanted from the house, I wasn't sure. Perhaps to alleviate my concerns. To remind me it was just bricks and mortar and it didn't change who Roane was.

The cab pulled up to the huge sandstone mansion, and my bravery faltered a little. It didn't do much to reassure me that Roane was an ordinary, down-to-earth farmer.

The house was set back miles from the main road, surrounded by fields. The lawns around the mansion were well kept and rolled for acres before turning into wheat and barley fields.

A dirt road turned into a gravel drive with a fountain in the middle.

An exterior imperial staircase led up to the front door of the grand home.

It was like a smaller version of Mr. Darcy's house.

"Holy fuck."

"Is this it?" the driver asked, staring up at the house in awe.

Just as I was about to step out, a figure appeared in the doorway. It was a woman dressed in a conservative pencil skirt and blouse. I waited as she elegantly walked down one side of the stone staircase, the gravel crunching underfoot as she approached the cab.

The driver rolled down the window.

The woman, who appeared to be in her midfifties, asked, "May I help you?"

"We're looking for the Alnster estate," the driver said.

"This is it." She looked at me. "I'm Mrs. Smith, the house-keeper. May I help you?"

I licked my dry lips.

Roane had a housekeeper.

Of course he did.

"I'm . . . I'm looking for Roane."

Her brows pinched together a little, as if she was trying to place me. "Mr. Robson does not reside here."

"Do you know where I can find him?"

"Perhaps you would favor me with a name first?"

Wow, Mrs. Smith was old-school posh. I wasn't sure I wanted to give her my name. I was afraid she'd know who I was and have us led off the grounds at gunpoint.

"I'm sorry to have bothered you." I tapped the driver on the shoulder. "Let's go."

We left the housekeeper staring after us, and I gave the driver the directions to the farmhouse.

Roane had been telling the truth. He really did live there and had a separate life from his parents.

Although my pride was still pricked, my trust still wounded, guilt niggled at me.

I should have stayed.

I should have listened.

Butterflies raged in my belly as the car meandered down the dirt road through the fields of sheep surrounding Roane's coastal estate.

When the farmhouse and the agricultural buildings surrounding it came into view, my breath caught.

Then I saw him.

He and Bobby were unlatching the ramp from the truck to transport the sheep.

My heart began to pound in my chest, and despite the breezy day outside, my palms and underarms began to sweat. Even the backs of my knees sweat.

"This it?" the driver asked as he pulled to a stop at the house.

When I didn't answer, he repeated the question.

I was too busy staring at Roane, who had frozen in place, staring back in astonishment.

"Yes . . . but can you wait? I'll pay you to wait."

"Sure, pet, but the meter's running," he warned.

I didn't care about the meter.

My legs were like jelly as I stepped out of the cab, my hands shaking as I rounded the hood of the car.

Roane moved away from the truck and took a few wary strides toward me.

We stared at each other.

For what seemed like forever.

I felt like I hadn't seen his handsome face in months. Those chestnut eyes . . . *kind* eyes. Roane might have lied about his age and the true extent of his fortune, but he'd never lied about who *he* was.

He'd doubted me when he struggled to tell me the truth, for fear I'd walk away.

But I'd made his doubts about me warranted by *running* away.

I shrugged helplessly, quite sure there wasn't a blameless soul between us. "I'm so sorry."

Roane blinked, momentarily surprised.

Then he was walking—no, racing—toward me.

His arms closed around me, and I found myself hauled against him as he slammed his mouth over mine in a hard, desperate kiss. It was bruising, ravaging, no finesse.

Yet it was the best kiss of my life.

My fingers dug into the muscles of his back like I was afraid at any minute he might be yanked away from me. He groaned, the sound delicious and thrilling, as his kiss slowly gentled.

Finally, he released me to press his forehead to mine. "Greer got my message to you then?"

Confused, I shook my head. "What message?"

"It took a bit of doing but I managed to track down her number. You wouldn't answer my calls so . . . I called her yesterday. Asked her for your address in Chicago. She wouldn't give it, but said she'd let you know I called."

"But I was already on my way here . . . didn't she tell you?"

Roane exhaled slowly. "No, she didn't."

Knowing Greer, she'd kept it from him to surprise him, even if it meant leaving him hanging in misery for a few more hours. I sighed, a sound somewhere between a laugh and a sob following in its wake.

"Do you forgive me then, angel?"

"I do. Does the call to Greer mean you forgive me?"

Roane lifted his head to cup my face in his hand. Those beautiful eyes of his shimmered as he gazed at me with all the love I'd missed so much these last few weeks. "I think I'd forgive you anything, Evie Starling."

I opened my mouth to reply, but his next actions stopped me.

He tugged on the neckline of his T-shirt and pulled out a chain. At the end of the chain was my engagement ring.

My vision got watery as emotion thickened my throat.

He'd kept it with him.

Seeing my expression, Roane gave me a chiding smile. "Don't you realize yet how much I love you?"

"I do," I promised on a choked whisper. "And I love you. You're my home."

"I know it." He unclasped the chain behind his neck and gently guided the ring down until it landed in his palm. "It devastated me to watch you leave, but I had to believe you'd come back. I had to. There was no other choice for me." Roane took hold of my hand and placed the ring back on my finger, where it belonged. "There's no escaping me now, angel."

"Only you could make stalker talk sexy, Robson," I cracked to ease the tension.

He chuckled, pulling me back into his arms and burying his head in my neck. We held each other, breathing each other in.

"Meter's still running, pet," the cabdriver's voice called to us.

Roane lifted his head while I buried my face deeper into his chest. "Bobby, can you help the man with Evie's luggage?"

"I need to pay him," I mumbled.

"Bobby will get him. We'll pay him back later."

I didn't know how much time passed as we stood in the middle of the yard just holding on.

It wasn't until a happy bark sounded seconds before a weight slammed into our sides that we stumbled apart to find Shadow jumping up on his hindquarters to get to me.

Laughing as he found purchase on my shoulders and his tongue found my cheek, I hugged the Dane in return. "Missed you, boy," I whispered, refusing to cry even though it was really hard not to.

"Down," Roane said gently, pulling on Shadow's collar after a while. "You've had your turn with the bonny lass." He rubbed Shadow's head affectionately before grinning at me. "Now it's my turn again."

I looked down at the hand he held out to me and took it with my left, the engagement ring glittering even on a cloudy day like today.

"Bobby," Roane called over his shoulder.

"Aye?" I heard him shout from one of the hoop houses.

"I'm taking the rest of the day off."

I could hear laughter in Bobby's voice as he called back, "Aye, tell me something I didn't already know!"

Giggling a little hysterically with the biggest relief I'd ever felt in my life, I followed Roane into the house and upstairs. As he reached for me, I complained I smelled like I'd traveled all day and didn't want him enduring that.

In answer he changed direction and guided me to the bathroom. Minutes later I found myself naked in the shower with my fiancé as he moved inside me, not caring that our reunion was hampered by a slippery bathtub or that our kisses were interrupted with muffled curses as we tried to steady ourselves.

All I cared about was that I was home.

And it was real.

Epilogue

Four months later . . .

Christmas songs played softly in the background, barely heard over the noise of our chatter as we sat in groups around The Anchor. Milly and Dex were hosting a Christmas pub quiz for the locals, and the atmosphere was relaxed and spirited as we competed in tabled groups to win the huge hamper of Christmas goodies they were giving away.

I sat with my chair pressed to Roane's, huddled into his side, his arm around me, fingers caressing the skin below the short sleeve of my blouse as we considered the latest quiz question.

Joining us at our table were Caro, Viola, and Lucas. As they discussed with Roane whether or not the Oasis single that hit number one in 1996 was "Some Might Say" or "Don't Look Back in Anger," I considered my youthful friends and how far we'd come in such a short period of time.

I'd love to say Roane and I fell back into our relationship with ease, but we'd both burned each other's trust, and there had been moments over the past few months when we'd been a little unsure of each other.

In those first few months I'd questioned him about where he'd been, what he was doing, not realizing that over time those questions began to feel like an interrogation. Finally Roane demanded I stop, and I discovered Roane didn't "do" loud arguing. He just walked out, thus putting an end to my raised voice.

I did apologize, and more self-aware than before, I promised him and myself that I'd let it go, that I'd do better.

And I did.

However, our wedding was last month, and when his parents made it clear they were unhappy about how quickly things were moving, Roane became tense around me, tiptoeing on eggshells. It finally occurred to me that he was afraid the conflict might send me running again. That hurt, but I understood his concern, and there was nothing I could do but prove him wrong.

Which I did. I smiled at the white gold band nestled beside my engagement ring, my gaze flickering to the wider white gold band on Roane's left hand.

He couldn't wear it at work, but he never forgot to put it on when we socialized.

Despite Roane's parents' concerns, they attended the wedding, they made nice, and they were coming back for Christmas, so I saw that as my chance to show them that Roane and I hadn't made a mistake marrying so quickly.

As for my mom and Phil, they adored Roane. We flew them over for the wedding, and they fell in love with Alnster and my husband as rapidly as I had. They'd already booked a stay at a holiday home in nearby Bamburgh next summer and were staying for three weeks. We'd told them they could stay with us, but I think they wanted not only to give us privacy but to have their own. I kind of got the impression that since Mom's return from rehab, she and Phil were rediscovering each other. And it was good.

Greer, of course, had the baby. A little baby girl she and Andre named Evangeline. I'd flown out to see my namesake four weeks before the wedding. She was cute as a button, but she cried a lot. Despite my "advancing" years, Roane and I had already tabled the kid discussion. We would try, but not for a few years yet. Seeing baby Evie scream and cry every other hour, I'd been grateful for that decision and in awe of my best friend.

We were sad she couldn't make it to the wedding, but Roane and I were planning a trip out there next year so we could visit them and then drive to Indiana to see Mom and Phil. And to show him where I grew up.

It was certainly different from where Roane had grown up.

I'd, of course, been inside Alnster House, that huge sandstone mansion belonging to my husband and his parents, named by the ancestor who'd built the place back in the seventeenth century. It had been added to and renovated over the centuries, and if I thought it was awe inspiring on the outside, it was nothing compared to the interior.

Marble floors and staircases, huge oil paintings, beautiful sculptures. The public rooms were like rooms in a museum. The family rooms on the second floor, although opulent with Aubusson carpets and Chinese silk wallpaper, were more comfortable and welcoming.

We'd had the wedding reception at the house, making use of the ballroom.

Yes, it had a ballroom.

The first time I walked into Alnster House, I'd felt Roane watching me anxiously. All I could do was hold his hand and smile reassuringly. That mansion wasn't him. That's why he lived in the farmhouse. The house, however, was his legacy, and maybe one day we'd have to move there with our kids, but for now I was getting a huge kick out of redecorating our cozy farmhouse. I'd even convinced Roane to hire an architect so we could start opening up the spaces to make it free flowing and modern.

"It's 'Don't Look Back in Anger,'" I said, tired of listening to the back-and-forth.

My friends stared at me, uncertain.

I huffed, holding up my hand. "Who is the only person here who remembers 1996? Some of us"—I turned to Roane—"had only been walking for, what, two years?"

He smirked.

"And some of us"—I looked at Caro—"were still in diapers." Then I gestured to Lucas and Viola. "And some of us weren't even born. God, why am I friends with you? You're making me old. Put down 'Don't Look Back in Anger.'"

"Words to live by," Viola said pointedly.

"Ha ha." I rolled my eyes as they grinned at my expense.

"I don't remember you being this touchy about your age." Caro tapped a finger against her chin. "I think marrying Roane has made you tetchy about your age."

Months ago, a joke like that might have fallen flat, but now Roane just winked at me and squeezed me closer.

"I don't know why." Vi snorted. "Think about it, Evie. When you're forty, your husband will still be a hot, young thirtysomething. You're like my hero."

Roane chuckled.

"He's lucky I love him." I scratched his beard playfully. "Or I would never forgive him for turning me into a cougar."

"Oh, you're not a cougar," Lucas said. "Roane would have to be fifteen years younger rather than ten."

"He's six and a half years younger," I corrected him.

Lucas grinned mischievously. "Oh, is he? My mistake."

As he and Viola fell against each other laughing, I mock glowered at them. "Why are you home for Christmas again? Just to torture me?"

"No, we're home so I can have a painfully awkward Christmas dinner with my loving mother and a father who won't talk to me." Lucas's lips twisted into an unhappy smile.

Vi covered his hand with hers. "At least he's letting you in the house."

"Aye, because my mam put her foot down. At last."

Although I saw a happy ending for Viola and Lucas, I wasn't sure there was one in the cards for Lucas and West. His father just couldn't let it go, and if it would mean losing his youngest son, then I pitied him. I pitied the bitterness that was choking the life out of him slowly but surely.

"Right, hand over your answers, you lot," Milly said, approaching our table with a beaming smile.

Roane handed them to her as I shot a look over my shoulder to make sure Shadow was okay. He was sprawled in front of the roaring fire and had been since we'd arrived two hours ago.

"Maybe we should pull him over to us." I turned to Roane. Shadow had a habit of staying in front of a fire too long.

"You know he'll move when he's too hot," Roane assured me as he always assured me.

Less than ten minutes later, Dex retook the mic to announce, "And the winner is Maggie, Annie, and Liz!"

We looked over at their table, pretending to boo at the same time we raised our glasses to them. Maggie blushed in delight as Dex placed the huge hamper in front of them.

"See," I said, "age and experience matter in a pub quiz. Don't"—

I raised a finger at Lucas, whose eyes were sparkling with some mischievous comment about my age—"even say it."

Choking on his laughter, he buried his head in Vi's throat as she grinned at me.

Roane's arm slipped down my shoulder to my waist, and I felt his fingers slip under my shirt to tickle me lightly. Shivering, I turned into him with a soft smile. "You feeling me up in public?" I murmured.

His dark eyes dropped to my mouth. "When am I not feeling you up in public?"

"True. You're very handsy. You should stop. I'm a married woman, you know."

"Oh, I know." He bent his head toward mine, seconds from stealing a kiss when—

"Evie, how's the new tenant working out?"

Roane and I moved away from each other as Dex pulled a seat up to our table.

"Good," I answered. "So far so good."

Once I'd bought the store from Penny and realized I'd have an empty apartment upstairs when I moved in with Roane, I had a new door put on the rear of the building and closed off the entrance to the bookstore at the back to separate the apartment from the store. I was intending to let it as a holiday apartment, but a guy called Bryan Holmes, some financial dude from London, paid me up front for three months' rent.

He said he needed a long vacation from London. When I'd met him, I'd thought he was a good-looking guy in his late forties. He was only thirty-eight. The stress of working in the financial hub of the country had led him to a bit of a midlife crisis. He'd decided the cold sea air in a tiny little village would do him good.

"I hardly ever hear him when I'm at the store." I shrugged. Not that the store kept me busy during the winter months. I only opened it a few days a week, and even then I spent most of my days working on edits for my clients.

It didn't matter. I trusted that between my rental income from the apartment and the good summer business, I'd make a success of my store.

Even if I didn't, I thought as I looked around The Anchor at the fairy lights and Christmas decorations twinkling above the heads of my friends, my dog, and my husband, I wasn't going anywhere. They were all stuck with me for good.

"Did you hear?" Milly appeared at the table, her hands resting on Lucas's shoulders as she directed her words at me.

"Hear what?"

"The truth has come out about why Erin and Peter Branston separated three months ago. Erin apparently played private eye when her husband started working late. She found him at the Newton Arms with his head between another woman's legs."

"Ugh, Mam." Viola made a face as Lucas's shoulders shook with laughter. "That's a sentence a daughter should never hear her mam say."

"Never mind that." Caro blushed but her eyes were filled with sympathy. "It's something a wife should never see her husband do with another woman."

"Poor Erin," Dex tutted. "And the kids."

Erin was the attractive blonde who'd ordered books from me all those months ago. I'd heard about the separation, we all had, but I marveled that it had taken this long for the truth to come out. "So they're getting a divorce?"

"Aye." Milly nodded in approval. "She says she's taking the bastard for everything."

"So she's single?"

"Aye, that's what divorce means, Evie."

I ignored her sarcasm. "You know, my tenant Bryan is single . . ."

Milly's eyes lit up.

Roane groaned and shot me a warning look. "Evie . . . don't even think about it."

Acknowledgments

While strolling through vacation listings, I came upon a bookshop holiday advertisement. To my delight I discovered there is a book shop in the lowlands of Scotland that offers exactly what Much Ado About Books offers in Evie's story. This got my imagination firing, and before I knew it, Evie's adventure in England was playing out in my head, desperate to be told. As for the story's setting, I have long since hoped to set a book in Northumberland. It's one of my favorite places in the world and one of the most beautiful counties in England. It was a no-brainer that *Much Ado About You* should be set there. It was a joy to send Evie there. When I wrote this book, I wrote it with the desire to create the ultimate romantic comfort read, and it was certainly a comfort write! I hope readers felt my love for the characters, the setting, and that it magically transported you all there.

For the most part, writing is a solitary endeavor but publishing most certainly is not. I have to thank my fantastic editor, Kerry Donovan, not only for helping to make me a better writer and storyteller, but for believing in me and in this book. Moreover, thank you to all the team at Berkley for your hard work on Evie and Roane's story.

The same must be said for my amazing agent, Lauren Abramo. Lauren, thank you for always having my back and for making it possible for readers all over the world to read my stories. I know how lucky I am to have you.

And thank you to my bestie and PA extraordinaire, Ashleen Walker, for handling all the little things and supporting me through everything. There are no words for how much I appreciate and love you.

Thank you to every single blogger, Instagrammer, and book lover who has helped spread the word about my books. You all are appreciated so much. On that note, a massive thank-you to all the fantastic readers in my private Facebook group, Sam's Clan Mc-Bookish. You're the kindest, most supportive readers a girl could ask for and I hope you know how much you all mean to me.

In case I don't say it enough, thank you to my family and friends for your never-ending well of support. I love you all so much.

Finally, to you, my reader, the biggest thank-you of all.

Much Ado About You

SAMANTHA YOUNG

Discussion Questions

1. When we first meet Evie, she's being stood up by a man she met online. At thirty-three, having dated for over half her life, she's exhausted by it. Have you ever felt similarly to Evie about dating?

2. Evie leaves her job after a decade because she feels her career trajectory has halted there. She also feels she's been passed over for a promotion because she isn't male. Do you think she was right to walk away for these reasons, or do you think she should have fought harder for the position she wanted? Have you ever been passed over for a promotion because of gender discrimination? If so, how did you deal with it?

3. Greer's pregnancy makes Evie feel as if she's being left behind—everyone else's lives are moving forward while hers stays still. Can you sympathize with Evie's fear of being the last single friend or have you had a friend in that position?

4. Life in her thirties isn't what Evie hoped it would be, and that's why she decides to take a break from it by traveling to England to run Much Ado About Books. Have you ever considered or actually done something similar? What was it? Did you find it helpful?

5. Evie's obsession with all things Shakespeare and Jane Austen led her to England. Have you ever been to the UK? Which part? What made you decide to choose that destination for your travels?

6. When Evie and Roane meet, there is an instant chemistry between them and a comfortable connection neither of them expected. Do you think Evie was right to friend-zone Roane because she was there to find herself, not love? Or do you think she should have engaged in a fun holiday romance? Have you ever had a holiday romance?

7. One of the deeper conversations Evie and Roane share is about Evie's feelings regarding "singledom" in her thirties. She's struggling to figure out if she's unhappy being alone because society dictates that she should be in a romantic relationship to be happy, or if she's genuinely lonely without a partner. Can you relate to Evie's struggle?

8. One aspect of Evie's personality is her inability to stay out of situations when people she cares about are involved. She gets involved in Caro's life; the feud between the Taits and the

Elliots; and Annie and Maggie's conflict. Do you think Evie is running away from her own problems all the while trying to fix everyone else's?

9. Alnster soon becomes much more than a vacation spot for Evie. What aspect of her time in Northumberland seduces Evie into staying? Or do you think it was a number of reasons?

10. Roane considers his lies to Evie "stupid omissions." Do you agree? Or do you think Evie was right to feel betrayed by the lies and by the village's group effort to keep the truth from her?

11. Evie's trust issues with everyone, including Roane, stem from her mom. Is that something you can relate to? Do you think broken trust from a parent can affect your friendships and romantic relationships?

12. Do you think Evie overreacted leaving Roane and England? Or do you think she needed to go home to Greer and her mom to understand what she'd left behind in England?

Don't miss Samantha Young's

FIGHT OR FLIGHT!

Available now.

Sky Harbor Airport, Arizona, March 2018

ood. Food and coffee. I knew those should be my priority. The grumbles in my belly were making that perfectly clear. And considering the purpose for my visit to Phoenix, it was no wonder I was marching through the terminal after having my bag searched in security, feeling like I might claw someone's face off if I didn't get a shot of caffeine in my system.

Even though I was hangry, my priority was to get upgraded to first class on my flight home to Boston. I could be hangry all I wanted in an airport. But as I was someone who suffered from mild claustrophobia, sitting in coach—with my luck stuck beside someone who would take their shoes *and* socks off during the flight— would be a million times worse than being hangry. I couldn't chance it. A pair of strange, hot, sweaty, smelly bare feet next to me for four and a half hours? No, that was a hell my current state of mind couldn't deal with. I shuddered as I marched toward the desk at my gate.

Seeing a small group of people crowded under a television

screen, I faltered, wondering what had drawn them to the news. I slowed at the images of huge plumes of smoke billowing out of a tremendously large mountain, my curiosity drawing me to a halt.

Within a few seconds the news told me that an unpronounceable volcano in Iceland had erupted, creating this humongous ash cloud that was causing disruption in Europe. Flights there had been grounded and consequently travel chaos ensued.

The thought of being stuck in an airport for an indeterminate number of hours—days even—made me shudder in sympathy for my poor fellow human beings.

I couldn't imagine dealing with that on top of the week I'd just had. I liked to think I was someone who was usually cool and collected, but lately my emotions were so close to the surface, I was almost afraid of them. I asked the universe to forgive me my self-absorption, thankful that I was not someone who wasn't going to make it home today, and continued on my path to the gate desk. There was no one in line, and the man behind it began to smile in welcome as I approached.

"Hi, I was wondering—*Oof!*" I winced as a laptop bag attached to a big guy whacked against my right shoulder, knocking me back on my heels. The big guy didn't even realize he'd hit me as he strode right past and cut in ahead of me.

Rude!

"I'd like tae upgrade tae first class, please," he said in a deep, loud, rumbling, very attractive accent that did nothing to soothe my annoyance with him for cutting in front of me.

"Of course, sir," the gate agent answered, in such a flirtatious tone, I was sure that if I'd been tall enough to see over the big guy's shoulder, I would see the agent batting his lashes at him. "Okay, flight DL180 to Boston. You're in luck, Mr. Scott. We have one seat left in first class."

Oh, hell no!

"What?" I shoved my way up next to Rude Guy, not even looking at him.

The gate agent, sensing my tone, immediately narrowed his eyes at me and thinned his lips.

"I was coming here to ask for an upgrade on this flight and he"—I gestured to my right—"cut in front of me. You saw him do it."

"Miss, I'm going to ask you to calm down and wait your turn. Although we have a very full flight today, I can put you on our list, and if a first-class seat opens up, we will let you know."

Yeah, because the way my week was going, *that* was likely.

"I was first," I insisted, my skin flushing as my blood had turned so hot with anger at the unfairness. "He whacked me with his laptop bag pushing past me to cut in line."

"Can we just ignore this tiny, angry person and upgrade me now?" the deep, accented voice said somewhere above my head to my right.

His condescension finally drew my gaze to him.

And everything suddenly made sense.

A modern-day Viking towered over me, my attention drawing his from the gate agent. His eyes were the most beautiful I'd ever seen. A piercing ice blue against the rugged tan of his skin, the irises like pale blue glass bright against the sun streaming in through the airport windows. His hair was dark blond, short at the sides and longer on top. And even though he was not my type, I could admit his features were entirely masculine and attractive with his short, dark blond beard. It wasn't so much a beard as a thick growth of stubble. He had a beautiful mouth, a thinner top lip but a full, sensual lower lip that gave him a broody, boyish pout at odds with his ruggedness. Gorgeous as his mouth may be, it was currently curled upward at one corner in displeasure.

And did I mention he was built?

The offensive laptop bag was slung over a set of shoulders so broad, they would have made a football coach weep with joy. I was guessing he was just a little over six feet, but his build made him look taller. I was only five foot three but I was wearing four-inch stilettos, and yet I felt like Tinkerbell next to this guy.

Tattoos I didn't take the time to study peeked out from under the rolled-up sleeve of his Henley shirt. A shirt that showed off the kind of muscle a guy didn't achieve without copious visits to the gym.

A fine male specimen, indeed.

I rolled my eyes and shot the agent a knowing, annoyed look. "Really?" It was clear to me motorcycle-gang-member-Viking-dude was getting preferential treatment here.

"Miss, please don't make me call security."

My lips parted in shock. "Melodramatic much?"

"You." The belligerent rumble in the Viking's voice made me bristle.

I looked up at him.

He sneered. "Take a walk, wee yin."

Being deliberately obtuse, I retorted, "I don't understand Scandinavian."

"I'm Scottish."

"Do I care?"

He muttered something unintelligible and turned to the agent. "We done?"

The guy gave him a flirty smile and handed him his ticket and passport. "You're upgraded, Mr. Scott."

"Wait, what—?" But the Viking had already taken back his passport and ticket and was striding away.

His long legs covered more ground than mine, but I was motivated and I could run in my stilettos. So I did. With my carry-on bumping along on its wheels behind me.

"Wait a second!" I grabbed the man's arm and he swung around so fast, I tottered.

Quickly, I regained balance and shrugged my suit jacket back into place as I grimaced. "You should do the right thing here and give me that seat." I didn't know why I was being so persistent. Maybe because I'd always been frustrated when I saw someone else endure an injustice. Or maybe I was just sick of being pushed around this week.

His expression was incredulous. "Are you kidding me with this?" I didn't even try not to take offense. Everything about this guy offended me.

"*You*"—I gestured to him, saying the word slowly so his tiny brain could compute—"*Stole. My. Seat.*"

"*You*"—he pointed down at me—"*Are. A. Nutjob.*"

Appalled, I gasped. "One, that is not true. I am *hangry*. There is a difference. And two, that word is completely politically incorrect."

He stared off into the distance above my head for a moment, seeming to gather himself. Or maybe just his patience. I think it was the latter because when he finally looked down at me with those startling eyes, he sighed. "Look, you would be almost funny if it weren't for the fact that you're completely unbalanced. And I'm not in the mood after having tae fly from Glasgow tae London and

London tae Phoenix and Phoenix tae Boston instead of London tae Boston because my PA is a useless prat who clearly hasn't heard of international direct flights. So do us both a favor before I say or do something I'll regret . . . and walk. Away."

"You *don't* regret calling me a nutjob?"

His answer was to walk away.

I slumped in defeat, watching him stride off with the first-class ticket that should have been mine.

Deciding food and coffee could wait until I'd freshened up in the restroom—and by freshen up, I meant pull myself together—I wandered off to find the closest one. Staring out of the airport window at Camelback Mountain, I wished to be as far from Phoenix as possible as quickly as possible. That was really the root of my frustration, and a little mortification began to set in as I made my way into the ladies' restroom. I'd just taken my emotional turmoil out on a Scottish stranger. Sure, the guy was terminally rude, but I'd turned it into a "situation." Normally I would have responded by calmly asking the agent when the next flight to Boston was and if there was a first-class seat available on that flight.

But I was just so desperate to go home.

After using the facilities, I washed up and stared long and hard into the mirror. I longed to splash cold water on my face, but that would mean ruining the makeup I'd painstakingly applied that morning.

Checking myself over, I teased my fingers through the waves I'd put in my long blond hair with my straightening iron. Once I was happy with it, I turned my perusal on my outfit. The red suit was one of the nicest I owned. A double-breasted peplum jacket and a matching knee-length pencil skirt. Since the jacket looked best closed, I was only wearing a light, silk ivory camisole underneath it. I didn't even know why I'd packed the suit, but I'd been wearing black for the last few days and the red felt like an act of defiance. Or a cry for help. Or maybe more likely an act of denial.

Although I had a well-paid job within an exclusive interior design company as one of their designers, it was expensive to live in Boston. The diamond tennis bracelet on my wrist was a gift on my eighteenth birthday from an ex-boyfriend. For a while I'd stopped wearing it, but exuding an image of success to my absurdly wealthy and successful clients was important, so when I started my job, I'd dug the bracelet out of storage, had it cleaned up, and it had sat on my wrist ever since.

Lately, just looking at it cut me to the quick.

Flinching, I tore my gaze from where it winked in the light on my arm, to my right wrist, where my Gucci watch sat. It was a bonus from my boss, Stella, after my first year on the job.

As for the black suede Jimmy Choos on my feet, with their sexy stiletto and cute ankle strap, they were one of many I was in credit card debt over. If I lived anywhere but Boston, I would have been able to afford as many Choos as I wanted on my six-figure salary. But my salary went into my hefty monthly rent bill.

It was a cute, six-hundred-square-foot apartment, but it was in Beacon Hill. Mount Vernon Street to be exact, a mere few minutes' walk from Boston Common. It also cost me just over four thousand dollars a month in rent. That didn't include the rest of my bills. I had enough to put some savings away after the tax man took his cut too, but I couldn't afford to indulge in the Choos I wanted.

So, yes, I'd reached the age of thirty with some credit card debt to my name.

But I guessed that made me like most of my fellow countrymen and -women, right? I stared at my immaculate reflection, ignoring the voice in my head that said some of those folks had credit card debt because of medical bills, or because they needed to feed their kids that week.

Not so they could live in a ridiculously overpriced area of Boston (no matter how much I loved it there) or wear designer shoes so their clients felt like they were dealing with someone who understood their wants better.

I bypassed the thought, not needing to mentally berate myself any more than I had since arriving back in Phoenix. I was perfectly happy with my life before I came home.

Perfectly happy with my perfect apartment, and my perfect hair, and my perfect shoes!

Perfect was good.

I straightened my jacket and grabbed hold of the handle of my carry-on.

Perfect was control.

Staring at the pretty picture I made in the mirror, I felt myself relax. If that gate agent had been into women, I *so* would have gotten that first-class seat.

"But forget it," I whispered. It was done.

I was going to go back out there and get a much-needed delicious Mediterranean-style salad and sandwich from one of my favorite food stops in Phoenix, Olive & Ivy. Feeling better at the thought, I relaxed.

Once I stopped being hangry, it would all be fine.

Photo by Mark Archibald

Samantha Young is the *New York Times* and *USA Today* bestselling author of the Hart's Boardwalk series and the On Dublin Street series, including *Moonlight on Nightingale Way, Echoes of Scotland Street, Fall from India Place, Before Jamaica Lane, Down London Road,* and *On Dublin Street.* She resides in Scotland.

Do you love contemporary romance?

**Want the chance to hear news about your favourite
authors (and the chance to win free books)?**

Kristen Ashley
Meg Cabot
Olivia Dade
Rosie Danan
J. Daniels
Farah Heron
Talia Hibbert
Sarah Hogle
Helena Hunting
Abby Jimenez
Elle Kennedy
Christina Lauren
Alisha Rai
Sally Thorne
Denise Williams
Meryl Wilsner
Samantha Young

Then visit the Piatkus website
www.yourswithlove.co.uk

And follow us on Facebook and Instagram
www.facebook.com/yourswithlovex | @yourswithlovex

PIATKUS